GENESIS VARIANT

BOOK 6, GENESIS SERIES

ABOUT THE AUTHOR

Eliza Green tried her hand at fashion designing, massage, painting, and even ghost hunting, before finding her love of writing. She often wonders if her desire to change the ending of a particular glittery vampire story steered her in that direction (it did). After earning her degree in marketing, Eliza went on to work in everything but marketing, but swears she uses it in everyday life, or so she tells her bank manager.

Born and raised in Dublin, Ireland, she lives there with her sci-fi loving, evil genius best friend. When not working on her next amazing science fiction adventure, you can find her reading, indulging in new food at an amazing restaurant or simply singing along to something with a half decent beat.

For a complete list of Eliza Green's books, visit

www.elizagreenbooks.com/books

BOOK 6 IN THE GENESIS SERIES

ELIZA GREEN

Copyright © 2019 Eliza Green

The moral right of the author has been asserted in accordance with the Copyright, Designs and Patents Act 1988.

All rights reserved. No part of this publication may be reproduced, stored in a retrieval system, or transmitted, in any form or by any means, without the prior written permission of the author, nor be otherwise circulated in any form of binding or cover other than that in which it is published and without a similar condition being imposed on the subsequent purchaser.

All characters in this publication are fictitious and any resemblance to real persons, living or dead, is purely coincidental.

ISBN: 9781096490227

Editor: Sara Litchfield
Cover: Deranged Doctor Design

Dedicated to the two people who still like me.

1

Marcus Murphy couldn't believe what Exilon 5 promised: sunshine, space and breathable air. That's what Harvey Buchanan said, the man who'd altered his appearance using facial manipulation techniques. Together they'd boarded the passenger ship with fake identities. The journey would take two weeks, just long enough for Marcus to get used to his new face.

Harvey sat back and folded his arms. 'You're a strange man, Marcus. You're reacting to news about Exilon 5 like it's the first time. Haven't you ever seen the promotional videos?'

It *was* Marcus' first time. The criminal factions who'd ruled over Earth for seven years before the people took it back mistrusted technology. All he knew was whatever Gaetano Agostini, his former boss, had deemed important enough for him to know. And before that, Exilon 5 wasn't even on his radar.

He looked around the ship's recreation room where they both sat. 'It's not like I ever dreamed of moving to the new planet. My old life was on Earth. Why waste time daydreaming about shit that might never happen?'

Harvey shook his head. 'I'll never understand you insular types.'

'What the fuck's that supposed to mean?'

'I.N.S.U.L.A.R.,' he spelled out. 'You know, people who are intolerant of anyone who exists outside of their tiny world. Those who never travel, never experience other cultures... never even get the bullet train anywhere.'

'I had nowhere to go.' Marcus' chest heaved at the accusation but he kept his anger in check. The semi-crowded conditions in the room helped. 'It's not like I had family I could visit in South America, for fuck's sake. Everyone I knew lived locally.'

His travel companion laughed too hard. 'Travelling isn't about burdening yourself on relatives. Is that the only reason you stayed put?'

'I had no reason to go,' he said with a shrug. 'What's your point?'

'It's about exploring and getting to know new cultures, which is exactly what you'll do when we get to Exilon 5. The cities are named after places on Earth—New London, New Tokyo, New Melbourne—and preserve the culture of those regions, but people from other cultures also live there. The land mass is vast with little to no ocean. The cities were built in a way so everything is connected by road or rail.'

Harvey talked to him like he was some intolerant prick from a backwater town. He lived in fucking Hunt's fucking Point, New York. Slap bang in the middle of city life. He may not have travelled farther than Boston, but he had street smarts. On Earth, where he worked for the criminal factions, that mattered more than tolerance.

He thought about the man who'd taught him how to fight: Gaetano Agostini. Enzo, Gaetano's son and a psychotic piece of shit, had taught him how to fight dirty.

Marcus hoped they were both dead.

It was only the second day on board the passenger ship and Marcus had yet to see anyone he recognised. He checked out the sea of grinning faces—people like him lucky to escape Earth. But he was escaping for a different, more dangerous reason. In the end, Marcus had betrayed Gaetano to save his own skin because Gaetano had set him up to fail.

It had been Agostini or him. Even Carl, his friend, had turned to the darker side to save his own skin. A small part of him wondered if Carl was still alive. A bigger part hoped his lying, cheating ass was burning in purgatory.

His gaze settled on a table with teenagers two over from theirs. Then he saw him. Marcus' eyes cut back to a frowning Harvey.

'You look like you've seen a ghost. What's wrong with you?'

'Ben Watson. That kid whose grandfather I kidnapped is sitting. Right. Over. There.'

He fixed his gaze on the table and pointed discreetly under his elbow.

Harvey glanced over, which drew a hiss from Marcus. 'What the fuck? He'll look over here and recognise me. Then he'll tell his little buddy Bill Taggart where I am and I'll be arrested the minute I step off this ship.'

Harvey returned his gaze to Marcus. 'Have you looked at your reflection lately? You're a different person. So am I. Stop your whining and just relax. He doesn't know who you are.'

Marcus straightened up. Harvey was right. He looked nothing like his old self. Gone was the Marcus Murphy with a neck scar so prominent he would be identified in a line up. In his place sat Martin Casey from

Richmond, just one of the many borrowed identities that Harvey had on file in his database of dead people. Marcus must have studied his reflection a dozen times since Harvey had completed the genetic manipulation changes to his face. Didn't matter what he looked like. Beneath, he would always be Marcus.

He leaned his elbows on the table and glanced over at Ben. The teenager sat with others his age, his eyes focused on the wall rather than the conversation happening around him. To Marcus, he would always be the dipshit with connections to Bill Taggart who refused to help him get on board this ship. If it hadn't been for Harvey...

'It's about time you accepted your new look.' Harvey leaned across the table. 'I didn't change your face so you could hide. You're here because I need you.'

'Not doubting your abilities, Doc. I still need time to get used to it.'

The procedure to rearrange his face had something to do with nanotechnology. Harvey had explained it to Marcus before he injected thousands of nanoids directly into the muscles of his face. The nanoids worked by increasing the cell structure count, adding new muscle outside what was genetically predetermined. Before Marcus could protest, he'd felt the crawlers add bulk to his hollow cheeks and take away cells from his neck to provide more definition. When the bandages came off, Marcus had washed his face repeatedly to rid himself of the nanoids Harvey said died in the process to make him more appealing.

A curious Ben glanced over suddenly, forcing Marcus to hide his face. Even with his new identity, this kid held too much power over him.

'Can't you do something about him? Like snuff him or something?'

Harvey looked over at Ben before cutting his eyes back to Marcus. 'You still don't get it, do you? This spaceship returned to Earth specially to bring that runt to Exilon 5. What would Bill Taggart do if the ship arrived and the boy was found dead in some closet? We'd all be stuck in detention indefinitely until the killer was found.' Harvey glanced over at Ben again. 'There's far more interesting things happening on Exilon 5. When you get settled, you won't even care if he's alive.'

'Really, like what? You got criminal gangs there too?'

Marcus hoped he wouldn't be put to work for another Gaetano.

'Criminals are crass. Too low level.' Harvey sat back. 'You're playing in the big leagues now. My sources say the peace treaty is on shaky ground and splinter organisations have formed on both the human and Indigene sides to disband it. They want to return things to how they were.'

Harvey had filled him in on the politics of Exilon 5 and the curtailed freedom the treaty afforded to the Indigenes. 'I thought the treaty was supposed to be a good thing.'

'For the ten board members maybe, and anyone working in the International Task Force. But with freedom comes fear. People feel that the Indigenes have too much freedom. Bill Taggart's primary role as Director of the ITF is to maintain that treaty. If we can break it, the ITF falls apart and any remaining power the board members have on Exilon 5 is dissolved.'

'So who takes over?'

'We do.'

'What, doctors?'

Harvey rolled his eyes. 'No, those of genetically

inferior quality who were never offered the chance to transform into a superior race.'

'I can relate to that.'

All his life Marcus had sat on the outside, not only from genetic programmes but any work programmes that required a greater intellect to his own.

Harvey's eyes flashed with anger. 'You and I are not the same. Get that into your thick skull right now.'

A surprised Marcus leaned back from the man. He sounded just like Gaetano.

'Know your place in society and you will get on just fine.'

'My place?'

'Yes, Marcus, your place. I plan to break apart the oppressive, autonomous power regime that exists on Exilon 5 and give real people a shot at turning Exilon 5 into a profitable, tech-dominant planet like Earth.'

'What's it like now?'

'The use of technology is discouraged in society. Yet, the government uses it. They kept all the good stuff that actually transferred.'

'Sounds like you need my experience, because that's how we survived and operated on Earth—in a technology vacuum.'

Harvey blew out a breath, as if irritated. 'The criminal factions waited for the World Government to leave before they climbed out of their sewers. You operated a regime of oppression and fear. That's not progress, Marcus. That's just as bad as returning to the dark ages.'

Marcus didn't appreciate Harvey's condescending tone. The factions did just fine.

He folded his arms. 'So how would you have done things differently?'

'For a start, I would have gained the trust of those below me rather than rule with an iron fist. People will do a lot more if they feel useful to a cause.'

Bullshit. 'What were *you* doing while the factions ruled Earth?'

'Waiting for you lot to kill each other. Your business model had a short life span. If you don't have trust you have nothing. You don't care whom you kill to protect your position. Power fluctuates amid a changeable environment of fear and suspicion. That's why trust is paramount. Take Bill Taggart, for example. While I despise the man, I have to admire him. He's done what few others have—he has the full support of the Indigenes.'

Marcus thought little of those bottom feeders. 'Then the joke's on him. Because they're worthless, blood-sucking vermin.'

'Clearly you haven't seen them in their natural environment.'

Marcus uncrossed his arms and leaned across the table. 'Neither have you. You said you've never been to Exilon 5.'

'Do you even know who I am?'

'Yeah, a doc who thinks he's better than everyone else.'

'Fucking dipshit,' muttered Harvey. He leaned closer. 'I was one of the original geneticists involved in their creation. I know what their potential is because I helped to design them.' He shook his head. 'You are a moron. That's why you'll never amount to much. Where you see weakness, I see opportunity.'

Marcus could see opportunity aplenty, but his experience of the half-dead, blood-draining, bald freaks that lived in the attic of the Deighton mansion had given him an insight he was sure Harvey didn't have. 'We'll have to agree to disagree.'

'That intolerant attitude of yours won't get you far, because when we get to Exilon 5 you'll be working with Indigenes. We won't break the treaty without their help. Some of them want change as much as we do.'

Fuck that. Marcus was his own man. He owed Harvey nothing.

'I have no ties to anyone, Harvey. I'll find my own way on Exilon 5.'

Harvey bared his teeth. 'Did you think that face came for free? I own you now and if you step out of line, I can put you in the ground just as easy as I kept you out of it.'

2

Bill Taggart paced the length of the corridor under the watchful eye of Laura O'Halloran. She looked a picture of calm. Why wasn't she concerned about the incoming spacecraft?

Laura's hand on his arm brought him to a stop.

'Will you stop pacing for one minute? You're driving me nuts.'

'I hate waiting around for other people.'

'No, really?' Laura rolled her eyes. 'Bill Taggart, you must be the most frustrating, infuriating man I know.'

That made Bill smile. 'So why are you with me?'

'Eight years on, I'm still asking myself the same question.' She kissed his mouth and it worked as the distraction she'd probably planned it to be. 'Turns out I like a challenge. And you're just that.'

She challenged him too, in a way that suited him. He thought back to the time she'd followed him through Sydney, right before she'd brought him to meet Stephen. The Indigene had opened Bill's eyes to the truth about his own government. Her stubbornness and determination to do right by the Indigenes had not only intrigued him but brought his own goals into focus. Bill had been so consumed with the search for Isla Taggart he hadn't thought to look at the people he worked for. Laura's bravery had blown open a conspiracy that could have resulted in the deaths of countless innocent Indigenes.

Bill had turned a blind eye at the time; their deaths would have been on his conscience.

The time to make amends was now. And it started with one teenager.

He leaned in for another kiss, making this one last. Laura moaned and his grip on her tightened. He glanced around the busy New London docking station. Ben Watson could wait a few minutes more. Isla's murder had been the worst thing to happen to him. But had she not died, he never would have found Laura.

She pulled away and took the moment with her. But the glint in her eye said, *Later.*

He'd make sure of it.

A burst of commotion separated them farther as the rarely used docking station in New London filled with extra personnel.

The passenger ship had arrived.

'Time to put on your best act,' Laura whispered in his ear.

He glanced down at the black uniform that identified him as Director of the International Task Force, a position awarded him after Tanya Li, former chairperson of the World Government, and some board members had narrowly escaped execution during a showdown with the Indigenes on Exilon 5. Tanya had agreed to certain demands rather than fight a superior race. One of Bill's demands had been to take charge of the ITF.

He became alert when a young soldier carrying a DPad approached him.

10

'Sir, we finally got the manifest,' said the soldier. 'A hundred people on board.'

His team had had no access to the manifest before or during the flight. When the World Government board members had arrived on Exilon 5, they had ordered all interstellar communications to be disabled. This hampered Bill's efforts to keep in touch with events on Earth. While Anton had found a back door to communicate with Jenny Waterson, his underground contact on Earth, the ships' logs had remained too encrypted to decipher.

'Show me.'

The soldier handed over the DPad. Bill scrolled through the short list of names. He had expected it to be longer. He donned his professional mask in the presence of the soldier; those under his command were still loyal to the ideals of the old ITF and World Government regime, which threatened the Peace Treaty. The Peace Treaty gave Indigenes the freedom to surface safely. But suspicions on both sides around what that freedom meant had created splinter groups who opposed the accord.

He found the name he wanted and nodded at Laura. Slipping into her official role as head of ITF communications, she nodded back.

Bill handed the DPad back to the soldier. 'One of the passengers will come with me. He has knowledge of this world prior to the Peace Treaty. We need to question him.'

'One of us can question him, sir.'

'No, I'd rather take care of it myself. ETA for the spacecraft?'

'Ten minutes. His name, sir?'

'Ben Watson.'

The soldier nodded. 'I'll make sure he's brought to you.'

The young man walked away to the area where the spacecraft ferrying passengers from the ship was due to arrive.

Laura moved closer to Bill. Just having her near calmed him.

'Are you worried about meeting Ben?' she said.

He nodded. 'What's this going to achieve, other than put that teenager through hell again?'

'It will give you and Stephen closure.' She squeezed his arm. 'But more important, it will give Ben Watson some answers.'

☼

Ten minutes passed before the young soldier returned with a lanky teenager almost as tall as Bill. The teen walked with confidence but his eyes revealed his wariness.

Ben said nothing when the soldier introduced him to Bill.

'Thank you, Dunne.' He ignored the teen's gaze on him. 'Please organise accommodation for the remaining passengers after you've processed them. Ms O'Halloran will see personally to Mr Watson's accommodation requirements.'

'Yes, sir.'

The soldier left and Bill noticed Ben's brow lift, possibly at the formality.

Laura offered her hand to the teen. 'Ben Watson. I've heard so much about you.'

Ben hesitated before he shook it.

'Let's get you out of here. And cover your eyes until we get to the vehicle.'

She led the way to the exit with Ben close behind her. Bill brought up the rear, grateful to have Laura there.

He'd avoided social situations for most of his adult life. But this one he couldn't escape. He had no idea what to say to the boy whose life he'd ruined to get information on Stephen.

They returned to their vehicle, parked on the side of the station that overlooked a replica of St. James' Park in London. It was midday and the park buzzed with lunchtime activity. Bill and Laura climbed into the front of the driverless vehicle, with its command console and hidden steering wheel, while Ben, half hidden under his coat, got in the back.

'Did you move the docking station?' Ben said.

Laura turned round. 'No. We built around it.'

'The last time I was here, the station was in the desert with nothing around for miles. You had to get a bus to it.'

'Things look a lot different to when you were last here. New London was more of a town than a city,' said Bill.

He looked at the regal buildings that lined the streets to the side of the park. Beyond them were areas retaining the charm of the old world but with a New London twist. In eight years, New London had gone from a span of ten miles out in all directions from its centre to twenty-five miles in all directions—about half the size of the city on Earth.

'The architects designed this park and the streets just beyond. What do you think?' he said.

Ben ignored him and stared out the window. Bill faced the front again; he hated rudeness more than small talk.

Laura gave a command to the car to drive to a location just outside the luxury area of Whitehall. When the self-driving car moved, she nudged Bill with her elbow.

'Talk to him,' she whispered.

Bill coughed and turned round in his seat again. 'Eh, Ben, you probably don't remember me.'

'I remember you.' They boy's eyes cut to Bill. They looked almost black under the car's interior light. 'You got me kicked off this planet.'

'I didn't personally get you kicked off—'

'But you helped. You and that Indigene who I've been told is a friend of yours. Maybe you were both scheming together.'

Bill scrambled to defend himself. 'I was monitoring Stephen. I didn't know him at the time.'

'But you used me to get closer. You put me on the government's radar.'

'Well, yes, that's what happened, but I didn't mean —'

'To get me kicked off this planet?' Ben folded his arms. 'I know. But it didn't stop you using me.'

'I didn't... shit.' Bill rubbed his jaw. 'Laura, a little help please?'

But Laura stifled a laugh.

He stared at her. 'What's so funny?'

Her laugh bubbled to the surface. 'I rarely see anyone put you in your place. It's a joy to witness.' She turned to Ben, looking contrite. 'I'm not undermining how things played out back then. But you must know your contact with Stephen was the best thing that could have happened. It led to the formation of the peace treaty.'

'Didn't feel like it was the best thing,' said Ben. 'I was only eight.'

Laura reached out a hand for Ben. He shifted away from her.

'I'm sorry for how the government treated you,' she

said pulling back. 'And if Bill had been in charge back then, it wouldn't have happened. He's helped to get you safe passage back to Exilon 5.'

'Eight years later. And this is my home.'

'Better late than never.' The calm slipped from her voice as she adjusted her position in her seat. 'We know all about what happened to you on Earth, and according to Jenny Waterson your connection with the Indigene Isobel changed the outcome there. You're a wilful kid, boy— young man. Our government treated you badly, but your positive experience with Stephen changed him and led to you to give Isobel a fair go. Don't blame Bill for the direction your life took. It's done. You can't change anything. You must decide where you go from here.'

Bill stared at the woman he'd asked to marry him more than three times. Time and again she'd refused on the basis of it being an outdated practice. He didn't know why she'd finally agreed on try four, but for him marriage proved his commitment to her. Listening to her defend his stupid actions, he'd never loved her more.

Ben uncrossed his arms and stared out the window again. 'I suppose it's not his fault. Or Stephen's. But still.'

'I'm sorry for what happened,' said Bill. 'You were in the wrong place at the wrong time. But also in the right place.'

'Okay.' Ben kept his eyes on the fast-moving scenery. 'Where are you taking me?'

'To your accommodation in New London but we need to make a small stop first.'

The car continued on the road that crossed the boundary lines of the city and travelled deep into the undeveloped, stony wasteland beyond.

Ben looked around. 'Where are we? I don't recognise this place.'

One of the designated hunting zones came into view, encased by the faint shimmer of the environmental bubble.

'Many things have changed on Exilon 5 besides the size of New London,' said Laura. 'When you were last here, only humans resided on the surface. That's still the case, but they now share the land with the Indigenes.' She pointed at the shimmer. 'That's one of the hunting zones—safe areas for the Indigenes to hunt without humans tracking them.'

'What happens if they go outside the zone?' said Ben.

'It's at their risk,' said Bill. 'The Peace Treaty only covers the zones, not the areas outside.'

'The Indigenes are fast,' said Ben.

Bill smiled. 'Yes, they are.'

'So who runs this planet?' Ben switched his focus from the scenery to Bill. 'Are the ITF still in charge?'

'Yes, and I'm their director. Laura works as my head of communications.' Laura's ability to read minds due to her partial transformation years ago qualified her for that role. 'She's also our "official" Indigene liaison.'

'What happened to the World Government? I thought all the board members relocated here after the last ships left Earth.'

'They did, but they don't control anything. Not any more.' Bill concentrated on a group of mountains in the distance. 'They and a group of individuals live on the outskirts of town—a place beyond the hunting zones.'

'What, in a new town?'

'Sort of,' said Bill.

'So why don't they want to rule any more?' said Ben. 'They never struck me as the types to give up power.'

'They still have power, just not the kind you and I

Genesis Variant

have,' said Laura.

'I don't understand.'

Bill sighed; he hated talking about them. 'The board members and a select group of two hundred people came to Exilon 5 and lived a hermitic life in the mountains. Over the next five years, the board members conspired with genetic doctors to experiment with advanced procedures they'd learned about on Earth. The numbers accompanying the board members whittled down to one hundred. The GS humans live in a place that feeds their advancement.'

'What's GS? And where, like on a farm?'

'GS stands for genetically superior. And no, not a farm. They're no longer human, thanks to the experiments. They're like Indigenes, but they're also not. Their group is evolving at an exponential rate.'

'Holy shit!' Ben leaned forward. 'Can I see one of them?'

'Not unless you want to die. The best thing you can do is stay away from those murdering freaks.'

Marcus waited in the holding area of the passenger ship as just one available spacecraft, carrying about twenty of the one hundred people on board, shuttled between the ship and the docking station. He and Harvey, travelling under pseudonyms beginning with the letter "C", were next in alphabetical order to travel on the craft. With the surname Watson, Ben should have been in the last group, but the military had picked him out of line and put him on the first craft. Marcus pressed down his bitter rage for the teenager who, just two months ago, had been under his command. It appeared the boy had friends on Exilon 5.

The spacecraft returned to the hold a short time later and he and Harvey climbed on board. Marcus strapped in tight, remembering the journey at the start to the ship stationed above Earth's atmosphere. He'd almost decorated the seats with his lunch. The five-minute journey down didn't feel as rough, but when the craft landed Marcus scrambled to be the first to exit. He would never set foot in one of those things again.

A dozen receiving stations similar to those on Earth beckoned. Marcus entered a different station to Harvey and queued airside for his identity chip to be scanned.

The officer motioned Marcus forward and Marcus passed through the barrier to landside. While he waited for Harvey, he saw a man in his early fifties with greying hair escort Ben to the exit. A blonde-haired woman too scrawny to be Marcus' type was with him.

Harvey joined him. 'No issues?' Marcus shook his head. 'Good. Let's go.'

He'd planned on ditching Harvey as soon as he made it through the receiving stations, but with freedom just moments away Marcus had no idea where to go. He followed Harvey to the exit, looking around for the box of gel masks that usually sat by the entrance. But all he found was a shallow dish on a table containing strange-looking eye wear.

'Where are the masks?'

Harvey picked up a pair of dark eye glasses and pressed them to his eyes. 'Don't need them here, but you will need a pair of these.'

Marcus glanced at the bowl of glasses, then at the exit door made of tinted glass that gave the outside world a dark, ominous look. He picked up a pair but didn't see why he had to wear them. The lack of gel masks and oxygen canisters worried him more.

Harvey approached the door and it opened. Marcus held his breath, not sure what to expect. Fresh air and a brightness to which he was not accustomed assaulted him.

He shielded his painful eyes. 'Holy shit.'

'That's what the eye wear is for,' snapped Harvey. 'Put yours on.'

Marcus put the glasses on without complaint. The heat on his skin felt strange, but nice; he was used to a much colder climate on Earth. But it didn't take long for that feeling to switch to discomfort. The heat reminded him of the old food replication terminals where the air conditioning couldn't cope with the numbers.

He walked on but something jerked him to a stop. 'What the hell—?'

Harvey pulled him back to the entrance and nodded at a car that Ben Watson was getting into. 'I know the man and woman with the boy. I don't want to see them right now.'

'What, the skinny bird and the jackass?'

'The very same. I have a past.'

Marcus never doubted that for a minute; Harvey Buchanan didn't strike him as a pushover. Yet, on Earth, Marcus had power while types like Harvey kept a low profile. It encouraged him to learn more about the weaknesses of the man who claimed to own Marcus' ass.

Marcus dropped his idea to ditch Harvey. He would play along for a while, get a feel for things and see where he fit in this world.

The sun felt like it cooked him from the inside. He draped his arm over his face. Even with the eyewear in place, his eyes pinched. At least the air tasted fresh. He pulled new oxygen into his lungs—not as pure as the canisters the criminal factions used, but good enough.

The vehicle carrying Ben and the pair Harvey avoided pulled away from the parking spot next to the station. Harvey emerged from his hiding place and walked to the same parking area, where two buses were parked. Marcus took in the rolling, green park the station overlooked. It reminded him of Astoria Park in Brooklyn, the place where Gaetano Agostini had run his operations.

Marcus followed Harvey, who approached the first of two buses. A sign on the front of each read: *Processing*.

A woman with a DPad waited by the first bus. 'All passengers will be taken to the detention centre for processing, medical care and assignment.'

'Detention Centre? Assignment?'

That wasn't part of the deal. Marcus had agreed to a new face and a better life.

'We have to blend in,' said Harvey. 'We can't exist outside of the system. ITF rules. Everyone must be useful in society.'

'So what kind of assignments are we talking about?'

Please don't say cleaner. It had been his old job before he worked for Gaetano Agostini and he had hated every fucking minute of it. He'd been someone important on Earth. No way would he start from the bottom.

'Whatever they need. Mostly construction jobs. There's a lot of ongoing work, a lot of undeveloped land.'

The line moved forward and Marcus shuffled with it. 'I didn't agree to this, Harvey. I have no interest in being a lackey here. I've got skills. Management and such.'

Harvey leaned in close to his ear. 'Lesson one: Keep your mouth shut. You're not supposed to be here. I had to pull strings to activate your identity and put it on the grid. Don't fuck it up for yourself. And don't call me Harvey in front of the officials.'

Marcus almost blurted out to Harvey that he was full of crap, and that he'd never work for him. But Marcus accepted the rare opportunity handed to him to live with a new face and a new identity on a world where no one wanted him dead. Carl, that backstabbing piece of shit, wouldn't have made it this far. His choice to side with Gaetano probably got him killed.

Couldn't have happened to a nicer asshole.

Marcus owed nothing to nobody, least of all Harvey. But he'd play along for now because, for all his ambitions and ideas, this world felt alien to him. To familiarise himself with his surroundings, he had to trust people who knew the lay of the land. He could fake it with Harvey. Or should he say John Caldwell.

'Okay, John. Whatever you say.'

Harvey patted him on the head. 'Good boy.'

Genesis Variant

Please stop for two minutes.

Stephen ignored Serena's thoughts in his head and paced inside the Council Chambers in District Three.

Serena switched to her voice. 'Stephen!'

'What if he doesn't remember me?'

'Of course he will. Why wouldn't he?'

He stopped pacing. *What if the boy won't forgive me?*

Serena pressed her forehead to his and replied to him telepathically.

It was a long time ago and he's a teenager now. He's just survived one of the worst moments in Earth's history. How could he not be happy to see you?

That thought unsettled Stephen and he wore out the same section of floor again. Shelves decorated one wall, filled with books Pierre had collected during his time as elder. Since Pierre's death eight years ago, both he and Serena had carried on the elder's tradition and collected enough books to fill several shelves. Stephen stopped at a bookcase and picked up one of Pierre's books, hoping some of the elder's wisdom lingered and might transfer to

23

him.

His scientist's mind shook off the idea. Pierre and his wife Elise had both been killed by Charles Deighton. Elise had been killed by an imprint of the late Deighton who had inhabited Anton's body and taken over his mind. Now, no traces of the pair remained. No afterlife existed as they had once thought.

Stephen frowned at the book in his hand, then shook his head and laughed. 'Look at me, a Council leader and scientist no less and I'm terrified of what a teenager thinks of me.'

'It was a crucial time in your life. He was important —a catalyst in the relationship between the Indigenes and the humans.'

I treated him no better than a dog.

Serena smiled. *Throughout history, dogs were considered man's best friend. Maybe that's a compliment.* She held out her hands. *Do you want me to work my magic on you?*

She referred to her ability to influence the people around her, to make them think and do what she wanted. She could also calm a room, similar to how Elise, an empath, used to when she was alive. His friend Arianna had taken over the position of most powerful empath in the district.

'No, I must deal with this my way. I can't take the easy way out. I need to face him.'

'Okay, but whatever happens, I'll be with you.'

Stephen gently gripped the sides of her head and pressed his forehead to hers. 'As you've always been from the moment you came into my life.'

Serena had shown up in District Three at the same time Anton had returned home after months in human captivity and with a bomb set to kill the Indigenes. Elise had called Serena an Indigene in her own right, but an anomaly that required further investigation. That investigation had led them to uncover what she was—a human scientist whose DNA had been merged with Anton's—a second-generation Indigene—to create a new Indigene. Not only could Serena control other Indigenes but also the Nexus—the place that healed their bodies and enhanced their natural abilities like telepathy and influence, and Stephen's "reader" ability.

After Pierre's death, Serena had chosen a life with Stephen over a return to her human life.

'And I'll be here as long as you still want me.' Serena's eyes cut to the open chamber door. She stood back. 'They're here.'

Stephen's heart pounded fast in his chest. He wasn't ready. When would he ever be? His meeting with Ben Watson eight years ago had gotten the boy extricated to Earth. Most of the boy's life had been spent under the control of the criminal factions who'd taken over after the World Government had abandoned the planet in favour of Exilon 5.

He breathed in and out deeply; it did little to calm him. 'How can I command an entire district, but I'm terrified about meeting one boy?'

Serena touched his arm. 'Because you had a connection with him, albeit it a fleeting one. He represents who you used to be and who you have become.'

Stephen's eyes flashed to the door when he heard three sets of footsteps approaching the Council Chambers.

He took one last deep breath and waited. Bill Taggart appeared first, followed by Laura O'Halloran. The boy trailed behind. He was taller and more sullen than Stephen remembered. All three wore gel masks in the thin, tunnel air that suited the Indigenes most.

Stephen walked over to Bill and gave his friend a hug.

'You nervous?' Bill whispered by his ear.

'I don't know why.'

'You and me both. I almost left the docking station before he arrived. Laura had to talk me into staying.'

Stephen chuckled, feeling his own load lighten. He hugged Laura next. 'I'm glad you're here.'

'That's what Bill said to me earlier.'

Stephen pulled back. 'He knows what he's talking about.'

Laura smiled.

Can't put this off forever, said Serena.

He dropped the delay tactics and zeroed in on the boy who leaned against the wall, hands in his pockets, doing his best not to look at him.

But Stephen sensed his curiosity.

'Hello,' he said.

Ben glanced at him. 'Hey.'

'Do you remember me?'

Ben kept his gaze elsewhere. 'Yeah.'

The reply lacked emotion, but Stephen felt the hidden anticipation, excitement and anger that rolled off Ben in waves.

'Do you want to sit down?'

Stephen pointed to the table and chairs that he'd had put in specially. Humans preferred to sit—unlike Indigenes.

Ben folded his arms. 'Nah, I'm okay here.'

A fuzzy feeling came over Stephen's thoughts. He looked up at Serena to see her concentrating on Ben.

'Stop it,' said Ben, his eyes cutting to her. Serena blinked once and Stephen felt her influence drop away. 'I know what it feels like to have one of you in my head.'

'Sorry, I was just trying to help,' said Serena.

She wasn't used to opposition; humans found her hard to resist. But Ben appeared to be a good match for her. He wondered if the boy could help Serena sharpen her skills. It had been a long time since she'd met a challenging opponent.

The boy pushed off from the wall and walked over to the bookshelves. His fingers grazed the covers of two hardback books on Earth's history.

Serena joined him but kept a small distance. 'I didn't mean to upset you.'

'It's just been a long time since I've seen him,' Ben said to Serena, nodding to Stephen. 'I need to process what I feel on my own, not have you fix it. That's what got me into this mess in the first place. I thought I needed others to fix my problems, but I had the power to do it all along.'

Ben looked around the room. Bill and Laura's silence, their anticipation of how the boy would react, made the atmosphere tense and awkward. Stephen both sensed and saw Ben's hesitation. It manifested as a yellowish grey aura.

'How about we leave these two to talk?' Serena suggested.

Stephen sensed that Laura battled against her abilities. They flowed more freely in the district. He had felt for some time that she could influence like Serena— though not to the same degree. But he could no longer read her thoughts, not since he had treated her for her Seasonal Affective Disorder. It had ignited a change on a cellular level within her, though Laura still refused to accept that she was part Indigene.

A hesitant Bill didn't move until Laura steered him out of the room. Bill still had questions for the boy—either that or he sought the same forgiveness that Stephen did.

Eliza Green

When just he and Ben remained, Stephen closed the heavy, oak door that sealed the soundproofed room. Pierre had held many secret discussions here that had only led to mistrust within District Three. After his death, Serena and Stephen had adopted an open door policy. But not today. Today, this discussion would remain private.

Stephen sat at the table and a nervous-looking Ben did the same.

'I never thought I'd get the chance to speak with you again,' said Stephen. 'You must have questions for me.'

'Are you responsible for getting me passage off Earth?'

'Partly. Bill had a lot to do with that.'

'Well, that makes us even.'

Stephen sat back, surprised. 'You're forgiving me, just like that?'

Ben folded his arms, but his wariness dropped a little. 'Isobel told me I was the reason you changed your mind about humans. Is that true?'

'Yes. You were the catalyst. I didn't know what you were. We called you Surface Creatures. Then you revealed that you were human.'

'I don't understand. Why was that such a big deal?'

'Because we are also human, but we hadn't used the term for what we thought was centuries.' Stephen leaned forward. 'The term Indigenes had stuck over the years. Though, given our origin, and the fact that our species had only really existed for fifty years, it's possible the Indigene name was just a memory implant.'

'So you changed your mind about humans because of my revelation?'

Stephen smiled and shook his head. That wasn't even close. 'You must have sensed my wariness of you at

28

the time. Our meeting was just a mission to gather information on your species. We had minimal success with other humans. Most were aggressive towards us.'

'Then you met me...'

'You were innocent. A blank slate. You called me a friend without even knowing anything about me. That had not been my experience of your species up to that point.' Stephen shifted in his seat; he would never get used to sitting. 'Do you know why I met you the second time?'

Ben shrugged and clasped his hands. 'Because I hadn't given you the answer you wanted?'

Stephen laughed, just as Ben frowned. 'You were astute back then. I see you haven't lost that.'

'I may have only been eight, but I knew stuff. My life was complicated then and it is now. Difference is I know better.'

Stephen stood up and paced, relieved to be out of the confines of the chair. 'I met with you again because your innocence intrigued me. You reminded me of our young. Less developed mentally than our Evolvers, but innocent like they are. I saw my young self in you. Curious. Caring. Trusting. Truth was I didn't like the comparison.'

Ben's eyes tracked his movements. 'Why?'

'You reminded me of me, and even though we looked different it pained me to admit we were the same underneath. We were ready to fight you humans, which made us no better *than* humans. It began to feel like we were at war with ourselves.'

Ben concentrated on his clasped hands. 'I was so excited when I met you. I was really into spy stories at the time. Did I tell you that?' Stephen shook his head and Ben smiled. 'I thought you were a spy.'

Stephen remembered. 'You asked me if I knew

your mother.'

'Yeah, stupid kid stuff.' Ben's aura had a tinge of red to it. 'I needn't have worried so much. She didn't care about me. Don't feel bad for what happened. I brought it on myself.'

Stephen stopped pacing. 'Why do you think that? None of it was your fault.'

'I had silly notions that my father would return one day, and he would rescue me from my mother. She wasn't exactly parent of the year. But my father never came and nobody questioned my mother's lack of parenting skills. Then I met you. I not only found a father figure, but a friend. You were interested in what I had to say. I don't blame you, only me. If I had heeded the only advice my mother ever gave me, which was to never talk to strangers, we wouldn't have met.'

'Well, I'm glad you ignored her advice. I'm not sure how things would have played out had I not discovered the true name of your species—and ours.' The red in Ben's aura deepened. Stephen changed the subject. 'How's Isobel?'

Ben smiled and his aura switched to green. 'She's helping to integrate the Indigenes into life on Earth. They don't need masks like the humans do. It's weird, but Earth is the perfect place for them.'

Stephen laughed at a very old memory. 'I said the same thing when my friend Anton and I arrived on Earth for the first time.'

'Huh, ironic.'

'Ironic indeed. Are you pleased to be home?'

'Maybe... I was born on this planet. But Earth had become my home.' A grey colour overshadowed the green. 'But my family is dead now.' Ben looked around the chambers. 'Your home is nice and all, but I'd rather

Genesis Variant

live up there, in the sunshine. I've had enough of dark places to last a lifetime.'

'Agreed. You can't breathe the air down here anyway. The surface is safer. Laura has arranged special accommodation for you. It's a place that helps young men and women to adjust to life on Exilon 5 and to find work, or continue their education. Whatever's required.'

'And that's where I'll live?'

'Yes.' Stephen sensed the boy's hesitation. 'You don't approve? It will give you more freedom than you had on Earth.'

'I had a chance to help when I was there. I would like to be useful to whatever cause you need here. I helped to bring down the criminals.' Ben's aura glowed orange, showing his pride. 'Use me, or I'll disappear.'

He gestured for Ben to stand. 'It's late so you'll spend the night here.'

Ben tapped his mask. 'Do I have to wear this all night?'

Stephen shook his head and opened the door. 'We have created special rooms for such occasions. The insignia rock can draw air from the surface. You will be comfortable.'

'Then you'll find something for me to do?'

To give him no purpose on Exilon 5 would be a worse fate than to have left him on Earth.

'I'll speak to Serena and Laura. No promises.'

5

This feeling of contrition surprised Bill. He normally did what pleased him, only answering to the people who mattered most. In the early days it had been his first wife, Isla. But since he'd met Laura and Stephen, a gnawing need for self-improvement followed him like a shadow. His stomach clenched as he waited alongside Laura and Serena for Stephen and Ben to finish their talk.

He kept quiet over how much Ben's lack of interest in him bothered him. Nor had the boy offered thanks to Bill for rescuing him from that hellhole called Earth—a description that Jenny Waterson used often to describe his former home.

Bill shook his head. Why should Ben thank him? Hadn't his actions extradited him to Earth in the first place?

A kiss from Laura on his cheek snapped him out of his melancholy.

'Stop it,' she said.

He looked at her. 'Stop what?'

'You've gone to that pessimistic place of yours.'

He tried to look cool. 'No, I haven't.'

'Even Serena can sense it, but she's too polite to say anything.'

Serena looked somewhere else.

'I know when you're working yourself up in knots.'

Bill huffed out a breath. 'It's your fault, you know.'

Laura's eyes grew large. 'Mine, how?'

'You made me care about more than just me.'

The Council Chamber door opened before she could answer, but the smile on her face was all the reply he needed. Bill focused on Ben and braced for an irate teenager. It surprised him to find a calm one. Stephen joined Serena and they pressed their foreheads together.

Serena pulled away and spoke to Ben. 'It's late. I'll show you to your quarters.'

Ben nodded, holding on tight to his satchel. 'Got anything to eat?'

Serena looked unsure and glanced at Laura.

'I think I can rustle up something,' said Laura. 'I'll follow you shortly.'

When Ben had left with Serena, Stephen returned to the Council Chambers. Bill and Laura followed him inside to see the Indigene stood in the middle of the room. He turned to face them.

'How did it go?' said Bill.

He may not have Stephen's ability to sense moods or see them in colours, but his profiler past taught him how to read body language. The lack of tension in his friend's shoulders said it had gone well.

'I never thought I'd have this chance to put things right,' said Stephen. 'What a coincidence that Isobel ended up with his adopted grandfather. We couldn't have planned that better if we'd tried.'

'A fucking miracle if you ask me.' Bill ran a hand over the three-day stubble on his face. The arrival of this day, this moment, had dominated his thoughts. 'I nearly chickened out of meeting him in the docking station.'

Stephen nodded. 'I sensed your edginess when you brought him here. He didn't have the worst life on Earth. From what he told me his guardian, Albert Lee, was a very kind man.'

Bill walked over to the table and sat down in a chair. 'Dead now?'

'Yes and his step brother. Both killed by the faction overseeing their neighbourhood. Ben's all alone now and very eager to help out our cause.'

Laura stood next to the bookshelves. She rarely sat down, unless they were at home—a side effect of her rapid change into an Indigene before having that change reversed.

'You still need to talk to him, Bill,' said Laura. 'He may have forgiven Stephen but I sensed he's unsure about you.'

'You should use your detection skill more,' said Stephen.

Laura shifted, as if uncomfortable. She rarely used her Indigene skills around people except for a trusted few, including Bill. Laura had regained her human appearance and kept her ability to detect dishonesty in others. The combination made her the perfect candidate to become Bill's chief communication officer.

'I agree with Stephen,' said Bill. 'I don't understand why you keep it hidden. In the last eight years you used it, what, half a dozen times, and only when I've insisted.'

Laura crossed her arms. 'It feels as if I'm being deceptive. The people I use it on don't know I can see their lies.'

Stephen smiled. 'You get used to it, believe me. When it's all you know, you work around the ethics of knowing more than others.'

'Maybe.' Laura didn't sound convinced. 'I mean, it's not like I can influence people like Serena, or see the future like you. Or see the inner workings of tech without opening it, like Anton can. Or know what it means to be an empath, like Arianna. You all have very important skills.'

'You've developed a supercharged sixth sense—a heightened perception of deception that none of us have,' said Stephen. 'It's an extension of who you were as a human.'

Laura huffed. 'If I had that skill when I was just an office worker in the Earth Security Centre, I might have saved myself a lot of grief.'

'It was your ability to see past my appearance that led me to trust you,' said Stephen.

'And me,' added Bill.

Laura rolled her eyes. 'Great. I've got the power of trust.'

'Don't give up on your ability. The more you use it the more it will make sense,' said Stephen.

'Maybe.'

Laura's head whipped round at a speed that used to alarm Bill. She stared at the door and Bill knew she'd heard something.

'Do you hear that?' said Stephen. 'Sounds like a low rumble.'

Laura smiled. 'That's the sound of a hungry teenager. I'd better go before he starts to eat the dirt off the floor.'

She left Bill and Stephen alone.

Stephen joined Bill at the table. 'She could be even more useful if she stops fighting her Indigene side.'

Bill couldn't agree more. But any time he brought the subject up, Laura shut the discussion down. 'It's no use either of us telling her how useful her deception skill is. She has to experience it.'

'Laura's feelings about her being an imposter are potent. Serena senses that better than I can.'

'Do the other Indigenes feel that way about her?'

'Some do. They still fight their origin. That's natural.' Stephen stood up, restless. He picked a book off the shelf and studied the spine. 'But we've got bigger problems to deal with.'

Bill nodded. 'Like the genetically superior humans?'

After the peace treaty agreement, the board members had arrived from Earth with two hundred selected humans, dozens of Earth doctors and data detailing new genetic practices from their study of the Indigenes. Five years of experimentation had followed and the numbers had whittled down to just one hundred. Bill had established the new numbers through ITF monitoring and Tanya's own confirmation. During that time, Tanya had continued to preside over ITF matters and the peace treaty. Three years ago, the group had relocated to a set of caves in a mountainous range. Their genetic experiments to improve the code in a select few appeared to change them physically. Tanya Li had aged significantly and showed no further interest in protecting the treaty. Her lack of interest had allowed rogue elements on both the Indigene and human sides to test the strength of that accord.

'When they arrived on this planet, we didn't interfere with their plans.' Stephen returned the book to the shelf. 'Their activities were of no concern to us. The treaty gave us what we wanted: the freedom to hunt without persecution. But in the last few months I've detected an increased presence outside the caves they

36

rarely left before. That makes the Indigenes uneasy and it has led some to attack humans.'

The attacks were a problem; they violated the treaty.

'I don't know why the GS live in isolation or why they built that environ,' said Bill. 'I haven't spoken to Tanya since she relocated to the caves.'

Stephen had reported back on the movements of the GS while out hunting. A prediction had hit him three months before it happened: He'd seen them build the environ, covered in white tarpaulin, located two miles from the caves. Stephen had no answers for Bill as to why they'd built it.

Bill continued. 'In the last few days, my team has reported a small drain of power from New London's solar station. It appears the GS have infiltrated the feed by running a cable from the base station to the city.'

'What are they using the power for?'

'No idea. The cable leads back to their environ. Whatever they have inside needs energy.'

'Have you tried disconnecting it?'

Bill nodded. 'I sent out a group of engineers to take a look. The GS are using an interactive cable that's embedded into the main supply at a halfway point. We need to do more analysis on how the cable has attached itself to the feed. If we just yank it out, we risk shutting down the power to the city.'

'What about your former boss, Simon Shaw? He's one of them. Why not ask him what's going on?'

Bill hadn't seen Shaw in almost eight years, not since he first came to Exilon 5. Bill had introduced him to Stephen, who had given him a tour of District Three. That was before Bill had learned of Simon's involvement in Tanya's GS human experiments. Simon had been a friend

37

once who'd helped him out on more than one occasion. But now, Bill had no idea what the experiments had done to him.

'I can't be sure if the Simon I knew even exists any more.'

'A quiet group of genetically enhanced humans can't be a good thing, Bill.'

He had to agree. 'But the splinter groups forming on both sides worry me more. Groups of who knows what size preparing to fight each other? We could be facing another war, worse than what happened eight years ago.'

The war eight years ago between board members, their soldiers and the Indigenes had ended Pierre's life, but had also cemented an uneasy treaty.

'That time was different.' Stephen paced. 'That dissent amounted to nothing. Pierre had abandoned his leadership duties after Elise died. The district was in turmoil. None of us knew what would happen to our race.' He stopped pacing. 'But when he died, Serena and I secured a future through the treaty. Dissent while things are good doesn't make sense. We are in a better position than before the treaty.'

Bill stood up and joined Stephen by the bookshelves. 'It appears some don't agree with you. To be honest, that damn treaty is held together with paper and glue. One hundred genetically enhanced humans with numbers too small to do damage on their own evolve every day. But with a new race comes a new set of problems. What are they becoming? Where do they fit into society? Will they issue demands?'

'I know. It's the Indigene situation all over again.' Stephen sighed. 'Give me some time to analyse the root of this new Indigene dissent.'

Despite his investigator background, Bill preferred

action and real solutions over analysis. But Stephen knew best how to handle the situation with his charges.

'What about the unrest on the human side?' said Bill.

That was Bill's problem. How to handle it? He'd no idea.

'We need spies,' said Stephen.

Bill perked up at that actionable idea. 'Anyone in mind?'

'Well, Laura for a start.'

'No. Absolutely not.'

'Come on, Bill. She should put her Indigene skill to use and weed out the liars.'

'It wouldn't work. They all know she works for the ITF.'

'How about we alter her appearance so she's unrecognisable?'

While Bill liked the idea in general, he hated it for Laura. He'd almost lost her once, during her Indigene transformation.

'There must be another way.'

'I can't think of one and we have to act soon, Bill.'

'I'll give it some thought.'

'I thought you preferred to move fast on ideas?'

Bill almost laughed at the irony. But when it came to Laura's safety, he had all the patience in the world.

Stephen held his hands up. 'I sense your unease. We can talk about other solutions. I might have an idea about something else.'

'What?'

'The boy, Ben. He wants something to do, a reason to live. It could help to heal his wounds.'

When his first wife Isla had died protecting the Indigenes, Bill had found solace in ignoring others' problems. Life had been simpler back then. But Laura had come along and shown him a better life, one where he didn't turn his back on society.

He would see the boy right. He owed Ben that much.

'I'll see what I can find for him to do.' Maybe Laura would have a use for him. 'Jenny Waterson said he was good at gathering intel and staying off the radar. She found him hiding in the back of their car once. Didn't even know he was there—' Bill stopped talking when Stephen's expression brightened. 'What?'

'I think we should call a meeting with the representatives to discuss the GS and the splinter groups. I've just thought of a better idea.'

6

Laura stopped off at one of the rooms near the exit to the surface where she'd left her backpack. She rummaged inside the bag and pulled out a sandwich she'd made for Bill that morning: ham and cheese. Her husband barely ate unless she forced him—or steak was on the menu. She also took out an unopened bottle of water and caught up to Serena and Ben.

She didn't have to go far, picking up Ben's scent in one of the tunnels close to her location. She stopped at one of the special rooms built to accommodate human visitors. Inside was a bed and bedside locker. The faint bubble from the insignia rock that drew clean air from the surface shimmered around both items. Only those with superior sight could see the outline. Laura had seen many new things since her transformation eight years ago.

Serena stood by the door while a quiet Ben sat on the bed, leaning forward and staring at the ground. His energy was a contrast to the boisterous teens she'd encountered on Exilon 5. Through Jenny Waterson's recounts, Laura understood what horrors the teen had seen on Earth. The criminal regime had been days away from starving the residents or shooting them. If it hadn't been for Isobel, things might have been far worse. Jenny had credited her for shifting the balance of power back to the ordinary people. And saving them.

Ben held his mask in his hand. A mobile amplification machine sat next to the bed and drew out pockets of trapped air inside the insignia rock into a contained bubble. The environmental barriers surrounding the hunting zones worked along the same principles, except in reverse.

Laura pushed through the membrane and handed the sandwich and water to Ben. 'Here you go.' Ben took the items from her and she popped off her mask. 'It's not much, but you'll only be here for tonight. We really should get a replicator down here.'

She looked back at Serena, who nodded.

'I'm sure Anton could find a way to power it,' she said.

Ben examined the room hewn out of bare rock.

'Your accommodation is located in New London, a shared property run by a lovely lady, Annette. Someone will take you there in the morning.'

Ben put the sandwich and water down on the locker and looked up at her. 'So you can dump me there and forget about me? I won't stay there. I want to be of use. Stephen promised.'

Laura sat beside him. 'No, not dump. You need to live somewhere other than underground. If Stephen promised, he'll deliver. But you must be patient. This planet is not how you remember it.'

'You mean the genetically superior humans?'

'Among other things.' Laura stood. 'Eat your food and get some rest. There's a bathroom two doors down.'

She put on her gel mask, pleased to see Ben had at

least unwrapped the sandwich. She exited the bubble. Serena nodded for her to walk outside.

'You're good at that,' said Serena when they were far enough away from Ben that he couldn't hear.

'At what?'

'Calming people. You're a natural.'

Laura didn't agree. She shrugged.

A strange feeling came over her when Serena invaded her mind and tugged at the privacy wall she'd erected around her thoughts.

'You could just ask, you know,' said Laura. 'It wasn't that long ago you were also human.'

Eight years ago Serena had been altered using some of Anton's code. Serena was a perfect human-Indigene hybrid because she could switch between her human and Indigene side at will.

'I didn't mean to intrude,' said Serena. 'But I wonder why you maintain such a high privacy wall around us. You've had the same length of time as I have to get used to your abilities.'

'I may have been Indigene for a half a second, but that wasn't long enough to feel like one.'

Serena shook her head. 'I disagree. It doesn't matter how long you are something; it matters where you feel you belong. I had been Indigene for only a short time before Stephen showed me my files. It felt natural to remain as one.'

Laura fiddled with the oxygen flow on her canister. Serena's astuteness bothered her. She didn't want to admit to how lost she'd felt for a while now. Accepting it could mean major upheaval in her life and she couldn't do that to Bill.

'You know, that gel mask may not be necessary,' said Serena.

'It feels necessary,' said Laura.

'After Isobel's genetic reversal, her lungs adapted in a way we never thought possible. The reversal changed the lung tissue's rate of oxygen absorption. She could move between environments without the need for the air filtration device or the gel mask.'

Jenny had said as much in her report. Laura had glossed over that detail on purpose.

Serena continued. 'We reversed your genetic mutations. We may have given you the same ability.'

Laura readjusted the mask on her face despite its already tight seal, as though the action would put an end to this conversation. 'Maybe I'll test it someday.'

Her reply was short and clipped, much like her temper these last few months. Serena pushed against her privacy wall a second time.

'Stop, please. I don't like it when you do that. If I wanted you to know something I'd tell you.'

She felt Serena's exit, like a flutter of wings against her skin.

'I'm sorry. It's just you haven't talked much about your brief time as an Indigene, and my influence doesn't appear to work on you.'

Laura stopped walking. 'There's nothing to say about it. I'm fine.'

Serena stopped too and grabbed her hands. 'Aren't you curious to know what abilities you unlocked, to know your real self?'

'My real self is human, Serena. I don't know how else to say that.'

'I've seen glimpses of your speed, how you pay greater attention to some people than others. You use your senses as if you're a child figuring them out. You've worked out some, but you won't embrace the ability you've mastered the most. Instead, you hide it.'

Laura sighed. Sometimes it drained her to be around the Indigenes, who felt and sensed too much. Maybe if she told Serena something, she would back off.

'I can tell when people are lying. It feels like a tiny shudder in the air between us. But it's not just that; the lie also manifests as an impassive, dark figure or shadow behind them. When the person lies, the figure moves almost imperceptibly, like an adjustment.'

It was the only thing clear to her.

'A dark figure?'

Laura nodded. 'We all have one, but others can't see it. The more we lie, the farther the shadow misaligns from the original. When we tell the truth, the shadow stays perfectly aligned to our corporeal form.'

Serena's smile told Laura she'd only heightened the elder's curiosity, not dampened it.

'I'd like for you to work with Arianna in the Nexus. She helped me after Stephen brought me there for the first time. Her empath ability sensed a new connection between me and the Nexus. It had to do with the different energy I put out. The Nexus changed the same day I used it.' She tapped a finger against her lip. 'I'd like to see how it reacts to you. There are other tests we can perform, lab-based ones. Stephen performed similar ones on me—'

Laura put her hand up. 'I really appreciate your interest in this, but I don't want to explore anything. I know what I can do, and I'm happy with that.'

She strengthened her privacy wall when she felt Serena push against it a third time. Truth was she hadn't been happy for a while.

Serena backed off. 'I promise not to push, but I am curious and I will ask again. Because the GS humans are up to something and we need everyone at peak ability fitness. We've no idea what they're planning.'

'And you will have my help. Mine and Bill's.'

Serena turned and listened. 'Stephen's calling me. We should head back.'

Her connection with Stephen impressed Laura. To her, Bill's thoughts sounded like a gentle hum. She couldn't read them, or sense when he was lying. His mind was closed off to her. But wasn't that a good thing?

Maybe love blinded the truth.

They walked back to the Council Chambers.

Along the way, Serena said, 'You'll have to face it at some point. If you don't it will consume you.'

'And I will,' said Laura. 'But not now.'

Never, if she had her way.

Because accepting just how Indigene she felt would force her to face another truth: She'd outgrown her human life.

Where would that leave her and Bill?

7

The vehicle destined for the detention centre passed through a steel perimeter and pulled up outside a dome-shaped building on the edge of the city with a rusty sign that read: *Biodome*. The place reminded Marcus of the condemned buildings on Earth that were no longer fit for purpose. The cracked tarmac road to the facility showed further signs of neglect as weeds pushed through the fissures. A layer of red dust covered the white dome made of glass and the tarpaulin that partially covered it.

The area buzzed with activity as men in green uniforms patrolled the vicinity. Marcus waited his turn to get off the vehicle.

'Inside please.' A solider gestured to the entrance of the building. 'And be ready to scan your identity chips.'

Marcus followed the other "detainees" inside the building. It felt like an internment camp in the presence of so many soldiers. The dome interior was a large, open space with a long table at the back wall where several people sat with DPads. The air had a faint smell of dung to it, and even though the space had been cleared, Marcus could see evidence by way of holes in the floor that the space used to be sectioned.

He'd heard the biodomes on Exilon 5 housed and cultivated several breeds of animal resurrected from preserved DNA following their extinction on Earth. The rusty sign and faint smell told him the animals had been moved on some time ago.

Now, those in charge used the space to herd a different animal. One day, Marcus would show them just how much of an animal he could be.

He moved only as fast as the person in front of him and reached the long trestle table where a woman with a DPad waited. A scanning flat plate on the table tilted outward at a forty-five-degree angle.

'Press your left thumb on the plate,' she said without looking up at him.

Marcus did and watched his identity chip produce a fake picture and details about the alter ego that Harvey had created for him on Earth.

She turned the plate back to her and swiped the information off screen to the left.

'Mr Martin Casey, you will be assigned a construction job. Please wait over there.' She pointed at a group gathered under a sign that read: *Construction*. 'Someone will take you to the safe house soon.'

Safe house? Like the type they used for reformed addicts and criminals just out of prison with no place to go? Marcus would not let some woman order him around. He'd been Gaetano's right hand man for fuck's sake. Or at least he would have been if his son Enzo hadn't muscled his way into the family business. Enzo had been nothing more than a pretty boy asshole and lazy, psychotic fucker who couldn't organise an orgy in a brothel.

Marcus levelled a glare at her but she returned him a look filled with boredom and apathy.

'Is there nothing else?' he said. 'I'm more qualified than that. Check my credentials.'

He'd given Harvey a list of his qualifications: strategist, management, right-hand man.

She turned the plate outward to show him the second page of information from his chip. He nearly threw up in his mouth when he saw only one thing under skills: *Construction*.

Harvey, the lying bastard. He searched for the man, finding him in another queue and paying him no attention. He turned back to the woman.

'This is a mistake. My skills are listed wrong,' Marcus stuttered. 'Check again.'

'No mistake. The chips never lie. Please stand over there. Next!'

She pointed off to the side and tended to the next person. Her disinterest irritated him more than Harvey's lies about his skills. What kind of world put bitchy women in power and men like him at the bottom of the career barrel? The sooner he got out from under Harvey, the better.

He gritted his teeth and stood alongside a group of able-bodied men. Marcus could do manual fucking labour in his sleep. But it was beneath him. His true skills lay in his mind and he would put that to the test soon.

Harvey scanned his thumb and joked with the woman in charge. Ever since he had changed Marcus' face, the man acted like he owned him. Harvey Buchanan did not compare to a man like Gaetano Agostini. Marcus would not follow a glorified geneticist for long.

Harvey joined him under the *Construction* sign.

'What the fuck, man?' Marcus hissed out of earshot of the others. 'I didn't agree to this. What happened to my other skills, the ones I told you to put down?'

'What, strategist, management?'

'Yeah.'

'Can you read?'

'A bit.'

'Can you write?'

Marcus didn't see how that mattered. 'I didn't need either when I was on Earth. So why here?'

'Because this is not Earth. Your lot aren't in control here. The ones with brains are, get it? You need to slide in under their radar.'

Marcus puffed out his chest. 'I'm ten times better than these assholes in charge.'

'But you're uneducated and scrappy. You lose your temper over the most ridiculous things. You are unstable.'

'Who fucking said that?' Marcus hissed.

'You just did. Most people just get on with it, but you think everyone owes you something because you once held a shaky position of power on Earth. Well, here's the kicker. You only got that position because the educated relocated here. You're no match for them. To be somebody on Exilon 5, you'll have to prove yourself.'

Marcus gritted his teeth and kept the name he wanted to call Harvey to himself.

One of the soldiers came over and spoke to them formally. 'I'll be taking you to the safe house. The shared accommodation is nothing fancy, but you'll be comfortable. Follow me, please.'

Marcus and his group followed the soldier out of the animal den and into a waiting vehicle. The soldier got in the front and laid a set of coordinates into the dashboard console. The self-driving vehicle drove away from the abandoned biodome and headed west along a road that left the city behind.

The contrast between the developed city and the

land beyond shocked Marcus. Inside, carefully constructed roads and iconic buildings sat next to green spaces filled with trees and flowers. Outside, it looked like the world had fallen away. Except for the odd mountainous range in the distance, the single road appeared to run straight through a flat, stony landscape. Marcus stared into the distance. If there really were other cities on Exilon 5, he couldn't see them.

The car turned left suddenly on to another isolated road and stopped outside a half-constructed neighbourhood, identifiable by the rows of unfinished houses in various states of build. From what Marcus could see, this build appeared to span an area covering approximately fifty acres. The vehicle pulled up outside a three-storey house made of brown brick—the only one that looked finished. The start of the city wasn't far, maybe a mile or so.

'You must scan your chips upon entry and exit,' said the soldier from the front seat. 'Your landlord is waiting inside.'

Marcus got out and entered the house. It looked nothing like the Deighton mansion on Earth. The house, with its wooden floors, white walls and basic, grey furniture, looked more like Albert Lee's tavern than it did a home.

He missed the opulence of the mansions on Earth abandoned by those with money and power and occupied by the criminal factions. He hadn't given up power to become a lowlife like the Waverley rejects he'd controlled there.

Harvey stood beside him. 'It's not that bad. I've lived in worse.'

'Not bad?' Marcus looked around the place that reminded him too much of his rough childhood home in

Hunt's point. 'This is a fucking nightmare.'

'Cheer up; things could be worse,' said a tall man who appeared from another room.

The man had long, brown hair tied back in a ponytail and glasses. He looked around at the faces in the room.

He pulled a bunch of envelopes out of his back pocket and shuffled them in his hand. 'Welcome, everyone. We've been promised more bodies for a while now. This neighbourhood build is six months behind schedule.' He handed everyone an envelope. 'My name's Ollie Patterson. These contain your assigned rooms, your schedule, when you work, when you eat.'

'How much do we get paid?' one man asked.

'You're paid in food and board.'

'Shit,' said the man.

Marcus couldn't agree more.

'Get settled in. Work begins at 7am.'

Ollie left the room and the group tore open their envelopes.

Marcus opened his white envelope with a red dot in the left-hand corner. It contained a key to room four on the first floor, and a card with a holographic interface showing his schedule for the next day. He picked up the card and tried flicking the information on, like he would with a DPad, but only one screen existed. Then the schedule changed and something new popped up for that evening. It read:

Meeting at 10pm. Flip the card over and wait at the red location.

Marcus turned the card over and a map appeared of the building zone showing him his current location in green and another marked in red.

The others headed off to their rooms.

Harvey stayed behind and examined his room key. 'Room 5. Looks like we're beside each other. Isn't that cosy?'

'You can forget about coming into my room at night. I like girls.'

Harvey glanced at the card in Marcus' hand. 'See you at ten. Don't be late. And don't scan your chip when you leave.'

He walked off before Marcus could ask him what the meeting was for. What happened at ten?

☼

At ten minutes to ten, Marcus left his room. The directions that had disappeared right after he'd seen them had appeared on the back of his information card five minutes ago. They showed a path between his location and his destination. It looked to be two streets over—less than five minutes' walk.

The place was empty when he crept downstairs. A scanner sat by the door. The soldier had said they must scan their chips upon exit and entry. Marcus slipped out the front door without scanning his, as Harvey had instructed.

The cool air felt weird on his face and panic hit him. Marcus groped for the mask he'd forgotten to bring. He searched his pockets, the ground. He clamped his hand over his mouth to limit the toxicity. It took a few controlled breaths and nothing bad to happen for him to remember where he was. He peeled his fingers away and drew in a little of the fresh air that made his lungs ache.

Fucking idiot, Marcus.

It felt strange, yet liberating not to wear a mask or check if his canister still had oxygen. The Indigenes, the ones the factions had put to work on Earth, had produced decent versions of the canister that were an improvement on the leaky versions given to the neighbourhoods.

Marcus followed the directions, passing by unfinished properties he guessed it would be his new job to build. In the distance, idle machines sat behind wire fencing. He wondered what they were for. With no experience in construction and no clue how to use a hammer for more than bashing people's skulls in, he wondered how long it would take for Ollie to figure him out.

But the more he thought about it, the more he admitted Harvey was right. His inability to read and write precluded him from many jobs. Before he became somebody, before the factions had risen to power on Earth, he'd been a genetic reject. Gaetano Agostini hadn't cared if he could read or write. But this wasn't Earth and he didn't know where he fit in.

Yet.

He arrived at the location—an open-air storage area with bricks, roof tiles and metal girders—to find a group of men gathered at the metal fencing. A black vehicle waited. Harvey was already there talking with Ollie.

Curious, Marcus moved closer to hear Harvey speaking to Ollie in Russian. He settled at the back of the group of seven men and listened to the language most black-market dealers on Earth spoke. The Agostini faction's biggest rival gang had been a group of Russians with no empathy and little patience.

Ollie and Harvey shook hands.

Then Ollie pointed to the vehicle. 'Everyone get in. We're taking a little trip out of town.'

Marcus sat in the back with the seven men, while Harvey and Ollie sat up front. Nobody spoke during the fifteen-minute journey, except for the two men up front who spoke in Russian to each other.

The car pulled over and Harvey turned around. 'Everyone out.'

Marcus stepped out and looked around at the remote location. He hated remote places. He knew what happened there.

Harvey and Ollie stood before them. Neither man had a weapon, but that didn't mean snipers weren't positioned to take them out. He hoped he'd done enough to convince Harvey to keep him around.

Ollie spoke. 'Those of you looking like you're about to crap your pants, it's not your time to die. So relax.' Everyone exhaled, including Marcus. 'You all know my name. The man to my left is John Caldwell.'

Harvey's alias.

Ollie continued, 'John and I need recruits for a new splinter group to disband the peace treaty and this man—' He pointed at Harvey. '—has identified each of you as suitable candidates. The treaty has done nothing to improve life on Exilon 5. The rich stay rich while the poor build houses for the rich. The ITF says this world has no class divide, but that's not true.' Ollie paced in front of their group. 'The Indigenes have liberties we do not enjoy. For starters, they have permission to hunt and kill animals in special zones where the bigger biodomes exist. We are now the second-class citizens the Indigenes once were. Their zones encroach on human boundary lines and limit access to other areas we use. We are not permitted to cross their land. It's like the land is hallowed ground. This is our world and we will no longer live by these restrictions.'

'The class divide is like this.' Harvey demonstrated with his hand. 'The genetically-superior humans, International Task Force, Indigenes, animals, then us. You see how wrong that is? And some Indigenes feel the treaty is bad. Some see privileges going to a special few, namely elders and anyone with a special connection to those elders. To help change things on this planet, we've joined forces with the other side.'

Other side? Marcus looked around.

'We've brought some guests to meet with you,' said Harvey.

Marcus couldn't see much in the dark but he recognised their forms.

He froze as he counted at least ten Indigenes. 'What the fuck are they doing here? Don't you know what they can do?'

He stumbled back from their unchained presence. The last time he'd seen an Indigene it had been locked up in the attic of the old Deighton mansion, and Marcus had used a shock collar to keep it under control.

'Yes, we do,' said Harvey.

Of course he did. Harvey had said he'd created them.

'They're here to help us. Our goals are aligned. We will find new volunteers to join our cause. These Indigenes will convince more of their kind to join our cause.'

The Indigenes didn't move but Marcus sensed their uneasiness.

'Since the peace treaty and the creation of the GS humans, this planet has gone to shit,' said Ollie. 'We plan to stop the demise and return things to the way they were, pre-treaty.'

'What do you want us to do exactly?' said Marcus.

'In their pursuit of GS evolution, the board members have created a void,' said Harvey. 'We will oust the ITF and replace it with a new police force that treats both the humans and Indigenes equally. And we will begin by discrediting Bill Taggart.'

Marcus had no problem with that.

'But to understand both sides of the issues we face, each of you will pair with an Indigene.'

Ollie pointed to an Indigene, then to one of the men.

One Indigene stepped forward, a tall freak with yellow-flecked eyes and a hard stare. He stopped in front of Marcus, towering over him by a couple of feet.

'Looks like I'm stuck with you,' the freak said.

Fuck.

8

Stephen stood at the top of the Gathering room, a soundproofed meeting space used often by his elder predecessors and mentors, Pierre and Elise. The raised platform no longer existed. He and Serena had converted the room into a more informal space with a circular table and chairs to make their human guests feel welcome. Spare chairs were stacked against the walls to cope with larger numbers, but Bill usually capped the numbers of humans visiting the district at any one time.

Stephen looked around the room. Pierre never would have permitted a group of humans to meet inside his district. Elise, who had been more open-minded, probably would have convinced him. It had been the biggest change under his and Serena's command. He may be a pure bred born of two Indigenes, but Serena and others like her had once been human. It felt wrong to exclude people with whom Serena still shared a connection.

The Gathering room had been Pierre's idea, set up to discuss matters in private with a select group of representatives from District Three—and sometimes with other districts. Since taking up the role of elder—a label Serena confessed to hating—Stephen had operated an open-door policy on all matters.

No more secrets. Secrets had led to cracks in their democratic society. Secrets had circulated rumours and challenged their way of life. And though splinter groups opposing the peace treaty had formed within other districts, Stephen had not heard of any recruits joining from District Three. He credited that to his refusal to exclude his charges from matters concerning everyone.

But tonight was the exception, because Serena had insisted on it.

The representatives were due to arrive shortly. Serena, Bill and Laura waited with him inside the room with its door closed while Anton and Arianna kept watch outside. Their role: to occupy the human group until Stephen was ready to receive them.

'What we need now is a controlled group that can keep a cool head,' said Serena. 'If we open this idea out to everyone in the district, we'll create mass panic.'

Stephen rarely disagreed with her but this time it felt like the wrong decision. It surprised him when both Laura and Bill agreed with her.

'I don't like it, Serena,' said Stephen. 'I promised my charges—our charges—we would no longer keep secrets. Yet here we are whispering in private, just like Pierre used to.'

'Keeping this discussion between us is necessary,' said Bill. 'We have no idea who among the districts is riling up the others, recruiting them for these splinter groups. If we don't control the numbers in here today, we lose control of the rogue groups out there making a nuisance. Plus, we don't know if your open-style democracy has helped or hindered the creation of those groups.'

'I don't think it matters if you have an open or closed style, Stephen,' said Laura, glancing at Bill. 'Pierre operated a closed-door policy and many wanted to turn rogue then. The Indigenes will make up their own minds. Some will disagree with your open-door policy as much as Pierre's closed one and use it to their advantage. But Bill is right. It's too early to share our ideas. We need to control the message. Force the groups to reveal themselves.'

Stephen relented with a sigh. 'I just want to do what's best for the district.'

'Let's begin this the right way and take it from there.' Serena touched his arm and her influence reached out for him. But she didn't use it because she had promised never to use it on him. 'When we know what we're dealing with, we'll report back to the others. That's both an open-and-closed-door policy.'

Stephen smiled at the only Indigene who could make him see sense so fast.

'Okay, closed door it is.'

Commotion outside ensued. With that, Serena opened the door and said, 'We're ready, Anton. Bring them in.'

Stephen fidgeted as ten Indigene representatives filed into the room and stood behind the chairs around the table. Ten humans followed and occupied the chairs. All ten had been selected by Bill and Laura, people who had both worked for the government on Earth and who'd silently opposed the treatment of the Indigenes. Now they wanted to do something to change that. Bill and Laura's trust of them was enough for Stephen.

The mix of male and female humans all belonged to an underground movement similar to the one Jenny

Waterson ran on Earth. When the treaty had first come into existence, Stephen had been naive to think it would give the Indigenes equal rights on Exilon 5. Instead, the hunting grounds they had secured as part of the deal served only to reduce their activities to these controlled zones.

But an important part of the deal had been fulfilled. They'd received files on their human origins and secured an agreement to reverse the genetic mutations of any Indigene who requested the change. The reversal treatments were carried out by former Earth doctors in specially built labs on the outskirts of the cities.

Everything looked good on paper and in practice.

But Bill and Laura remained sceptical about the deal that curtailed Indigene's movements more than it freed them. Bill's taking up the role of Director of the ITF and Laura as chief communication officer had been an orchestrated move to keep control of matters. That's how this group of ten humans had come to be—a group of intelligence gatherers under Bill's command with eyes and ears in many places.

Arianna followed Anton inside the room and closed the door. Anton nodded at Stephen, indicating his agreement with the privacy. In a district full of mind readers, Stephen had learned to read his friend's signals.

The humans shifted in their chairs and glanced back at the Indigene reps with hesitant, yellow auras who occupied the space around them. Prior communication usually happened in the central core with plenty of space and one side facing the other. This was the first time both sides had been in a room this small.

Serena started. 'Why don't we go around the room and everyone can say the one thing that's bothering them. Let's start with our human friends first, followed by the Indigenes.'

'Must they stand this close to me?' one human said.

'I don't like how this one keeps staring at me,' said another, glancing back.

One Indigene with an intimidating brawn and height pinched the end of his nose and said, 'They smell funny. And if they don't stop thinking I'm going to kill them then maybe I will, just to shut off their thoughts.' He stared at one shocked man. 'Yes, that's right, human. I can hear you.'

Very few Indigenes could read human thoughts unless granted access, Stephen almost said. But then he caught the grins on his friends' faces and smiled at the unintentional icebreaker.

The human male held his hands up. 'I'm grateful to be included in these discussions, but I have no wish to die today. I just want to make that clear.'

'If I wanted to kill you, human, you'd be dead already,' said the Indigene.

The male slid lower in his seat. 'Okay, just so we're clear about that.'

Laughter erupted on the human side. Silent laughter rippled through the mind readers. Both Anton and Serena smiled while a tense-looking Bill ran his gaze over the stony-faced Indigene reps. But the laughter had relaxed the Indigenes, a change so minor the human eye would not see it. Stephen nodded at Bill to reassure him.

'We know you're not used to being crammed into such a small space,' said Stephen. 'Up until now we've conducted our affairs in the central core, a more public space, I think you'll agree. But the rogue groups on both sides are making trouble and we must claw back control before things get out of hand. We would like your input on the direction this is taking.'

'What about the genetically superior humans, aren't

they a bigger threat than a few rogue elements?' asked one human.

'The one hundred GS are still committed to honouring the peace treaty,' said Bill. 'We don't believe they're responsible for the splinter groups.'

'That's not what I meant. You must have seen their new environ, a few miles out from the caves they live in? What's it for?'

'The GS are a concern but one problem at a time. The rogue groups are attempting to disrupt the peace treaty —'

'Serena said earlier to say what bothered each of us,' said the human. 'Right now, the GS group concern me.'

The room agreed.

Bill removed a device from his pocket that Stephen recognised to be a 3D image recorder. He'd used a similar one to perfect his humanisms before meeting with Ben Watson eight years ago. Bill placed the recorder in the middle of the table and activated it. A large 3D image displayed above the recorder showed the mountain range where the GS "nested".

He said, 'We all know they've lived at this location for the last three years, right around the time their genetic experiments began to yield results. The numbers whittled down from two hundred to just half that. We never recovered their bodies. Their diet is blood-based, similar to the Indigenes. But what you don't know is that we have a list of missing people who were last seen in the area. We have reason to believe their diet may have evolved beyond animals.'

Stephen assessed the humans' reaction to Bill's news. He sensed some were disgusted by the idea of cannibalism, while others were not surprised. The Indigene representatives remained unsure what to make of this new being—a distant cousin.

Bill continued. 'We took this image three months ago. And this one last week—' He flicked from an image of an empty plot of flat land to a dome covered in white material. 'I'm not sure when this went up, but it's been erected for a reason.'

'Why don't we send in recon to check it out?' suggested one human.

'It's impossible to get close without detection,' said Bill. 'I was inside their caves once. Just inside the entrance they have an entire wall covered in screens that monitor several miles around the caves.'

'What about one of us?' suggested an Indigene.

'They aren't fussy about who they kill,' said Stephen. 'Human or Indigene, it means nothing to them. They are neither.'

'Previous to last week, they continue to live like hermits,' said Bill. 'We paid them no attention because the treaty was our main concern. Then we discovered this.'

Bill flicked over to a grainy image that showed an exposed cable running from the GS environ to a point outside of the solar power base station, where the main feed ran from it to the city.

'What is it?'

Bill gestured at the image. 'The GS connected this power cable to the main feed for New London. For the last few days they've been drawing amounts of power so small we didn't notice it. Then yesterday, the power drain doubled. Engineers checked on the base station this morning and tracked the issue to the buried main feed. That's when they discovered the extra cable.'

'What are they using it for?' said one of the Indigenes.

Genesis Variant

'To power their environ. Beyond that, we have no idea,' said Stephen.

'So we just sit here and wait for them to tell us?'

'No, we discuss a plan,' said Stephen. 'These new photos show we've been too passive where the GS are concerned. The room agrees they must become our primary focus.'

'So do we walk up to the caves and ask them?' said another human.

'And get killed in the process? Great plan, human,' said the brawny Indigene.

Maybe they could obtain the information in a safer way.

'We came here to discuss the rogue groups on both human and Indigene sides,' said Stephen. 'Their actions concern us as much as this new development in GS land does. Just because they've maintained a separation from the GS humans doesn't mean they haven't been watching them.'

'What do you suggest, Stephen?' said Bill.

'The rogue groups on both sides oppose the treaty. They've already come to blows a few times but recently they've been quiet. Can we offer them anything in exchange for what they might know about the GS humans?'

'What about asking the human doctors?' said Serena. 'The ones who carried out the genetic mutations on the GS?'

'I tried but they've been sworn to secrecy,' said Bill. 'The GS still have influence here, even if they don't actively participate in politics. The experiments and tests were all done in secret. It's likely the GS threatened the doctors to keep their mouths shut. It's a dead end.'

'How do we know the doctors aren't siding with the

splinter groups?' said Laura. 'We should sound out groups on both sides, keep our options open and get as much information as we can.'

Stephen sensed the representatives had no issues with approaching the splinter groups comprised of humans. But engaging with the GS intensified the fear in the room. Neither side was ready to deal with the genetically altered race yet.

The humans chattered nervously while the Indigenes' telepathic conversations sounded like a rush of words in his mind. Stephen still believed that Indigenes from District Three had not joined any of the splinter groups. Although the other Indigenes in the room did not agree.

He clapped his hands to bring order to the chaos in the room. 'Anton and Arianna, you two ask around, find out how many rogue elements operate out of the other districts. Serena and I will speak to the elders there, to see if they know anything about where their rogues meet.'

'And here, Stephen,' said Serena. 'We can't assume the problem hasn't extended to District Three.'

'Fine, and here.'

'I think we should attempt to speak with the GS,' said Bill. 'I had direct access once.'

Stephen shook his head. 'It's too dangerous. We don't know what drives them in their current form.'

But Bill was persistent. 'And we won't know unless we ask them. Simon Shaw used to be an ally before the board members included him in their test group. Let me reach out, see how this new species differs from yours.'

'What about ITF privileges?' said Serena. 'Have you any special clearance on information the doctors might have?'

Bill shook his head. 'Our remit doesn't extend to

Genesis Variant

anything involving the GS, human or otherwise. That means no access to their medical data.'

One human said, 'How can we help? Maybe we could get close to members of the splinter groups on the human side?'

'No, we can't risk revealing the identity of this group,' said Bill. 'We must keep all interactions at the highest level. I'm already known to be a rogue operator and Laura is devious most of the time, so our enquiries won't be suspicious.'

Laura swatted his arm and he grinned.

'He's right,' she said. 'This group works best when you operate freely. Your covert findings will be crucial to this process. Let Bill and I meet with the groups and the GS.'

Stephen detected a growing confidence from Bill that he could get through to Simon Shaw.

While the group continued their independent discussions, he pulled him aside. 'It's a risky plan, Bill. Your former boss may no longer recognise you.'

'And then again he might. We should still talk to the splinter groups and you to the elders. The more information we have, the better.'

Stephen nodded. 'One thing's for sure, the Indigenes and humans who oppose the changes on Exilon 5 are working together. We must convince both sides the treaty is good for everyone and we are not the enemy.'

'Agreed. If the treaty falls apart, who knows who or what might fill that void.'

9

Simon Shaw checked the machine inside the purpose-built environ powered by the electricity supply from the solar power plant for New London. A few days ago, he'd attached an insulated cable to the main feed to the city to siphon off its power. He checked a screen displaying data for the supply. It fed a contained ball of energy no bigger than his fist inside the machine.

He searched through the Elites' whispers for a clue as to when they might use the machine but found only voices similar to his. It had been that way for three months now. The Elite ten, former board members of the World Government, had been silenced by the extensive tests carried out on them. The remaining one hundred who'd survived the brutal experiments could once hear the Elite's thoughts. People like Simon with no family, no official title on Exilon 5 and nothing to lose.

Initially, Simon had hoped the changes would preserve his individuality, but the experiments on his body had changed more than his cellular structure. They had changed the way he thought.

The transformation of the original two hundred GS

made up of board members, ITF directors and supervisors at the now defunct World Government and Earth Security Centre was supposed to happen at an equal pace.

The geneticists from Earth had used rapid genetic sequencing to map out the genes of the two hundred. Then they tailored changes to the unique code in each person. But the early extensive testing had been too much for some genetic structures to handle, including the Elite board members. The Elite had pulled out of the early testing, choosing instead to work with the geneticists to weed out the problems. Alteration from human to Indigene had already been done. The Elite hunted for the next step in evolution.

It soon became clear to Simon that the Elite's goals differed from the remaining one hundred. The new changes to his code gave Simon a longer life. But that wasn't enough for the Elite. They wanted everlasting life. New tests changed their appearance to make them paler and leaner than the remaining one hundred. A hierarchy followed that Simon should have expected, which began with the Elite referring to the remaining one hundred as the "Conditioned".

The Conditioned resembled humans more than the Elite, who looked closer to Indigenes in appearance. Simon had endured five years of experiments as a human, and three more in the changed body of a Conditioned.

Why? Because Tanya Li had promised him a better life and Simon had fallen for her lies.

He checked the display on the machine and recorded on his DPad how much power the cable siphoned from the grid versus what the machine stored. A slight loss in power occurred during transfer. They could have stolen sixty gigawatts—over half of the daily collection—but that would have alerted the ITF to their plans. Tanya Li, Elite

One and former chair of the World Government, had requested Simon to gradually drain the power to minimise disruption to the city's supply.

Simon had never worked with electricity before. He'd been a paper pusher in his former role as ITF Director of the London office on Earth. But thanks to a process called memory mapping, he'd become a temporary expert. The machine he'd built with his genetically superior mind allowed him to map any experience to his mind—in this case, an electrician's. Once he'd completed work on the mind mapping machine, he mapped the skill of a geotechnical engineer on to his brain so he could build the environ.

Mind mapping had been fun at the start. For a time he spoke ten languages, but the new knowledge forced Simon's brain to work harder. The headaches had started a few months ago to match his increase in knowledge. It felt as though his brain outgrew his skull, even though brains didn't grow because they contained more information. They just worked harder.

Inside the environ, a blissful silence filled his head, except for trace thoughts of the Indigenes hunting close by and the two Conditioned posted outside.

It must be the machine. Maybe its contained power could disrupt thought processes.

Whatever the reason, he felt human again with only his thoughts for company.

It had been too long since he'd felt any peace. The soundproofing omicron rock that the caves were built from worked well to mask the thoughts of the Conditioned he could hear. But the second he crossed that threshold, the same rock irritated his mind like buzzing bees.

Simon studied the black shell of the machine. It held a circular containment field at its core that stored the stolen power. This power would not help the Elite to achieve everlasting life, but heal their bodies enough so they could reach transcendence, or a superior state. The Elite's bodies would be discarded, but transcendence required a viable body that could withstand the rigours of that final stage. Rigorous testing had aged the Elite to the extreme and Earth geneticists had tried and failed to reverse the effects. But there was one thing they hadn't tried: using the stored power to attract the healing power of the Nexus.

When Simon had arrived on Exilon 5, he'd still been human and in touch with Bill Taggart. The Indigene called Stephen had given him a tour of District Three. Stephen had explained the Nexus to him in detail, detail he'd relayed back to the Elite at the right time.

Simon finished his work and pressed his thumb to a biometric scanner by the door to unlock it. His two Conditioned escorts flanked him as he walked back to the caves located two miles away. The pair conversed to each other telepathically. Simon didn't join in. Even after three years as a Conditioned, he still felt like an imposter— neither comfortable with the changes made to him nor the silent intrusion of others.

If Tanya Li pressed him for an answer, he'd say life as a Conditioned was no different to how he'd been treated in his old job on Earth. Daphne Gilchrist, the CEO of the Earth Security Centre, who had been murdered by Charles Deighton, had always favoured the stronger males in meetings—a point she made with him often. Just because Simon didn't cut people down before he'd heard all sides of the story didn't make him weak.

His escorts were necessary. The trek back to the caves carried risks and Simon kept a lookout for trouble. Few dared to get close to the heavily monitored, three-mile radius around the caves. Humans or Indigenes, it didn't matter. The Elite considered everyone to be a threat. An unaccompanied Conditioned was a target. One with backup was less appealing. Tanya had wanted to build the environ closer to the caves, but Simon had argued for a new location, one where the amplification recording of the gamma rock was most intense. He knew from his tour of District Three that the Nexus thrived in gamma.

While Simon kept a steady pace, he thought back to his earliest conversation with Tanya Li about the genetic testing that, in her words, "will blow your mind".

'This is an exclusive group and I want you to be a part of it,' Tanya had said. 'Charles Deighton spoke highly of you and I need strong-minded people. If this new genetic testing works, it will open up your world to unimaginable possibilities.'

The offer had tempted him even though Simon knew Deighton thought as little of him as Gilchrist.

'What if I change my mind?' he'd asked.

Tanya smiled. 'You won't. Trust me on that.'

Tanya had been right. The early tests had blown his mind. Set a few months apart, each trial had made him stronger for a while. Soon he had craved more. Simon had felt the changes drag him further from what made him human. His greed, his desire for more, increased with every change. Then one day, the doctors under Tanya Li's command announced their discovery of the code that would give their minds everlasting life.

'Live forever?' Simon had said when Tanya called him in to discuss the next phase in the testing.

Tanya smiled. 'Isn't that what our former colleagues—God rest their souls—worked towards? We can become something special. The Indigenes are superior to humans but still primitive. Our predecessors started these trials to create a better version of ourselves.'

'Everlasting life is not all it's cracked up to be.'

A life with no end to it? His life hadn't been all that great to begin with.

Tanya laughed. 'Are you speaking from experience?'

'Of course not. What I mean is if there's no end to life, how do we battle the urge to stop growing, learning, exploring? These are things we do *because* life is short.'

But Tanya didn't agree. 'Why must we grow, learn or explore at all if there's no end to life? We can just live it however we please.'

Simon hadn't signed up for this. A better mind in a hardier body? Yes. But that change came with a price attached: the ability to hear others' thoughts. He endured that torture daily.

The sight of an approaching figure broke Simon out of his thoughts. He stopped and watched the hunched-over figure shuffle across the land between the caves and the environ with an accompaniment of ten Conditioned behind her. Two assistants pushed a hover chair behind her. Tanya Li, Elite One, wore a white cloak with a hood that covered her thinning hair and her frail body, worn from all the changes. In human years, one hundred and eight wasn't old. Just three years ago she'd had a head full of jet-black hair and walked tall. A set of sharp eyes staring out from a withered, skin bag were all that remained of the old Tanya Li.

She met him halfway between the caves and the environ.

'Show me the energy figures,' she said.

'I can do that from inside the caves.' Simon glanced around. 'It's not safe for you to be out here.'

Tanya waved him off. 'My sharp mind will outwit

my opponent. I need to see the machine. I need to feel its power for myself.'

Simon turned back and walked alongside Elite One. The environ was just a mile away, but halfway there Tanya gave up walking and slumped into the hover chair.

He unlocked the door and opened it wide enough for Tanya's chair to fit. One of her assistants joined them in the small space. He closed the door on the remaining Conditioned, who set up a tight perimeter around the enclosure.

'How much energy is the machine drawing from the city's feed?'

Tanya slid off the chair to stand. Her naturally short frame looked even smaller with her pronounced spine deformation.

'Fifteen megawatts of power. Only a fraction of what they use.'

Tanya touched the machine he'd built. Simon still retained the knowledge of a geotechnical engineer and an understanding of the mechanics of soil and rock. The machine build, which he'd started in the caves, had to be finished in the environ when it got too big.

'If the gamma rock can amplify our stolen power, we shouldn't need much to attract the Nexus to us.' Tanya stared at the bright ball of energy at the machine's centre. 'We should minimise the amount of power we take. I don't want Bill Taggart and the ITF checking out this place.'

Tanya had courted him for the genetic trials after Simon had seen District Three. He still believed that his insider knowledge was why Tanya had picked him. Not because of his strong mind.

'They're curious about this place,' said Simon. 'I can sense their thoughts. Bill Taggart and Laura O'Halloran will visit here soon. I am a point of contact, someone Bill thinks he can trust.'

The only person Simon trusted was himself.

When Tanya nodded, Simon released a quiet breath, grateful her telepathic abilities had diminished. Transcendence wielded a double-edged sword: the rigorous tests and preparations had rendered her telepathy useless. All the Elites were similarly affected.

'The Elite can no longer read minds' said Tanya. 'I must stay with them and gauge their reaction to our experiment. It has been some time since I've met with Bill Taggart on ITF matters or the peace treaty. I'm sure my new appearance will come as a shock to him. My weakened state may put his mind at ease that we are not a threat.' Tanya pulled the loose skin on her arm tight. It crinkled when she released it. 'How soon before they get here?'

'They plan to visit here tomorrow morning.'

Tanya nodded. 'You will meet them and escort them to our home, where I will demonstrate how little they have to fear. The caves will serve as a neutral space. I will tell them about the machine and its basic purpose. That is all. Nothing will interfere with plans for the Elite's transcendence.'

10

'How do we get close enough to the GS one hundred to speak to them?' Laura said.

The meeting with Stephen and the representatives had wrapped up and Bill had ordered the vehicle to drive him and Laura back to their apartment.

It was getting dark when the car pulled up outside a block that overlooked New Belgrave Square. On his first mission to investigate the Indigenes, Bill had been posted to one of the apartments there. Back then the area had suffered with issues ranging from waste to rent-dodging tenants. While the park and the surrounding replica nineteenth-century houses hadn't changed much, management of the area had improved. He and Laura had looked at several apartments in New London but none overlooked a park—something Laura wanted to be near. They had secured a penthouse apartment on the west side of the park, double in size to his old lookout apartment two blocks down.

'I thought we'd figure that out over a late dinner,' said Bill. He grabbed his bag. 'I'm hoping that if we turn up, they'll have to see us. Plus, I've spoken to Tanya

76

before about ITF matters so it shouldn't look suspicious.'

'The last time you met with her, she and the others still looked human. Neither of us has seen them since they ramped up their genetic experiments. We have no idea what the changes have done to them.'

Bill exited the car and Laura did the same. 'Look, we won't know how they've altered until we see them. But given everything that's happening, I think we should find out.'

He closed the door and the self-driving car drove off to park in the apartment block's underground space.

People passed them in the street.

Bill ushered Laura to the main door. 'Let's finish this discussion upstairs.'

He had no desire to discuss such sensitive matters in public.

Their block had a set of stairs and no turbo lift. Laura jogged up the five flights of stairs while Bill followed, wishing for an easier way to the top. Just two apartments existed on the top floor and they owned both of them. Laura unlocked the door using her identity chip. Bill followed her inside the double-sized space.

A noise assaulted them. 'Welcome home, Mr and Mrs Taggart.'

It was the avatar on the Light Box.

Laura thumped him on the arm. 'I thought you changed that.'

He rubbed the spot where she'd hit him. 'What, you don't like your new title?'

'So, I'm a label now? I've lost all my individuality?'

'Yes. I own you now, Mrs Taggart.'

Laura grinned and thumped him a second time, but the pain was worth it to see his beautiful wife's smile.

77

'The day I lose my individuality will be the day I become just like one of those GS one hundred. That's not why I agreed to marry you, Mr Taggart.'

'Then it must have been for my insatiable love-making skills, or my ability to ruin dinner. Or my witty conversations. Take your pick.'

'Yeah, the last one.'

Laura stepped close enough that he could smell her perfume. He buried his nose in her neck and inhaled. A giggle erupted from her.

'I love it when you wear that scent,' he said.

The perfume was an exotic blend of native white and blue flowers from Exilon 5—his first wife Isla's favourite flower. The scent connected the only two women he'd ever loved.

Bill nuzzled Laura's neck again. 'We can skip dinner if you'd like.'

She giggled again and made a half-hearted attempt to pull away. 'I sense your intentions aren't honourable.'

'I hope not.'

'Normally I would give in to you—you're an impossible man to refuse—but with this meeting looming over our heads I wouldn't be able to concentrate.'

Bill kept kissing her neck and worked up to her lips. He pressed his lips to hers until she groaned. 'When you're right you're right. My new wife distracted me.'

'Ugh.'

Laura twisted again to escape his clutches.

He held on tighter. 'You don't like being my wife?'

'No, I love it. Turns out it's the same life as before. Go figure. But I'm not used to the "wife" label yet.'

'But I'm your husband, so I get the same label.'

Laura perked up at that. 'Yeah, I forgot about that. Hmmm...' She pointed to the kitchen. 'Husband, make me

Genesis Variant

something to eat.'

Bill mock-bowed and scurried to the kitchen. It contained an oven they never used, a replicator and a H2O machine.

'Of course, wife.'

He punched in numbers on the replicator and removed a plate of chicken and rice. Then he replicated a second one and set both down on the kitchen table. Laura stood by the entrance to the kitchen with her arms folded.

'I'll need something to wash all that down.' She nodded at him. 'Get me something to drink.'

Bill filled two glasses of water from the H2O machine and set them down on the table. 'Anything else, wife?'

She stared at the glasses. 'Did I say you could get something for yourself?'

Bill played the submissive role. 'I'm sorry, wife. I assumed it would be okay, since I'm bigger and stronger than you and I need to keep up my strength.'

Laura lifted a brow. 'Stronger? Are you sure?'

She sat down at the table and prepared to arm wrestle.

'Now?' Bill looked at the plates of food. 'But I've been slaving away in the kitchen all evening.'

'Yes, now.'

Laura pushed both plates off to one side. Bill grinned and set his elbow on the table.

He gripped her firm hand and steeled his grip against hers, waiting for her command. 'Ready? Go.'

He pushed against her arm. It felt like an immovable rock.

'How long are you going to draw out my humiliation?' he said. 'You're emasculating me.'

Laura winked at him. 'As long as it takes until I'm

79

satisfied.'

Bill's arm strained against hers but it didn't budge. 'Could we hurry this along please? I'm starving.'

Laura sighed. 'Okay.'

She gave one quick push and his arm yielded with the slightest of pressure. The first time they'd arm wrestled like this was just after Stephen had turned her fully into an Indigene. She'd nearly put his arm through the table. As half-Indigene half-human, her strength was no less impressive.

'I give in, O mighty wife.'

'And so you should, husband.' She stretched across the table and kissed him on the cheek. 'Did I hurt you?'

Her voice was soft.

'Only my pride, love.'

They pulled the back the plates and Bill carved off a piece of chicken too big for his mouth and ate it. When he got this hungry, his manners took a back seat.

'Do you think you'll get a read on them tonight?'

Laura squirmed in her seat. 'I've no idea. As humans, maybe, but if their experiments succeeded who knows what they can do? Let's just wait and see.'

She cut a piece of chicken and popped it in her mouth.

'Anton says the cave they occupy has the highest density of omicron rock on the surface.' Omicron was mostly found below the surface. 'Because of its soundproofing ability, the Indigenes have been unable to get a read on their thoughts or activities.'

Laura nodded and cut another piece of chicken. 'And this new environ they've built. What do we know about that?'

'Only that its location is directly over one of the tranquillity caves. There's a high concentration of gamma rock.'

'So, they're using the gamma rock to amplify something, maybe the power they're stealing?'

Bill shrugged and raked his fork through his rice. 'I can't see what else they'd need it for. But the real question is why steal the power? I mean, they could probably make their own, build their own solar plant. But their actions indicate urgency.'

'Does the omicron rock also mask the environ?' said Laura.

'Anton says the gamma rock concentration is so strong it amplifies anything within a five-mile radius. That covers the environ and the area surrounding their caves.'

'Do we know what abilities they might have? Are they telepathic? Will they see us coming? How fast are they?'

'Neither Anton nor Stephen can confirm that. We're flying blind on this one, I'm afraid. I'm hoping Simon Shaw still recognises me so we can use our prior connection to talk rationally.'

'So, remind me why you and I volunteered to go alone?'

'Because, one, I trust you to keep us both safe and pull us out of there if you sense trouble. And two, because it's Simon.'

Laura stared at her plate. 'Do you think he'll remember you?'

Bill shrugged. 'They have no reason to erase the memories of the GS, like they did the entire Indigene population.'

Laura looked at him. 'What if Tanya Li comes to meet us instead?'

It had crossed his mind. He had a volatile history with the former chair of the World Government who'd secured Laura safe passage to Exilon 5 when she'd transformed from human to Indigene so fast. But on Exilon 5, Tanya had used Laura to bargain with the Indigenes. What Tanya hadn't known at the time was Laura and Bill had the protection of the Indigenes.

'I've avoided that woman for years and barely spoke to her in the early days as ITF Director. She's been too busy working with the geneticists.' Bill shook his head. 'I can't see how she'd want to speak to me. I've probably surpassed my usefulness to her.'

'Just in case, we should prepare as if we're meeting her, not Simon.'

Bill finished his meal and cleared away the dishes as soon as Laura put her knife and fork down. 'If she doesn't come, I'll be interested to see who she sends and how many. Numbers will determine how important she considers us to be.'

'Or how much of a threat we are.'

'Let's get going.' He grabbed his coat off the chair. 'I don't know how long we're going to be out.'

Laura stood. 'Unlike you, Bill, I am built for stamina.'

☼

Their vehicle drove him and Laura to a location twenty miles from New London's city limits and a spot three miles out from the caves. Old access roads resembling dirt tracks marked the spot where Tanya had brought excavation equipment in to begin work on the caves. Those roads had since been dismantled and access blocked by large boulders that formed a ring around the open sides to the mountainous area where the caves existed. The cordoned-off area was a neutral space that ITF law had no jurisdiction over.

Only six cities and few arterial roads had existed when Bill first arrived on Exilon 5. Now, two hundred cities were connected by roads, containing radar, lidar and sonar sensors to facilitate automated cars, and high-speed Maglev trains. Development had been slow at first due to a lack of raw materials. But infrastructure had soon caught up with immigration numbers. Rapid developments and a fast-growing population made it impossible for Bill's ITF teams to police all neutral grounds.

The vehicle idled by one of the original arterial roads, now decommissioned because it cut through one of the safe hunting zones outlined in the peace treaty. Bill grabbed a torch from the glove box and flicked it on.

'Use the night vision on the magnification glasses,' said Laura. 'If the GS can see as well as the Indigenes, the torch will make us easy targets.'

Bill looked out at the pitch-black landscape he was sure contained predators of all kinds. 'The range on the glasses is too limited. I need the torch. Unless you want to take the lead?'

Night vision was one of the Indigene traits Laura had retained.

Laura shook her head. 'Bring the torch.'

They exited the car and Bill took the lead. He slipped the glasses on and flicked on night vision. A few feet of the landscape ahead changed from black to green. Laura trailed behind him as he shone the light at the ground. Cloud dominated the night sky and masked the double moons that might have provided some light. A wolf bayed in the distance. In a panic, Bill waved the torch around. It picked up dozens of shining eyes, watching them.

'We're not alone,' he whispered.

'I know.'

'Wolves?'

'Only one, but the rest are Indigenes. I'm guessing rogue. They're watching to see what happens.'

'Are we in any danger?'

Bill flicked off his light and the bright eyes beyond the range of his glasses vanished.

Laura slowed. 'I don't know.'

He looked back at her. 'Can't you just sense them or something?'

'I'd rather not. Look, we already know what the Indigenes can do. Let's assume the worst and keep going. And keep the light off. It's only attracting them to our location.'

Bill pocketed the torch and relied on the night vision glasses. 'Indigenes can see in the dark. What difference does a torch make?'

'They can see the colours that exist in white light. The rainbow acts as a beacon for our location.' Laura sighed. 'That's what I see when you turn it on.'

'Point made.'

Laura passed him while Bill watched every step he took. They reached the boundary point to the GS land marked by large boulders. Laura scrambled over the top while Bill followed, slower and less sure footed than his wife.

She dropped down the other side on all fours and Bill eased himself to the ground. He landed with a thud and wiped the dust off his trousers.

'They're following us,' she growled.

'Can we divert them off our scent somehow?'

'No. These Indigenes are doing recon. I sensed them following us as soon as the car left the city borders. They've been sent to track us.'

Genesis Variant

Who controlled these rogue Indigenes? Maybe Stephen could find out.

'Let's get this over with.' Bill set off walking into the neutral ground, home to genetically superior beings. 'The sooner we meet with them, the sooner we can go home.'

The idea of hostile Indigenes on one side and cannibalistic GS beings on the other terrified him.

Laura marched on ahead and Bill lost sight of her. A mile inside the perimeter he caught up to her again. She'd stopped and was sniffing the air.

'What can you pick up?'

She glanced at him, looking embarrassed. 'Nothing. We're close.'

Bill didn't buy her act. 'How far out are they, Laura?'

She pointed into the darkness. 'A mile in that direction.'

'I'll take your word for it.' Even with his torch, he wouldn't see much. 'Do they know we're here?'

Before she could answer, a new voice replied that Bill hadn't heard in a long time.

'Yes, we do.'

Four tall, ghostlike figures dressed in white approached them.

Bill tensed while Laura dropped into a half crouch —a hunting stance he'd seen Stephen use before.

'How did you sneak up on us?' said a shocked Laura.

The leader stepped closer and Bill barely recognised his former boss, Simon Shaw, in the pale shell before him. 'We move lighter than air, so you would not have heard our footsteps. We can block our thoughts at will. I sensed Laura was hunting for mine so I made my

85

presence known to her, but omitted my location.'

Bill stared at Simon. 'You can switch off your thoughts to those around you? Is that one of your abilities?'

Simon smiled and nodded. 'It's no different to being human, Bill Taggart. Humans can't communicate using thought alone. Indigenes have that ability. We simply have both abilities and can toggle between the two. Does that interest you?'

'Yeah, I guess it does. I wasn't sure what to expect when I saw you,' said Bill.

'I'm still the Simon Shaw you knew, but a better design. My memories are still intact. I remember where I came from.'

'What happened to the people who disappeared from this location?'

Simon wanted to talk and Bill wanted answers.

'We took them.'

'Where?'

'Back to the caves. We hadn't eaten in a long time.'

Bill felt Laura shudder beside him. His own stomach swirled at the thought.

He shook off his disgust and said, 'Why are you stealing power from the grid? What do you need it for?'

'I will explain, but not here.' Simon looked around. 'Tanya wants to see you. I'm to bring you to her.'

Bill glanced at Laura, who looked as surprised as he felt. This was too easy.

But his curiosity won out. 'Okay, where?'

'The caves. It's a ten-minute walk from here at your pace. I will walk with you while the others run ahead and prepare for your arrival.'

'Prepare?'

The three that had accompanied Simon disappeared

in a blurry haze while Simon and Laura matched Bill's slow pace.

'Yes. We live in isolation. We don't get many visitors.'

Bill said, 'So what's changed, Simon? Why are we to be your guests of honour tonight?'

'Tanya wishes to talk to you about the Elite's changes. They—we—need your help.'

'Help how?'

'I'd rather not get into it out here. The caves offer protection from prying minds and you brought company.'

Simon looked around and Bill knew he referred to the Indigenes who followed.

'They aren't with us.'

They walked in silence. Bill found it odd to meet Simon in this new guise. His former boss had helped him and Laura out on more than one occasion. He wondered if the morals of the man he once knew still existed.

'How are you, Simon?'

Simon frowned at him. 'Why do you ask?'

'Because you adopted this way of life very fast. I was too busy with my new position to talk to you about it. My interactions with Tanya were to update her on the treaty, nothing more. I haven't spoken to you in years and now I want to know how you are.'

'I'm fine, Bill Taggart. I feel like I have a purpose,' said Simon.

'Really?'

Simon's glare was so fierce, Bill shank back from it. Laura, who watched the ground while she walked, hadn't noticed it. He hoped she was putting her Indigene abilities to use. No better time to start.

'My *purpose* is to support the Elite and GS to achieve evolution. We are working to perfect the code that could eliminate disease. That is a decent purpose.'

Bill agreed, but he didn't buy it. 'A noble one, if it can be achieved.'

Simon's reply was clipped. 'It is within reach.'

The entrance to the caves appeared—a large arch with a door inset back from the stone. The door was closed. Bill tensed at the idea of entering a space no Indigene could read and no human had left.

'Don't worry, Bill Taggart, we can control our urges. An earlier genetic experiment messed up our code, starved us to the point where we needed human blood. Now we eat something else.'

'What?'

Simon left Bill without an answer as a DNA scanner similar to the ones the Indigenes used bathed Simon in a blue light. The door opened and he led Bill and Laura inside the caves. The first corridor was small and hewn roughly from the rock but it led into a large room of contrast. Smooth, rendered walls met the equally smooth, tiled floor. Large lights hung overhead that brightened the space more than the Indigene districts or any space in New London. Bill noted one wall was covered in screens that displayed images of the outside. Two of the tall figures that had accompanied Simon pointed to objects on the black screen that Bill could not see.

The camera footage gave the GS 100 a perfect view of their surroundings. Even if Simon hadn't detected them, he would have seen them from the moment they climbed over the boundary boulders.

A platform or altar marked the back of the room. A white, privacy screen behind the altar covered a third of the wall space but Bill saw a gap that indicated the space carried on. His suspicions were realised when three figures appeared from behind the wall.

Laura gasped. Bill stared at three bags of skin so old and withered, he couldn't be sure they contained people.

'Hello, Bill.'

While she looked nothing like her former human self, Tanya's voice and gaze were as distinct as ever.

He stepped closer to the frail figure held up by two young males. Her skin was so wrinkled it almost swallowed her appearance.

'What happened to you, Tanya?'

'The genetic transformations have weakened my body,' she said with a smile.

'Shouldn't that be the case for Simon too? Yet he looks okay.'

'The Conditioned have had less aggressive tests to the Elite. Our mortal bodies can take no more experiments.'

'So what was the point in all of this?' Bill didn't understand. 'Why do you need power from the grid?'

Tanya clasped her hands to the front, an action that reminded Bill of the late Charles Deighton, Tanya's predecessor. 'We need it to power a machine that will heal our bodies. We don't have access to the Nexus like the Indigenes do. But as you see from my appearance, we need it.'

'The Indigenes heal naturally,' said Laura. 'The Nexus just speeds up that process.'

Tanya's eyes cut to Laura. 'Our bodies are transforming faster than they can regenerate. That's why we need a little power, to stop time.'

A plausible excuse, but Bill suspected this was just the beginning of their power drain. 'I'm afraid I can't allow it. What you're siphoning off now interrupts the feed to the city.'

Tanya slid her eyes back to Bill. 'Do you see Tanya Li through this withered, dead shell? Because I haven't for some time. We need the power to heal—that is all. If you won't give us more, then we must make another request.'

'What?' Bill feared Tanya's next words.

'We want access to the Nexus. We've made do with our own version, but the Elite grow weaker by the hour and we need a more stable way to heal. So far we've drawn a small quantity of power, which we've amplified using the gamma rock. It's certainly not enough to interfere with the city feed.'

Bill smiled. 'I've known you long enough, Tanya. Do you really expect me to believe you're using the power just to heal?'

'Believe what you want, Bill Taggart, but that is the truth,' said Tanya.

'I want you to remove your cable from the main feed.'

'No. Without that power, we will die.'

Bill was no monster. 'Then I'll agree to a daily draw of power less than what you've taken so far. No more.'

'I don't know how much the Elites will need. I can't agree to a specific number.'

'Then I'm sorry, Tanya, this arrangement won't work. The city needs every watt of power with none to spare. If you need power, we can provide you with the materials and labour to create a grid separate to ours.'

'We are fine with what we have, Bill Taggart. But thank you for your concern. What about access to the Nexus? You haven't answered my question.'

Bill couldn't see Stephen and Serena agreeing to it. 'It's not my decision, but I highly doubt it. You were responsible for the Indigenes' creation. You represent everything they despise in humans.'

'We are no longer human.' Tanya pointed at Simon. 'And you gave this Conditioned access to their district.'

He glanced at the altered man stood off to the side. 'That was different. Simon was human then and a friend once.'

'He's still a friend, Bill Taggart,' said Tanya. 'That's why you came here, because you trust him. And we can be friends too, if you drop your prejudices. We wish to live without constant pain. Would you deny us comfort?'

'Under normal circumstances, no.'

Tanya nodded to Laura. 'I hear congratulations are in order. You two were recently married.'

Bill nodded.

'And yet your wife is one of them.'

Laura growled. 'I am human, Tanya.'

'As were the Elite and the Conditioned once. And yet you both commit your time to preserve the Indigene way of life. Well, look at me. I'm a new species—we all are—and we demand the ITF's help.'

'The difference is the Indigenes have earned our trust,' said Bill.

Tanya nodded. 'Then so must we. Tell me what it will take to earn it.'

He could think of nothing. 'I'll let you know.'

Movement on one screen caught Bill's eye. Simon studied the image that showed several figures about a mile out from the cave.

Simon spoke to Tanya. 'They brought company.'

'I told you, they're not with us,' said Laura.

'Please leave now,' said Tanya. 'Your presence here has drawn too much attention.'

But Bill had more questions. 'We'd like to come

91

back, to keep in touch with your plans.'

'Unless you return to grant us access to the Nexus, we have no further business.' She nodded at the Conditioned pair beside her, who stepped towards Bill and Laura. 'You know the way out.'

Bill attempted to stall their exit. 'We really should discuss the peace treaty and the rogue elements attempting to destroy it.'

He didn't know when he'd speak to Tanya again.

'The Elite will relinquish all control to you if you'll grant our request for more power. The Nexus or the power grid, it doesn't matter.'

The Conditioned pair pushed Bill and Laura towards the exit.

'Wait! I want your help to maintain the treaty.'

Truth was, the treaty held on by a thread and Bill had no idea how to stop the rogue group activity from breaking it apart.

Tanya held up a hand and the pair stopped pushing. 'How?'

'We need your voice of support. If the rogue humans and Indigenes see us working together, they might back off.'

It was worth a shot. The rogue human groups with a loyalty to the old World Government regime would listen.

'I'll speak to the other Elite. But to be honest, there is only one thing we need. Grant us our request.' She nodded to the pair. 'Please see our guests out.'

'We know the way out, Tanya.'

Bill and Laura returned to the entrance without assistance. Simon released the door and let them out.

'Time for you to go,' said Simon. 'Unless you're willing to meet Tanya's demands, we're done here.'

'What's the power really being used for?' said

Laura.

'To heal, just as Tanya said. Their bodies are too frail to regenerate on their own.'

'Nothing else?' said Laura.

'I would tell you if there was.' Simon glanced behind him. 'I'll be watching you on the monitors to make sure you clear the area.'

Laura and Bill re-entered the black night. Bill gripped Laura's hand as she relented to her ability and navigated for both of them. Neither of them spoke until they'd made it over boundary wall.

'Tanya's reason for the power sounded genuine enough,' said Bill. 'What did you make of her?'

'I'm not sure.'

'Please, Laura. I need you to use your ability.'

She shook her head and sighed. 'I can't read her. Her mind has transformed beyond her physical body. But I'm certain she's lying. Whatever their reasons, they need the power for more than its healing properties.'

11

Exits to the left and right of the platform led to a large, excavated space containing the remainder of the habitat for the GS, including their domiciles. Simon watched from the screens while Tanya's two assistants helped her off stage and through one of the exits.

He glanced back past the screens to the only entrance to the cave. One way in, several ways out.

The omicron rock vibrated; it felt like a buzzing in his mind.

One screen showed Laura and Bill returning to the boundary wall in an area the cameras didn't cover. What areas the cameras couldn't see the Conditioned took turns to patrol. He moved closer to the screen and the buzzing intensified enough for him to fight off the intrusion. As a Conditioned, omicron sucked.

Simon had sensed Bill's scepticism over Tanya's explanation for the use for the power. Laura had been harder to read. She'd been an Indigene once, if only for a brief time, long enough for her to retain Indigene abilities. But if she had any skills, he couldn't tell.

Take me back. He heard Tanya's order moments

before she returned to the observation room in her hover chair. Her two assistants followed but Tanya still had enough strength to commandeer the vehicle. The Elite had yet to test the power from the machine to see if it could reverse some of their ageing. Simon had only been gathering it for a few days. If Simon could get the machine to work, Tanya might drop plans to beg the Indigenes for access to their Nexus—a more complicated solution.

Tanya's gaze, still sharp despite her frailty, met his.

'What do you make of those two?' she said. 'I'm unable to read either of them. Damn side effect of superiority, I suppose.'

'Bill is sceptical, but that's no surprise. He's always been hard to convince of anything. He was a difficult employee when he worked under me.'

'And Laura?' Simon shook his head, to which Tanya nodded. 'No matter. We don't need to convince her, only him. If the power we have isn't enough, we will take more power from the grid.'

'If you assist with the peace treaty, Bill may be more amenable. That's why he came here.'

'The Elite has no interest in that agreement.' Tanya waved her withered hand. 'To be honest, I'm surprised it lasted this long. We only agreed to it to keep the Indigenes off our backs when we moved to this planet.'

And it had worked well. But Tanya missed the point.

'You don't understand, Elite One. By keeping the treaty alive, you gain his trust and access to more power. If you don't show an interest, Bill Taggart and the ITF will cut you—us—loose.'

Tanya nodded. Her neck bent too much for it to support her head.

'I'm sure I can invent something else to keep Bill

Taggart interested,' she said. 'In the meantime, the minimal draw of power will not stop us from proceeding with our plans. Dr Jameson will soon tell me what I already know—that my body won't last much longer. And I've got nine bedridden Elites. Our shells won't support the next phase of transcendence.'

'The machine is as ready as can be,' said Simon. He hoped the machine would use the gamma amplification to attract the Nexus to the stored grid power. 'The Indigenes said the Nexus is organic, so it doesn't have the same constraints as a manmade machine. We may be able to coax it away from its confines.'

Tanya shifted in her chair and her head lolled to the side. 'It has to work. The Elite are out of options.'

They were also out of time.

'I've no idea how much power we'll need to make this work,' said Simon. 'But be prepared that what we have might not be enough. We may need the Nexus after all.'

Tanya laughed but it came out as a growl. 'I'd rather die than ask the Indigene vermin for a favour. They killed one of my bodyguards without any thought. But my survival trumps my pride on this occasion.'

Simon had read the report from eight years ago about the time when Tanya and several board members had travelled to Exilon 5 to meet with the Indigene leaders. Simon had secured Bill an audience with Tanya which led to both Bill and a sick Laura travelling with the party. The battle on Exilon 5 had come close to shifting the balance permanently in the Indigene's favour.

She continued. 'Before I lost my ability to read minds, I could sense the Indigenes would rather die than to speak with us. And some wish we were dead now. While I don't enjoy doing anything for that race, I agree it's

Genesis Variant

prudent to keep Bill Taggart on side. The Elite will pretend to support the treaty. No matter anyway; it will fail on its own. By that time, the Elite will no longer exist in corporeal form.'

Simon wondered what would happen to the Conditioned when the Elite transcended; Tanya had promised him longer life but he had no cast-iron proof that his altered code honoured any such promise. When he'd asked to see the research, speak to the doctors, Tanya had refused him access. Simon was beginning to think his purpose stretched only to protecting the Elite until they reached transcendence.

Tanya slipped down in her chair. When she couldn't adjust her posture, her assistants helped her.

She groaned when they pulled her up in her chair. 'This is humiliating. The sooner we use the machine the faster I can reclaim my dignity.'

Her body was frail, not her mind.

'Have the doctors considered a new body for you, just until the process is complete?' said Simon.

Tanya shook her head. 'I'm stuck with this body until the end. They don't know how to integrate a live consciousness in another's mind.'

'But it was done before by Charles Deighton, when he invaded Anton's mind.'

'That was an imprint. We're talking about swapping out an actual consciousness and making it work with another brain, not sticking a bland copy into a mind that's already occupied.' Tanya pushed on a lever and her chair moved past the screens, closer to the front door. Her two assistants followed. 'I want to try the machine now. The others are too weak to try this so I must be the guinea pig. We have no choice.'

Simon agreed with a nod. 'Let's go.'

97

☼

Simon sprinted ahead of Tanya to the environ while Tanya's assistants accompanied her in her chair. He unlocked the door and held it open while Tanya steered her chair inside the space. Her assistants entered with her.

A restrained ball of energy crackled at the centre of the black machine and illuminated the space in a soft, orange glow. Simon's temporary mind mapping gave him the knowledge of an electrician to work the machine and that of a geotechnical engineer to understand how the machine related to the earth. But the harder his mind worked to retain both sets of information, the more he felt it slip from his mind. Regardless, he still knew enough to see that the stored grid power might not be enough to attract the Nexus to restore Tanya.

Tanya shifted in her chair but only produced minor movements. 'How is this going to work? Do I need to stand for this?'

'The machine will activate the stolen power and the gamma rock will amplify its reach. I hope it will be enough to communicate with the Nexus.'

Tanya frowned. 'Communicate how, by talking to it?'

Simon understood her scepticism. She'd never experienced the raw potential of the Nexus. Neither had Simon, but he had felt the raw and excitable hum beneath his feet when he'd stood in the tranquillity cave that one time.

'The Nexus is organic in nature and does not follow parameters and structure. It is constantly evolving. I had my team drill several conduits in the rock to pierce one of their tranquillity caves. I'm hoping the amplified power will coax it along one conduit, like a moth to a flame, so to speak.'

'If you say so. Let's see this thing in action.'

'You'll need to get close enough to the machine to touch the protective field around the stored energy,' said Simon.

Tanya barely moved until her two assistants hooked their arms underneath hers and lifted her up to stand. They extended her hands out until her fingers almost touched the field.

Tanya pulled back a little. 'How dangerous is this?'

'The energy may loop back around and provide a kick back through the field.'

Tanya drew in a breath.

'Don't worry; you'll be fine,' said Simon. 'The field acts as a dampener around the energy. It won't hurt, but you might feel a jolt of power when the Nexus discovers it.'

Tanya released a slow breath and rested her fingers on the outer field.

Simon turned the machine on and it visibly vibrated Tanya's arms.

'How long do I need to wait?' she said.

Her dark eyes, barely visible beneath skin folds, watched the machine.

'Not long, I hope. The vibration the machine is emitting will act like a beacon. If the Nexus is listening, it should pick up the sound.'

Tanya closed her eyes just as the ball of stored energy grew brighter. The brightness sparked and shot to where Tanya touched the field. Tanya yelped and tried to break contact.

'No, don't let go.'

Simon lunged for her and steadied her arms to keep

them rigid.

A thin rope of bright, white energy poked out from the conduit and appeared to look around. It snaked through the stored energy and pierced the field without trouble. Simon froze when the tendril wrapped around one of Tanya's arms and licked at his hands. The bright rope delivered a sharp shock to him. He gritted his teeth against the pain and held on to Tanya.

Tanya's head jerked and she yowled when the rope slithered farther down to encompass her body and legs. Simon released her. The tendril held her in place. Tanya's muscles spasmed where the rope appeared to squeeze her. She grimaced and panted. Then, after a few minutes, the rope retreated through the stored energy and disappeared inside the conduit. The stolen energy that had glowed bright at the start had lessened to a minuscule amount and barely glowed.

'What the hell was that?' said one of Tanya's assistants.

Tanya slumped forward in Simon's arms, exhausted. He helped her to her chair.

'I don't know. The closest I got to the Nexus was when I toured one of the tranquillity caves.' One assistant helped Simon lower Tanya back down. 'I believe that when they connect to the Nexus, tendrils similar to that one pull them inside. But it's all in their mind. It happens on a different plane to the physical one.' He stared at the machine. 'I may have accidentally designed a machine that gives the Nexus form in this world.'

'Did it fix Elite One?' said the second assistant.

'I don't know,' said Simon. And he didn't. He looked at Tanya, who had her eyes closed. 'Elite One, how do you feel?'

Tanya's appearance was serene, peaceful. Her eyes

Genesis Variant

flashed open and she stood up without help. Her skin, so wrinkled it had almost swallowed up her appearance, looked tighter and smoother.

'I feel... good.'

She swayed a little. Simon supported her.

'That was... powerful. I feel like my old self again. I mean before all the changes, not the decrepit sack of skin I am now.'

She walked unaided out of the environ, leaving Simon to marvel at the machine. He had had no idea it would even work.

Tanya gained strength with each new step. She waved off the chair and her assistant's help as she walked back.

'I'm excited by this,' she said. 'Let's heal the other Elite before the Indigenes notice we've got access to their precious Nexus.'

12

Laura stayed up all night combing over the details of the meeting with Simon and Tanya while Bill crashed on the bed. Her telepathic and empathic abilities weren't as strong as others' in District Three. She hated using them, feeling like imposter for using something she had only got through a rapid transformation of her mind and body. She'd asked Stephen to reverse the changes straight away and return her to human, as if her appearance disgusted her.

How could she look human and use abilities she had no right to keep? How could she claim to be something she was not?

Not that it mattered much. She hadn't gained much insight from Simon. She'd felt him block any attempts she made to link with him telepathically. Her efforts had left her drained. At least Bill had been happy to talk. But while Simon had been a closed book, she'd sensed something from Tanya. When Laura looked at her it was like she saw two versions: one in her white robe, the other a black figure that peeked out from behind Tanya any time she promised Bill something.

She'd seen her ability in action before. It usually occurred right before a person's nervous twitching alerted her to a lie. It was how Bill used to profile criminals and still did, using telltale habits that people could rarely hide. But with Tanya, it was different. The shapeless black mass representing the lie took form and looked straight at Laura.

Laura shook her head. She'd been another species for half a second eight years ago. And now she had a skill the others didn't? It didn't make sense. But this new manifestation prompted a desire to discuss her changes. Serena and Arianna came to mind. As did Margaux, the elder from District Eight with an ability to see what others didn't.

Bill snored in the bed beside her. She snuggled under the covers, careful not to wake him. He rarely slept through the night.

Morning came a few hours later and Laura left a cosy looking Bill to sleep. Since she had started to see black shapes as lies a few months ago, her own sleep had suffered. Maybe her Indigene side needed less sleep than her human one.

In the kitchen she started on breakfast. She replicated the raw ingredients for an Irish breakfast—sausages, bacon, eggs—and set the pan on the heat. Few people cooked like this any more, even on Exilon 5 where raw ingredients could be sourced cheaper than on Earth. Laura found cooking therapeutic. She set a pot to brew in the coffee machine. Her husband's favourite.

'Something smells good.' Bill appeared at the door. He slid into a seat and rubbed his eyes. 'You should have woken me. I'd have made you breakfast.'

Laura shrugged. 'No trouble. As soon as the sun's up, I'm ready to go.' She pushed half the sausage, bacon and scrambled eggs on to his plate and the remainder on to hers. 'Besides, I enjoy the alone time.'

'You thinking about last night's meeting?'

Laura poured a mug of coffee. She placed it in front of him. 'Among other things. I think we should find out more from the splinter groups, see what they know. I got a weird feeling last night.'

'Me too.'

He ate too fast and drank half his coffee in one go.

Laura sat down and nibbled on her eggs. They had a slightly better flavour from being replicated raw and cooked.

'You'll get indigestion eating like that.'

'I want to get in early. I've got some snooping to do.'

Laura ate quicker. 'Okay, give me a minute to finish this and clean up.'

Bill got his DPad and called the car to pick them up. When they exited their apartment block, the driverless car idled outside. Bill climbed into the driver seat in front of a console with a hidden steering wheel. Laura sat beside him.

The car passed through the city that covered an area half of London's size on Earth. Laura looked out at replicas of smaller parks and pretty streets with the prefix "New" attached to their old-world name.

Ten minutes east of the docking station and New St James' Park, the car pulled up outside a large, glass building. The offices were located in the Whitehall/Shoreditch area known as New Shorehall. The area contained the best of replicated British architecture, from the old war office building to Westminster. But among the opulence sat warehouse spaces that once housed goods. They had been converted into glass monsters for use as luxury apartments and office spaces.

Bill said the warehouses reminded him of the Shoreditch area in the real London, which had become a virtual tech hub in the late twenty-first century.

Laura got out and looked up at the glass building with six floors nestled between replica nineteenth-century buildings. The ITF occupied the entire building but only operated on three of those floors. She glanced at the entrance to a nearby MagLev train station that connected them to the other cities on Exilon 5.

In the foyer, they scanned their security chips at the security station—a tradition of the old regime. It didn't matter that things were less volatile on Exilon 5 than on Earth. She and Bill had both agreed to keep the security in a world not comfortable in its own skin.

Laura headed for the stairs that would take her to the first floor and her team. She shook her head when Bill called the lift to take him to the top of the six-floor property.

'Oh, I meant to ask... I promised Stephen I would,' said Bill, with one hand on the open lift door. 'Ben Watson wants something to do. Is there anything you can give him?'

Off the top of her head, Laura could think of nothing. But she remembered Jenny had sung the boy's praises, said he was great at research.

'I'll give it some thought. He'll have to sign a confidentiality agreement.'

'We can give him access to non-classified information.' Bill stepped into the lift. 'I'll do some independent research on these splinter groups, see what turns up.'

Laura nodded. 'I'll do the same and let you know.'

She jogged over to him before the door closed and kissed him on the cheek. Then she tackled the short climb to her floor. The brief burst of exercise did little to settle her nervous energy.

She exited the stairwell and entered a large, open-plan office with a dozen hot desks with monitors. Her team of fifteen often rotated between monitors depending on the work they did. To the left was a glass-walled boardroom. At the back, another glass-walled room: her office. A forensic analysis station took up the rest of the space.

'Morning, Laura,' said Julie, her second in command.

'Morning. Let's meet in the boardroom in ten minutes.'

Julie nodded; her blonde hair, shorter than Laura's, bobbed. She announced it to the rest of the room while Laura slipped into her office with a view of the entire floor.

She sat down and activated her monitor. A list of documents appeared on screen and for a moment it transported her back to her old job in the Earth Security Centre where she had filed paperwork on the population and never asked why the ESC and government kept a paper trail on them.

While she still kept notes on the population, at least her reason was to help innocents.

The sun streamed through the window and caught Laura in its glare. She squinted and reduced the brightness in the command-activated glass with a flick of her hand. Lately, her eyes had become more sensitive to light. It had begun around the time she started to see the manifestation of lies. Maybe she'd never get used to sunshine. She'd suffered from Seasonal Affective Disorder for so long before Stephen treated her. And while the condition no longer afflicted her, she still wasn't used to the sun.

Laura looked out at her team who read and listened

in on conversations in the pursuit of peace and order. When she and Bill had first moved to Exilon 5 eight years ago, the ITF operation in New London had been much bigger. The board members with security detail to match the original numbers of the GS had still been human and active in the operations on Exilon 5. But as their interest, more notably Tanya's, shifted to the geneticists they'd commissioned to work on their code, the resources went with them. Bill had had no choice but to scale back the operation. He and Laura had agreed to mirror the underground operations that were happening on Earth. Without Tanya's knowledge, he'd reassigned men and women to work as undercover operatives who continued to this day. Their identities would remain known only to a few, including Stephen and Serena.

One of the roles of the underground operatives was to monitor the peace treaty on the ground, to get a feel for things. Things were not good.

Boxes divided up her inbox filled with chat-room conversations sent over interstellar wave that she and her team had hijacked. The illegal chat rooms used interstellar wave to transmit communication on Exilon 5, something that had been used to communicate between the two planets. The conversations rarely lasted long, disappearing seconds after they'd been posted. The rooms required round-the-clock monitoring. If anything of interest appeared, one of her team would take a screenshot and send it to her. Nobody liked the onerous task. Her team could spend hours watching data that yielded nothing. Ben Watson came to mind. Could this be a job for the boy?

Laura was in an enviable position. She saw the most interesting conversations, or moments of time, without having to trawl through the clutter.

Today, a screenshot showed a man discussing an

attack on one of the power grids outside New Tokyo. She forwarded the snapshot of the terrorist threat to the ITF office in Tokyo. Another was of a group of three discussing ways to get inside the Indigene tunnels. This type of chat happened on a regular basis and never amounted to anything, but Laura took each threat seriously. She forwarded any chat referring to the tunnels to Anton.

Was this trio chat from one of the splinter groups working with the rogue Indigenes? There were plenty of humans who hated the Indigenes just because they existed. She couldn't assume it was without a verification of the source. To do that, she'd have to locate the start of the group thread and find the original poster. If the poster was a recruiter, there could be some place they regularly met.

The sun disappeared behind a cloud, plunging her already dark office into a deeper grey. Laura looked out at the open-plan office. Julie had gathered her team in the conference room bar five including Mike, her senior analyst, who stayed behind to monitor the Wave.

Julie gave her a nod. She got up and joined the remaining ten in the boardroom and closed the door to give Mike and the others privacy. Members of her team, including Julie, sat around an oval, glass table, DPads at the ready.

She stood at the top of the room next to a large screen on the wall, sensing her team's anticipation and excitement. They had no idea of her abilities or her alteration into another species. Laura had thought about telling them, but with the increased activities of the GS 100 and the splinter groups, it never felt like the right time.

'We discussed yesterday how to locate the meeting areas where the human groups and rogue Indigenes meet. There seems to be very little chat about it over the Wave.'

Julie leaned forward. 'It's possible they're staying off the Wave because they know we monitor it.'

'So what does that tell you about this group?' said Laura.

'That they're cautious?' one of her team suggested.

Laura nodded. 'Yes, but they're also familiar with how the Wave works and what we do here. Not many know how the Wave works. These people could have been high-level operatives on Earth. Not every specialist on Earth was assimilated into the GS 100 fold.' She folded her arms. 'We know they're in the cities but not using the Wave, which means they've found another way to communicate. What do we do?'

'If we can't monitor their activities online, we have to do it offline,' said Julie.

'That's what I'm thinking. Suggestions?'

'Old-fashioned detective work,' said one. 'Feet on the street. Talk to the locals, sound out activity of any large groups meeting in their establishments.'

'A good suggestion,' said Laura. 'But as soon as we talk to locals, we tip off the groups and they move elsewhere. How do we pinpoint the activities of a group of men and women who have managed to evade us?'

The room fell silent and Laura sensed their frustration at the lack of progress. Actually, she felt it like goose bumps on her arm. She shook off the weird feeling. She'd never had it before.

Maybe it was one of her Indigene traits.

They had concentrated their efforts on locating these groups but now their work took an urgent turn with the GS 100's new environ and drain of power. If she could locate just one group with knowledge of the GS 100, maybe she could shed some light on Tanya's plans.

Her team's tension sent a shudder through her

bones.

'What about the ships?' said Lisa, one of her operatives.

Laura's head whipped round to look at Lisa, drawing gasps from the room. She'd turned too fast. Only Julie knew what she had once been. The more she denied her abilities, they more they appeared to come out naturally.

She diverted attention to Lisa. 'What *about* the ships, Lisa?'

The team looked at their colleague.

Julie gave her a discreet nod that the others didn't see. Laura released a tiny breath.

'The passenger ships. Is it possible that the passengers arriving here are being recruited for these groups?'

'It's possible. Check that out,' said Laura.

She hadn't considered that avenue but fresh bodies and minds would be too tempting to pass on. She and Bill had been at the docking station just yesterday, too preoccupied with Ben Watson's arrival. Were the groups recruiting from Earth? Had they used the ships to *ferry* their people to Exilon 5? Plenty of criminals with a desire to escape Earth would jump at the chance to join a fight.

'Do we know where the group from the recent ship went?'

Julie checked her DPad. 'Straight to the processing centres. They were assigned work based on their skills and taken to the safe houses.'

'It's possible these safe houses are a cover for a recruiting drive.' Laura paced the room. 'Can someone pull up the manifest for the last ship please?'

'I can,' said Julie.

She hit a few buttons on her pad and set the device

in the middle of the table. She pulled the image out with two fingers and the manifest, listed in alphabetical order, rotated three-sixty degrees.

Laura stopped pacing and read it. 'Does anyone recognise the names on that list?'

Ben Watson's name was at the bottom.

Julie pointed to a name. 'This guy used to be a ship engineer, and this woman worked in tech.'

Laura nodded. 'Good, it's a start.'

Julie shook her head. 'No, you don't understand; the emphasis is on "used to". They're both dead.' She tapped two new names and brought up their images. 'These two are travelling under false names. And if they are—'

'Then others are too.' Laura stared at the photos of the supposedly dead travellers. One was of a man called Martin Casey. The other travelling under the name John Caldwell was a face she'd never forget. 'Harvey Buchanan.'

Shit.

'Who's Harvey Buchanan?' said Julie.

'Someone who was a big deal on Earth.' Laura had to tell Bill. 'Locate his chatter on the Wave and we'll find the head of the splinter group. And be careful. Use your fake identities to lurk. This man is dangerous.'

Laura ended the meeting and took the stairs two at a time to the sixth floor. She entered the partitioned space. The evenly spaced desks and chairs allowed no free movement, unlike her open-plan space.

She offered good mornings as she walked through the space to the back of the room where Bill's office stood, with four solid walls and a closed door. Bill had always preferred privacy over intrusion. But Laura had spent too long working in a tiny booth in the ESC that offered no interaction. For communications to work best, Laura relied on collaboration.

She knocked on his door, just like any other employee. Bill owed her no favours and she would never take them.

'Enter!' he said gruffly, his distracted tone permeating through the solid wood.

She opened the door and he lifted his hard gaze from the monitor to her. Then it softened.

'Close the door and come here.'

With her DPad in one hand, Laura stood behind Bill's chair. A drone shot of the environ belonging to the GS 100 was on screen. The image was overlaid with schematics from Anton showing the highest concentration of gamma rock.

'Tanya wasn't lying about the concentration of gamma rock. She's using it to amplify something.'

'The power from the grid. She already said as much,' said Laura. 'Can't we just give them a monitored allowance?'

'Not without compromising our own supply.' Bill tapped the screen twice with his finger. 'Besides, I want to know why she really wants it.'

'They want it to heal. I sensed that much from Tanya. From Simon I learned the Elite are in a bad way and will not stand more genetic experiments done to them. It's possible they want to strengthen their bodies to continue with the experiments. A powerful mind in a weak body is not a good outcome for them.'

'They've gone through all these experiments, why —to live longer in a body that will eventually die?' Bill shook his head. 'Tanya doesn't aim low. There's more to her request, I can feel it.' He glanced at the DPad in her hand. 'Did you find out something?'

Laura nodded and pulled up Harvey Buchanan's photo from his identity chip. 'I did and you won't like it.'

She turned the DPad around and Bill released a breath. 'Shit, I thought he was dead.'

'With facial manipulation and stolen identity chips, who knows any more?'

The man who'd created false identities for Bill and Laura eight years ago when they needed to travel to Exilon 5, who'd almost killed them to gain their knowledge of replica identity chips, was on Exilon 5.

'What's he doing here?'

Laura sat on the edge of the desk. Bill rubbed the back of her leg.

'We think he's got connections with whoever is running the main splinter group out of West London. People have arrived on the ships travelling under false identities. We think the groups might have brought people here, or at least targeted people coming off the ships. Then Harvey Buchanan turns up, travelling under a false name.'

'Where did he go?'

'Assigned to a construction job in the west quarter. That can't be a coincidence. We've never looked into these safe houses before. I think we should now.'

Bill stroked her leg with his thumb. 'Who's the foreman in charge there?'

Laura checked her DPad. 'Ollie Patterson.'

'Can we arrange a meeting with this Ollie, tell him we want to talk?'

Laura didn't like the sound of that. 'You want to negotiate with terrorists?'

'They haven't done anything yet, love. They've been passive until now.'

'A quiet group is never idle, Bill.'

They'd both seen the repercussions of their own

government's silent operations. They'd ended with a bloody battle with the Indigenes.

'I agree, but what if we meet them on neutral ground?' said Bill. 'If we can offer them something small, they might share what they know about Tanya's plans. If they know anything at all.'

Laura stood up. 'Of course they know something. Harvey's with them. Now you want us, you and me, to meet with a potential terrorist? What if something goes wrong?'

Bill stood too and grabbed her hands. His confidence sent a tickle up her spine and drew her closer to his foolish plan.

'It has to be just us, love. We don't know for sure if Harvey's involved, but this Ollie Patterson definitely won't agree to talk if we go in there with numbers. Besides, we have your Indigene abilities to help us if anything happens.'

Her skills wouldn't stop a Buzz Gun blast or a bullet. But maybe the manifestation of deceit as a separate black shadow would give them an advantage. She'd only use her skill as a last resort.

Laura squeezed his shoulder and smiled. She would not saddle him with more worry.

'I'll get Julie on it and have her set up a meeting for later.'

She left his office knowing that after this meeting, she needed to face her personal problem head on. Was she human or Indigene?

Stuck between two identities, she felt as if she belonged to neither.

13

Bill received word from Laura about Julie's success in contacting Ollie Patterson. She had arranged a meeting for him at 9pm that evening in the disused biodome on the edge of New London.

'There's just one condition,' said Laura.

'What's that?'

'It has to be just you.'

He leaned back in his chair. 'That's fine.'

'No, it's not. You're not going in alone.'

'Laura, love, this is how these things work. These people are a secretive bunch. They won't want an audience.'

Laura paced the room. 'Maybe I can stay close, keep an eye on things.'

While Laura's skills would prove useful, he'd changed his mind about her going. 'No. He's not going to do anything to me. He needs me. And he might not show up if I bring you.'

Laura stopped pacing. She didn't look convinced. 'When it was both of us going, I was fine with the idea. But just you? I don't like it. It could be a trap. A group followed us last night on our way to meet Simon. What makes you think this Ollie Patterson will come alone? He'll probably bring backup with him.'

Bill didn't see what other choice he had. They needed more information on the splinter groups and the GS 100. If there was even a slim chance he could learn something new from this meeting, he had to risk it.

'Last night was different. You said the Indigenes who watched didn't want us. They were there to observe only.'

Laura leaned over a seated Bill. She fussed with his jacket, straightened his tie. 'At least let me tell Stephen.'

'No, love. Stephen is worse than you for worrying. He'll only order a troop to follow. If this Ollie has Indigenes working with him, they'll detect if there's more than just me.'

Her hands stilled on his tie. 'So that's it? We just accept these meeting conditions with no safeguard?'

Bill sighed. 'What else can we do?'

Laura's expression brightened. She smiled and let go. 'What about Serena? She could influence those who work for this Patterson character into keeping quiet about her presence.'

Bill hadn't thought of Serena. It could work, and the idea of meeting this Ollie Patterson alone didn't appeal to him.

'Okay, but only she can come. Stephen needs to stay out of this.'

Laura looked relieved. She checked her watch. 'It's 8.30pm now. If I run I'll make it in twenty. That will give her ten minutes to get there. She's fast. She won't need that long.'

'I thought you didn't like to use your abilities.'

His wife's face darkened a fraction as she walked to

116

the door. 'Only in emergencies.'

She disappeared from his office and the vacant, sixth-floor space so fast he almost missed it. While he'd picked up on the edge to her mood that struck whenever he mentioned her abilities, Stephen had warned she needed to embrace that side of her. If she didn't, she could risk getting stuck between her human and Indigene identities. Stephen had said he'd *seen* her conflict, most recently when they'd met with the underground operatives under both Bill and Stephen's command. But how could he broach the subject with Laura when she kept changing the conversation?

He idled in his office for the twenty minutes Laura had said it would take for her to reach Serena. While he waited he ran a search on Ollie Patterson. Little information came back on him and there was no photo on file. The name was probably an alias anyway. Bill expected the supposed head of the splinter human group in New London to bring with him a list of demands.

Next, he pulled up Harvey Buchanan's photo. The image of a man with sandy hair, a piercing gaze and a faint smile looked back at him. Bill had known Buchanan on Earth during his days as investigator. Bill had brought down a leading figure in technology manipulation who happened to be a close colleague of Harvey's. The move had damaged Harvey's side business of selling failed prototypes from Nanoid valley to the seedy underworld.

But Harvey had also helped Bill and Laura gain passage to Exilon 5 to find Stephen when word about the captured Anton had dried up. In the same breath, Harvey had also betrayed them to their own government to help his cause. He was someone Bill would never trust.

With ten minutes to go till the meeting, Bill waved his security chip over the screen to lock it. He called his automated car on the way out and found it waiting for him by the kerb.

He climbed into the front seat and ignored his racing heart. 'East London biodome.'

The car took the shortest route to the biodome, located on an old perimeter line of the city. It used to house animals before the ITF relocated them to heavily monitored habitats that could cater better for their growing numbers. Before the peace treaty, the Indigenes had hunted the animals close to extinction. A new one-kill-per-hunting-party rule gave the animals time to breed and replenish their stock.

The car pulled up outside the biodome that had been closed for more than a year. Bill got out and looked around the abandoned space with its high, chain-link fences and weed-covered path leading to the dome entrance. The dome itself, once bright and white, had lost its gleam under a thin layer of dirt.

ITF had used the biodome just yesterday to process the passengers off the last ship. Bill looked at the building that Harvey Buchanan may have been in as recently as then.

It was too dark to see anyone in the vicinity, but he knew how these meetings worked. Someone was watching.

He approached the locked facility that not long ago had buzzed with his people. But the place was not a regular ITF haunt and a man like Ollie probably knew that.

Had Serena arrived yet? Just knowing she would come put his mind at ease. He would never see her though. Serena was the master of illusion.

He reached for the handle just as the door opened. A man with long, brown hair tied back in a ponytail and glasses greeted him.

'Bill Taggart. I recognise you from the news feeds. Glad you took my advice and came alone.'

News feeds? There was probably a whole file on him.

'I said I would. Ollie Patterson, I presume?'

'The one and only. Come in.'

The eerie quiet of the abandoned building made the hairs on the back of Bill's neck stand up. He hated being penned in. And although he couldn't see anyone else, his skin prickled with the feeling they were not alone.

Maybe he'd been hanging around Stephen for too long. Or maybe he'd always been a paranoid bastard and would remain that way until he dropped dead.

He followed Patterson to the main room, where he saw a trestle table at the back of the room. Two chairs to the front of the table faced each other.

'Take a seat, Bill.' Patterson motioned to the chair and took the other one. 'Were you expecting more than just me?'

Bill sat down. 'The fact it looks like we're alone doesn't mean anything.'

Patterson laughed. 'I forgot what you used to do, Investigator. Director of the ITF on a peaceful planet must be a real step down for you.'

'It has its moments. Where people exist, opportunity and deceit usually follow.'

Patterson touched a hand to his heart. 'Is that what you think our group is—opportunistic and deceitful?'

Bill leaned forward. 'Yeah, I'd say that sums you up.'

'So you think the peace treaty works?'

'It keeps the cities in check.'

Patterson smiled. 'And the Indigenes.'

'We all have to follow rules.'

Patterson paused for a moment. 'But the treaty appears to weigh more in the Indigene's favour than ours.'

The Indigenes had certain perks, but nothing that tipped the scale in their favour. It was a small demand, given how humans had almost wiped them out. Bill didn't see how their concessions affected someone like Ollie.

'The peace treaty favours both Indigenes and humans.'

Patterson crossed his legs and rested one arm on the table. 'I assume you know the Indigenes hunt outside of their hunting zones, which is in direct violation of the treaty?'

Bill nodded. 'As long as it doesn't affect the one-kill-per-group rule, I have no issue with that.'

'Of course it matters!' Patterson grunted. 'They're breaking the rules, testing the boundaries of what they can get away with. And for the record, the kills are sometimes two or three.'

Animal welfare felt too low a concern for Patterson. What did he really want?

'Are you sure the Indigenes killed all the animals? Man has a history of hunting. Meat is expensive in the cities. Those animals can fetch a fair price. Maybe you find it easy to use the Indigenes as scapegoats for bad human behaviour.'

Patterson examined his nails. 'The Indigenes have confirmed to me that they broke the rules on purpose. And the humans I represent don't like having to tiptoe around their own land. God forbid we should go where the hell we like.'

'And yet you engage with Indigenes of your own free will.'

Patterson locked Bill in a stare. 'A business arrangement that benefits both sides. And now the GS humans are making a nuisance of themselves. What do they want, a piece of the action?'

Bill released a small breath. He had thought he'd have to coax Patterson more to talk about them.

'What dealings have you had with the GS 100?'

'None. We keep our distance.' Patterson uncrossed his legs and leaned forward. 'Did you know they've built an environ just beyond their caves?'

'Yes. Do you know why?'

Simon had already told him its purpose but Bill wanted to know what Patterson had heard.

'I know as much as you, I'd imagine. You probably know I'm the foreman for the construction site in the west quarter.' Bill nodded. 'Some of our stored materials were stolen recently. My men and I fear the day the GS 100 come looking for more than materials and equipment. We need to protect ourselves.'

'Protect?'

'Yeah, weapons, Bill. Whatever you can spare. We've heard the rumours of what the GS 100 like to eat.'

Bill leaned back, curious to know Patterson's real agenda and how Harvey Buchanan fit in to this. 'I can assign troops to protect you while you work.'

Patterson shook his head. 'They won't be there twenty-four-seven. We must protect ourselves round the clock.'

Patterson's rejection of his offer didn't surprise Bill. 'Sounds like you expect a war.'

'Sometimes we do.' Patterson released a slow breath that felt for show. 'We're vulnerable on that build site, isolated from the city. But what would you know about it in your ivory ITF tower, protected from such attacks? Your offer means nothing to us. We need weapons to show the GS 100 that we are not sitting ducks.'

Bill stood up. 'I can't give you what you want, Mr Patterson. But we can provide extra troops if you meet me halfway on this.'

Patterson mirrored him. 'We want guns or nothing. And we'll go on strike if we have to.'

'Are you sure that's how you want to play this?'

'Bill, we'd rather not resort to other measures to get what we want.'

'Is that a threat?'

'No, it's a promise.'

The lights in the biodome flickered before returning to full brightness. Bill frowned at the light in the ceiling.

'That's happening because of your friends in their environ. They've doubled the draw of power. Did you know that?'

'Since when?'

'Two hours ago.'

Clearly his and Laura's talk with Simon and Tanya had been for nothing. What did Tanya want with the extra power?

'My team and I will deal with it.'

Bill walked away.

Patterson followed him to the exit. 'And if you can't, remember this. You'll want us on your side, not against, when the time comes.'

Bill left the biodome and climbed into his waiting car while Patterson watched him from the door.

The car drove out through the open section in the chainlink fence. Bill glanced back to see Patterson speaking to a man. Harvey Buchanan. The men shook hands. Bill almost ordered the car to turn around.

Buchanan on Exilon 5 wasn't a surprise, nor was his connection with Patterson. It only proved there was more to this union than an irritation over the peace treaty. For one, Harvey hadn't been on Exilon 5 long enough to feel its effects.

One thing was clear: Bill would not put weapons in these men's hands. They wanted something else, power most likely, similar to Tanya and her followers. But this power did not come from the grid. It came through spilled blood and temporary alliances.

And destroying the peace treaty would be the fastest way to upset the regime.

Bill had to be careful. If Harvey was involved, he should expect a fight on his hands.

14

Stephen watched Anton at work in his laboratory. Serena had left with Laura an hour ago and he needed a distraction while he waited for her to return. He hated it when she went out alone but Laura had insisted it was the only way to help Bill.

Anton melted a lump of silver metal in a bowl. Next to the bowl was one of Anton's moulds, but Stephen had no clue what the mould would make.

You could help me instead of brooding over there, said Anton.

I need to know she's okay. We've no idea what these humans want.

Anton laughed. *You're worried about Serena? I think the humans should be worried about her.*

Stephen switched to his voice. 'Don't mock me, Anton. I'm not in the mood.'

'I'll stop mocking you when you start making sense. Now, quit your sulking. Serena can look after herself.'

Stephen sighed and shuffled closer to Anton's work. Anton was right, but his bond with Serena was stronger than the one Anton had with Arianna. Sometimes when they were separated, he felt her pain.

A noise at the door drew his attention. Arianna entered the room wearing a pair of gloves that reached her elbows. She carried a three-litre container of liquid nitrogen.

She glanced at Stephen and his melancholy lifted.

Damn empaths. Can't hide anything from you, he said.

Arianna smiled. *No, you can't.*

Anton pointed to a free space at the end of his workbench. 'Set it down over there, Arianna.'

She set the container down gently and removed her gloves before turning to Stephen. 'Why is your heart racing? Why do you look like you're about to be sick?'

Stephen studied his friends' auras; Anton's was a happy green while Arianna's was an indecisive yellow. He imagined his own to be closer to grey than a calming blue.

He hated feeling so out of control when Serena put herself in danger. In the beginning it had been easier to convince her to stay out of trouble, when she was still figuring out her influencer ability. But the more she understood the ability that gave her temporary control over humans, and, to a lesser degree, Indigenes, the more he knew Serena would want to help.

Her gift was a double-edged sword; it made her both unique and invaluable. She was gifted to the point where sometimes only Stephen watched out for her safety. She had been human once, but her genes had been altered using Anton's mutated DNA. She had become a unique creation with the abilities of all Indigenes—part empath like Arianna, part envisionary like Stephen—but only in small measures. Her ability to influence the minds and actions of others stood out above all else.

'Did you tell him she'll be fine?' Arianna said to Anton.

'I did, but he'd rather brood than believe me. Stephen, she'll be back before you know it. Can't you see it?'

'Not down here.'

Never in the District, not with the omicron rock acting as a buffer to his envisioning abilities. But to go up top would show Serena he didn't trust her. She'd warned him to stay below, that if she caught him checking up on her, she wouldn't speak to him again. He'd broken her rule once and she'd ignored him for a whole month. The silence in his head had been the worst punishment ever.

But there were other barriers to his envisioning ability than the omicron rock. He'd succeeded before in using his ability below surface, eight years ago to be exact, when Charles Deighton and a few board members had visited Exilon 5 to start a war. His vision had given the Indigenes a few weeks' notice to prepare for their arrival.

But the existence of the genetically superior humans that lived in the caves had changed how his ability worked. Ever since their creation, ever since the human and Indigene splinter groups had joined forces, Stephen had felt a physical block on his ability. He couldn't be sure it was something the GS had done, or if the groups had created a device to counter his efforts.

Whatever the reason, he was flying blind.

'What if the GS humans are at this meeting with Bill?' he said.

Stephen settled next to Anton, who checked the progress of the melted silver.

'Then she uses her ability on them. Relax, Stephen.'

Anton slipped on heat-proof gloves and lifted the bowl with the molten silver off the heat. He poured it into the mould that Stephen saw held a microprocessor separated from the base by a small, metal lattice. The metal took the shape of the mould and swallowed up the microprocessor.

Anton's answer didn't satisfy him.

'The GS humans are evolving too fast and we have absolutely no data on them. I can't get a read on them. It's like they're blanks. Plus, they don't venture outside of their caves long enough for me to predict their future.'

He omitted the part about the block on his ability.

'That's why I'm making this,' said Anton.

'What is it?'

Stephen leaned on the bench. The mould rocked, forcing Anton to steady his experiment.

'Watch where you put your giant hands. I'm building a neurosensor using amorphous metal. It's a neural detection device that should be able to monitor brain activity.'

Using a set of flat pincers, Anton picked up the mould and placed it on a platform set over the container of liquid nitrogen. He lowered it slowly into the nitrogen and left it there for just a few seconds. When he pulled it out, the metal had solidified to a glossy finish. The end result was flat and round—a perfect shape to attach to the side of the head. But Stephen still didn't understand its usefulness.

'If we can't access their minds, how does the neurosensor give us an advantage?' he said.

'Through specific genome evolution, the GS humans may have found a way to block all telepathic communication at will,' said Anton. 'We know they have the ability—it's a given if they used our genetic code. This disc has a dual purpose: to monitor the brain activity of the GS while amplifying our thoughts to stimulate theirs, so we can locate a weak point in their barrier. Ferromagnetic metallic glass has a low magnetisation loss, which makes it a high efficiency transformer that will facilitate electrical energy to transfer between two circuits, or brains. If we can get close enough to the GS, the device might enable us to hear snippets of their thoughts. Like eavesdropping.'

'So how do we get close enough to hear them?' said a new voice.

Stephen turned at the sound. Serena stood at the door, arms folded. Stephen ran to her and almost knocked her over with the force of his hug.

He pulled away and studied her face, pressing his forehead to hers. *I was worried.*

Have faith in me that I won't break, she said.

'It's not that. I just can't stand the thought of losing you.'

Serena smiled. 'And I hate it every time you hunt. I worry that some animal will finish you off, or worse, a hostile human who knows how valuable you are to this district.'

Stephen returned the smile. 'So we're agreed; we'll never leave this district again. We'll live out our remaining years in the Council Chambers?'

'Fine by me.'

Stephen grabbed her hand. 'Well, before we become recluses in our own home, tell me how your meeting went.'

Serena led Stephen over to Anton, who stopped what he was doing. Arianna joined them.

'The meeting was between Bill and a human called Ollie Patterson, the foreman of one of the construction sites in the west of the city. They disappeared inside the biodome and spent no more than ten minutes talking. Ollie requested guns from Bill to protect their construction site, where their safe house is also located. Ollie accused the

GS humans of stealing their stock.'

'What did Bill say?' said Anton.

'He refused to agree to his demands. Then he left.'

'What did you sense from Ollie?' said Arianna.

'Enough to know he's lying and the guns aren't for protection. I sensed he's planning a revolt.'

'Did any Indigenes show up?' said Stephen.

Serena nodded. 'But not from this district. They were from District Eight, Gabriel and Margaux's territory.'

That was bad news. If Indigenes were travelling from other districts, it meant the groups in New London had gained notoriety. 'That's where Serena and I must go next, to speak to Gabriel and Margaux and understand the problems they face there. This is worse than I thought.'

'What about me and Arianna?' asked Anton.

Stephen nodded at the neurosensor. 'Can you make more of them?'

'It will take me a few days to make more micro processors, but yes.'

'First, I need your help with something else, Anton,' said Stephen.

'Anything.'

'We need to find out who is inciting this rogue element. Just because no Indigenes from this district turned up at the meeting doesn't mean they're not involved. This problem is not limited to one district and I suspect it may have started here, considering we're the closest district to the GS humans. I'd like you and Arianna to talk to the youngest Indigenes, those who've just exited their Evolver stage. Maybe they're bored, or feeling let down by the treaty. Maybe they were too young to understand what the treaty meant at its creation, or to understand what life was like before it existed. Peace creates restlessness and the chances of them speaking to

Serena or me as elders are slim.'

'What makes you think they'll speak to me?' said Anton.

'Because you're more approachable than I am. You're like a younger version of Gabriel. We live in different times to Pierre and Elise. Being an elder doesn't hold the same respect as it once did.'

'I seem to recall the others didn't accept Gabriel when he came here,' said Anton.

Stephen remembered the time well. Elise had just died and Pierre had locked himself up in Council Chambers. Gabriel and Margaux had volunteered to help, but their presence had only angered the Indigenes.

'They clam up around Serena and she's better at conversing than I am,' said Stephen. 'So get them talking. Irritate them if you have to; be the source of their anger. We often reveal too much when we're angry.'

Anton nodded and picked up the neurosensor disc, rolling it between thumb and forefinger. 'We can try. But I'd like to test the neuro sensor first. I don't know how much range it will give me.'

'How long will you need?'

'A day to test it.'

Stephen frowned. 'On who? We can't risk getting close to the GS humans and tipping them off about our new invention.'

Anton smiled at Serena. 'How about the only Indigene who can block us?'

'This evening, I promise, Anton,' said Serena. 'As soon as Stephen and I get back from District Eight, I'm all yours.'

15

What a joke. Marcus had pictured a different future on Exilon 5 to the one Harvey Buchanan had in mind. Instead of doing great things, Harvey thought pairing him with an Indigene would be a good idea.

Fucking bottom feeders.

Their first meeting had been in the middle of nowhere, when Ollie and Harvey had introduced him to the fuckers. The second had been just an hour ago, different meeting location, same middle of nowhere. The tall freaks and their shining devil eyes watched him like he was their next fucking meal.

What had happened to the pecking order on this planet? Since when did people trust the Indigenes?

But cool-as-a-cucumber Harvey had divided up the groups of humans and Indigenes and paired Marcus up with a male Indigene called Clement, who had the freakiest blue eyes he'd ever seen.

Harvey's earlier warning that he owned Marcus rattled around his head.

Looks like you got me, you dipshit.

Ollie Patterson had gathered their group to discuss

the meeting he'd just had with Bill Taggart. Harvey stood by his side.

'I demanded weapons—to defend our construction sites,' said Ollie, glancing at Harvey. 'But Taggart said no.'

That didn't surprise Marcus. People like Taggart were no different to those who ran the factions back home. They liked power too much to just give it away.

Harvey instructed the new human-Indigene pairings to monitor all activity in the region.

'If those GS 100 or Taggart sneezes, I want to know about it,' said Patterson.

Harvey nodded. It was subtle, but the nod told Marcus that Harvey controlled things, not Patterson.

Marcus watched him, the man who did Harvey's bidding. He couldn't be sure what Ollie got out of the arrangement. Harvey was easier to read. A man who rivalled Gaetano Agostini's ambitions should never be crossed.

Patterson recounted other details of his meeting with Taggart. It sounded like a chat about nothing. But as he stood there, Marcus knew now would not be the best time to break off on his own. A few days on Exilon 5, that's all he'd had. He knew nothing about the planet other than what Harvey and Ollie had shown him. But one thing was clear: The wrong people ruled.

That didn't mean no place existed for a man like Marcus Murphy. He would prove to Harvey he could toe the line just like everyone else, even if that meant working with a bottom feeder.

Marcus' day would come.

The meeting disbanded and Marcus began his surveillance with Clement. He perched on a rock that formed part of the boundary wall and observed the landscape with a pair of magnifying glasses. The area included the GS 100 caves. Clement stood still and listened.

Marcus shivered at the creepiness of his "partner", who'd said nothing more than *yes* to Marcus when he'd asked, 'Should we go over there?'

Not much had been happening around the caves until an hour ago, when three freaks dressed in white, hooded cloaks had emerged from a cave his glasses couldn't reach. Clement had confirmed it. The trio moved fast to the environ.

Clement pointed in the distance. 'Over there.'

Marcus readjusted the magnification and saw four new entities slumped in hover chairs being escorted by another three of the GS.

'This is ridiculous,' said Marcus. Clement didn't respond. 'I mean, look at them. They're like two hundred years old. A ten-year-old girl could take them out.'

Clement made a noise.

'What?'

'You humans are too linear in your thinking.'

He spoke in a cold tone that made Marcus shiver.

'Linear, how?'

'You look at the outside and see weakness. Their strength lies in their mind.'

Marcus didn't get his point. 'So? If the body dies, the mind dies with it.'

Clement waved his hand. 'Again, you only see what's on the outside.'

Marcus put the magnification glasses down and looked at Clement.

He kept a safe distance between him and the blue-eyed weirdo, who had shifted closer to him. 'Okay, I'll play. What do you see?'

133

The Indigene looked into the distance. 'I can't read them. Their minds are closed off. That means they can hide their true intentions.'

'So? I can't read your mind. Doesn't mean I'm weak.'

Clement smirked at Marcus. 'You humans are weak. I could access your mind if I wanted. I know what you're thinking.'

Marcus panicked and thought of something boring. 'Fuck off out of there. My thoughts are none of your business.'

The Indigene levelled a glare that unsettled him. 'You believe you're destined for greater things. You despise, yet admire, the human called Harvey and you're wary of the other one called Patterson.'

'So? You don't have to be a mind reader to get that vibe. We humans call it instinct.'

Clement sneered. 'But you have one thing going for you.'

Marcus folded his arms. 'What's that?'

'You're afraid.'

Marcus laughed. 'Fear? And they call you super humans?' He blew out a breath. 'More like imposters. I'm not afraid of anything.'

'Healthy fear keeps you from making stupid choices. To say nothing scares you reveals your stupidity.'

Marcus was close enough to hit Clement, but his fear kept his clenched fists by his side.

'I can see it in your eyes,' said the Indigene. 'Hold on to that fear, because you'll regret the day you fight me.'

'I wasn't going to do anything, bottom feeder.'

He pretended not to care, but he could feel Clement crawling around inside his head.

He uncrossed his arms and slipped on his glasses

Genesis Variant

again. He'd had enough of Clement's mind games. He watched the able-bodied GS and those in hover chairs disappear from view inside the environ. He removed the glasses and rubbed the bridge of his nose.

This was just like working with Enzo Agostini all over again, sent to do recon on properties and people. Except Marcus had been able to stand the humans he'd worked alongside.

This Indigene, not so much.

'The feeling's mutual,' said Clement.

Marcus cursed. 'Now you can read my mind?'

'Only when your guard is down.'

Marcus raised the drawbridge in his mind. 'Why are we even here, for fuck's sake?'

Surely Harvey and Ollie had a better use for him than to do these crap jobs.

'To keep an eye on the new species.'

'Why are *you* here? I thought you hated humans.'

Clement stared at Marcus. His bright, blue eyes shone under the moonlight. 'To keep an eye on you. We have our own reasons for agreeing to this alliance.'

'Then why am I here?'

'To keep an eye on me.' Clement looked off into the distance. Marcus wondered what he looked at. 'Do you wish to know what Buchanan and Patterson think of you?'

Marcus already had an idea. 'Not really.'

'Patterson doesn't even know who you are. You're a faceless individual in a sea of ordinary. A nobody. You're not even on his radar.'

Marcus seethed at hearing that. The last time someone had called him a nobody, he had blasted him with a Buzz Gun.

'Harvey is keen to control you. He knows you're itching to break away but you can't. He has plans.'

135

'Plans?'

'To take over the ITF building and become the new power in this land. Patterson doesn't know. When the time comes, only a few will matter to him. You're not one of those few.'

Marcus paced. 'Fuck! And you got that all from his mind?'

'No. I overheard them talking to others on their communication devices.' Clement smirked. 'But I could be wrong. Harvey is familiar with our abilities. He could have planted the idea in my head.'

Marcus was sick of people using him for their own gains. 'Well, whatever the truth is, I won't be anyone's puppet.'

Clement shrugged. 'You could go along with his plans or you could help me and, in the process, achieve something I know you want.'

'And what the fuck's that?'

'To become like me.'

Marcus laughed. 'I don't know what you've been snorting but that's the last thing I want. Read my mind.'

He pulled up the memory of him torturing three Indigenes in an abandoned warehouse.

Clement didn't react. 'Not like me, exactly. You want power, to become untouchable. I can help you get it.'

'How?'

Clement had to be lying.

'Help our side to gain the advantage here. We want rid of the GS humans and the treaty. The humans don't want to share power with us, so we'll take it. Help us to get all three.'

The idea intrigued him.

'Untouchable, how?'

'As in, physically stronger—' Marcus made a face.

'—than the humans who command you.'

The idea made Marcus smile. 'What do I need to do?'

Clement stared into the distant landscape. 'Fill Harvey and Patterson's heads with lies. Start with the ones I'm about to feed you.'

16

Dressed in dark clothing and with air-filtration devices in place, Stephen set off running with Serena for District Eight. They passed through the environmental barrier of the closest hunting zone and ventured farther into the land with no treaty protection. District Eight was located a hundred miles north of their location, close to the human city of New Singapore. Between them was too much land without ITF protection.

An hour ago, Laura had contacted him, saying she and Bill wanted to discuss their meeting with Ollie Patterson. While Stephen wanted to hear Bill's side of it, he'd put the meeting off until he and Serena had spoken to Gabriel and Margaux. Bill had offered to drive them both there, but Stephen didn't want to be seen with a human and further stoke the Indigenes' mistrust, even if it was just Bill.

'What's Gabriel going to say when we get there?' said a panting Serena.

Stephen kept a steady pace with her even though he could run faster. 'The same thing we have, that this is more serious than we first thought.'

It worried him that Indigenes from District Eight had been spotted near New London and were working with local humans. This showed just how far these splinter groups had recruited.

'I thought the peace treaty would be a good thing, but it has only fuelled suspicion,' she said through a flurry of breaths.

'The concept behind it still stands. But the treaty created gaps and those with different intentions want to fill them.'

'Is that what's happening here?'

Stephen was sure of it. 'Yeah.'

A short distance off to the west, Stephen saw the now familiar white tarpaulin covering the GS 100 environ that contained their power-stealing machine. Stephen stopped suddenly, forcing Serena to skid to a halt. This close, he tried his envisioning ability.

'Anything?' said Serena.

'I can't see them—future speaking, I mean.'

Serena concentrated on the west. 'We're too far out for my influence to work. I'm worried that if I try, it will be me that falls under their spell, not the other way around. They were created out of my code. They must have my abilities.'

They ran again. Stephen picked up the pace to put some distance between them and the GS 100. 'I agree. They used the genetic information from your creation and improved on it in ways we know little about. We must not take for granted any change in their behaviour, no matter how small.'

I agree, said an out-of-breath Serena.

They kept to the hunting zones as much as possible, marked by a translucent, shimmering environmental field. Occasionally, when the zone ended, they had to exit into unprotected territory. While Bill had assured Stephen they would not be harmed if the military caught them beyond the hunting zones, it was the vigilantes Stephen worried about most.

He and Serena could outrun any human threat. But an Indigene vigilante? That posed a different problem.

The environmental barrier made his skin prickle as he slipped from safety to danger, and back to safety again. It carried on like that for another seventy miles until Stephen spotted the visible entrance to District Eight that had been built above ground. The peace treaty no longer required them to hide the locations of their districts with rocks and camouflage. But a handshake agreement rarely stopped violence and the elders still took precautions.

Serena slowed her approach to the door set into the tall rock face. The door was made from omega, the strongest rock on Exilon 5, and covered in a metal shielding. An electrical charge coursing through the door nipped at Stephen's skin. Amid the irritation, they both looked up at the scanner set into the rock face. The scanner projected an ultraviolet light that only Indigenes could see. It scanned their forms before it disappeared, taking with it the electricity.

The door slid open and Stephen followed Serena inside to a stairwell that tunnelled deep into the earth. The door closed behind them and they descended the stairs until they met a second door, also made from omega. The second door opened and Stephen felt the familiar light resistance of the environmental barrier as he passed through.

A young, male Indigene waited.

Gabriel is waiting for you both in Council Chambers, he said. *I'll take you there.*

The hostility from the young male rolled off him in

waves.

We know the way, said Stephen.

The male nodded and left. Stephen and Serena took the south route to the Council Chambers. Serena's aura was a calm blue, he noticed, with a hint of yellow uncertainty.

Both he and Serena had been here before, but this was the first time either of them had felt anything other than respect. He walked faster, keen to hear what Gabriel had to say.

The tunnel layout, similar to home, made District Eight feel familiar, but this district gave off a different acoustic vibe. Stephen grazed his fingers along the tunnel wall and felt the strong thumping that attuned to the negative mood of the Indigenes. The farther into the district they ventured, the harder that thumping became. Stephen glanced at a surprised Serena. What had happened here?

They reached the Chambers to find an open door and a space inside twice as big as the one in their district. Gabriel had turned the chambers into his and Margaux's private dwelling. According to Gabriel, it was the only place where they could find a sliver of peace in the district, and the only place the district could get a break from Margaux. She had a habit of meddling in the minds of others.

Two mattresses lay side by side on the floor in the open space. It had no bookshelves, unlike Pierre's old space. A timepiece sat next to the beds. A table had been shoved up against one wall before the beds. There was a board on top with a set of drawings, or possibly blueprints, pinned to it. Stephen and Serena entered the space to find Gabriel and Margaux arguing in silence. The wild gesturing and expressions on their faces gave Stephen his first clue. A third Indigene stood off to the side. He turned to look at them when they entered. He was around Stephen's age, with striking, blue eyes similar to Serena's.

He nodded at them. Stephen caught Serena staring at the male.

Don't get any ideas, teased Stephen. *I'll fight him to win you.*

Serena turned to him. *No, his eyes... they're so blue, like mine.*

I noticed that too.

Serena tickled Gabriel's mind—the telepathic equivalent to a tap on the shoulder.

The tall elder turned fast, his eyes wide. 'Ah, you're here. Give me a minute, and shut the door.'

Stephen obeyed Gabriel, who turned back to his wife. 'You can't do that. It's too dangerous.'

'It's only dangerous if you don't know where to look. I do.'

'But what if you get caught, Margaux? I mean, it's one thing to watch them, quite another to pry. I can't control the younger ones and it will only get worse.'

Margaux folded her arms. 'I'm not doing anything to them. Besides, they're young; they'll get over it.'

Gabriel grunted and turned away. 'Talk some sense into my wife.'

But the erratic-minded Margaux appeared to be lucid. This was possibly the most lucid Stephen had seen her.

'What's going on?' said Stephen.

His envisioning ability, if it wasn't broken, should have given him a glimpse of what Margaux had done and what she planned to do.

He thumbed at the male Indigene. 'And who's this?'

Genesis Variant

'This is Clement,' said Gabriel. 'He has managed to infiltrate one of the human groups near New London. I trust him.'

Clement nodded and Stephen's gaze found Gabriel again.

'The young are restless and Margaux is taking matters into her own hands,' said the elder. 'There is massive unrest here. You probably feel it too. She thinks that if she eavesdrops on the younger adults' discussions about joining the splinter groups, she can use their strategies against them. I tried to tell her it's pointless and dangerous, that what she's doing is risking Clement's infiltration. The young despise rules and her interference will only push them to rebel against our district's order.'

'That's why we're here,' said Stephen. 'Some from this district travelled to New London to meet with human groups there.' His eyes cut to Clement. 'I guess we know who at least one of them is. What are the human groups planning?'

'It's not clear. They have paired each of us off with a human. They have expressed an interest in power and the GS 100. I don't know what they want with the latter.'

'How do they propose to get that power?'

Clement shrugged. *By driving a wedge in the peace treaty for starters.*

'What about this human you've been paired with?' said Serena.

'They call him Martin Casey. He is a lowlife from Earth, but an idiot. A different name flashed in his mind and he showed me an image of him torturing Indigenes there. But he has an overactive imagination, so I can't say if he showed me that to scare me or if it really happened.'

Even idiots can be dangerous, said Stephen. *We shouldn't rule him out as a threat.*

143

'I agree,' said Gabriel with a sigh. 'The young in this district are uneasy and I don't know what to do about it. So far, none of them have been recruited to the New London group, according to Clement. But still, something big is happening here.'

'When did it the unrest start?' said Serena.

'About the time the GS 100 crawled out from their caves and showed the world what they are. But it probably started long before that. We're just feeling the effects of it now. Those on the cusp of adulthood listen to their peers more than their elders. Tradition is being cast aside in favour of smaller groups with younger voices.'

'How young?'

Gabriel shrugged. 'Those too young to know what the peace treaty meant eight years ago. Now that they're adults, they view the treaty as a bad thing that represses the movements of our species.'

Just what Stephen had feared. 'That's one way to look at it, Gabriel. The other is that the treaty gives us a freedom we never had before.'

'But we can't venture outside of the zones,' said Gabriel.

'Bill Taggart assures me there will be no penalties if we do.'

'That's hardly progress, Stephen. I hate to admit it, but there's some sense to disbanding the treaty.'

'What? No. The treaty protects us from extinction.'

Gabriel paced the room under the watchful eye of Margaux and Clement. 'Okay, not disband. Perhaps renegotiate? Margaux and I are too far removed from the newest generation. Even you and Serena are dinosaurs to them, so that also rules Clement out. The young blame us for their restrictions; they believe humans have no rights to this planet. All it will take is the right word in their ears for the treaty to fall apart.'

Clement spoke. 'I don't know much, but some males from this district align themselves with the policies of the group I've infiltrated.'

'How many from this district are in your group?' said Stephen.

'Ten in total; just me from here.'

'Are you the only undercover Indigene there?' said Serena.

'That I know of.'

'What do the other Indigenes in your group want to achieve?'

Clement shrugged. 'They want to break apart the treaty. The humans want the power the ITF have. That's all I've learned from the followers. The leaders have found a new way to block me from accessing their thoughts.'

But the answer didn't satisfy Stephen. 'Then what?'

Gabriel sighed and shrugged.

'That's why I follow the younger ones!' said Margaux.

Gabriel stared at his wife. 'And it's dangerous.'

'Not the way I do it.'

Margaux folded her arms and Gabriel grunted. Stephen probed her thoughts but Margaux placed a new block on her thoughts, preventing him from accessing them. She was through discussing it.

'Is there anything we can do here?' said Serena. 'We could try speaking with the young, gauge the level of their hostilities. I could influence them, get them to open up.'

Gabriel shook his head and walked to the door. 'Clement has already tried.'

How? said Serena.

'Oh, didn't I tell you? Clement has your ability.

145

Well, part of it anyway.'

'Excuse me?'

'He was changed using your DNA.' Gabriel watched her. 'I thought you might have guessed from his eye colour. You're the only two Indigenes with blue eyes that I've ever met.'

Serena touched Clement on the arm. 'Is that true?'

'My files state I was changed shortly after you. My influence does not reach very far. I can only influence the person next to me.'

Serena shook her head and smiled. 'It's nice to meet you, Clement.'

Clement bowed. 'And you. Gabriel and Margaux speak highly of you.'

'But not me?' Stephen huffed. 'Thanks, Gabriel.'

The elder responded with a laugh and a wave. 'Your head is big enough as it is.' He rested his hand on the door. 'Go back to your district. You can't do anything here. I'm sorry you've had a wasted journey, but I'm worried your presence will only fan the flames of anarchy. I'm sure you felt it coming in.'

Gabriel opened the door and a rush of emotions hit Stephen as word of his and Serena's arrival spread.

'I'm sorry, Gabriel. We'll leave immediately.'

Stephen and Serena walked back to the exit amid a disturbing level of increased whispers and new collusions.

'What the hell, Stephen? Another like me?'

He felt her giddiness flutter against his mind. Another, indeed, with the power to influence whom he liked.

Where would it all lead?

17

Twenty-four hours ago, Simon's machine had acted as a conduit for the Nexus to heal Tanya's frail and withered body. She had looked fitter, stronger and had walked around unassisted. Simon and those whom Tanya had picked to assist her had brought the rest of the Elite to the machine to repeat the process. Each session, the white light had passed through the concentration of energy at the machine's centre, curled around the Elite's arms in a rope-like fashion and passed its healing energy to them. Their bodies, on the precipice of death, had kicked and fought against their predisposed demise but the Nexus had restored them to a state where they had control over their bodies.

Simon then witnessed the physical degradation reverse in each Elite before him. Each session had required the power to be replenished, which meant taking more power from the grid. But it appeared that while his machine needed power, the Nexus contained an infinite supply of energy.

However, for all his efforts, just twenty-four hours later, Tanya showed signs of her prior physical weakness again. Simon gathered alongside three human doctors in the Elite's staging room, a large, circular space beyond the observation room with ten beds. Before the Elite reached transcendence, Tanya wanted them to lie in repose and think about how the treatments had altered their minds. Tanya had said it would prepare them to live without their bodies, which, if transcendence worked, they would no longer need.

Ten headboards followed the curve of the wall attached to ten beds, the ends of which pointed towards the centre of the room. Tanya shuffled around the unoccupied space, large enough to hold twenty people, while her assistants followed with her hover chair. It wouldn't be long before she needed the chair again. The nine remaining Elites had joined the discussion and sat on their respective beds.

Simon stood alongside the lead geneticist assigned to herald in this great change: Dr Jameson.

'This is ridiculous. The power from the grid isn't enough. The reversal results are just temporary,' said Tanya. 'How much longer do we need before we can fully transcend?'

'We need more time. The treatments are aggressive for a reason,' said Dr Jameson. 'If we slow the treatments down, we won't push the mind to accept total transcendence.'

Tanya grunted. 'So we're stuck in these useless bodies for how much longer?'

'Indefinitely,' said Dr Jameson. 'We can't carry out more treatments on any of you until we're sure your bodies can endure them. They alter your genetic structure, speed up ageing. If you are to beat this ticking time bomb, you must outrun the changes.'

Tanya pressed her gnarled fingers to her temple.

'Simon, the power isn't enough. It's taking too long to repair all the Elites. How much can the machine store?'

'We can try doubling it, but I haven't been able to test it except for the amounts we've taken so far.'

Simon knew that taking too much would alert Bill Taggart and his ITF men and possibly lead to their experiment being shut down too soon.

'Double, that's all?' Tanya groped behind her for the chair within her grasp. Her hand missed the edge; one of her assistants helped her to sit. She sighed when her backside found the seat. 'Double gives us, what, two days of age reversal? Then what?'

Jameson stood with his hands behind his back. Simon remembered the man from some old World Government footage. He'd been the lead doctor to test a young Indigene who had been captured. Since then, Jameson had had his extensive knowledge of genetics upgraded, courtesy of the mind-mapping machine.

Rapid mind advancement had its perks.

'The next stage of the treatment is extremely aggressive. I don't know if two days of healing will work, but we can try. All we can hope for is to reach the stage prior to full transcendence.'

Tanya nodded, looking hopeful. 'Okay, we'll try that. But if it doesn't work we may need to take a lot more power. The Nexus has proved to be a formidable healing source but it can't do much if we only give it a narrow conduit to reach us through. We need more power and to widen that channel.'

Simon didn't know how much power the machine could safely contain. He wasn't keen on overloading it without testing it first. 'If we slam too much power into the machine, we might break it. Then it won't be of use to us. There's also the risk the Indigenes will detect our access to the Nexus energy. If they figure that out, they might block our access to it.'

Tanya grunted. 'We cannot control their actions but this is a matter of life and death.' She hovered closer to Jameson. 'We need the power to live, am I correct, doctor?'

Simon caught the small step back Jameson took from her withered appearance.

'Yes. If the body dies before you complete transcendence, you will lose the consciousness forever.'

Tanya's steely gaze cut to Simon. 'See? We must try everything, Simon. You were always too cautious, even in your human form.'

And for good reason. His cautiousness had allowed Simon to survive in a world that harboured dangerous humans like Charles Deighton, and now Tanya Li. The power Tanya and the Elites could yield required him to keep pace with their plans. If he didn't, he risked being left behind.

Guns didn't win wars; planning and strategy did.

'The Nexus wasn't the least bit fazed by the volume of people it had to heal,' said Tanya. 'In fact, it seemed to want to do more.'

Simon felt his caution stir, in the pit of his stomach. 'The Nexus is organic. We must be careful how we use it. We cannot control it like the power in my machine, should anything go wrong. I would warn against giving it access to more power without testing.'

Tanya seemed to consider it; Simon held his breath. The other Elite sat in silence on the edge of the beds, hunched over and watching the discussion. Their eyes shifted from Simon to Tanya and back. Simon couldn't read the Elite's minds, nor could they read his, but he was sure they could communicate telepathically with each other.

'Okay, we start with double for each of us,' said Tanya after a moment. Simon released his breath. 'We'll take it from the main feed to New London.'

Simon nodded. He'd won this argument for now. 'We must proceed slowly. If we take too much in one go, Bill Taggart could shut off the power to the city and our access.'

Tanya grunted as she hovered in her chair. 'He wouldn't disable the city like that. Too many things rely on power. The food replicators for one. Their Light Boxes for another.'

'The latter is not a necessity,' said Simon. 'The humans are adaptable. They can live without many things. They can learn to live without power. We must give them no reason to try.'

In the infancy of the transfer programme, the World Government had wanted to create a simpler version of Earth on Exilon 5. That version began with no technology to pollute the minds of the people, as had happened on Earth. They would start again. But illegal tech had flooded the market and infected the minds of the people until Exilon 5 had become no different to Earth. The world was too far gone to change things now.

One of the Elite turned towards Tanya. She appeared to listen.

'Seven wants to know if we've ruled out storming the closest district. We could demand access to their Nexus.'

Tanya shook her head as if her mind were being pulled in different directions. Another Elite's attention was on her.

'No, you're right,' she said, then turned to Simon and the doctors. 'Six says we must not storm the district in our current state. We would be unable to overpower the Indigenes.' Tanya huffed out a breath. Simon saw the effort it took for her to speak aloud in her current form. 'We must be stronger before we try. At least fifty per cent more than we are now.'

Simon ran through the options available to them. 'Say we steal more power from the grid and Bill shuts off access. That's our access gone. The second option is we allow him to build a separate solar grid that will give us whatever power we need—'

'We don't have time for that option,' interrupted Tanya. 'I'm not prepared to wait months to transcend.'

'Okay, the third is we make it impossible for them to disconnect our power cable without blowing the supply. I used responsive materials to design the cable. Responsive materials can take commands. If I program our cable to remain connected to a power source, it would take more than a few engineers to remove it.'

'There's a fourth,' said Tanya. 'We widen the conduits to the Nexus and access more of its power.'

Simon still had the knowledge of a geotechnical engineer. To access the Nexus, he had drilled three precise and narrow holes that punctured the area where the largest concentration of gamma existed.

'To be honest, I'm surprised they haven't noticed we've accessed their Nexus,' said Tanya.

'When they connect to the Nexus they do so subconsciously,' explained Simon. 'If the Nexus is redirecting some of its reserves to find our machine, they may not even be aware of that action.'

Tanya shook her head and smiled. 'Isn't it ironic that the Indigenes were once the species closest to extinction? Here we are a new species with such advanced minds that we could cure all known illnesses. But our bodies weaken us to the point where none of that matters. If this doesn't work we may not see out the rest of the week. You're lucky we still need you, Simon.'

Her chilling statement put Simon on high alert. Since the machine had become operational and the Elite had increased their efforts to reach transcendence, he had wondered what his role would be when it was all over.

Tanya stared at him, which prompted him to say, 'The only option readily available is to take more power from the New London grid.'

'There's one other option we have yet to consider,' said Dr Jameson.

Tanya turned her chair to face him. 'And that is?'

The Elite had perked up, Simon noticed.

'We know full transfer of consciousness is not possible yet, but Charles Deighton transferred a copy of his personality and memories into the young Anton's body eight years ago.'

Simon frowned. 'You want to preserve the Elite's minds in the Indigenes?'

Jameson shook his head. 'Not the Indigenes, but younger bodies than theirs. That could ensure the Elite are strong enough to reach transcendence. We must preserve the mind. Otherwise, this will be for nothing.'

Tanya seemed intrigued by the idea and, judging from their almost imperceptible smiles, so too did the rest of the Elite.

Simon feared where this conversation was headed. 'I think we should try the power idea first.'

Tanya waved her hand dismissively. 'We can try, but this is looking like the better option.' She narrowed her eyes at him. 'How old are you, Simon?'

'Fifty-two in human years.'

'And would you say the extensive testing has

strengthened or weakened your body?' Tanya waved her hand again. 'No matter, Jameson can determine your physical prowess and that of other Conditioned, isn't that right doctor?'

Jameson nodded. 'We would need to match the right mind to the right host.'

Tanya's laugh came out soft and feathery. 'I wouldn't fancy my copied mind living in an unbearably dull host.' She glanced at Simon and added, 'Don't look so worried, Simon. We would only be sharing your mind. Temporarily.'

Nothing to do with transcendence felt temporary. This wasn't what Simon had signed up for when he agreed to be altered. A longer life in a stronger body—that's what Tanya had promised. He'd viewed the Elite's achievement of transcendence as an end to his contract with the former board members. But if he heard right, Tanya would use their mind-mapping machine not to transfer skills to his already overworked mind, but a copy of an entire consciousness. Could his mind take it? Or worse, would the intrusion destroy what little peace he needed to function?

When Charles Deighton had hijacked Anton's mind, Anton had almost lost himself to the more dominant personality. That's what Bill Taggart had said and Simon saw the same potentially happening to him.

His mind was not the strongest. And assuming Tanya had Simon in mind as her host, her more aggressive one would prevail. He would become a casualty in Tanya's pursuit of transcendence.

He'd been okay with the idea when Tanya risked her own life.

But now? He needed outside help to preserve what remained of his humanity.

18

The blinding sun made Marcus' eyes water. He wiped away the tears with his sleeve, but it only made them water more. Through blurry eyes, he examined the blistered hands that clutched the shovel Ollie Patterson had given him. Ollie had told him he'd run out of gloves. Bullshit. He'd seen him put a pair in his pocket earlier.

A giant hole. That's what Ollie wanted him to dig. Alone. He couldn't see the reason when they had machines, diggers even, that could save him from sweaty, manual labour. The same machines the other men used to transport bulkier building materials from one location to the other.

Not by hand. By machine.

Marcus stopped and straightened out his back, stooped after a morning of digging dirt. This was the same work he used to do for Gaetano, except his holes had been the size of a body. This one couldn't fit a body lengthways. He'd have to bend it to make it fit.

This useless hole had no purpose other than to punish Marcus. He'd seen Ollie and Harvey chatting about it, glancing his way when they thought he didn't notice.

He had, and he'd even asked Harvey about it.

'Dig a hole? What the fuck for? What have I done?'

'Nothing,' said Harvey. 'And that's the problem. You laze around when the other men get to work. You're late to the job and you talk back to the others. In a word, you're a liability. But Ollie can't get rid of you because the ITF assigned you to this job, so you'll dig holes until you learn some respect.'

Marcus tossed the shovel to one side and sat on the pile of dirt he'd been working on all morning, yesterday evening and into the night. He'd been supposed to do recon with Clement last night, but Ollie had assigned the Indigene to someone else. Clement had asked him to spread a lie among their group that the Indigenes wanted to switch allegiances permanently to the human side. Clement said it was to lower Harvey and Ollie's guard around them. Not his first preference, to help an Indigene, but Clement had promised him something neither Harvey nor Ollie had: a chance at power. He'd spread the rumours among the other men at dinner last night.

'Apparently the ITF are closing in on a splinter group near New Melbourne. Looks like they've got a lead on the head of operations there.'

'Bullshit. Who told you that?' said one man.

'I overheard someone talking about it.'

'One of the Indigenes? They'd say anything to scupper this deal.'

Marcus shook his head. 'A human with a vested interest in keeping this deal alive: Bill Taggart.'

The men had shown little reaction to Marcus' news, but he was confident word would spread back to Ollie and Harvey.

That morning, though, he might as well have said nothing for all the good it did him. A hip flask would be

Genesis Variant

nice right about now, with a hit of something to numb his aches and pains. But Ollie was a former evangelist or some other bullshit because the house was dry. Not a lick of booze to be found anywhere.

This job was a joke and Marcus would make Ollie Patterson pay for humiliating him. He was nothing more than a lanky son of a bitch with airs and graces that made Marcus want to puke. What he hated more than defectors were people who lied about who they were, who put on a show with some fabricated bullshit version of themselves to fit in with everyone else.

Sounded a lot like what Marcus did on Earth.

But his alter ego was about survival, not being a prick. Ever since Harvey had altered his face and turned him into Martin Casey, he could feel his real personality slipping away. He'd have to work extra hard to keep Marcus Murphy alive.

A vehicle sped past, forcing Marcus to his feet and to resume digging. He didn't need to see past the tinted windows to know Ollie Patterson rode in the vehicle. While Marcus didn't fear him, he continued to pretend to be the man Harvey had made him—a mild-mannered office worker with no balls, who was as dead as a dodo.

The vehicle stopped and Ollie got out. Ollie gave him a wave, which Marcus reciprocated with a salute. But what irked him more was seeing Harvey emerge from the other side of the vehicle.

The hierarchy only strengthened Clement's accusations that the men didn't care about Marcus. But Marcus had picked up a few things about lying cheats from working with Gaetano Agostini and his rabid son, Enzo.

Never show your hand to the enemy.

Ollie Patterson was a lackey and he hadn't decided

157

what Harvey was yet. Sure, he shunned the spotlight that Ollie occupied, but Marcus could see how Harvey pulled Patterson's strings, especially at meetings.

Sweat trickled down his back as he tossed dirt from the hole to a pile behind him. What he wouldn't trade for a long, hot bath, a case of gin and a knife to stick in Ollie's gut until he squealed. But more than that, he would love to know where Ollie went while they worked.

When it looked like Ollie and Harvey were on their way over, Marcus removed something from his coat pocket and resumed his dig.

'That hole is looking mighty good, Martin,' said Ollie. 'Keep it up.'

Marcus straightened up and looked the squealer in the eye. 'How big do you want it?'

Ollie shrugged while Harvey looked elsewhere. 'I'll let you know when you're done.'

'Whatever you say; you're the boss.'

He slapped Ollie on the bare arm, much to the man's surprise.

Ollie glanced down at his arm and laughed, then walked to his car. Harvey didn't react but when Ollie's back was turned, he gave Marcus a quick thumbs-up and a smile.

What the fuck was that? It irritated Marcus that he couldn't get a read on Harvey's hot and cold signals.

Ollie and Harvey climbed into their vehicle. Marcus waited until the car drove back the way it had come in. He waited some more for it to disappear from view.

Marcus tossed his spade to the side and told the foreman he was taking lunch. He walked the mile back to the safe house. There, he collected his DPad and turned on the remote tracer. The tracer picked up the micro locators hidden in the almost invisible receiver Marcus had slapped on to Ollie's arm—a gadget from the Agostini regime. He had until that evening to track Ollie before he washed the receiver down the drain.

Marcus ran to the next block over and discovered a vehicle lying idle outside one of the finished houses in the build. These vehicles were identical to the ones the criminals used on Earth. And he knew how to pick their locks. Marcus got inside the vehicle and overrode the commands to recognise his identity chip. The vehicle moved as soon as Marcus gave it a command to follow the route Ollie and Harvey's vehicle had taken.

It wasn't long before his car came upon their vehicle. It sat on the side of the road on the approach road to the power base station. Marcus ordered his car to drive past the stationary vehicle to park behind a cluster of rocks tall enough to mask his location. He got out and used a pair of magnification glasses to spy on Harvey and Ollie, who were still in their vehicle. A moment later, they got out and trekked into the flat, stony plain past the fenced-off field of solar panels. They had to be meeting someone.

Marcus stayed behind a cluster of rocks and turned up the magnification on his glasses. A few minutes later, he saw an Indigene dressed in a white cloak dash towards the pair. Except it wasn't any old Indigene. It looked like one of the GS humans. Ollie shook the freak's hand, then pointed to the vehicle. The GS human shook his head and pointed towards the power base station in the distance attached to the field. Then both men returned to the vehicle while the freak took off running in a new direction.

The car drove off after the GS human. Marcus returned to his car and followed them past the station to an undulating section of land between it and New London. He kept the car hidden, back from where the hill peaked, and crawled to its brow to watch.

The GS human studied a cable that was part exposed to the elements. Harvey and Ollie stood watch while the GS removed a DPad from his robes and entered commands Marcus couldn't see. Then he hunkered down and disconnected a secondary cable from a primary cable. Marcus assumed the primary one delivered power from the grid to New London. The GS stood up and handed Ollie money hidden inside his robes. Ollie shook his hand and turned away to count his bills.

Since when were Ollie and Harvey helping the GS humans? Was their speech about fighting the GS humans just a load of bullshit? Marcus made to leave but something new caught his eye. Ollie had just turned his back when Harvey handed something to the GS human, a piece of tech in exchange for what looked like a microdisk. Harvey glanced back at Ollie, who still had his back turned.

A secret deal? For what?

The GS human ran off and the men had a brief conversation. But what interested Marcus most was the disk Harvey hid in his pocket.

Interesting.

Marcus returned to his car and set off before the others reached theirs. He had to be back on site before Ollie or Harvey returned.

The GS humans working with Ollie and Harvey? An interesting turn of events since his and Clement's role had been to watch the subversive group of super humans. He'd read about the group that included the former board members of the World Government. They had a reputation for being as ruthless as Gaetano Agostini. Maybe Marcus should do his own deal with them.

But what could he offer them? What did they need?

He returned the stolen car to the house one block

Genesis Variant

over, but not before he wiped the car logs. Confident in his abilities to steal, lie and manipulate, he returned to his digging hole and waited for Ollie and Harvey to return to site. Neither man showed up, leaving Marcus to wonder where they'd gone. Whatever was on that disk, Harvey wanted to keep it secret.

7pm came around and, with no sign of Ollie or Harvey, Marcus clocked off. He kneaded his tight, sore muscles on the way back to the house.

Dinner was served at 7.30pm sharp. No do-overs. If you were late, you didn't eat. Marcus washed as fast as he could.

He joined eleven other men at the dining room table with room for fourteen. Of the twelve, Ollie had picked just three to join the private splinter groups to watch the GS 100. He checked his location card. It indicated no jobs for that evening. But it was early and Ollie could still change his mind.

An older, stern-looking woman carried dishes of food in to the table. Everything had been replicated and there would be no more. Besides Ollie and Harvey, the woman had the only pass code to operate the replicator.

To Marcus' surprise, Ollie entered the room with Harvey. Both men laughed like they were best friends. But Marcus knew better and he would discover Harvey's secret.

The men sat in the two remaining seats. Ollie lorded over the table of hungry men, who waited for their master to issue a command.

'Okay, let's eat!'

Everyone swiped at food like rabid dogs tearing into flesh. Marcus grabbed whatever dish wasn't being hogged and scooped mashed potato on to his plate. He fought for the bowl of chicken breasts but a younger man

161

also held on to the bowl.

Just like old times in the Deighton mansion. Except in this house, there wasn't nearly as much shoving and pushing involved.

'Let go, and I won't stab my fork into your eye,' he hissed at the man.

The man's eyes widened and he let go. Martin Casey may look like a mild-mannered accountant, but Marcus Murphy, with a scar proving his bravery, lived inside him.

He took two chicken breasts—one more than his allowance—and tossed the bowl into the centre of the table. He felt confident. The young man took the remaining tiny and shrivelled breast; it probably looked like the man's dick and balls.

The woman brought out two plates piled high with food and gave one each to Ollie and Harvey. A pang of jealousy flared in Marcus' chest. It should be him getting a special plate. Marcus hadn't travelled to this planet to be a lackey.

Harvey stared at him. 'You need something, Martin?'

Yeah, what the fuck is on that disk? Does Ollie know you're a lying motherfucker? Does he know you used to work for the GS humans?

Marcus dropped his eyes to his plate and tore off a piece of chicken. 'Nope, all good.'

'Glad to hear,' said Harvey.

His condescending tone turned the chicken into a lump which Marcus forced down.

He listened to the chatter as he ate, mostly from the men who weren't doing extracurricular jobs for Ollie. All came from Earth and were people Marcus had once ruled with an iron fist, weak men who would likely squander their second chance through a banal existence. Men who worked nine to five, went home to spend the evening with their boring wives, only to repeat it the next day.

Not Marcus. He would never let a woman tie him down.

Dinner usually ended when the food did. Nobody lingered after the housekeeper cleared the last of the plates and bowls. Marcus retired to his room and lay on his bed to digest his meal, wishing for something better than replicated food.

He picked up the location card and turned it over. No new commands flashed up to indicate more surveillance that night. His thoughts went to Harvey and his mystery disk. Harvey was definitely a Gaetano type, maybe not as intimidating as Gaetano, but no less dangerous.

Not a problem for Marcus. He knew how to spot dangerous men a mile off; he'd worked with enough to know how to handle them. He would make his move against Harvey soon. As soon as he figured out what his move would be. Clement's offer to get him power became more tempting the longer he lay there.

The card flashed with a red dot and a time, indicating a job in two hours. Marcus sat up slowly, wondering if he'd be paired with Clement again. As much as he hated those freaks, the Indigene had been more company than the people he worked for.

He went downstairs to find the place was quiet. He spotted Harvey outside, sitting on the porch swing chair.

It had been two days since he'd spoken to Harvey without Ollie being present. His desire to learn more about Harvey's motivations fuelled him as he stepped outside.

The swinging chair creaked with Harvey's motion. He looked up when Marcus approached.

'You're a bit early. Job's not until later.'

Marcus shoved his hands into his pockets. 'I fancied a bit of fresh air.'

Harvey laughed once. 'And yet you got nothing but fresh air today.'

'Digging a hole don't give you much time to enjoy it.'

He leaned against the gable wall.

The swinging stopped and Harvey leaned forward, resting his arms on his knees. 'I heard a rumour from the men that the Indigenes want to switch sides to the human cause. Is that true?'

Clement's lie. 'Yeah, as far as I know.'

Harvey appeared to think about that. 'So tell me about your life on Earth. I don't think we talked much about it.'

Marcus shrugged. 'Nothing to tell. You were there.'

'What were you attempting to achieve with your factions?'

'The same thing the World Government was: power. The people needed leaders. We assumed that role.'

'At the expense of common sense? You won't get respect if you don't give it.'

Respect was for weaker men. 'Better to just show them their purpose. The people in those neighbourhoods were weak and pathetic.'

Harvey leaned back and crossed his legs. 'Yet, they now thrive under their own steam and you've been exiled here. That didn't work out too well, now did it?'

Marcus clenched his fists. Fuck Harvey. What he did on Earth mattered.

'Those Indigene freaks ruined everything. We were outnumbered.'

Harvey laughed. 'You were always outnumbered. A

few Indigenes didn't tip the scale. Your days were numbered. You want to know what I think?' Marcus didn't. 'You were a bunch of children fighting in a grown-up war. You all wanted the same toys in the playground, pushing and shoving each other to get them. All that got you was a bunch of cranky, gun-happy morons who shot anyone who got in their way.'

'It was more complicated than that.'

'No, it wasn't. I used to work in your line of business.'

'What happened to that?'

Harvey shrugged. 'Didn't like the hours.' He changed the subject. 'You fought like a school-kid bully over chicken earlier. If you don't grow up you won't last long here. The power here is different to that on Earth.'

'Don't seem like much has changed.'

A small cluster of people fought for power like the factions, except the factions had had the good sense to wait for the right moment to make their move

'Of course it has.' Harvey cursed. 'Shifting power away from the Indigenes by targeting their peace treaty will cause ripples in the International Task Force. And while Bill Taggart scrapes around to save his precious deal, he won't notice when we slip in and take control of their operations.'

'What, like a takeover of their headquarters?'

'More subtle than that. Ollie says they monitor chat over interstellar wave, so we send them bad intel, create diversions where we can. They'll lose control of policing and the trust of the people. That's when we offer the people an alternative, a better, more secure way of living.'

'What, like an army?'

'More like a security firm that offers protection.'

Marcus liked the idea but he refused to tell Harvey.

Instead, he shrugged. 'Why weren't you changed, you know, with the rest of 'em who came here? You had connections there, yeah?'

Harvey stared up at the double moons that gave off an odd, blue illumination. 'They didn't deem me important enough.'

'So this is revenge to get back at the GS humans because they rejected you?'

Harvey flinched. 'The GS humans are not as important as they think they are, or as infallible. The day we erase those mutations from this planet will be a good day for everyone.'

19

Stephen's visit to District Eight left him with an unsettled feeling. Things were bad there. Whether Gabriel wanted it or not, Stephen would find a way to help him. How did his own district stack up against the animosity he'd felt in Gabriel's? He hoped Anton and Arianna could find out.

Serena had retired for the evening, but sleep would not come for Stephen. He walked the tunnels like Elise used to do; it made him feel more connected to the former elder. His charges were nowhere to be seen. Not surprising since they'd given him and Serena a wide berth ever since the GS humans built their environ three months ago. Their murky, yellow-grey auras indicated their unrest and disappointment at Stephen and Serena's inaction against the GS.

What could he do? He didn't know what abilities the GS had. To go in guns blazing would be a bad idea. So far the GS hadn't done anything, but that didn't matter to some.

Stephen encountered three Indigenes older than him on his walk through the tunnels. He sensed an edge to their moods, as though they expected everything to fall apart.

He greeted them with a nod and kept walking. He hated not knowing what was coming. His envisioning ability usually gave him some indication. How had he coped before that ability manifested? Maybe Anton and Arianna could get a clearer view on the situation.

He sensed his two friends in a distant part of the district but couldn't get a read on them. Not unusual since Serena had taught Anton and Arianna how to mask their feelings from others, including their auras from Stephen. It had frustrated him that he could neither feel nor see his friends' moods. But his lack of foresight irritated him more.

What blocked his ability, kept his visions too far out of reach? It had to be the GS 100. Nothing had changed as dramatically as they had. Yet the others still had their abilities, including Serena.

Stephen passed through the core of District Three, normally a hotbed of activity ranging from Evolver classes to a social space for older Indigenes. But that evening, it was unoccupied. The sound of his footsteps echoing from the rough, stone floor to the rounded ceiling made him shiver. He quickened his step when it felt like unseen eyes watched him.

He entered a tunnel that would lead him to the Council Chambers where he would soon meet Anton and Arianna. His stride, normally long and even, became short and fast. These days he couldn't switch off his cluttered mind. It had been over a month since he'd used the Nexus to heal, but he never had the time.

The chambers came into view and he entered through the already open door. Anton and Arianna waited with Serena.

He frowned at his mate. 'I thought you'd gone to bed.'

'Arianna came to get me.' Serena laced her fingers through his. 'I want to be of use.'

So did he. Stephen kept his gaze low as Serena pulled him farther inside the room. His lack of envisioning skill made him feel obsolete. Auras were all he had left and Anton and Arianna had none to help him understand their mood. He loved Serena, but by passing her mind tricks on to his friends, she had emasculated him.

Stephen pulled his fingers out of hers and pressed them to his head.

'Are you okay?' said Serena.

He kept his thoughts private. 'Nothing, I'm just tired.'

He sounded like Pierre, who used to keep things from Elise. He shook the comparison from his head and engaged with the others.

'What did you discover?'

Serena closed the door.

'It's not good,' said Anton.

He paced while Arianna kept still, except for her eyes, which tracked him around the room. She had to feel Anton's anxiousness. That's how it was for empaths. They felt everything. Too intensely, according to Arianna.

'The younger Indigenes take their guidance from those older than them and younger than us. When the GS humans came into being, the young wanted to see what the new species looked like. But their peers talked them out of it, said they would see them soon enough when they came to this district to kill everyone.'

'That's a pack of lies,' said Stephen.

'It is, but it's the lies they've been told.'

'And they told you this, willingly?'

Anton stopped pacing. 'No. I read fragments of their thoughts. Arianna sensed their mood, which they really couldn't hide from her anyway. They're too young and unpractised at hiding much from an empath. On the walk here, Arianna and I pieced together the knowledge we both had and came up with this.'

Stephen preferred cold, hard facts, not guesswork. 'So this might not be a true account of what happened?'

'We both know how to read the Indigenes. Arianna and I are in tune with each other's thoughts.' Anton stared at Stephen. 'If you could stop acting like a control freak for two seconds, I'll tell you what else we learned.'

Stephen matched his friend's stare. 'Go ahead.'

Anton rolled his eyes. 'As I was saying, the young are being fed lies about the GS humans' intentions. They allow the older ones to control them.'

'What about the Indigenes taking control, Anton?' said Serena. 'What are their reasons?'

'Initially, it was to stop the young from acting out, from doing something stupid. So they scared them into behaving themselves. Their curiosity about the new species was getting out of control.'

Stephen looked away. It was his job to control his charges.

'And now they trust the older Indigenes, not me.'

'Exactly.'

Arianna continued. 'While we questioned the young and got nothing from them, one let his thoughts slip through. Their peers have been going out on nightly vigils to watch the GS humans. They saw a group of humans doing the same thing. They watched the group for a few weeks before approaching them. Naturally, trust issues and hostility presented on both sides, but when they realised their issues were the same, some of the older ones joined them.'

'This is how the groups came to be?' said Stephen.

Genesis Variant

'I believe so,' said Arianna.

'You saw all that in this young Indigene's mind?' said Serena.

Arianna nodded. 'He witnessed it when he followed the older ones to the surface. It was his memory of the event.'

Anton paced again. 'The older ones meet regularly with the humans to discuss mutual goals. One of those goals is to weaken the hold the GS humans have on this planet.'

Stephen couldn't see how they might achieve that. 'By what means? We cannot read the GS humans' minds, so that rules out an attack.'

'By more conventional means, Stephen,' said Serena.

'Exactly.' Anton stopped pacing but Stephen sensed his wild energy. 'The rogue humans want to overthrow the ITF policing structure, which will weaken the influence the GS has over matters.'

Stephen smiled and shook his head. 'That won't work. The GS have no interest in matters on this planet.'

'He's right; they don't,' said Serena, looking at Anton. 'What can they gain from that?'

Anton had no answer. But Arianna suggested one. 'What if the humans have no interest in the GS humans, but are using it as an excuse to gain the Indigenes' trust?'

'For what purpose?' said Stephen. 'Why take over the ITF? It will make no difference to the activities here.'

Anton's eyes grew large. 'What if the rogue humans don't care about the ITF hierarchy, Stephen? Maybe they just want to destabilise the treaty and ITF, to upset the balance.'

Arianna continued. 'So a new power can take over?'

171

Anton smiled as though something clicked into place. 'Just like what happened on Earth.'

At least Stephen understood one side's motives in this. 'So this is about power. The GS and their lack of interest in affairs have created a natural crack in society. Some elements, one of whom Bill Taggart has met with, wish to widen the crack. Forget about Earth. We all know what happens when humans rock the status quo. We end up a casualty in this war.'

Everyone nodded. He recalled the events of eight years ago that had led to the treaty's establishment.

But he still didn't understand the motive of the rogue Indigenes. 'We know what the humans set to gain in this disruption, but what do the Indigenes get by disbanding the peace treaty?'

Arianna stepped closer and lowered her voice, even though the room was soundproofed. 'I felt something from them as strong I feel your worry, Stephen. They're sick of being told what to do. The younger ones don't remember the issues during Pierre and Elise's reign, only the events that have happened since the treaty came into force. They don't see its purpose. They're restless and on the hunt for a new way to live.'

It didn't surprise Stephen to hear that. Gabriel faced the same issue in District Eight. 'That's the young's motives sorted, but their peers who remember life before the treaty—what do they want? Don't they realise the treaty is a good thing?'

Serena touched his arm. 'Don't take it personally, Stephen.'

'I don't.'

He eased his arm away. He had negotiated the treaty but should he have pushed for more? For equal rights to the humans?

'The older ones want what we do: equality,' said Arianna.

'It's not possible.'

He'd negotiated the best deal available at the time.

'Yet we are friends with the powers who run this world—the ITF.'

Stephen shook his head. 'The ITF does the bidding of the old system, of the GS humans. Bill and Laura do not operate with autonomy. There is no government here, only a police force. There's no way to make a new treaty stick. We do not live in a democratic society, or even an autocratic one. Our society sits atop a shaky treaty that's about to be ripped apart by radicals on both sides. Ironically, we need the GS humans. If they didn't exist, the ITF would have been overthrown years ago.'

'So why not overthrow it now?' said Anton. 'Why meet with Bill in a civilised way when it would be easier to demand his power?'

'Because this isn't Earth,' said Stephen. 'The criminals aren't in the majority here. Enough good people live here to keep our treaty alive. And Bill has his underground contacts. These radicals have to know about them, just not who they are.'

Serena folded her arms. 'I sympathise with both sides, but can't we find a solution to suit both parties?'

Stephen didn't know if it was possible. But one question remained unanswered. 'Anton, Arianna, did you find out anything about the GS humans' plans from your dealings today?'

To his disappointment, they both shook their heads.

'Besides stealing a bit of power, nobody knows more than that about them,' said Anton.

At least they had someone on the inside of the rogue groups. An Indigene called Clement.

20

After a night of restless sleep and a day spent worrying, Stephen needed to clear his head. Maybe a hunting trip would do just that. He dressed in a grey tunic to match his ashen skin. It would blend him in with the surroundings. While Serena used the Nexus, he used the alone time to take stock of the situation they faced.

He climbed the stone stairs leading to the hatch that protected their main access point to District Three. The hatch squeaked open and Stephen stepped outside into the environmentally-controlled hunting zone that encompassed not only an area of three miles squared but also the entrance to their district. Inside the bubble, they didn't need the air-filtration device to breathe. Stephen patted his pocket where his own device was—a just-in-case measure, because animals rarely followed the rules of the zones. Not only that, but the wolves had learned to recognise the change in atmosphere signalling the perimeter, and kept their distance.

Stephen stretched as he prepared to enter hunt mode. He sniffed the night's air to pick up on any nearby scents. When he couldn't find any, he strode to the edge of the zone and stepped outside where his sense of smell was stronger.

There you are.

The scent was faint. He stepped back inside the zone. He and Anton had crossed the boundary several times during their hunting trips, but it was easier to hunt when he wasn't fighting for air. Stephen dug his filtration device out of his pocket and popped the pieces in both nasal passages and the back of his throat.

If the animals wouldn't come to him...

The soft encasing of the zone yielded to his form a second time. Leaving the zone felt like walking through a stiff breeze. There was resistance but not enough to stop him.

With his device controlling the air to his lungs, he sniffed the air again. But the scent had vanished. Either the animals were too far out or his sense of smell wasn't working. Maybe his instincts were off. Maybe he'd been out of the Nexus for too long. But his speed still worked and he ran several miles out, following the arc of the zone's circumference. His vision still worked and he saw several beams of light in the distance that presented like a prism of colours. The humans' torches acted like beacons to the Indigenes. But he couldn't hear the humans.

The still night, with no breeze, felt odd. Ever since the GS humans had built the environ, Stephen had felt out of sync with his abilities.

He continued to move farther from the edge of the three-mile circumference to the land where he knew the animals liked to roam. It was why the hunting zones had been set up here, in the areas where the animals were most active. The hunting patterns of the Indigenes forced the animals to adapt.

So where were they now?

175

He looked around, sniffed the air again. No trace of them.

A low growl set his nerves on edge and he turned to see a pair of shining eyes close to his location. A lone wolf stalked closer as it hunted him. Stephen sniffed the air again, still not picking up the wolf's smell, let alone its fear. What was wrong with him? It had to be a defective air-filtration device.

His thoughts slowed him down enough for the wolf to edge closer without him noticing. Stephen switched to hunt mode, crouching low. He'd hoped the animal would set more of a challenge—he needed to let off steam—but he'd take what he could get.

The wolf stopped and watched his movements with the same precision of his own observations.

Hunter against hunter.

But the wolf lunged and caught Stephen off guard. He stumbled back when the wolf's teeth clamped on to his arm. It hung on with bared teeth, digging farther into his flesh. Stephen muffled his cry, not wanting to draw attention to his location. The wolf shook his arm, unclamped its teeth, then lunged for Stephen's leg. Stephen scuttled back while the animal stalked him. He scrambled to his feet and ran for the zone. The wolf followed as far as the perimeter, then broke off when Stephen passed through to safety.

Stephen watched the pacing wolf outside the zone, clear Indigene blood dripping from its bared incisors. His heart raced as he examined his arm and leg wound. Neither wound was healing at the speed he knew it should. He removed the air-filtration device on his way back to the district and the hatch. Inside the district, Indigenes gasped as a limping Stephen passed them. He moved as fast as possible, not wanting to hear what they thought of their inadequate leader.

He searched for Serena's voice only to find a whisper of her in another part of the district. Their normally strong connection had become paper thin, but more so since they had returned from seeing Gabriel. Clement came to mind. Another like Serena? Stephen didn't want to think about what that meant. He shuffled along trying to mask his pain from others. Clear fluid leaked from his wounds and stained his grey tunic, but at least the flow from both bites had stemmed since the wolf's attack.

How had he not sensed its presence?

Stephen reached the nearest tranquillity cave, the one above which the GS had built their environ. He used the stone steps to climb into one unit and positioned his aching body on the floor. He calmed his thoughts and closed his eyes, concentrating on the golden lattice that replaced the solid wall. The Nexus sent a lone tendril through the lattice. It wrapped around his arm and pulled his energy inside.

The Nexus had changed since Serena's arrival to District Three. Before, the connection points and the Nexus had been separated by a black chasm. Discord had existed inside the space that Stephen hadn't noticed until her presence had ignited a change. The Nexus, a young, evolving, organic being, had reacted sharply to Serena the first time she'd entered it. But her presence had not been a threat. She had given the Nexus something it could not get from other Indigenes: the ability to learn and evolve. Serena had taught the Nexus to make better use of the space, to increase its efficiency.

Now, the Nexus wall no longer separated the connecting energies. It enclosed the units where the energies connected to the space. Stephen slipped from his

Eliza Green

unit to the centre of the surrounding Nexus wall where a bright ball of energy collected. Before the change, energies used to be scattered far and wide and didn't always connect with the Nexus wall. Now, he could find them easier and use their combined energies to heal faster—a much more efficient use of his time.

His wounds healed on the outside, but his mind refused to let go of the tight band of worry that encased it. The energies healed him. But he also sensed a trace of hostility from them. Stephen deflected the negative energy back to the Nexus so it could cancel it out.

Stephen lost track of time while inside the Nexus. Three hundred minds connected at one time provided a powerful source of energy to draw from. Adding his own energy to the mix gave back what he took from others—a trade of sorts. But the energy around him felt weaker than normal.

He focused on the Nexus wall surrounding the collected ball of energies at its centre. It seemed no different than usual, pulsating in time with the active minds, acting like the conduit it was. But weak points in the wall presented themselves where the Nexus appeared to not shine as bright. Stephen floated away from the energies towards the part of the wall that had caught his attention. Only then did he see them: tiny micro strands of light, similar to the tendrils that pulled his energy inside, reaching up to the ceiling of whatever confined the Nexus. His gaze followed the strands that extended to an unseen point in the black expanse above him.

In the Nexus, not everything was as it seemed. Blacks were not black. Oranges were not orange. Space was relative, or irrelevant. He had no idea what the Nexus space looked like other than how his mind interpreted it. The strands looked like tiny hands reaching for something

178

—or someone.

Stephen floated away from this extrication of energy that appeared to be attracted to some outside force. The micro tendrils continued to draw away from their original purpose to another undisclosed place.

He returned to the centre, to the healing on offer. Then something clicked into place. The GS environ sat above this very tranquillity cave. Bill said they had stolen energy from the New London main feed to power something in that environ. Now, that something drew micro tendrils from the Nexus wall.

The Nexus was such a powerful healing entity; others would kill to access it.

An agitated Stephen ignored the calming energies in the centre of the Nexus urging him to join them. He needed to get out.

He disconnected from the Nexus with one long breath and climbed out of the hole. He startled to see Serena at the top, waiting for him.

'Are you okay, Stephen?' She helped him out of the unit. 'I felt you inside the Nexus. I felt your anxiousness.'

'You were inside?'

Why hadn't he sensed her?

'Yes, I sensed you connect,' she said. 'I was worried about you so I disconnected shortly after you. What's the matter?'

Stephen straightened up. 'I know what the GS are doing.'

'What?'

'They're stealing power from the Nexus to heal.'

'What? How?' Serena's eyes grew large. 'I didn't think it was possible for the Nexus to exist in the real world.'

'Their machine, their collection of power. It's only

minor draws but I saw it for myself, in there.'

'If it's just a small amount, that's good, right?'

Stephen shook his head. 'You don't understand; at some point they'll want more. They always do after they experience the true power of the Nexus. This district might not be in danger now, but trust me, that won't be the case for much longer.'

'Have you seen it?' said Serena.

It would be easier if he had.

'No. I have no timeline for when it will happen. But the GS have sampled what the Nexus can do. Imagine if they had access to its full power?'

21

'We're getting a visitor.'

Laura looked up when Bill shook her shoulder and popped one bud out of her ear. They had spent the evening relaxing together in their apartment—if she could even call it relaxing. Bill did research on his monitor while Laura listened to a backlog of communication chatter from the Wave that Julia had recorded before it got erased.

'Who?'

Bill shrugged. 'Stephen.'

'Really?' She stood, feeling anxious. She had no idea why. 'When?'

It had been years since Stephen had set foot in her and Bill's apartment, once at the beginning of their move to Exilon 5, and again when he was doing recon. But Serena, Anton and Arianna had agreed it would be safer for Stephen, one half of District Three's leadership, to remain close to his charges in the district. Any trips to the city could be construed as a conflict of interest among those Indigenes who didn't understand the history Stephen and Bill shared.

'He says he needs to talk. Plus, he was after a

Eliza Green

change of scenery.'

Laura glanced at the clock. It was 11pm. 'Well, at least it's dark outside. We should prepare for his arrival. When's he due?'

'Any minute now,' said Bill.

'Now?'

A flustered Laura turned off the main lights until a gentle glow filled the room. Bill wasn't wrong about the timing of Stephen's arrival. A minute later, she heard a soft knock on the door. Bill opened it and a tall figure dressed in a long, brown trenchcoat and Fedora entered.

Her eyes raked over his appearance as Bill closed the door behind him. 'At least you look the part.'

Stephen removed his hat. 'Bill said I should dress like a human. It raises fewer suspicions.'

'It must feel strange to wear human clothes again.'

The last time Laura had seen Stephen in this attire was eight years ago. He'd followed her back to her apartment in Sydney. She'd thought Stephen was going to attack her, but then he'd surprised her by asking for her help to locate Bill.

'I remember that.' Stephen nodded and smiled as his mind fluttered briefly against hers. 'But this is not strange.' He swept his hands over his outfit. 'Nostalgic, maybe.'

Bill pointed at the coat. 'Is that the exact outfit you wore?'

Stephen nodded. 'When this all began. I don't know why I kept it. Serena understands because she remembers her human life. Anton, Arianna and I don't have human pasts like Serena. Anton told me to get rid of it for weeks after Pierre's death, said it was a bad omen. I don't know why I kept it.'

He brushed his hand over the tan-coloured material.

Genesis Variant

Bill gestured inside the room. 'Please, take a seat. Can I get you something to drink?'

'Unless you have animal blood, I'm fine. This won't take long. I'm already feeling uneasy about being inside the city. I'd like to get back to the district.'

Bill sat down on the sofa, an action Laura would have mimicked, but with Stephen present she felt drawn to her Indigene side and remained standing, like him.

'What can we do for you?' she said.

'I came for a few reasons, but first tell me how your visit with Patterson went.'

Bill sighed and rubbed his face. 'He's playing me, wants me to get him weapons. Says the GS are being a nuisance and he wants to protect his property.'

'And what does he really want?' said Stephen.

'I don't know,' said Bill. 'But it's not to protect property, that's for sure. I offered to send some security to the site, but he refused. There's something else. He confirmed that the GS humans are drawing double the power from the grid.'

'We know,' said Stephen.

Laura frowned. Bill had only just found out and he hadn't spoken to Stephen yet. 'Where did you hear about it?'

Anton and Arianna told me. Stephen switched to telepathic mode. *They learned it from reading the minds of the younger Indigenes.*

Laura saw the lie manifest as a shadow behind Stephen. Something else had tipped him off. The silent communication between them felt like a tickle on her brain. Laura didn't like using her Indigene skills, least of all telepathy. She was married to a human and she still thought of herself as one. She was about to tell Stephen to use his voice when Bill beat her to it.

183

'Hello? Non Indigene in the room. Could you speak out loud?'

'Sorry,' said Stephen before repeating what he'd said to Laura.

'Thank you.'

Bill stood up and Laura sensed his unease at being left out of the conversation.

'We don't know why the GS are draining more power,' said Bill, standing next to Laura. 'I plan to send a crew out tomorrow to dismantle their cable from the main feed. If they won't follow directions, we'll cut off their supply.'

Laura sensed new trepidation from Stephen. The increase in stolen power wasn't the only reason he had come.

'I think I know,' said Stephen. 'I was using the Nexus this evening and noticed micro tendrils drawing out from the wall and up to the ceiling. The stolen power feeds the machine inside the environ and the tendrils are drawn to something. I'd say that source of power.'

'They're stealing the Nexus' power?' said Laura.

'That's what I thought at first, but the Nexus has the ability to heal many users at once. The GS using it wouldn't cause much disruption. They requested access to our caves and we said no. All they're doing is accessing it in another way.'

'So if they're using the Nexus to heal and it's not causing problems for your district, what's the issue?' said Bill.

'Don't you see the connection?' said Stephen. 'If they need power to attract the Nexus and recently doubled their power draw, it means what they've taken so far isn't enough. The Nexus can be highly addictive for anyone who uses it. It can make you strong, powerful. And for

Genesis Variant

someone who is neither, they may not stop until they've accessed it in its pure form, not through some makeshift environ.'

Bill shook his head. 'We will never grant them access to the Nexus the traditional way. Maybe the sample *will* be enough to satiate them.'

But Laura saw the point Stephen made. 'They'll keep taking from the main feed, Bill. The more energy they use, the more the Nexus will be attracted to it. So where will they stop? Stephen's right. We shouldn't underestimate their plans. They may go beyond simple healing.'

Bill paced the room. 'Shit, I thought they'd get a little power to heal and when they were finished, they'd disconnect.' He stopped pacing. His eyes flitted between the pair. 'So what now?'

'We start by disconnecting the power supply,' said Laura. She turned to Stephen. 'I'm not sure what you can do to stop them from accessing the Nexus though.'

She'd seen the Nexus once, back when she was caught between human and Indigene and fighting for her life. Arianna had brought her there to complete her transformation and to stop further damage being done to her human body. She'd only used it that once, even though Stephen had said she could use it whenever she wanted.

'The Nexus is organic and doesn't obey the normal rules of society,' said Stephen. 'It is a living thing with instincts of its own. It is drawn to energy, like a moth is drawn to fire. We cannot tell it what to do.'

'But Serena can,' suggested Laura.

Arianna had told her about Serena's first use of the Nexus where she had controlled it and changed the way it worked.

Stephen nodded. 'I had thought about it. I will talk

to her, and we can try, but I'm not sure if it will help.'

'Okay, so we have a plan,' said Bill.

He prepared to see Stephen out. But when Stephen didn't move, a sick feeling lodged in Laura's gut. She sensed Stephen wanted to talk about more than the Nexus and the power supply.

'Actually, there's one other reason I'm here.' He faced Laura and her heart thundered in her chest. 'I need to ask you a favour.'

'Anything.'

She smiled but knew Stephen could sense her trepidation, the way she could sense his.

It's nothing bad, Laura, but I notice you fight your Indigene side. Why?

'I don't know.' She walked to the other side of the room, for some space. 'I don't feel entitled to call myself one.'

But you clearly show abilities that prove you are. And that could become more if you accepted them.

'It's not that, Stephen. I... well, it doesn't feel right.'

Why not? You are as much of an Indigene as Serena, said Stephen. *She was human once. Now she is both, but she embraces her Indigene side. I can feel your struggle and how unhappy it makes you. You don't want Bill to know, I understand that, but to fight it will make you sick, both mentally and physically.*

'It's not as easy as that.'

She glanced at Bill to see him staring at her. He looked away and she switched to telepathy.

Okay, yes, I've been feeling out of sorts. I don't know what I am any more. I feel human and yet I don't. This isn't fair to Bill. He's my husband and I can't talk to him about this.

Why, because he'd tell you to do what makes you

Genesis Variant

happy?

Exactly. Laura huffed out a breath. *He would tell me to become an Indigene and forget about him, because he loves me so much and he wouldn't want to hold me back.*

So why don't you explore your Indigene side?

Because I'm afraid that the minute I do, it will end our relationship. That he will no longer be enough for me. Laura shook her head. *I'm not ready for that.*

Stephen nodded. *You can't keep fighting it either. You need to let whatever is inside you emerge. Then you can take it from there. To deny a part of you that exists is to exist only partially.*

Laura switched to her voice. 'I know, Stephen. Give me some time.'

'We don't have time,' he said, sounding frustrated. 'I need you to use your ability now.'

'Why?'

'You're the only one who can get a read on the GS. Our abilities don't seem to work around them. Plus, they don't care for our kind. You can at least sense when they're lying.'

'I've already tried. Bill, tell him.'

Laura looked over at him but he pretended to be interested in something on his monitor.

When she persisted, Bill looked up and nodded. 'She tried, Stephen. But it wasn't enough. She should give it another go.'

She couldn't read her husband's mind but the tension in his jaw told her Bill was annoyed by their silent conversation.

'I'll try again, Stephen. That's all I can do.'

She hoped her promise would put an end to the conversation.

187

Stephen shook his head. *Try harder, Laura O'Halloran. Then find your place in this world.*

He put on his hat and Bill showed him out.

With Stephen gone, a worried Bill turned to her. 'What was all that about?'

'What?'

'The silent conversation between you.'

She sighed, hating that she kept secrets from Bill. But she didn't know how else to do this. 'He wants me to start using my abilities more.'

'I heard that bit. I meant the part I didn't hear.'

'It was nothing, Bill.' Laura pushed a bud in her ear and returned to the communication chatter, leaving one ear free. 'Don't worry; it was nothing.'

But Bill didn't look convinced.

He returned to his desk and monitor. 'Are you sure?'

'Of course I am.'

Laura faked a smile and slipped the second bud into her ear.

22

Bill got no sleep that night thinking about Stephen's visit and his and Laura's secret conversation. His wife had been feeling lost for a while now, but he had hoped with some time she'd figure out what she wanted. The day she had agreed to become his wife had been the happiest of his life. Her acceptance had eliminated all doubts in his head about her wanting him. But last night, seeing how tense she had been while she and Stephen talked brought back all his insecurities.

Laura slept soundly next to him in the bed. He leaned over her and tucked a strand of her blonde hair behind her ear, then pressed a soft, feathery kiss to her cheek. He loved this woman so much it hurt. It differed to the love he'd had for Isla, but was no less intense. Isla had been taken from him. Bill would not make Laura stay in a place or situation where she wasn't comfortable.

With just the bare amount of sleep under his belt, Bill got up a few hours later. A headache plagued him that rivalled his worst caffeine-induced migraine. He slogged to the shower and attempted to wash away his discomfort, then dressed and headed for the kitchen to get a coffee. It was his worst addiction and he couldn't shake it.

He slowed when he saw Laura at the replicator. She turned and gave him a smile as bright as the sun that streamed through the window. His doubts eased a little; whatever had been on her mind the night before had vanished in the morning light. He smiled back, albeit his feeling forced, and set to make some coffee.

'That's not going to sustain you. I can make some porridge. You want some?'

Bill wrinkled his nose. 'Nah, coffee will do me.'

Laura shrugged. 'Okay, but don't blame me if you keel over from hunger later this morning.'

Laura never skipped breakfast; she couldn't function without food in her belly. Low blood sugar, she called it. Bill, on the other hand, regularly forgot to eat, especially when his diet of caffeine and adrenaline sustained him.

'I've lived this long. I'll survive.'

She turned back to the replicator and Bill noticed her smile fade.

He couldn't bear the tension between them. 'You feel okay after last night? You seem... stressed.'

His wife nodded, concentrating on the food replicator as she punched in a code for porridge. 'Everything's fine, Bill. Please don't worry. Let's just work on a solution to stop the GS from taking more grid power.'

Her answer didn't satisfy him. 'You'd tell me if something was wrong? I don't want you to think we can't talk about this stuff.'

She turned and gave him a smile too wide to be natural. 'I know, Bill. And I promise if there was something to talk about, we'd talk about it.'

'Okay.' Bill collected his mug from the coffee

machine and drank the bitter liquid that matched his mood. He had a feeling this wasn't the end of their talk. 'I'm heading to work. You need a lift?'

Laura carried her bowl of porridge to the table and set it down. 'No, you go ahead. I want to check through Julia's recordings of the communication chatter some more, see if there's anything worth investigating.'

Bill finished his coffee in three gulps and left her to her breakfast.

He arrived at the office, staying only long enough to contact the head technician responsible for maintenance of the power grid. He asked him to meet him at the base station. Frank, his technician, had already been in touch with Bill about the cable when it first appeared. Until now, Bill had instructed Frank leave it alone. But today, he would go there to tell Frank to disconnect it.

His car drove through New London and travelled along an old access road that took him beyond the city limits. Twenty-five miles from the boundary and in the opposite direction to the GS caves and District Three's entrance stood a field of high-tech solar panels spanning an area close to two hundred square miles. Next to the field was a base station from which technicians controlled and monitored the power feed to the city. Surrounding the entire operation was a chain-link fence that Bill knew to be electrified. Similar stations to this, using molten silicone to store electricity, fed the other cities on Exilon 5.

The car pulled up to the fenced-off entrance and Bill got out of his vehicle. He pressed his security chip to the plate by the humming gate. It brought up his photo and credentials on screen. The humming dropped away as the gate de-electrified and opened. Bill returned to his car, which drove through and parked in a bay outside the base station. There was no sign of Frank.

191

Bill got out and entered the station. Just inside were a dozen wall monitors all showing data on them. On one monitor, Bill saw Frank at the location where the GS had attached their cable, a plot of land a few miles out that would remain undeveloped while the feed ran underground.

He returned to his car and caught up to Frank at the site. Frank had hunkered down and was scanning an exposed part of the cable for the main feed where one section attached to another. A different, smaller cable was attached to the connector at a forty-five-degree angle. Frank continued to scan the cable even after Bill joined him.

'What if we just yank it free?' said Bill.

Frank shook his head. 'I would advise against that. I originally thought pulling it free would be enough, but if we interrupt the supply, we risk a city-wide blackout.'

'So we don't pull it free.'

'I didn't say that. I need to see how it's connected first. That's what the scans are for. We should take these back to the station so we can analyse them properly.'

Bill examined the cable. It was not a natural fit for the connector, but somehow had found a way to work with it. He was no electrician, but the cable, crude in design and with exposed wires, looked dangerous.

Frank visually inspected the connection. 'We know it's siphoning off the power.' He continued to scan the connection points with his DPad. 'But I won't say any more at this stage.' Frank stood up. 'We'll continue this back at the station.'

They drove back separately to the base station. Inside, Bill stood next to Frank while he transferred the scans over to the main computer and screens.

Frank cursed, shaking his head. 'See this?' He

Genesis Variant

pointed at the infrared images of the cable and its components. 'There are two parts to the cable. One part sits on the main feed while the other, the sub feed, mines the power back to the GS humans. The sub feed is reliant on the existence of the first part. Both must exist to work.'

'So we disconnect one or the other.'

Frank pointed at the image, specifically the part that sat on the main feed. This has somehow integrated itself into the main feed. We disconnect it, we blow the main feed. See how the ends merge with the primary cable feeding power to the city? The GS appear to have designed this intelligent cable to think it belongs there.'

'So we have no choice?'

Bill would not give in to GS demands. He had to stop them from destroying New London's energy supplies.

'We could try laser cutting it, but given how the interactive cable works, we could be cutting the main feed too.'

'Let's try that. You got cutting equipment in that truck of yours?'

Frank frowned. 'I do. You want to try now?'

'No time like the present.'

☼

They returned in separate vehicles to the location of the compromised cable. Frank pulled a machine out of the back of his truck twice the size of his chest. He set it down next to the secondary cable attached to the connector.

He snapped on a pair of rubber gloves. 'These will protect me from any surges, but I'd suggest *you* stand back.'

Bill did. He watched from a safe distance as Frank turned on the laser-cutting machine. A red beam shone

193

from the tapered end and made a high buzzing noise as Frank cut the cable mining the power back to the GS. Five minutes later, he turned off the machine and stood up. Bill saw he had successfully cut the cable. The pieces lay separated from each other.

'That should do it, until the GS attach a new cable... what the hell?'

Frank jumped back and Bill saw the two severed ends of the cable wriggle in the dirt.

'Shit!'

The cable slithered along the ground searching for its other half. Bill lunged for the cable and yanked it back, but it squirmed against his efforts. The reconnection sent sparks dancing over his hand and up his arm. He went flying on his ass.

'Stay back,' Frank warned.

Bill scuttled back as the cable reattached itself fully to the severed part. The insulating rubber around the cables melted and reformed to fill the cut Frank had made.

Frank picked up the machine and attempted to cut the cable a second time. But this time, the laser barely made a dent in the rubber casing.

Frank huffed out a breath. 'If it wasn't welded before, it is now.'

'What the hell is it?'

'It's an organic, biomolecular, energy cable. I've never seen one, but I've read about them. It feeds on energy and won't disconnect unless the right code, command or biowave is given.'

'Can't we just try pulling it from the actual connector?'

'No, this thing is protecting itself. In the face of danger, it only strengthens its connection. If we keep attacking it, we risk the entire feed.'

'So we shut down the power to the station. Cut off its access.'

Frank scanned the connection point again. 'That will kill power to everything, including all of your computers. You might lose everything, you might lose nothing, but you'll be flying blind.'

'Shit, so what do we do now?'

Frank returned the laser cutter to the truck bay. He turned round and perched his fists on his hips. 'Convince the GS to stop mining power. Or call their bluff. Threaten to shut down the grid. They might back off.'

A frustrated Bill thanked Frank, who got into his truck and drove off. Bill returned to his vehicle and drove to the boundary wall that marked the start of the GS grounds. He sat in the cabin and observed through magnification glasses the white, dome-shaped environ and the mining cable that ended at the back of it.

When he'd said no more power, the GS hadn't listened.

He needed to pay Tanya another visit. And this time, Laura would use her damn abilities to the full.

23

'I'm coming to get you. Where are you?'

Silence greeted Bill on the other end of the line.

Then Laura answered him. 'In the office. Why? What happened?'

'We need to speak with Simon and Tanya again. This situation with the power is getting out of hand. I'll explain what I just saw when I pick you up.'

Bill hung up while the car drove him away from the dirt road and GS boundary wall towards the city and civilisation. He didn't know how to contact Simon a second time, or what to say to convince Tanya to remove her cable. He should have known; a little power would never be enough for someone like her. She would keep giving him the run around, mining more power until she compromised the power grid operations. And Frank had no way to disconnect the power. The ITF would slip under the old board members' command, just like the bad old days.

The car pulled up outside the offices, where Laura waited.

She climbed into the front seat beside Bill. 'So what's this all about? Why the urgency?'

Genesis Variant

Bill barked a command to return to the boundary wall and the car moved. They would wing it from there like the last time.

He told her what had happened with the cable.

Laura cursed. 'So Stephen was right about the GS seeking access to the Nexus. The only way they can do that from up here is if they increase the power to their machine.' Laura stared out at the fast-moving scenery before turning back at Bill. 'How will we find Simon?'

'The way we did the last time, by walking into the area their cameras monitor and hoping they come get us.'

'And if they don't?'

They would. They'd be too curious not to come.

'Tanya will want to know why we're there.'

Laura settled into the front seat. 'I hope you're right.'

'There's one more thing,' said Bill.

His voice cracked and he cleared it. She frowned while he fumbled for the right words to ask his next question. He'd no idea how she would reply.

Her frown turned into an impatient stare. 'What is it? We're almost there.'

'I need you to tap into your Indigene skills, the ones I know you have.'

Laura picked at her sleeve. 'I don't know, Bill. They're buried deep. I don't even know what my skills are.'

'Bullshit. You fell into silent conversation with Stephen without even blinking.'

Laura levelled a glare at him. 'Doesn't mean I know what they are. Some are instinctual, others not. You know I don't like using them. I've told you why.'

'Have you?' Bill turned his body. 'Look, we don't have many opportunities to speak to Tanya and I'm

197

running out of options to stop them. I want to try one last thing. And I'd like your help with it.'

Bill kept his mouth shut, waiting.

Laura sighed and shrugged. 'I don't know how I can help you.'

'Yes, you do. You can see when people are lying. You can probably do much more than that. I've known Stephen long enough to read his body language. I could guess he wants the same thing I do.' The car arrived at their destination but Bill wasn't ready to get out. 'He told you to embrace your Indigene side, but you refused, didn't you?'

'Stop pressuring me, Bill.' Laura rubbed the back of her neck. 'If I don't feel Indigene, I can't just pretend I am.'

'You don't need to pretend. I see the way you slip into it, then pull back out when you think I've noticed too much. Love...' He turned more and grabbed her hands. 'I don't want you to be something less than you are. If you feel Indigene, don't hold back on my account. I don't want to be the one to hold you back.'

'You're not, Bill. I love you. You're my husband.'

'And I love you too, but you need to deal with this. Because if you don't, it will get between us anyway, and as much as I love secrets and intrigue, this is one secret that we need to talk about.'

Laura pulled her hands out of his. 'If there was something to talk about, Bill, you'd be the first to know. But there isn't.' There was an edge to her voice. 'If it makes you feel better, I'll talk to Stephen. He's worrying over nothing.'

She gave Bill a smile that looked too forced to be genuine. Bill dropped the conversation with a sigh. Whatever his feelings, right now he needed Laura's skills.

Simon might be here shortly, and he wanted to play his lie just right.

They got out of the car and stood at the circle of boulders that encompassed the GS land beyond. He climbed over one and dropped to the other side. Laura took longer and he got the impression she was being slow on purpose. In silence, they made the short trek into the unremarkable, rocky land that held both the environ and the caves.

Laura walked at a normal pace next to Bill. Until his wife figured out what she wanted, nothing between them would be resolved. Bill would try to give her space to make that decision.

Their feet navigated rock-strewn land for half an hour until they reached a flat area close to the edge of the environ. Last time, they'd travelled under the cover of darkness. But it was mid morning and visibility was good.

The sun bounced off the environ, causing Bill to shield his eyes. Laura slipped on a pair of shades to protect hers; they were more sensitive than Bill's. So many things connected her to the Indigene way of life. He couldn't understand why she continued to pretend none of it mattered.

They slowed when they got close to the white, tarpaulin-covered dome. Bill saw the caves in the distance, just a dot and at least a couple of miles away.

'Someone's coming,' Laura hissed.

Bill looked around but saw nothing. Then a white object sped towards them and came to a stop.

He groped for his Buzz Gun but Simon already had his hand on it. 'Not a good idea.'

Bill relaxed his hand enough to appease Simon. His former ITF boss wore a white robe with a hood draped over his head. It was already twenty degrees Celsius out, and Simon's skin looked similar enough to the Indigenes that he wondered if he could tolerate the sun.

'We need to talk,' said Bill. 'To Tanya.'

Simon frowned. 'About what?'

'You know about what. About the extra power you continue to mine from my main feed.'

'It's not enough power to affect your operations,' said Simon. 'You still have plenty in reserves. I checked the numbers before I initiated a new draw.'

'So you designed the cable?'

'Yes, why?'

'What the hell is it? It has a life of its own.'

'It's an intelligent cable,' said Simon. 'Since we can't be there to monitor it day and night, I designed it to reattach itself in the event of disconnection.'

'Well, I need you to detach it. Right now.'

Simon shook his head. 'Tanya won't agree to it, Bill. The power is helping the Elite to heal. Not by a lot, but enough that it will prolong their life for a few more months. The Elite's bodies are too fragile to support them for longer than that.'

Laura shook her head. 'I don't understand; you said the healing is supposed to fix any issues with their code, to reverse the damage.'

'Yes, but their bodies weren't designed to be tested so much then rapidly healed. Their cells are dying.'

'So what happens when Tanya decides she wants double what you currently have, or triple?' said Bill.

'I don't know,' said Simon. 'I didn't build the machine in the environ to store infinite power. Nor do I know how much it can safely store. Too much healing seems to be counterproductive to them. The healing effects are already reversing. That's why Tanya didn't come to meet you herself. She isn't strong enough.'

Genesis Variant

'Reversing? You mean the healing doesn't work?' said Laura.

Simon nodded. 'It would appear so. We tested it with a little power and it gave them back their strength for a day. Then we doubled it and gave each of them two sessions with the machine. But that only healed them for a day like before—three days less than what we expected with a double dose and double the power. Their bodies appear to have a limit to how much healing they accept.'

Bill was confused. 'So what you're saying is they no longer have a use for the power?'

'No, they still need it to heal, no matter how short the benefits. I just don't think the power will do more than give them back a few days of strength.'

They still wanted the power. That was all Bill needed to hear.

'Remove the cable, Simon, or I'll order my men to shut down the power.'

Simon smiled. 'Didn't you just hear me? They just want dignity and to feel normal in their twilight years. That's not too much to ask, is it, Bill?'

Bill wasn't sure how to answer. What harm was there in helping a group of people to heal for a while who would otherwise die?

'And what about you? Have you not required healing?'

'No. My body is still strong. We Conditioned have not been intensively gene manipulated like the Elite have.'

'Conditioned?' said Laura.

'It's what the Elite call us. The extensive testing done to our bodies has conditioned them to be harder than the Elite's.' Simon shrugged. 'It's just a name.'

'A name like that sticks you on a lower tier to the Elite,' said Laura.

201

'I disagree. We are very important.'

Laura removed her shades and stared at Simon. 'So why do I see deceit in you? Your heart rate is elevated, and you're sweating.'

'I just ran here. And it's hot out,' Simon said with a smooth smile. 'You're reading too much into this. I'm telling the truth. But you have kept something important from me. You can read me. Tanya would not have agreed to let you inside the caves had she known what you are. She's unable to read humans or Indigenes. I can sometimes read the latter.'

'But you didn't know what I was,' said Laura.

'Not until now. I witnessed your initial rapid changes but it didn't occur to me that you might have held on to your new Indigene skills. Skills you hide from him.' Simon nodded to Bill. 'You're scared to face them, because doing so would mean letting things in your life go. Am I right?'

Simon's words made Bill squirm. He stared at his wife in an attempt to gauge her thoughts. All he discovered was a poker face wiped clean of emotion—just like an Indigene's.

Laura folded her arms. 'I'm not hiding anything, Simon. But you are. The Elite didn't meet us here for another reason. And I'm sure that if we saw them, we would see the healing worked better than you've let on.'

Simon shook his head. 'Why would I lie to you about that? The Elite are not long for this world. You saw that for yourself. All we're doing here is giving them some dignity.'

Bill no longer bought the act. 'The Elite didn't go through a major genetic alteration to end their lives like a bunch of old people in a home. And when they achieve whatever it is they've planned, where will those plans

Genesis Variant

leave you and the other Conditioned?'

Simon shifted his weight from one foot to the other. It was the first reaction Bill had noticed since he'd shown up.

'You're mistaken, both of you. This is only about preserving life for as long as possible.' Simon sighed, as if the conversation bored him. 'You need to leave our land now. You are no longer welcome here.'

'What about the power? It doesn't belong to you.'

'Sorry, Bill, but I have no control over that.'

'Well, I do. Expect your power supply to vanish soon.'

He turned away.

'And I'll instruct my business associates with access to the base station to turn the power back on.'

Bill turned back. 'What did you say?'

'There are other humans happy to do our bidding, for the right price.'

'This won't be the end of it, Simon.'

He pulled Laura with him as he walked away. She complied.

'No, it won't be. I'm certain of that,' said Simon.

Bill stopped, but Laura urged him to keep going.

'Leave it,' she said.

He couldn't. He turned to face his old boss—a man he had respected once. 'What happened to you?' He pointed at the caves. 'Those people don't respect you and never will. This can't be your life.'

'It *is* my life. And I must accept what I cannot change.'

'Who says you can't change it?'

Simon smiled. 'Nice to see you again, Bill.'

He ran off. A blur of white trailed all the way back to the caves.

203

With a huff, Bill turned back around and walked on. His frayed temper poked at the edges of his nerves. He ignored it long enough to ask Laura what she thought.

He kept his tone cool, businesslike. 'What did you sense from him?'

'I saw his lies manifest, especially when he talked about the Elite and their plans for healing. There's more to this than simply giving the Elite a few more days, or months, of dignity. They're up to something and they will take more power if it serves their needs. And one other thing.'

'What?'

'Simon can't keep me out of his head. Before, he could protect his thoughts from others and turn off the telepathic connection at will. But I couldn't feel any shield. I still can't read his thoughts but his defences are weak. Whatever changes he's undergone recently have weakened him.'

Bill nodded and kept walking. A new silence mounted between them.

Laura said after a moment, 'Don't listen to anything Simon said about me. He's got it wrong.'

Bill stopped. 'Has he? You're hiding things from me.' He strode away from her, forcing Laura to catch up. 'I don't need to be a mind reader to pick up on that.'

'Come on, Bill. That's bullshit. This is you and me. Let's talk about this.'

Bill stopped again and folded his arms. 'Okay, why are you denying your Indigene side?'

Laura hesitated. 'I'm not.'

Bill dropped his arms and walked on. 'Wrong answer.'

'Come on, Bill. Talk to me.'

The walk back to the car was torturous. Bill kept his

Genesis Variant

stone wall up while Laura pleaded with him.

By the time they reached the car, she had given up. They got in.

'So what now?' Laura said, her voice barely above a whisper.

'Now?' He turned to her sharply. 'Pack up your things and go visit Stephen. Deal with this shit you refuse to deal with and don't come back until you know what you want.'

'You're kicking me out of my home?'

He issued a command and the car moved.

'Damn right I am, starting today.'

'You can't do that, Bill. That's my home.'

'Stop, Laura.' He pressed his fingers to his temple. 'Just fucking stop and deal with it. Please.'

Laura shut her mouth and stared out the window.

He hated the silence more than the secrets, but he refused to hold her back. If he was no longer enough for her, he might as well be an asshole now. It would make the separation easier on them both.

24

Simon returned to the caves after leaving Bill and Laura to find their way out of the flatlands. He walked into the observation room where several Conditioned watched the pair on screen. Simon saw Bill and Laura looking less than pleased with each other. He hadn't meant to put a wedge between the pair but Tanya had insisted he distract them somehow to take their focus off the power mining.

A noise sounded close by. He turned his head just as one of the Conditioned appeared at the back of the raised platform.

'Tanya wants to see you now,' he said.

Simon hopped up on to the platform and followed the Conditioned through the roughly hewn tunnel behind the partition on the right. The tunnel led to an open area covered in white panels that gave the space a laboratory type feel. Three doors, one to the left and two to the right, led to the staging room and accommodation for Tanya's assistants. The tunnel carried on straight to a similar open area and the location of the ten Elite's accommodation. Similar areas accessible through the left partition behind the platform led to the majority of the Conditioned's accommodation and the laboratories where the Earth doctors carried out their tests on the Elite. It was also the space for Simon's mind-mapping machine and any inventions he or others created. The staging room to his left acted as the only central space with immediate access to both the left and right tunnels.

Simon sensed Tanya's excitement but didn't see her. One of Tanya's assistants appeared like a ghost from the dark tunnel ahead of him.

'In here.' She gestured to the staging room. 'Elite One wants to show you something.'

Simon opened the door and walked inside alone to see Tanya, dressed in a hooded robe similar to his, stood in the middle of the circle of beds. She had her back to him.

'Simon,' she said, her voice barely a whisper.

She rarely spoke telepathically these days, not since the last, and most aggressive, treatment had weakened her ability. If Bill and the Indigenes knew how vulnerable the Elite really were, they would have taken them down already.

Tanya turned slowly. Simon gasped when he saw her. Elite One smiled and swept her hands down her body. Then she drew a circle around her face with her finger.

'What do you think?'

Tanya was no longer the withered skin bag he'd seen the day before, but a vibrant woman who looked closer to eighty than one hundred and sixteen. Definitely not the two-hundred-year-old she'd resembled for the past three months.

'What happened?'

'The Nexus healing.'

'But it didn't work as well as we thought. It only gave you back thirty-six hours.'

Tanya laughed. Her eyes, wide and observant,

crinkled slightly at the corners. 'Turns out the healing needed more time to work from the inside out. The skin ageing reversed itself just an hour ago.'

'And the others?'

Tanya nodded. 'All of the Elite have seen tremendous results. We need more power from the grid. Who knows how long these changes will last?'

Simon was confused. The changes were only to facilitate transcendence so the Elite could ditch their bodies in exchange for everlasting life.

'The power was to give you enough strength so you could continue with your treatment. Besides, it may not matter much if we can't access much more of the Nexus than we do. Let's wait and see how long these changes last before—'

Tanya waved her hand dismissively. 'I don't want to wait, and neither do the other Elite. We want to access all of the Nexus. If that small amount did this to us, can you imagine what the whole thing would do?'

'And how are you going to get inside the district? What about your plans for transcendence?'

'They're linked. Dr Jameson says it might be possible to transcend with minimal power, but the Nexus would guarantee success.'

'And my other question?'

'That's where the Conditioned can help. I may look good, but I'm not as strong as them. If Dr Jameson can transfer the Elite's consciousness, or at least a copy, to the Conditioned's consciousness, we can piggyback on it to physically enter the Nexus. We need them as a power source. The Nexus is proving our best chance make this happen.'

Using the Conditioned in this way? Simon's skin prickled at the thought. 'What will happen to the

208

handpicked Conditioned during this "transformation"?'

Tanya walked over to him and gripped his face a little too tight. 'They will be a sacrifice, Simon. A worthy sacrifice. But before we can use the Nexus for final transformation, we must reach stage two.'

Simon released a breath when Tanya let go of his face and walked to the other side of the room. In their current state, Tanya and the others could reach that stage sooner. But at least it gave Simon time.

☼

Simon was on observation room duty that afternoon, a task he rarely minded. But today, all he wanted was some space to think about what was about to happen.

He shielded his thoughts from the pair of Conditioned on duty and thought about Tanya's renewed vigour. No longer did Tanya's plans for transcendence include a promise to leave the Conditioned with a better quality of life. No, Elite One had tasted power again and would push hard for transcendence, even if it meant trampling over others to get it. He saw that now. What would it mean for others? The Indigenes, the Conditioned —it didn't matter. Tanya would take it all.

She had not picked her ten subjects yet, but her reliance on Simon pointed to her choosing him. Simon would resist any plans she had use his body in this way. But he feared that when the time came, he wouldn't be asked.

He could run. To where? He had no money, no accommodation except for the caves.

Bill might give him refuge. To live as what—a freak in New London? No, he had turned his back on that life when he'd agreed to the first treatment.

209

Was he stuck? It felt like it. But maybe he could still turn Tanya off her idea to piggyback. How, he didn't know. At least he still had her trust.

An unenthusiastic Simon watched the monitors covering a three-square kilometre radius of bare land. Before they had built the environ, few trespassers had ventured into their monitored area. But in recent months, since their emergence and increased activity with the environ, their activities had drawn the attention of groups of Indigenes and people who had banded together. Simon perked up when he saw one group stood close to the boundary wall made up of the large boulders. They wore magnification glassed and appeared to be watching the environ.

Simon turned to the other two on duty. 'I need to check the machine, take some readings.'

'You're not supposed to leave your post,' said one.

'I won't be long.' He picked up a scanner for recording data and waved it at the other two. 'I'm worried about power fluctuations. Cover for me.'

The pair shrugged then went back to monitoring the screens with a similar lack of interest to him.

Simon ran all the way to the environ where he unlocked the door with his thumbprint and slipped inside. He closed the door and removed the scanner from his bag. He ran a quick diagnostic on the containment field and the machine. Everything was within normal safety parameters, just as he'd expected. To the rear of the environ was a second access door. This one wasn't within the camera's visual range. Simon opened it a crack and observed the prying eyes peeking over the top of the boulders.

He suspected they were part of the rogue groups Bill had mentioned. Their mission: to destroy the Elite and Conditioned, according to Bill. Simon smirked at the irony; it was far more likely Tanya would beat them to that honour. While Tanya and the rest of the Elite saw no threat in these groups, Simon had worked with the ITF long enough to know a quiet group was never an idle group. He'd witnessed how fast things had turned against the Indigenes when the board members had discovered Serena's existence. All they needed was motive. While he didn't know what this group wanted beyond watching the GS, he refused to wait for them to make their move.

To walk up to the group wearing a white robe would be a stupid move. To assume he could talk to them, human to human, was an even more ridiculous idea. Simon considered mind mapping. The device had many levels and types of experience recorded on it. He could mind map the skills of a negotiator on to his brain.

But the device was all the way back in the cave.

He closed and secured the rear door.

Simon gathered up his things, left the environ through the main entrance and returned to the caves. He found the bored Conditioned pair where he'd left them, still watching the screens. Simon looked at the images. He no longer saw the group on the monitor. A wolf had wandered inside the zone and was sniffing at the ground.

The pair looked up at Simon. He waved the scanner at them. 'I'm reading some slight anomalies but I'm losing my ability to decipher what it means. I need to do a fresh map of an electrician on to my mind so I can do something about it.'

One of the Conditioned sighed. 'How long do you need in case one of the Elite asks?'

'No more than an hour. Tops.'

He reckoned that would be enough time to meet with the group and return.

Simon hopped up on to the platform and followed

the left tunnel past one of the access points to the staging room to a new open-plan area. This was where the doctors worked and the location of the laboratories. A tunnel ran straight. To the left was a tunnel leading to the Conditioned's accommodation. He ignored it and followed the straight tunnel to a new area smaller than the first with just three doors to his left. He entered the last room, with a long bench against the wall, where they kept most of their equipment.

The mind-mapping device sat on the bench, hooked up to a monitor and power source. Simon scrolled through the list of skills on screen and found what he needed. He slipped the lattice cap made of silicone on his head. It's web-like pattern held several connection points. He initiated the process from the monitor and felt a jolt in his brain as the skills of negotiator flooded his mind. Other skills he already had, electrician and geotechnician, lessened to accommodate the new skill. After, he would need to redo both skills sets and remove the negotiator skill.

Simon disconnected and wiped the memory logs before leaving the room for his own. He slipped inside his private space, which held little more than a bed and chest of drawers, and opened a drawer of the chest nestled in one corner. He pulled out what remained of his wardrobe as a human. Tanya had thought it trivial for him to hold on to his human past, but Simon hadn't been ready to give up on his old life.

He opened his backpack and stuffed what clothes he needed into it. He then placed the scanner on top.

Simon left his room and nearly had a heart attack when he ran into Tanya.

Her sharp gaze eyed his backpack. 'Where are you going?'

'The machine is showing an anomalous reading. I just wanted to check it out, make sure everything's okay.'

'I'll come with you.'

'No!'

Tanya looked at him, surprised.

'I mean, it's probably nothing. We get glitches occasionally. I don't expect to be long.'

Tanya narrowed her gaze. He took some comfort knowing she couldn't read his mind.

'Be back in ten minutes. There's a group hanging around just outside our camera's range.'

'I will.'

Simon ran out. There wasn't enough time to learn the group's motives. He would have to settle for giving them a message. He ran to the environ, locked the door and dressed in a pair of trousers and a white shirt. His skin was not at translucent as the Indigenes, so he hoped he could pass as human.

He stole out of the rear of the environ, sniffing the air. The wolf still roamed the vicinity and was probably being watched by the pair monitoring the screens. He ran fast to the edge of the perimeter where the cameras could not reach. He hoped in his new attire and this far out, the group would mistake him for another human.

He sniffed the air again and picked up on the group's scent. He climbed over one boundary boulder farther back and approached their group.

A man in his thirties spoke to what appeared to be an all-human group.

One man poked the leader in the shoulder and pointed at Simon. 'Who are you?'

'They sent me from another city,' said Simon. 'Am I late?'

'Which city?' The leader narrowed his eyes. 'How

did you get here?'

'New Singapore. And by car. I parked it out of sight. We're close to their property.'

He nodded to the environ and caves.

The leader hissed. 'They don't own anything.'

Simon didn't have much time. Tanya expected him back in less than eight minutes. 'I have a message for you, from my group.'

The leader folded his arms. 'Yeah? And what's that?'

'The peace treaty is a good thing and we should preserve it.'

'The treaty is bullshit. Are you from the ITF?'

'No, I'm from New Singapore. I told you.'

'And how did you know we'd be here?' said the leader.

'We have eyes everywhere.'

The leader nodded to the environment. 'Even on that?'

'Yes,' Simon lied.

'So what are the freaks doing in there exactly?'

'We're not worried. It's nothing that will harm you.' The leader stared at him, prompting Simon to add, 'or me.'

'How can you be sure?'

'I just know, trust me. Please go back to your groups and tell them to stand down. There's nothing going on here.'

'Except you're here telling me to go, and I don't even know who the hell you are.' The leader stepped forward and grabbed a fistful of Simon's white shirt. 'You tell your ITF buddies and Indigene lovers we can't be bought with lies. The treaty serves only the Indigenes and the GS humans, and this is our chance to weaken their hold on this world. Put it back in the hands of its rightful owners.'

'The treaty is a good thing,' said Simon.

The leader twisted his shirt more. 'If you don't want a busted nose, get the hell out of here and go back to wherever you came from.' He let go. 'We know what you are. You can't fool us.'

Simon stepped back when one of the larger men came closer. He'd hated violence as a human. He hated it even more as a Conditioned.

The large man grabbed him and pinned his arms behind his back while another man punched him in the stomach. One blow wasn't enough to hurt him, but several were. Simon groaned and doubled over. He waited for the man to run out of steam.

Simon coughed and crawled away from the retreating, laughing group. The men didn't follow. He got to his feet and climbed over one boulder, hidden from view. Stumbling, he made it back to the environ. Inside, he undressed and put on his robe, but not before he examined the multiple bruises beginning to form. The Conditioned could heal fast, but not as fast as the Indigenes. Simon would need to keep his bruises hidden until they healed.

His return to the caves took longer than his trip out. Inside, he was surprised to find Tanya waiting alone at the monitors. The pair of Conditioned was nowhere to be seen.

'What were you doing out there?'

'I was monitoring the power fluctuations; I told you.'

Tanya shook her head and pointed to the hidden area where he had met the men. 'No, there. I saw you climb over the boulder. What were you doing?'

'I saw an opportunity to convince them the treaty is good for Exilon 5. More important, it offers us the same protection as the Indigenes.'

Tanya released a puff of air. 'The treaty means nothing to us. We no longer involve ourselves in human matters. All that matters is transcendence and when we reach the final stage, a human-Indigene treaty won't matter to anyone. We will have transcended our human bodies. Nothing can stop us.'

'But what about the Conditioned? What will happen to us?' said Simon.

Tanya walked away and Simon winced from the pain of his beating.

'The Conditioned must learn that not everything is free. At some point, they will have to earn their place in this world.'

Simon stared after Tanya as his last hope for a better life slipped away. If the Elite transcended, there would be nothing to stop others from taking the Conditioned down. The Elite had protected them throughout their changes, passed down strength and resilience to their charges. But since the environ had been built, Simon had seen no further effort made to protect them, especially from Tanya,

As a slower moving Tanya disappeared around a corner at the back of the raised platform, Simon vowed to stop this transcendence from happening.

Tanya wanted more power. He would start there.

25

Bill was being his usual stubborn, silent self. How dare he tell her what she felt or didn't feel? Or that she should abandon their home to work out what she wanted? Laura knew her own mind.

But on the ride back, while a tense Bill pretended to do work on his DPad, she couldn't stop thinking about what he'd said. Yes, she wanted to know what this all meant for her. She'd felt unsettled for years now, and even gone so far as to hide her Indigene skills. But as the problems with the rogue groups mounted and the GS increased their activities, her instincts were at their strongest.

The car swapped the undeveloped landscape and new building sites for the developed metropolis of New London. Bill still pretended to work. She'd seen him pissed off before, but never this angry.

'You're acting like you're done with me.' She watched for his reaction, unable to read his mind. Something she was glad for, because she didn't want to know Bill's thoughts during one of his silent treatments. 'Are you ever going to talk to me?'

His lips, a thin, white line, twitched. 'Of course.'

'So why the silent treatment?'

Bill sighed. 'I'm working.'

She hated this distance between them. She could usually get him to drop the silence with a joke or a laugh, but lately not much worked.

Her denial of her Indigene side had put a wedge between them. Bill was right. She needed to deal with it if they were to get past it. But Laura worried that getting past it might not include Bill. She had to know.

'How long do I have to decide this?'

Bill shifted in his seat, not taking his eyes off the screen. 'I need you gone as soon as possible. I can't stand this any more.'

She touched his arm, feeling his tension lift a fraction. 'Bill, look at me.'

'I can't.' His voice cracked. 'If I do, I'll change my mind.'

The car arrived back at their apartment and parked outside. Laura stayed in the car, determined to get through to her pig-headed husband.

'Bill, look at me.'

He huffed out a breath and looked at her. She saw tears in his eyes and the sight almost broke her.

'I don't have to go yet,' she whispered.

He rested his head against the seat, keeping his soft gaze on her. 'Yes, you do.'

'I could leave this evening.'

Bill closed his eyes for a moment. He reached for her and brought her hand to his cheek. 'I don't want to spoil our good memories. This has to be it.'

Laura snapped her hand back. 'Stop saying that. I'm only going for a while, just to sort things out.'

'No, you need to deal with your feelings, like I

must.' She heard the new break in his voice and almost changed her mind about going. 'If you decide that you don't want me any more—'

Her heart thumped against her ribcage. She leaned forward and held his face with both hands. 'I will always want you.'

'You've been unhappy for a while and I've been ignoring it.' He pulled her hands away. 'When I saw you with Stephen, you looked so natural.'

'I haven't been unhappy with you. True, I've been repressing my Indigene side, but so what? That doesn't mean this is the end.'

Laura swallowed back a lump in her throat.

'I don't know what this means.' Bill stared at his hands, which still held hers. 'Whatever happens, I'll accept it. I won't hold you back from the life you need.'

'You're what I need.'

'I love to hear you say that, but you need more. Please, Laura, don't make this more difficult than it is.'

Laura pulled her hands back a second time and slumped in her seat. 'How long do I have?'

'The sooner you leave the better. I can leave the car for you.'

'That won't be necessary.'

Laura used what little time they had together to look at Bill, to commit his face and the sound of his voice, even the smell of him, to memory.

She nodded, dried her tears and opened the door. 'I'll be out by the time you're finished work. Will you explain to Julie that I'm taking a few days off?'

Bill didn't respond but she felt a tiny displacement of air on her skin that told her he'd nodded.

'This isn't the end, Bill.'

She got out before he had a chance to refute her

statement. *Damn it.* Bill was right; the part of her she'd denied for years was finally coming between them. She was stuck. She needed get unstuck and see what part of their relationship they could still salvage.

The car drove off with Bill in it; he was probably heading to the office. With a heavy heart, Laura climbed the stairs to their apartment on the top floor. She opened the door to an instant greeting from the LightBox. She swiped at her eyes and commanded it to turn off. It didn't take her long to pack a few clothes, but she took some time to search for the perfect photo of Bill, for when her memory of him faded.

She stopped mid search. What was she doing? She was only going for a few days, not long enough to forget her husband's face. This wasn't the end. It felt like the beginning of something else. Would there be a place for Bill when it was all over?

Laura tucked the photo inside her bag alongside a few changes of clothes and some personal items. Then she left the apartment and began the thirty-mile journey to District Three.

☼

Laura took the Maglev train for New Singapore as far as the border ten miles away. The next stop would be the new city. She covered the last twenty miles on foot using her Indigene speed to get her there faster. An hour later she arrived at the main hatch that accessed the underground tunnels. Laura descended into the cold, dark pits of Indigene life.

The dark had used to bother her once. That had been before Stephen had treated her Seasonal Affective Disorder, which had mutated her cells and almost killed

Genesis Variant

her. To counteract the change, he'd forcibly changed her into an Indigene then reversed the effect when she'd wanted to become human again.

It was the reason she was here. Even though she looked human, it felt like someone else shared her body.

She stood outside the access door to District Three. A bioscanner embedded in the rock face scanned her. Her Indigene mutations cleared her for entry. The door, made of the impervious omega rock, opened and she walked through the environmental barrier protecting the air inside the district.

The air thinned, forcing her to use her gel mask. She slipped it from her bag and pressed it over her nose and mouth. It conformed to her face to give it a tight fit. The oxygen canister she wore on her hip, which connected to the mask with a thin tube, stirred memories of her time on Earth. She didn't miss that world. And neither did her mother, who lived comfortably in New Taiyuan and who was learning Chinese from a pair of immigrant women hailing from the original city on Earth.

A blur of light rushed towards her. Laura smiled as Arianna, with her elfin face and grey eyes, hugged her. She looked different to Serena, who was tall and had the most beautiful blue eyes she'd ever seen. But Arianna had a quirky style to her that Laura thought gave her a unique look. She saw why Anton adored her.

She pulled back, her eyes wide. 'Laura, is anything wrong?'

Laura felt her search through her thoughts. She gave her partial access as she looked around. 'No, yes. I don't know.'

Arianna stared at her. 'Bill knows you're here.'

It was more of a statement than a question.

'Yes. And you now know what I can't say out

221

loud.'

'I saw it in you a long time ago,' said Arianna. 'So did Stephen, but there was no point us telling you. You had to feel it.'

Laura stood there with her bag of clothes, feeling stupid for dropping in on friends like she needed a place to crash.

'This is your home, Laura. Never feel uncomfortable here.'

'That's just it. I don't, even though I've arrived unannounced.'

Arianna smiled and tapped the side of her head. 'I sensed you outside, your hesitation.'

Laura smiled back at Arianna, the Indigene who liked to fix others.

'I do not,' said Arianna.

'You do, but it's what's so lovely about you. You care about everyone.'

'Well, I suppose that's my empath side. It gives me insight into others' feelings to the point where they become my own. For my world to feel right, I need to fix theirs. That help doesn't always go down well. Come.' Arianna hooked her arm in Laura's and they walked. 'Let's get you settled first before you talk to Stephen.'

'I'm sorry. I don't mean to be a nuisance.' Laura slipped her arm out of Arianna's. 'I know you have a lot going on and my timing could be better.'

'Stephen won't mind. He could use the distraction.' Arianna reclaimed Laura's arm. 'Works too much as it is. Serena's always thinking it.'

Laura grinned at the problems of her Indigene friends, which were similar, if not identical, to her own. Bill was the worst workaholic she knew.

'I think that's why Stephen and Bill are friends,'

said Arianna. 'Because they share the same work ethic.'

'I guess so.'

Thinking of Bill made her feel sad.

'This isn't the end, Laura. It's the beginning. I feel you opening up to new possibilities, to the idea of your Indigene side. This visit has been a long time coming. Stephen will be pleased to learn you're here. If he's not too preoccupied with other things, he may already have sensed you.'

They walked a short distance until they reached a part of the underground network the Indigenes had converted into space for their human visitors. It was the same space that Ben Watson had used when she and Bill had brought him here to see Stephen. Laura entered the room and passed through a new environmental barrier surrounding the bed. She put her bag down. This would be her home for the next while. She might as well get used to it.

'Don't worry,' Arianna said from the other side of the barrier, 'you're going to feel right at home.'

'That's what I'm afraid of.'

'No point in denying it. Explore your Indigene side. Now, come with me. It's time to see Stephen.'

26

Simon slept so little these days. Ever since the last mutation three months ago that had given him the ability to hear others' thoughts, he couldn't shake the extra voices from his mind. The voices of the Conditioned sounded like a stream of noise that played on repeat. The Elite's thoughts were mostly about transcendence and what would happen when they reached it. Those thoughts were interspersed with new discussions about Tanya's idea to use the Conditioned as vessels that would store a backup of their consciousness.

Tanya's words still rang inside Simon's head: 'We need more power. We must tap into it more.'

She referred to the Nexus.

Simon had a good idea how far Tanya would go to access more of the Nexus and reach transcendence. But he didn't know yet if he would be one of those selected for the task.

Even from inside his room, Simon's mind could detect Tanya and the other Elite, but he limited their chatter. It drained him too much. He felt Tanya's frustrations, heard her cries in her bedroom on the far side

Genesis Variant

of the staging area. The effects of the Nexus' healing were wearing off.

More power. That's all Tanya thought about. Her desires became a chant that drowned out the other Elite voices.

He had met with Ollie Patterson and Harvey Buchanan the day before to hire them to protect the cable. With some minor adjustments to the cable connectors, Simon had reprogrammed it to mine double the power. But each change in command required him to visit the isolated site and disconnect the cable. It left him and the cable vulnerable. The men had spotted him connecting the cable the first time round and offered their services. All they wanted in return was GS protection from the ITF. Simon had given them a promise, but in truth it was an empty one. Tanya cared nothing for the operation she once commanded or the people she once controlled. Harvey, who had taken payment in worthless, early, medical data from tests conducted on the Conditioned, wanted something extra: immunity from the GS—a deal he hadn't shared with his colleague.

But for all his efforts, double the power wasn't enough for Tanya.

She called out to him; it sounded like a roar in his head. He tried to shut her out, but she only roared louder. What would happen when Tanya and the others transferred a copy of their consciousness into selected Conditioned with fitter, more robust bodies? Bill had told him years ago about the effect a similar transfer had had on Anton. The Indigenes had almost lost him to the dominant imprint of Charles Deighton. Simon was certain Tanya would choose him, and he was even more certain her personality would take over the second her copied consciousness had a chance.

225

Tanya used her voice. 'Where are you, Simon?'

Telepathy that only worked one way, out not in, drained her too much. Every day, when she pushed too hard, he felt just how much. What he didn't tell her was his efforts to keep her out drained him too. She exhausted him.

He got up, feeling less like an individual and more like a pawn these days. The closer Tanya and the others neared their goal, the less space and freedom she afforded him.

'Simon, come. I need you.'

Simon took his time to reach the area beyond the staging room that housed Tanya's accommodation and separate rooms for the remaining Elite. He opened her door to find a hunched-over Tanya sitting on the edge of her bed. Her room was decorated similar to his, with just a sideboard and a mirror on the wall above a dresser. It took her some effort to look up at him. What he saw didn't surprise him. Her eyes had almost disappeared behind the deep wrinkles and saggy skin. There wasn't a sound in the room, but inside Simon's head Tanya wouldn't shut up. If only he could flick a switch to turn off his telepathic skill.

'What is it, Elite One?'

She licked her lips and pointed feebly at the dresser. 'I need water.'

Simon saw a jug and some glasses had been set out. Tanya had assistants for this work. She didn't have to wake him for this. He poured her a glass, grateful she couldn't hear his thoughts like he could hers. The intensive testing had destroyed the Elite's ability to communicate both ways.

Tanya mumbled out loud, but roared in his head. *Where is it?*

Simon handed her the water, wishing she would

shut up for one minute. She grabbed it between two withered hands and tipped it back. The water ran down her face and neck, soaking the collar of her white robes.

He took the half-finished glass from her when she thrust it at him. He set it down on the sideboard.

'I can't return to this life, not when I had new mobility just yesterday,' said Tanya. 'The machine, the double power... I need more. The Elite need more.'

Simon released a soft breath, relieved to learn Tanya still wanted to try the machine in the environ to regenerate. 'I'll arrange to visit the site of the cable.'

She wagged a finger at him. 'See that you do. I want to be twice as strong today as I was yesterday.'

Simon had no desire to tell Tanya the machine and the Nexus' ability to heal may have reached its peak. She would figure it out sooner or later. By then he hoped she would be too weak to carry out the command to imprint herself on Simon.

'Right away, Tanya.'

He headed out before Tanya could change her mind. He had no official way to contact either Ollie Patterson or Harvey Buchanan, but Simon had a vague idea of where they might be. They had promised him protection from human or Indigene attacks, something a team of Conditioned couldn't give him, and the work to program the cable took long enough that Simon would be vulnerable.

He tried the construction property first and watched from a distance as men worked on building houses. He observed another man isolated from the others who cursed while digging a giant hole. Simon wondered what he'd done to deserve that punishment.

Neither man was there, so he tried the power station next. He found Harvey sitting in his car scouting out the base station. Simon wished he could read human thoughts. But his mutations only gave him access to the thoughts of other Conditioned, and the Elite.

He approached the car and Harvey startled. He rolled down the window.

'I need you,' Simon said.

'Get in,' hissed Harvey.

Simon slid into the front seat. Harvey turned to stare at him.

'Where's your friend?' said Simon.

'Busy. What do you want?'

'I need more power. I have to do some adjustments to the cable again. Can you guarantee my protection?'

Harvey frowned at him. 'How much power?'

'Double again.'

He didn't want to take too much and risk Tanya seeing the fault in the machine's design: that the Nexus using it as a conduit couldn't do what she wanted.

'Double your double? What's the matter, your leader getting all withery again?'

'Something like that.'

Harvey smiled. 'I was actually looking for you. Turns out, I need more of your medical data.'

Simon had given him outdated data on the early tests performed on the Conditioned.

'I can't get you more.'

'Then we can't help you,' said Harvey. 'It seems that we're at an impasse.'

Simon would not risk working on the cable without protection. 'You don't understand; we need this extra power to work the machine.'

Simon needed it to stall Tanya.

'Because your grandma is getting withered and old without it? Yeah, I know how it works. But here's the

228

thing.' Harvey leaned closer, showing he didn't fear Simon. 'I went through the data you gave me and it's all outdated. Plus it doesn't address the tests performed on the Elite. I want to know what makes them much weaker than you, and why you built the machine, not them. If they underwent advanced testing, then that should make them superior beings, no?'

Simon didn't disagree. 'I guess the changes were too extreme for their bodies to handle.'

'Yes, it broke their evolutionary code. And I'd like to know how,' said Harvey.

Simon was curious to know why Harvey needed the information. 'Why is it important to you anyway? You can't do anything with the information. The doctors have all the equipment.'

Harvey clucked his tongue. 'Not for you to know, Simon. If you get me information on the Elite, Ollie and I will offer you protection out there.'

He nodded to where the cable ran.

'I told you it's impossible.'

He couldn't go back without double the power they had. Tanya would run with her alternative idea for transcendence.

'You accessed information on your changes, so you can figure something out. Until then...' He nodded at the station and made a cut off sign with his finger. 'Work with what you already have.'

'I'll see what I can do.'

Simon gritted his teeth and got out of the car.

He set off running and contemplated his options.

Option one: Get the medical information for Harvey. Impossible, because he'd already tried; the data was locked away somewhere.

Option two: Continue to heal Tanya using the

quantity of power they could mine.

Option three: Reprogram the cable alone and risk attack from the humans or Indigenes. Without Ollie or Harvey's help, they had no deal.

Option four, and the most likely outcome: Tanya would order the doctors to proceed with the imprint and Simon would be stuck with Tanya inside his head.

No, the last option couldn't happen. Maybe there was a fifth option. Could he increase the size of the access point to the Nexus, tweak the machine's numbers to make it seem like he'd mined more power? Tanya might still believe the machine would help her reach transcendence in her own body.

But it was just a delay tactic before Tanya realised what he'd done.

He needed some way to see what would happen. Simon knew of only one with the ability to see into the future. The time had come to ask for outside help.

27

A nervous Laura followed Arianna through the tunnels and the core of District Three. They passed by several Indigenes who greeted her with a mix of apprehension and politeness. She'd never felt at ease in the district; it was as though the Indigenes thought her to be an imposter. It's how they made her feel. Bill used to say, 'It's all in your imagination, love.'

But it wasn't. While her telepathy wasn't strong enough to read minds, she could sense, and sometimes see, the lies the Indigenes hid from her.

She was a fraud.

Arianna must have sensed her mood because she looped her arm in hers and pulled her along.

Her smile reached her eyes. 'Almost there.'

Laura said nothing while they passed through the core and exited the other side into a tunnel. From there, she let Arianna lead her to wherever Stephen was.

Arianna was a second-generation Indigene like Stephen and Anton. Her mother had worked with Elise back when they were both human, in the time before they had both been changed. Arianna had taken the longest to come round to the idea of hosting humans in the district. From what little Laura sensed from this strong empath with the ability to hide her emotions, Arianna no longer felt that way.

They arrived at a laboratory with a long bench against one wall and another that cut the room in half. Medical equipment was dotted on the various surfaces. At the back of the room, Laura saw a bed with a machine attached to one end; an arm from the machine extended over it.

'It's a 3D-image body scanner,' said Arianna.

Laura took in the rest of the room. 'What are we doing here?'

'Stephen has picked up on your presence. He asked me to bring you here. He's on his way.'

Laura walked inside the room and ran her fingers over the equipment that looked similar to items she'd seen in Harvey Buchanan's facilities on Earth. 'What *is* all this?'

'Anton's work. He's building a neurosensor.'

'A neuro-what?'

Arianna chuckled. 'It's a device that will allow us to read the GS humans' thoughts. They can block us. Or maybe block is the wrong word. It's possible their minds cannot be accessed with their specific genetic mutations. But either way, Anton has been working on the device to see if we can bypass whatever blockade they have.'

Laura stopped at the main bench and examined a round, black disc sitting on a piece of cloth. 'Is this it?'

A voice sounded from the doorway. 'Careful, I haven't tested it yet.'

Laura turned to see Anton enter the room. He wasn't as tall as Stephen and had a more relaxed energy to him.

232

'Sorry to frighten you. I rarely have guests while I work.'

Laura backed off from his work. 'I'm sorry, I shouldn't have...'

Arianna smiled, prompting Anton to do the same.

'You're always welcome here, Laura. Don't feel like you aren't,' he said.

Please excuse my one love for his insensitivity, said Arianna to Laura.

Arianna pressed her forehead to Anton's. He closed his eyes and smiled. Laura turned away from the intimate moment. Her fragile heart tugged as she thought of Bill: her husband, her confidante—her best friend. Would she still feel that way about him after she'd properly explored her Indigene side? It still shocked her he'd told her to go, and that she'd walked away, without a fight.

Arianna separated from Anton and cleared her throat. 'I'm sorry, Laura. We're being rude. Anton wants to know if you're his new experiment.'

Laura widened her eyes. 'I don't know. Am I?'

'Only if you want to be,' said Anton. 'To be honest, it's been a while since I've had a different mind to help test out my equipment.'

'Well, you're going to have to wait in line, Anton.'

Laura's eyes shot to the new visitors. Stephen and Serena stood at the entrance to the lab. All four approached her at once. Panic swelled inside her. She stepped back, feeling like the experiment Anton hoped she was.

She felt Stephen's mood darken as he said, 'Please, everyone, give her some space.'

'No, no, it's fine.' She stopped where she was, and tried to make light of it. 'I came here voluntarily. I'm intruding on your space.'

The others stayed put. Only Stephen approached, but he kept a small distance between them. While the others chatted silently, Stephen stared at her. His intensity became too much to bear.

She was about to break the mood with a joke when Stephen said, 'I sense your abilities; they're faint, but I'd like to study your brain connector paths.'

'My what?'

'Don't worry,' said Serena. 'He did this on me once. It doesn't hurt. It just maps out your brain, shows you what parts you're using, and what you're not.'

'What did you find out when your brain was mapped out?' said Laura.

'It showed me I used all areas, which is highly unusual.'

Laura didn't want to know how different her mind had become with her alteration, then rapid reversal.

With a sigh, she said, 'Okay, let's get this over with.'

Stephen gestured to the bed that, for some reason, scared Laura. A low hum of silent words from the others encouraged her to lie down. The others watched, like stone statues. She was used to the eerie stillness of the Indigenes. She'd caught herself doing the same while deep in thought. Bill had had to nudge her out of it once or twice. She wished she could read her husband's mind, and get a real sense of what he thought about her changes.

Stephen switched on the giant scanning machine and positioned the arm over her head. It hummed while the arm mapped out a perfect 3D representation of her brain in the space between the arm and the bed. Some areas on the image were lit up in red; others were darker.

She sat up and studied the image next to her. 'What does it mean?'

Genesis Variant

'It looks pretty normal,' said Stephen.

To Laura's surprise, that was disappointing to hear. She had expected to hear her brain was a little different. It would explain her ability to see lies as manifestations.

'No changes? I feel weird, I can see and feel when people tell lies, but you're saying my brain is normal?'

Stephen smiled. 'I haven't even begun, Laura. Patience.'

She swung her legs over the side of the bed. 'So what's next?'

'Now we push you to use whatever abilities you have, and see how your brain function changes. We'll start with simple telepathy.'

Stephen was suddenly in her head. *Talk to me.*

Laura frowned. *About what?*

Anything. I just want to get a baseline reading.

Okay... She paused. *I don't know what to say, Stephen.*

Okay, tell me about Bill.

I'd rather not, she replied quickly. *How about I tell you about my staff at the ITF?*

Okay, that will work.

Laura launched into an explanation of the work the ITF did and the staff Laura knew she couldn't function without. She mentioned Julie, the only person in the office who knew Laura's secret. She had rambled on for a while when Stephen stopped her with a hand on her arm.

'That's enough. Now, try to read my thoughts.'

Laura concentrated on Stephen's mind and met with an instant blockade. She tried to push past it. During her attempt, she sensed the others' curiosity, as though they, too, felt her attempts to reach Stephen's mind. Maybe they could.

She pushed harder against his blockade.

'What am I thinking about, Laura? Read my mind,' said Stephen.

She blew out a breath. 'I can't.'

'Okay.' Stephen studied the 3D image of her brain behind her. She turned and saw new parts of the image had lit up. 'Your ability to communicate telepathically comes easy to you, but only if others allow you access. To reach my mind is a step too far. That's probably why you can't read Bill's mind.'

'That's right. I can't read him. I never could.'

'But you are closest to him. You share a bond. I think, with time, you can.'

'What do you mean?'

'When I visited your home, I felt you try to reach him,' he said. 'But you hesitated, almost as if you didn't want to hear what he had to say. But it's not entirely your fault. Bill keeps his thoughts to himself and makes it difficult for others to reach him on purpose.'

That was true. Bill could be one stubborn human when he wanted to be. But talking about him hurt her too much.

'So what you're saying is I can communicate telepathically, but not very well?'

Stephen nodded. 'It's strange, but then again so are the Indigenes. We have become a bastardised lot. We don't know how the genetic changes manifest in some people. We're learning as we go. The GS 100 group is a perfect example of how little we know about the genetic experiments as a whole.'

But Laura needed a better answer. 'So am I Indigene or not?'

'Does it matter?'

'Yes. I feel human, then Indigene. I don't know which side to align to.'

236

Genesis Variant

'Why do you need to align yourself to one or the other?' said Serena. 'Why not embrace the best of both species?'

She wished she could. 'If I could, I wouldn't be here.'

Stephen turned off the scanning machine. 'I think the Nexus could help you. It's where Arianna helped Serena figure out what she is.'

The Nexus scared Laura. She had used it just once eight years ago, when she'd been caught between two species and close to death. The Nexus had healed her, or so Serena had said. Laura hadn't been conscious at the start of her use of it, but by the end, she had awoken to feel the most excruciating pain, like her joints were on fire. That's when Arianna had pulled her out of there. Laura wasn't too keen to return.

'Isn't there another way?'

'Well, you could hunt, test your skills that way,' said Stephen. 'Would you prefer to face down a wild animal that wants to rip the flesh from your bones?'

Laura did not. '*Fine*. The Nexus it is.'

'When you're done there,' said Anton, 'I would like Laura to test out the neurosensor. She is to us what we are to the GS humans. If she can break down our defences, then, theoretically, we should be able to break down theirs.'

28

'This is a pile of shit.'

'What is?'

Marcus leaned against a boulder along the GS boundary. 'Sitting here with you. Alone. In the dark. No offence.'

Clement, perched halfway up one boulder, spied on the environ. 'None taken. And I'm sure I would say the same if I could read your mind, human.'

Marcus ignored his Indigene companion and touched the neural blocker below his ear, the one Harvey had inserted under the skin that morning. Harvey said it could block his thoughts from the GS humans. Turned out, it worked on Indigenes, too.

He sighed. 'Like I said, no offence. And it's only fair since I can't hear you.'

Clement looked down at him. 'So what's the problem then?'

'I didn't come to this planet to be a grunt. I'm supposed to be someone important.'

The Indigene sneered. 'And you think you'll get there by following someone you don't even trust?'

How did he know...? Marcus looked up just as Clement tapped the side of his head.

'I caught all that before your new blocker started working. And I also know you only half followed my instructions.'

'I told him about your interest in switching sides.'

'It wasn't enough to weaken their suspicions against us. Your leaders still use the blockers.'

'I'm working on it.' Marcus sighed again. 'And no, I don't trust him. But that's not exactly fucking news.'

Clement turned back to the environ that Marcus couldn't see. 'No, it's not. But if you expect Harvey to promote you, you'll be waiting a long time. He doesn't trust you.'

Marcus stood back and challenged Clement. 'What do you mean by that?'

But the Indigene shrugged as if he'd just made a minor point. Since when was Marcus' life *minor* anything? He eyed the Indigene who he trusted as much as he did Harvey. It had been too long since he'd flexed his authority, shown people who was boss.

'What I'm saying is there are other options available to you,' said Clement.

'What, you mean joining your lot?'

Clement didn't look at him. 'It's not a bad life, Marcus. You would be well treated.'

The thought of becoming an Indigene didn't appeal to him, but a life of being Harvey's whipping boy appealed even less. At least Harvey's new blocker kept his thoughts and feelings private from his companion. It wasn't that long ago Marcus had commanded these creatures he thought of as inferior to him. But not on Exilon 5. Here, the Indigenes had more freedom than he'd expected.

His choices were to wait for Harvey to see his

potential, or consider another route.

'Thanks for the offer, but I don't fancy living in a cave and eating raw meat.'

Clement laughed once. 'There's more to us than that. For one, we live longer. We're physically stronger than the humans. Just think how you would match up against the likes of Harvey. But if you want that life, you must follow my instructions to the letter and report back about Harvey and Ollie's plans and whereabouts. I don't trust them.'

Ollie Patterson was insignificant in the scheme of things. Even Marcus could see he was no more than a *yes* man for Harvey. But he admitted to some curiosity about the life Clement offered.

'Why would you want *me* to join your little group of freaks anyway?'

'I wouldn't, but if you spy on Harvey, report back what he says, I'll put in a good word with my elders.'

Elders? Such an old-fashioned word.

Clement continued. 'I can't hear his or Ollie's thoughts any more because of the same style blockers they wear. I need to know what they both have planned.'

Marcus considered his options. 'I'll think about it.'

☼

It was after midnight when Marcus returned to the halfway house. His muscles still ached from the hole he'd been forced to dig for the past few days. No more proving himself to Harvey. Marcus had already done that with Gaetano Agostini.

He stopped in the kitchen to get a glass of water. The air on Exilon 5 was drier than the oxygen he'd become used to on Earth. He noticed the dining room door

240

Genesis Variant

was open. Marcus glanced in to see Harvey sat at the table engrossed in something on his DPad. He looked up when Marcus lingered by the door.

'How did it go?'

'Nothing happened. All was quiet in GS land.'

It was the truth. He and Clement had waited for two hours; no movement from the caves or the environ.

Harvey returned his attention to the DPad.

'I don't trust them,' he said.

Marcus recalled the exchange between Harvey and the GS human that Ollie hadn't seen. It was clear Harvey played both sides.

But Marcus just nodded. 'They're keeping to themselves alright.'

Harvey shook his head. 'Not the GS humans. The Indigenes.' He looked up. 'How did you get on with Clement?'

'Fine.'

'Did he try to convince you to go against me?'

Marcus shook his head. 'Why would he? They want the GS humans gone too. That's what you and Patterson want, isn't it?'

'Patterson doesn't have a clue.' Harvey looked off to the side. 'The GS humans are a genetic evolution and I can't help thinking we're protecting the wrong species—the Indigenes—from extinction.'

'What do you mean?'

'At least the GS can't read our thoughts.' Harvey waved his hand and resumed his study of data. 'Nothing. Get some rest. That hole won't dig itself tomorrow.'

But Marcus paused by the door. 'I wanted to talk to you about that. What's the hole for exactly?'

'Drainage,' said Harvey, a little too fast.

'Look, John.' Marcus addressed Harvey by his

241

alias. 'I came to this planet to better myself. And I know your background. You told me.' He lowered his voice. 'And I also know about your meeting with the GS human.'

Harvey's eyes narrowed. 'How do you know about that?'

'I followed you.' He shrugged. 'It doesn't matter. What I want is a meeting with them.'

Harvey scoffed. 'What for?'

'To see if it's a life worth pursuing.'

Harvey rocked with laughter. 'The GS humans— even when they were World Government board members —wouldn't entertain you on Earth, so why would they do it now? They are genetically superior beings. They eat your kind for breakfast, past and present. Now get that stupid notion out of your head.'

Marcus balled his fists to control his rising anger. 'So why don't you change me then? Into an Indigene? You know how.'

Harvey looked incredulous. 'You hate those things. You said so yourself. Now you want to be like one? Sorry, you'll have to do better than that to convince me.'

'I never said I hated them—'

'You tried to have them all killed on Earth. Remember who you're speaking to.'

How could Marcus forget? Or what Harvey thought of him?

'I want a better life here than I had on Earth. I don't want to dig holes the rest of my life. That's all I'm saying.'

Harvey levelled a glare at him. 'I told you before, I own you.' His voice dipped dangerously low. 'I tell you what you will become, not the other way around. Got it?'

Marcus nodded, if only to kill this conversation dead. Harvey resumed his reading. Marcus had gotten the information he needed. Carrying his glass of water in one hand, he climbed the stairs and planned his next move without Harvey.

29

Laura's unease never left her, not even when the pressure-filled day gave way to the quieter night. She followed Arianna and Serena to the Nexus, hesitating at the entrance to the tranquillity cave she'd only been in once before. She'd been a half-formed Indigene then, drifting in and out of consciousness. Her memories of her time then were just snippets. One thing she remembered was the feel of cool arms around her. Arianna said it had been Anton who'd carried her down the steps into the individual unit. She'd felt a strange blast of light followed by the sensation of being pulled into a hole. She had resisted, that much she remembered. The rest was a blur, except for the scorching pain that lit her joints on fire and made her want to hurl.

Now, as they stood outside the caves once more, Laura couldn't seem to get her feet to move.

'Are you sure about this?' she said to the others. 'Isn't there another way to test it? I mean, you have all that equipment. Maybe I could try the neurosensor thingy on Stephen.'

Arianna smiled. 'Later. Your fear is rolling off you in waves. This will not be like the last time. I promise. The

Nexus reacted to the human part of you. It saw you as a virus and tried to fight you off with heat.'

Laura's laugh came out as a hiccup. 'Is that what it was doing?'

'Come on,' said Serena. 'Arianna and I will stay with you the whole time.'

Laura shuffled forward, then a little more, until she was inside the cave and stood over one unit. She had to do this. Whatever the changes inside her, they were affecting her relationship with Bill. She owed it to him to find answers, to be honest about what she needed and wanted. And she guessed it started with the Nexus.

She looked at Serena. 'Do I just get in?'

Serena nodded. 'Arianna will accompany you to show you how to connect. It works better if it's just one connector per unit.' She waved at Laura. 'See you on the other side.'

Laura was about to retort with something smart when Arianna jogged down the stone steps into the hole. She followed her, using the cool wall to steady her descent. At the bottom, Arianna sat cross-legged on the stone floor and motioned for Laura to join her.

'It's easier if you sit,' she said. 'And try to relax.'

Laura did the first part. The second part gave her more trouble.

She drew in a deep breath, watching Arianna as she closed her eyes.

'Copy me, Laura, and try to think of positive things. The Nexus doesn't like negative energy.'

Positive things. She sucked in a deep breath. Easier said than done. She closed her eyes and thought of Bill, and the happy years they'd spent together. She smiled when she remembered how they'd met, when she'd followed him down a dark alley in Sydney only to have

245

him turn the tables on her. It had been the start of a friendship that would weather the stormiest of Bill's moods before it turned into love for both of them.

In her mind, the wall changed to a golden lattice. Something warm and bright snaked through the lattice and touched her arm.

She scooted back and opened her eyes. 'What the hell is that?'

Arianna, with her eyes still closed, touched her leg. 'Relax. It's just a tendril from the Nexus. Don't fight it. Let it pull you inside.'

Laura sucked in another deep breath and closed her eyes again. She watched the tendril wrap itself around her arm. A sharp tug first, followed by the sensation of falling, unsettled her. She tried to fight it but the momentum carried her through the lattice. On the other side, the tendril let go and her body—in the form of energy—felt light and free. She floated above a collection of bright orbs at the centre of a three-sided, orange and golden wall. The fourth side, where she'd come though, appeared to be hundreds of entry points into the Nexus. The wall of shimmering energy connected with the entry points to create a full circle around the orbs at its centre.

Laura laughed and a burst of energy, warm and gentle, rippled through her—different to the searing pain she'd felt before. She watched two new energies enter the Nexus. She sensed them as female energies; how she knew that, she didn't know. The Nexus must be exaggerating her ability to sense things. She recognised the distorted voices as belonging to Arianna and Serena. Their energies stopped next to her.

'It's the Nexus; it taps into the gamma rock and uses its amplification properties,' said Arianna. 'Everything inside here is enhanced.'

Serena floated closer to the wall. It sparked with unrestrained energy.

Laura panicked. 'What's she doing? It's dangerous.'

Arianna chuckled next to her. 'Don't worry. Serena has a special relationship with the Nexus that the rest of us don't. I'll be curious to see how it reacts to you.'

'Me?' She kept an eye on Serena's energy, which floated close to the sparks. 'Why?'

'We altered you fully then reversed your treatment to change you back to human. Yet you retain some Indigene skills and sometimes feel like us. I feel your connection to this life, even if you don't.'

Laura wanted to say she felt it too, but she didn't want to think about what that meant for her and Bill.

Serena's proximity to the sparks caused Laura to squeak, 'Watch out!'

She looked away from the wall but didn't hear anything. She looked back to see Serena had connected with the wall. The slow pulse the wall gave out changed into a deeper, rolling movement. The sparks that had appeared dangerous appeared only to fuel her energy. It was as if Serena had a symbiotic relationship with the Nexus.

'That's exactly it,' said Arianna, in response to her private thought. 'Serena tamed the Nexus and turned it into a more trusting entity. It follows her command and when she enters the space, naturally, the Nexus gets excited at her presence. It benefits the other users because when she's around, the Nexus puts out more energy.'

Laura hadn't expected any of this. 'Amazing.'

'None of us expected it. She and Stephen were using the Nexus at the time. She had a rough experience and the Nexus knocked her about.'

'What happened?'

'She was okay, but shaken,' said Arianna. 'I worked with her after, came back here. We soon realised the Nexus wasn't trying to harm her; it wanted a deeper connection with her. She can influence others. The Nexus was drawn to the raw energy she had yet to harness. I guess you could say they evolved together, found their true power. If I were to give the Nexus form, it would be a young wolf. It has bonded with her and follows her around.'

Laura continued to watch Serena's energy ride the wall's deep, rolling movement. The pulsations slowed until they returned to the gentle ripple they had been when she'd first entered. Serena disconnected and floated back to where Laura and Arianna waited, over the bright ball of energy in the centre of the Nexus.

'Sorry, I was just saying hello. He misses my energy.'

'He?' said Laura.

'To be honest, I'm not sure if it's male or female. Feels too boisterous to be female.'

'Are we ready to try some expressions?' said Arianna.

Expressions?

'Yes,' replied Serena. 'We're going to tap into the skills of other connected users, see how you express yourself in their company. The Nexus will boost any connection you make and it should show us where your best abilities lie.'

'I... okay. What do I do?'

'We need to move right into the centre of the ball,' said Arianna. 'This will work fast. Many things will hit you at once. Fight off what hurts, and embrace what feels easier. Do you understand, Laura?'

Genesis Variant

'Not really, but I'm here so let's try it.'

Avoid hurt; embrace easy. She could do this. They moved closer to the collected energies. They were so bright, it hurt her to look at them. The closer they got, the more she heard the murmurings that sounded like a collection of voices.

'Everyone's defences are weak at the centre of brightness, including the Nexus,' said Serena. 'We have to be careful about who gains access to this central space.' Laura felt honoured to be granted access. Serena pointed to the energies. 'Join the centre, and let's see what happens.'

See what happens? She hesitated at the edge of the collected energy, but not for long. Something drew her mass of energy right into the centre. Voices all around consumed her mind. The brightness dazzled her to the point of blindness. She couldn't see her way out. She grappled for something to hold on to, but found only air. Her body on the outside panicked the same as her energy on the inside.

Laura looked up just as the energies shifted their attention away from each other and to her energy. She tried to swim out, but the brightness surrounded her.

Voices felt like drills inside her head. *Fight the hurt. Embrace the easy.* That's what Arianna had said. She erected a barrier inside her mind and pushed against the pain. The voices lessened.

Next came the feelings. Her mind flooded with emotions that overwhelmed her to the point where she felt she might cry. It was all too much and it hurt. She fought against them.

The feelings lessened but the battle for control raged on inside her. Colours hit her next, yellows, greens and blues attached to other energies. Laura felt no pain, so she granted the colours access. They danced before her eyes.

But soon the bright display faded. A darker energy hidden beneath the brighter ones came for her. A gasp escaped her lips on the outside as her energy tried to escape from it. But the dark energy barrelled down on her position. She braced for impact. It passed right through her, leaving her winded, but otherwise unharmed. She turned to see the energy doubling back for her. This time she was ready. It slowed upon approach and merged with hers temporarily. Her own light lessened to accommodate the darker one. She had expected to feel pain, trauma, but she felt a weird connection to it, as though it were her missing piece.

The energy stayed connected for a few minutes before it detached and merged with the collected energy. Then the dark spot faded into nothing.

A route opened up and Laura floated out of the centre of energy. Serena and Arianna joined her.

'Let's disconnect first, then we'll talk,' said Serena.

Laura returned to her body. She opened her eyes and climbed out of her unit. Both Indigenes waited for her at the top

'How do you feel?' said Serena.

'Weird, if I'm being honest.' She turned to look back inside the unit. 'What the hell was that?'

'The others were testing you. Tell me what you felt.'

'Well, the voices hurt, and so did the emotions, but not the dark energy. That felt part of me.'

'The bad news is you're not a full Indigene,' said Arianna. 'You can converse telepathically, but it doesn't come naturally. Nor are you an empath, like me.'

Laura hid her surprise and disappointment. 'That's

the bad news? What's the good news?'

'The dark energy was your human side. It manifests as such because it can't convert into energy like the Indigene side does.'

'Is that a good thing?'

'It depends on whether you want to know if you're more one thing or the other.' Arianna shrugged. 'The answer is you're equal parts human and Indigene.'

Laura had suspected it wouldn't be that easy. 'So I'm stuck with partial abilities and a weird attachment to this life, but also my human life?'

'Not many people get the chance to skirt both sides of the fence,' said Serena. 'When the human doctors turned me from human to Indigene, I still felt a connection to my past life. Then, when I found out what I was, I had the choice to turn back. I chose this life because it felt right.'

'So how do I choose?' said Laura. 'I don't want to be unfair to Bill.'

'Why do you need to choose at all? Can't you just have both?'

'And leave him every time I have the urge to come here?'

She didn't see how that could work.

Arianna touched her shoulder. 'You did well in there. Why not stick around a bit longer, try this life on for size? Maybe help us test Anton's neurosensor?'

Laura needed a distraction now. Because going home while she felt this way, torn between two lives, wasn't an option.

She had no idea where home even was any more.

251

30

It had been forty-eight hours since Bill had spoken to Laura. As he paced his tiny office, it felt like longer. Stephen hadn't been in touch either. His attempts to distract himself with work had only worked for a short while. Just one question replayed in his mind: Should he have told Laura to go?

His head said yes; he'd noticed the changes for a while now, minor ones that had begun soon after her initial reversal from Indigene to human eight years ago. Not counting the changes in the lead up to Laura's forced transformation, she had been Indigene for just one day. Post reversal, she still remembered her life, but her reflexes had been much improved.

His head said yes. His heart said no.

It felt like he'd abandoned her when she needed him the most. He swapped his pacing for the window and stared out at the grand designs that dominated this part of town—a replica of the war office among the grandeur. The changes to her behaviour had been subtle: her restlessness, her preference to stand not sit, her ability to sense when others were lying. She'd told him the lie appeared to her as a physical manifestation of itself, like a black cloud that followed a person around.

With a sigh, he sat down and pulled up the Wave chatter that he'd asked Julie to forward to him in his wife's absence. He was grateful Julie hadn't asked any questions. She was the only person who knew about his wife's double life.

A knock on the door surprised him. It opened and Julie stuck her head round. 'Do you have a minute?'

Bill gave her a sharp nod and she slipped inside the room. The sound of intermittent beeping from monitors in the next room faded when she closed the door.

'There's a boy downstairs, says he needs to speak with you.'

'A boy? What does he look like?'

Julie tucked her blonde hair behind her ear. From some angles, she reminded him of Laura. 'More teen, I suppose. Tall-ish, lanky, black hair. Ben something. Says it's urgent.' She thumbed behind her. 'I can have security remove him if you'd prefer?'

Bill stood up. 'It's fine. I know him. I'll take care of it. Thanks, Julie.'

She nodded, but lingered by the door. 'If you have a moment, I could use you on the first floor. We've got a lot of chatter and not enough people to monitor it.'

Bill rubbed the tiredness out of his forehead and said, 'I'll be there as soon as I can.'

Julie left and Bill wasn't far behind. He took the lift to the ground floor. Given everything going on, Bill had forgotten about the boy for whom he'd gained safe passage to return to Exilon 5. He hadn't felt the need to check on him at his new accommodation. Mrs Hegarty was a tough landlady, but also kind.

The lift doors opened. He passed through the

security station and entered a room before security that was reserved for uninvited guests. He found a pacing Ben.

Ben turned when he entered and his expression brightened. 'Great, I didn't think they were going to let me see you.'

Bill's guilt reared its head suddenly. 'I'm sorry I haven't checked up on you. There's a lot going on at the moment.'

'I don't care about that. I just needed to chat to you for a minute.'

'How's your accommodation working out?'

'Yeah, okay. Mrs Hegarty's nice. It's a change from Waverley neighbourhood. I still have a curfew, but if I miss it, at least I won't be killed.'

Bill shuddered at the reminder of recent conditions back on Earth.

The boy waved his hand dismissively. 'But that's not why I'm here. I thought you could use my help.'

Bill had no time for this. 'I'm sorry, but everything we do here is confidential. I have no use for you.'

Ben grew angry. 'I told you when we met that I wanted to be useful. All I'm doing is sitting in the house, or going to school with kids way younger than me. I'm way past what school can teach me. Returning after eight years is too much of a culture shock. I can't be expected to live a normal life, not after what I've seen.'

'So you want practical skills training, is that it? I can arrange for Mrs Hegarty to set that up—'

'No! I want to work here.'

'I'm afraid that's not possible.'

'Why not?'

'I told you. The work is confidential.'

'So I'll sign a privacy waiver. I can keep secrets. Been doing it my whole life.'

'It's not that.' Bill rubbed his eyes. 'I just... this isn't a good time.'

'Look—' Ben stepped into his personal space, forcing Bill to step back. '—I know the trouble you're having with the Indigenes and the GS humans. It just so happens I'm good at finding shit out. Just ask Jenny Waterson if you need a reference.'

Bill had heard good things from Jenny about Ben's efforts to help break the criminal factions' hold on the neighbourhoods.

'I've heard and I know you'd be good, but I just can't accommodate—'

'Give me a trial run. You don't even have to pay me.'

Bill stared at the ambitious teen who reminded Bill of himself at that age. 'And if I say no?'

The boy's eyes danced. 'Then I'll keep coming back every day until you accept.'

The door opened suddenly, causing Bill to wheel round. 'What?'

Someone from Laura's team stuck their head in. 'Sorry to interrupt, but Julie needs you on the first now. Says it's urgent.'

'It's always bloody urgent. Fuck.' He stared at the teenager, who showed no signs of leaving. Bill relented with a sigh. 'Fine, but you sign a confidentiality statement first and you don't interfere with anything. Got it?'

Ben nodded with a grin on his face. 'Whatever you say, boss.'

☼

Bill brought Ben to the first floor after making him sign his life away and swear never to disclose anything he learned in the ITF. He found Julie sitting at her station.

She looked up, then frowned at Ben. 'We have a guest?'

'This is Ben Watson. I thought you might find a use for him.'

'He's a little young, Bill. What is he, sixteen?'

'Don't let his age fool you. This boy has seen a lot and he knows how to keep his mouth shut. While Laura's away, we could use the extra help.'

Julie shrugged. 'I guess I could put him on sorting.'

'No, put him on chatter.'

The others in the room looked up.

'Chatter?' said Julie. 'Are you sure? That's highly sensitive information coming out of there.'

'I'm sure. He's all signed up and he has a head for detail. He'll be fine.'

Julie shrugged. 'Okay, I'll get him sorted in a minute, but there's something I wanted to show you. A new discussion came through on the chatter just now.'

'Show me.'

Julie pulled up a screenshot of the chatter. 'There's talk about a meeting near a section of the power grid's cable. Ollie Patterson sent a few men to watch while one of the GS humans tampered with that intelligent cable you discovered. Another man was mentioned. A John Caldwell?'

Harvey Buchanan's alias.

Bill didn't like the sound of that. 'What were they doing out there?'

'Well, we have reports from Frank at the base station that the GS has doubled their mine of power.'

'Doubled their double? Fuck. Since when?'

'Since last night.'

Bill had ignored the goings on at the station—the

256

thing with Laura had distracted him too much. Truth was he couldn't concentrate while she was gone.

'Order the tech team to erect a localised force field around the damn cable and the station. Caldwell and Patterson may be accessing the station using hacked codes.' He turned away and bit his thumb. 'What the hell do the GS want with the extra power?'

It was clear he and Laura had received a version of the truth from Simon and Tanya at their previous two meetings. Bill now suspected the Elite's plans to grow old gracefully had changed.

He turned back and knocked on the desk. 'There's something more going on with the GS humans and I want to know what.'

'You got it. And Caldwell?'

Bill looked at an eager Ben. 'Consider this your first assignment. I want you to monitor every piece of chatter that mentions his name. It's an alias for Harvey Buchanan, so check for that one too.'

Ben nodded. 'Don't worry. I'm very good at finding out stuff.'

Bill slapped him on the back. 'I guess we'll find out.'

31

Simon wasn't sure how he'd managed it. Tanya's lead doctor had left his bag unattended in the staging room. In it was a DPad that most likely contained information on the changes to the Elite. Tanya must have asked Dr Jameson to bring the data with him. The information rarely left the New London clinic. When it did, the doctors used an encrypted channel and an isolated monitor to access the information on site via the lab area across from the staging room.

Simon stood in the Elite's room alongside Dr Jameson where he discussed Tanya's idea to use hosts.

To Simon's relief, Tanya said, 'Not until we've exhausted the grid's power and the machine's usefulness. I would prefer to try transcendence in my body first.'

Jameson frowned. 'You might not be strong enough to cope with that.'

'That's my decision.' She nodded to Simon. 'Simon will reprogram the cable to take more power today, isn't that right?'

He nodded when both Tanya and Jameson stared at him.

'And if he can't get it?' said Jameson.

'Then we'll discuss hosting again.'

Her eyes flickered to him briefly but it was long enough to send a shiver down his spine. Tanya's thoughts were quiet today; he put that down to her preoccupation with the human doctor. She was on her best behaviour. Good behaviour or not, Simon still didn't want her taking up residence in his head.

'There's no reason why he won't get it, is there?' Tanya said.

Tanya glanced at him and he responded with a shake of his head. To be honest, he had no idea if Buchanan would even show. He'd contacted the man last night, had said he had data and would trade it for protection from a few of his men. Simon wasn't buying protection so much as immunity from attacks.

'I need to examine you, but,' Jameson glanced at Simon, 'somewhere more private?'

'In the laboratory, then. Simon, don't go far, we won't be long and I want to discuss with you the limits on how much power we can mine.'

Simon nodded, keeping close to the doctor's bag, which lay on the floor.

Jameson strode over to his bag. 'Hold on. I forgot something.'

Simon cursed silently at the doctor's remembrance. He expected him to take the bag and when Jameson reached in and grabbed what looked like a medical scanner, he held his breath. Jameson closed the bag, tucked it under one bed and left the room with Tanya.

Simon huffed out, and turned around in the empty space. Should he take the bag to the tech room, try to access what was on the doctor's DPad there?

He knelt down and pulled the bag out from under

the bed. As quietly as he could, he opened the zipper. The instant he did, he heard Tanya's thoughts becoming more alert, until the doctor distracted her with something.

Simon lifted the DPad out of the bag and hid it up the wide sleeve of his robe. He closed the bag and returned it to its hiding place.

He had just minutes, maybe, to copy whatever he could. He ran to the tech room and hooked the DPad up to the monitor. He was right about his assumptions: The DPad contained a wealth of information on the Elite's tests. But there was too much to copy. He settled for a small file to copy, something to appease Harvey in exchange for his protection.

The copy process took too long. Simon willed it to hurry up. When it finished, he settled his racing heart and disconnected the DPad. Then he raced back to the room. It was still empty.

But Tanya's thoughts became more active and he knew they were on their way back. With his heart in his mouth, Simon slid the bag out and slipped the DPad back in. The door opened just after Simon had pushed the still open bag back in place and stood up.

Tanya's gaze lingered on him and he worked hard to neutralise his expression.

'All appears to be normal, Tanya,' said Dr Jameson. 'But you're still too weak to proceed with transcendence.'

'Yes, yes. Nothing I don't know already. Simon will sort it though.'

She glanced at him. He nodded and slipped the micro file with the copied data into the pocket of his robe.

Jameson retrieved his bag from under Tanya's bed to slip the scanner back into it. He paused and frowned at the open bag.

The doctor's fingers grazed the pulling tab. 'Did

you leave this room unattended?'

'No, it was just me,' said Simon.

Jameson glanced between him and the bag. He did a quick check of its contents and rubbed his chin. 'I must be forgetting things in my old age.'

'Maybe we should get you inside the machine,' joked Tanya.

'The power from the Nexus isn't compatible with humans. It would kill him,' Simon said flatly.

'It was a joke, Simon.' She rolled her eyes for Jameson's benefit. She tried too hard to impress the doctors. 'He's far too serious sometimes.'

The unsmiling doctor nodded. 'I'd better get back to the clinic. We have a bunch of schoolchildren coming in for their inoculations.'

'Inoculations?'

'This planet has different bacteria, different soil. Even native-born children aren't immune from diseases that occur naturally here.'

Tanya nodded. 'Thank you, Jameson.'

'Call me when you've used the machine again.' Jameson picked up his bag. 'Then I'll examine you and make my final assessment on your viability to transcend in your current body. I'll see myself out.'

'I don't want you to leave the caves, Jameson.'

The doctor paused. 'I have to get back to the clinic. You know the arrangement. I split my time between here and there. The clinic work is refining the work I do here.'

Tanya waved her hand. 'Go, and keep using the secret tunnel, but return later. From now until transcendence, I want you to remain on site. Remember who signed off on your work privileges.'

Jameson pursed his lips. 'Of course, Elite One.'

The doctor left Tanya and Simon alone.

'What time are you scheduled to visit the site?' she asked.

Tanya thought Simon just went out and fiddled with the cable a bit. He hadn't told her about his payment for protection, or that the process of reprogramming the cable to accommodate more power safely took time.

'In an hour.'

Tanya nodded. 'I want all the power you can take. Can your machine handle it?'

'Yes,' Simon lied.

If he told her the machine had possibly reached its potential, she might proceed with Jameson's recommendations. He'd do what he could to stall Tanya.

'Good. See you soon.'

☼

Simon met Harvey Buchanan about a mile out from the power station. He wasn't surprised to see Ollie Patterson hadn't come with him. Harvey leaned against the black vehicle, hands in pockets.

Simon walked up to him and wasted no time. 'I need to take more power. Do I have your men for protection?'

'How much power?' said Buchanan.

'What does it matter?'

Buchanan smiled. 'I want to know how long I'll be without my men.'

'An hour, tops.'

Harvey pulled out one hand and held it out. 'Payment first. This had better be good.'

Simon fished the micro file out from his pocket. 'I got this.'

Harvey stepped forward and plucked the black coin

from Simon's hand. 'What's on it?'

'Information on the Elite tests. I could only get some, it was short notice, but with time I might get more.'

Harvey spun the disc on the top of his finger, then pocketed it.

'Do we have a deal?' said Simon.

Harvey smiled. 'I need to check what's on the disc first. You could be giving me crap data on the Conditioned tests again.'

Simon didn't have time for this. 'I'm expected back soon. I need to do this today.'

Harvey leaned against the car once more, glancing back at the power station in the distance. 'Sure, we have a deal.'

'Great, let's get going—'

'There's just one problem.'

Simon clenched his fists at the delay. 'What?'

'There's a new force field around the site where your cable connects to the main feed. How long will that take to get through?'

'Since when?'

'Since this morning.'

That was a problem.

He couldn't return to Tanya empty handed. 'I'll figure it out when I get there.'

Harvey pushed off from the car. 'Figure a way through it, then call me. That will give me time to check what's on the disc. Okay?'

'No, that's not okay. I need to do this now!'

Harvey shrugged. 'I can't guarantee men for this job until I know how long it will take. You said an hour, but that was before the force-field issue.' He opened the door and climbed in. 'Talk to you in a few days.'

Before Simon could react, the car was driving away

and with it his only leverage with Harvey Buchanan. He had to risk going out to the site alone. It could be a trap, but he couldn't go back to Tanya empty handed.

It took him five minutes to reach the site of the exposed main feed connector and his intelligent cable. He felt the sting of electricity surrounding the area before he reached the spot. It stretched about a mile out from the site. A localised force field, which meant something close by had to be powering it. He searched the perimeter of the field and spotted the black box just inside it.

'Shit.'

Simon touched the field but yanked his hand back when the power bit him.

He shook his hand out.

The sound of wolves baying in the distance accompanied him on his walk back. Hunting had appealed to him in the beginning, but no longer. At Tanya's insistence, all the Conditioned used synthesised protein injections for sustenance. Simon hadn't eaten the old-fashioned way for some time. While he walked around the perimeter again, his mind juggled through options. One man, the biggest meat eater he knew, popped into his mind.

The solution was less than ideal, but he had to try something. First, Simon needed a change of clothes.

Simon ran west to a set of houses that were part of the new build just beyond New London's city limits. He stole round back of one occupied property and yanked a set of clothes off the line. The house, without owners present or an active Light Box alarm, made it easy for him to steal a backpack from the hall closet. He rolled up his robe and tucked it into the bag. He needed to look like his old self where he was headed.

Simon crossed the city boundary and walked the

Genesis Variant

twenty miles to Whitehall and the glass block containing the ITF offices.

A security guard stopped him inside the lobby. 'What's your business here?'

'I need to see Bill Taggart.'

'He's not in,' snapped the guard.

The man was lying. Simon sensed Bill on the premises.

'I know he's here. Tell him his old boss wants to see him.'

The guard looked him up and down. Simon knew that with the right attire, he looked close enough to human again. His skin was pale after the alterations, not translucent like the Indigenes' skin. It was mostly his mind that had altered, not his appearance.

'Wait in there.'

The man pointed to a room just before the security scanner. Simon could bypass their security if he wanted, but he followed the man's instructions. He entered the windowless room. It held a table and two chairs. He stood in one corner, one hand on the stolen satchel containing the robes that he'd need for when he returned to the caves.

Outside, the guard spoke to someone. 'Says he knows him.'

A few minutes later, Simon heard the lift open and the recognisable heavy foot of Bill Taggart.

'Where is he?' Bill said.

'In there,' replied the guard.

Bill entered the room and closed the door.

His voice a low hiss, he said, 'Simon, you're the last person I expected to see here.'

Simon nodded. 'I didn't have a choice. I need to speak with you.'

Bill frowned. 'Does Tanya know you're here?'

265

'No, and she never can.'

'What's this about?'

'My life is in danger. I've tried to put off the inevitable but without power, I can't.'

Bill smiled and nodded. 'Ah, so you discovered our little force field? I'm sure you'll find a way around it, in time.'

Simon was desperate. 'I don't have time for games, Bill. I'm here to ask you for a favour.'

Bill's smile became a smirk. 'What favour?'

'Drop the force field and let me take as much power as I need.'

'In exchange for what?'

'For everything I know about Tanya's plans for the Elite.'

32

Laura waited with Arianna in Anton's lab following her time in the Nexus. Arianna had asked for her help to test Anton's neurosensor. There wasn't much Laura wouldn't do for the Indigene whom she thought of as her sister. Serena didn't join them, saying she had "elder" things to discuss with Stephen. She'd rolled her eyes at the word, causing Laura to giggle.

'When this is all over, I'm changing that term for something that better fits my youthful appearance.'

Laura couldn't agree more. From her stunning, blue eyes to her gentle, oval face and lithe body, the term didn't suit her.

Arianna stood next to her with clasped hands while Anton bustled around the lab with the energy of a young wolf. Stephen, Laura had observed, was quieter in general than Anton. Serena's calm energy tempered his more serious side. Arianna gave off a lighter vibe that Laura liked. It offset Anton's energy perfectly.

On occasion, Anton would look up and smile at the pair.

'He loves an audience,' said Arianna. 'Especially

when he has some new tech to try out.'

Anton moved faster than her old vision could ever have detected. But her improved Indigene vision turned the motion into one long, steady exposure.

Anton picked up a small, black box and carried it over to them like it was about to explode. Laura stepped back.

'It's not delicate,' said Anton, handing the box to Arianna. 'I get like this with all my inventions. Just ask Arianna.'

She nodded. *A ritual.*

Anton removed a small, round, glossy disc from the box. He popped it into a casing that appeared to be malleable, like it was made of silicone.

'For better adhesion,' said Anton.

'Where does it go?' said Laura.

'Here.' Anton tapped the side of his head. 'To enhance the neural pathways so we can improve our reach.'

He lunged at Laura with the disc covered in silicone and pressed it firmly to the side of her head.

'Does it remap the neural pathways?' she said.

'That's the idea.'

She stiffened at the thought of losing more of herself. 'Permanently?'

Anton smiled. 'No, you won't lose more of yourself.' Damn him and his ability to read her thoughts. She felt herself blush as he added, 'It's only temporary.'

She felt Arianna push gently against her defensive wall.

Keen to move the focus off her and to stop Arianna from probing her thoughts, she said, 'So what do I do?'

'The idea is that the neurosensor will allow you to break through the barrier protecting others' thoughts. And since we know you're not particularly good at keeping us out...' Anton stood in front of her and puffed out his chest. 'Test on me. Try to read my thoughts.'

Laura lifted both brows. 'How?'

'Concentrate on my mind and try to read it. I've cleared my thoughts and I have only one thing on my mind.'

Laura took a wild guess. 'Arianna?'

'She's good.' He rolled his eyes at Arianna. 'No, too easy for you. This one will require some digging.' Anton closed his eyes. 'Okay, go.'

Laura did the same and made contact with Anton in the same way she'd done with those in the Nexus. She found his connection; it felt like a small prickle in her own. Some basic thoughts were easy to find, like those of open-minded Evolvers. But with age came the ability to hide their thoughts. Laura couldn't read the minds of Evolvers older than ten years old.

She followed the path Anton wanted her to take—the one of least resistance. But something pulled her off the path to a different location. When Laura tried to take a new route, she met with an invisible barrier. She sensed where she needed to go, but the barrier stopped her from crossing.

'I can feel you trying to cross,' said Anton. 'Allow the neurosensor to do the work for you.'

Laura frowned and concentrated on the barrier. She had never been good at reading minds. It was her least favourite thing—to snoop in the minds of others.

'Concentrate on me,' said Anton.

'Sorry.'

She switched her focus back to the barrier to see she'd drifted away from it. She resumed her new path and felt the resistance build again. She drew in a deep breath and tried to open her mind to the neurosensor.

The barrier yielded a little when she pushed against it. Without the neurosensor, it felt like cycling a bike up a hill. With it, hands pushed her up that same hill. She rode the feeling and pressed further into Anton's mind. The barrier yielded to her and she heard Anton grunt.

She backed out a little until Anton said, 'Keep going.'

So she did. Laura entered a blackened space, a void in his mind. Something bright in the distance caught her mind's eye. She moved towards it and came across a pedestal bathed in a bright light. A box sat on the pedestal. Her fingers flicked open the clasp to the front, a move that elicited a new grunt from Anton. She lifted the lid and looked inside.

Her presence was yanked back so fast, it felt like an elastic rope had been tied around her waist. With a gasp, she opened her eyes to see Anton doubled over at the waist. He gripped the neurosensor between his fingers. She touched the side of her head to find nothing there.

Arianna was grinning at her.

Laura rushed an apology while Anton recovered. 'I'm sorry, Anton. I didn't mean to do that. Are you okay?'

He waved her off and straightened up. She was relieved to see him no worse for wear.

'So what did you see in the box?' he asked.

'A bottle of red wine. No label.' Anton smiled, but she didn't understand. 'What does it mean?'

He straightened up fully. 'It was a smell I came to hate. I don't know what vineyard it came from but Charles Deighton used to reek of it. When he imprinted on my mind, he left behind a few memories of things he enjoyed, like this wine. He drank it in a place called Les Fontaines.

Not in France, but some place that was a version of the city.'

'A bottle of wine is very specific, Laura,' said Arianna. 'I sensed you edging closer to his secret.'

'It was easy with the neurosensor, not so much without.'

'Sorry about that,' said Anton. 'I didn't like the lack of control. It felt too much like the time when I had Deighton in my head.'

Laura understood his reluctance to keep going. 'So does this mean it works?'

'I'd say that was the best indication it does,' said Anton.

'So what now?'

'Now I make more and Arianna entertains you somewhere else while I work. It was easy for you to break my mind because we are the same. But it will be tougher to break through the mind of an unknown species.'

Laura left with Arianna. Outside the lab, her stomach rumbled.

'Human food okay?' said Arianna.

Laura nodded. With the changes, she hadn't lost her interest in normal food. But she supplemented her diet with raw meat on occasion, when she got a craving for it.

They walked on.

'Bill will be impressed when he hears about your progress. Did you want me to invite him for a visit?' said Arianna.

'No.' Her reply came out too fast. Laura hadn't meant for it to sound so harsh. 'I'm not ready to see him.'

'But you will be, soon. I can feel your need for him increase.'

Laura stopped short of rolling her eyes at Arianna's empathic reply, based on feelings, not logic.

'I don't know. I mean, how did you and Anton end up together?'

Arianna laughed. 'That was easy. We were meant for each other.'

'No doubts?'

'None. But I'm not the person you should be asking about that.'

'I told you, I'm not ready to see him.'

Arianna shook her head. 'Not Bill. Serena. She was once human, then Indigene. Why not ask her why she chose to remain Indigene?'

Laura had thought about it, but one thing stopped her. What if, after everything, she chose the wrong side?

33

Bill watched an edgy Simon refuse to settle in the interrogation room. It was midday and he had a ton of work to do, but he couldn't ignore the visitor who promised him a major piece of the puzzle.

'Do you want to sit?' He gestured to the chair. Simon shook his head. 'A glass of water, then?'

Simon's pacing irritated Bill. Why wasn't he talking?

'The power,' said Simon. 'I need the force field gone and as much of it as you can spare.'

'Why? To power your machine?'

'Yes?'

'And that's the only reason for it?'

Simon sighed. 'The only one guaranteed to keep me alive. Bill, do you know what transcendence is?'

Bill nodded. 'Conversion from physical matter into pure energy. What's that go to do with—?' He paused. 'Is that what the environ is for? Is that why you need the power?'

'Sort of.'

Simon's unsettled movements looked like one giant

273

blur. It gave Bill a headache.

'Could you please sit, or just stop moving for a second?'

Simon glanced at him, then at the table. He sat down, but didn't look comfortable. Bill sat opposite him.

'The Elite's minds have altered beyond anything that's been attempted before. Their bodies, unable to keep up with the speed of alteration, have experienced accelerated ageing. The tests have stopped, but the ageing continues. We originally used the machine to reverse some of the damage. We used the mined power from the main feed to attract the Nexus to us.'

Bill shook his head at hearing this. 'You drilled through the rock to access the Nexus power?' Simon nodded. 'I didn't think it existed outside of the mind. How is that even possible?'

'The Nexus is attracted to energy. We created a power source and "called" it.'

'And it came? Just like that?'

'Yes. It worked to heal Tanya and the others for a short while. But the problem I have is the machine may have reached its design limitation. The Nexus needs more power. I would have to redesign the model. That takes time.'

Bill was confused. 'So why do you need more power if your machine can't accept it?'

'To appease Tanya. I can store it in a backup area that the machine can't access. The base readings show the sum of the power in the primary and backup storage units. She'll just think I got more power.'

'Is that why you met with Harvey Buchanan today?'

Simon looked surprised. 'Yes, how did you know?'

'Harvey was a geneticist on Earth. Don't you

remember him at all?'

Simon shook his head. 'I never had dealings with any geneticists. How did you come by him?'

'He sorted out new identities for me and Laura when we first came to Exilon 5. He also gave me the stabilising shot that halted Laura's changes when it looked like the Indigene DNA might kill her.'

Simon's patchy brows lifted. 'He was your contact in Magadan?'

'The very same. What help was he giving you?'

Simon clasped his fingers and sighed. Bill waited for the rest of the story.

'I needed his protection or immunity from the humans and Indigene groups he and Patterson control. The cable I use to mine the data is intricate and needs careful reprogramming before we can take more power. That long in the outliers without backup, I'm a sitting duck.'

'Good to know, Simon. But what did Harvey want in exchange for that protection?'

'He asked for test data on both the Conditioned and the Elite, but specifically the latter. I couldn't figure out what he wanted with it, but if he's a geneticist, that makes more sense.'

'A black market one at that. Tanya wouldn't have known him, but I'm betting Charles Deighton did.' Bill wanted to discuss Harvey's interest in all this, but Tanya's plans took precedence. 'Tell me what Tanya wants to do.'

Simon unclasped his hands and wriggled in his chair. 'I can't believe I used to sit in one of these all day.' He shook his head as if dislodging a memory. 'Tanya and her doctors are floating the idea of using us—the Conditioned—as hosts.'

'Hosts?'

'Yes, transcendence requires a healthy body and

Tanya and the other Elites are far from it. So they're considering using us as vehicles to achieve it.'

'And what happens to you?'

'Death, most likely.'

Bill leaned back in his chair. 'So why not walk away?'

'It would be the easiest and the hardest thing to do. I'm no longer human and I wouldn't be welcome in the districts.'

'It's better than being dead.'

Simon leaned forward. 'Someone needs to stop Tanya. Her plans for transcendence are bordering on narcissistic. The other Conditioned have no idea what's coming. I'm using the power to stall her, hoping she'll give up on the idea of transcendence. But soon she'll realise the machine is almost at full capacity.'

Bill could guess where this was headed. 'If your machine doesn't have enough power to achieve this transcendence thing, where will she head next?'

'The Nexus.'

Bill laughed at that absurd idea. 'The Indigenes won't give you access.'

'No, but she will attempt it in my body.'

'So you stop her.'

Simon huffed out a breath. 'Bill, don't you remember what happened to Anton?'

He did, through Stephen's recount of that time, and Bill's encounter when he'd discovered Elise's body after the explosion. 'So she'll be like an imprint?'

'A dominant one.'

Bill looked off to the side. A solution came to him.

He leaned forward. 'You'll just have to convince her otherwise. Wait for her to give up on the idea. Tell her you need to modify the machine, make it bigger.'

Genesis Variant

'I won't be able to stop her if she hijacks my mind.'

Bill frowned. 'Why not?'

'I got an idea of the power of the Nexus once, if you remember?'

Bill nodded. It had been at the beginning when Simon had just moved to Exilon 5 and was still someone Bill thought he could trust.

'The second Tanya feels that power for herself, she won't want anything else.'

This was not good. 'And transcendence, the energy they plan to become, where will it go?'

Simon shrugged. 'The Nexus absorbs it, I guess.'

No way. Bill wouldn't let that happen. 'We have no idea what their energy would do to the Nexus, how it would change it. We can't let her get that far.'

'That's why I'm here.'

'I'm listening.'

'I need to speak with Stephen. He's an envisioner, right?'

Bill nodded. 'He can only see short-term futures. Why?'

'Well, if we can see how this will play out, maybe we can put together a plan to protect District Three from attack. And I'm willing to accept any help in that department. If Tanya transcends using my body, I will no longer exist.'

Stephen would know what to do.

Bill nodded and stood up. 'I'll make arrangements. Can you be back after dark, about nine?'

Simon stood too. 'Yes. I have to get back now. But I promise I'll do everything I can to persuade her otherwise.'

Bill showed him out. He would call Stephen and arrange a meeting to discuss this disturbing news. But the

277

thought of seeing Laura again so soon made him hesitate. What if she was done with him? He wasn't ready to find out.

☼

In his office, Bill ended a call with Stephen. He didn't see another choice. Tanya's plans took priority over any issues in his marriage. He agreed to bring Simon at 10pm to a deserted location near the entrance to the district. Stephen was understandably nervous about having Simon in his district again. If Tanya used him as a vehicle, all of Simon's experiences would be laid bare for her to use.

He sat back in his chair and thought about Laura. Was she okay? He'd wanted to ask Stephen, but chickened out.

A knock on his door jolted him out of his thoughts. 'Come!'

The door opened and he half expected to see Julie. But he straightened up when Ben came into the room.

'Julie sent me. I've been doing some monitoring on the Wave.'

'Anything on Harvey Buchanan?'

His conversation with Simon had piqued his interest. What did Harvey really want with the Elite's data?

'No, nothing on Harvey,' said Ben.

Bill sighed and returned his gaze to his monitor. But when Ben didn't leave, he looked up.

'Was there something else?'

The boy looked like he was about to burst. 'Nothing on Harvey, but there is mention of his alias John Caldwell. He was with another man called Martin Casey?'

Bill sat up straight. Clement had mentioned being

paired with Casey.

'Buchanan—Caldwell, whatever—and another man, Patterson, have been hanging around the base station. I think they have access to it.' That was not new information to Bill. 'There's talk among the workers at the camp that both men don't stick around on site when there's work to be done. One guy, Martin Casey—the one who travelled with him—has been actively talking with one of the Indigenes using the Wave. He's giving the Indigene a blow-by-blow account of this Buchanan's movements.'

'What's the Indigene's name?'

Ben shrugged. 'Just a number. 375.'

It was most likely to be Clement.

Bill sat back. Jenny Waterson hadn't exaggerated about Ben's usefulness.

'You told Julie this?' Ben nodded. 'Okay, keep doing what you're doing and have Julie send me a screenshot of the chatter.'

'Already done. I did it before I came to you.'

Bill noticed a new message in his inbox. 'Good work. If you keep this up, you might have a career in espionage.'

Ben headed for the door. 'I'm just happy to be useful.'

'Trust me, you are.'

Ben smiled. 'I'll keep at it.'

He left the room, leaving Bill to ponder their next move. Harvey had just moved to the top of his list of people he needed to watch.

34

Simon changed back into his robe and buried the stolen satchel and the clothes he'd worn to the meeting with Bill Taggart at the back of the environ. He still had a few hours before he was due to meet with Bill again. On the way back to the caves, he concocted an excuse to explain to Tanya his lengthy time away.

He entered the observation room to discover an agitated Tanya waiting for him. Two of the Conditioned propped her up in her much weakened state. Simon knew she would entertain no delay with the power.

'Where have you been? You've been gone for more than an hour.'

'Everything's good, Elite One.' Simon moved closer to her. 'There's a small problem out at the site. The ITF has erected a force field around our cable and the point it connects to the main feed. I have assurances that the barrier will be removed soon.'

'How soon? Do we have more power or not?'

'Tomorrow at the latest. I just came back from recalibrating the machine so it will accept the new quantity of power.'

'Tomorrow? How am I supposed to wait that long?'

Tanya wasn't happy. Simon had been afraid of this.

'We still have the original power, just not more. I can give you a treatment to take the edge off.'

Tanya looked away and muttered, 'I shouldn't have told Jameson to go. He's the only one who can see this through. But he's on an assignment that demands his attention for the next twenty-four hours.'

Simon relaxed, hearing of the doctor's unavailability. Tanya would not proceed without him. A day—even twelve hours—could be long enough to speak to Stephen and figure out his next move.

Tanya glanced at her helpers behind her. 'Someone get me my chair.'

Simon helped to prop up Tanya while one of the assistants got her chair. Tanya's hard, raspy breaths shuddered through his hands. Would that sound be what he'd hear twenty-four-seven if Tanya hitched a ride inside his head? Tanya's smell—ripe and unwashed—drifted his way. He turned his head away. From the moment her health had taken a downward turn, Elite One had stopped looking after herself.

Not a moment too soon, the assistant returned with the chair and Simon offloaded Tanya into it.

She settled in and released a long breath. Everything looked to be an effort to her these days.

'Take me to the machine, Simon. I need a hit.'

He nodded, happy to pander to any wish that had nothing to do with hosting. He moved to the back of her hover chair and waited for her to initialise the magnetic levitation.

With the hover function enabled, Simon pushed Tanya to the environ as fast as possible. Inside, he switched on the machine while Tanya's assistants stayed outside. The machine whirred and powered up. He was relieved to see a contained ball of energy waiting in the centre of the machine—their most recent draw from the power grid, and four times their original mine. Simon didn't need to check the numbers to see the machine, designed to hold a certain amount of energy, was at full capacity. Tanya would never know, and stood this close to the machine and its radiation, Simon could hide his thoughts easier from her assistants outside.

He helped Elite One into a standing position. He drew her hands forward until they touched the barrier protecting the stored energy. The energy jumped to her hand but it was useless without a matter converter. Within moments, an almost white strand of light shot through the energy and touched Tanya's connected hands. She closed her eyes and smiled. Simon imagined the Nexus healing her from the inside. Her outer appearance would show the effects of the healing last.

Tanya disconnected as soon as the Nexus did. The stored energy, even though it had been increased, seemed to fuel it for just one minute. Tanya stood tall with no need for the chair.

'It's like a drug.' She touched her face, but snatched her hands back when they found folds of skin. 'I only wish it worked faster to fix the exterior. I can't wait to experience what it feels like to be a part of it.'

Simon didn't understand. 'A part of what?'

'A part of everything. Transcendence.' Tanya touched the machine that stored only weak, orange energy after the Nexus' depletion. 'When the Elite transcend into pure energy, that energy needs to go somewhere.' She turned and frowned at him. 'What did you think all of this was for? To live, unrestrained, like a ghost?'

Simon had told Bill he assumed the Nexus would

absorb the energy, but in reality he had tried not to think too much about what would happen after. He'd been too busy trying to stop Tanya's plans for hosting.

'I don't understand. Did you plan to live in the base station?'

Tanya rocked with laughter. 'You have such low ambition, Simon Shaw. I'm not sure why I picked you to be changed.' She paused. 'No, I am. We wanted you for your DNA, not your ambition. Plus, I also wanted your limited knowledge of the Nexus. To exist inside a suitable technology would give us ultimate control and infinite power.'

Simon tried to keep his mood light. 'I'm sorry, Tanya. I don't think much about these things.'

'Of course you don't.' She walked towards the exit. 'That's why we're Elite and you are not.' She opened the door and commanded her assistants to get the chair. 'I want to walk back. I could use the exercise.'

Simon followed Tanya, and kept tight control on his thoughts around the Conditioned pair.

'I want you to take the other Elite, give them a dose of the machine,' said Tanya.

'As you wish,' said Simon. 'Later, I'll need to do some calibration on it, get it ready to receive a full dose of power from the grid.'

Tanya turned. Her eyes were wide. 'All of it?'

He'd thought that would catch her attention. 'That's what they said.'

'What did you give them for the power?'

'The promise of longer life,' Simon lied.

She shook her head and smiled. 'It would appear trust can be bought after all.'

35

It was only 6pm—four hours before he had to bring Simon to see Stephen—but Bill couldn't settle his nerves. He had promised to give Laura space and even though they wouldn't meet inside the caves, he'd be close enough that she could detect him. What if his presence moved up her decision to live an Indigene life? He wanted Laura to make up her own mind without him camping outside her door.

It was at this very hour when he and Laura normally headed home. But Bill couldn't face the apartment without her. Two days had passed since he'd forced her out. Her absence left a gaping hole in his heart. And the fact that she hadn't tried to contact him, to let him know she was okay, hurt more than he would admit.

Bill distracted himself with just one screenshot of Wave chatter that Ben had sent, the one that discussed Harvey Buchanan's alias: John Caldwell. Harvey's recent meeting with Simon had piqued his interest, in particular the trade of information on the Elite in exchange for Simon's protection at the site of the cable. But with the addition of the force field around the site and the base station, Bill knew the trade would have been one-sided.

Nobody would get near either location without the codes to command the field generator. And they were inside the base station.

His communication device vibrated on the table.

Bill grabbed it and stuck it in his ear. 'What?'

If his patience had been thin before, it was nonexistent now.

'Bill?'

'Yeah, who's this?'

'Don't you recognise my voice after all these years?'

The hairs on the back of Bill's neck stood as he listened to the only man who still rattled him, even after all this time. 'Harvey Buchanan.'

Harvey chuckled. 'The very same. I'm calling you directly because your communication device is encrypted.'

'It is, but it's also off the band width. How did you get it?'

'I have ways of getting what I want, Bill. You of all people should know that.'

He did.

'We're not on Earth any more, Harvey. I run things here. There are no higher authorities to pay off for your protection.'

'I know, Bill, which is why I'm calling. I have something I think you'll want to see.'

'What is it?'

'Medical data listing the tests carried out on the GS humans.' Harvey paused. 'You know I have it. You've been monitoring the Wave for my name. Good job in finding me by the way. I guess it was bound to happen sooner or later.'

Bill trusted nothing Harvey said. Call it intuition. Call it full-blown experience.

'And what do you want in exchange for this information?'

Harvey laughed hard. 'That's what I like about you, Bill. I don't have to explain myself. You already know this isn't a one-way trade. Can we meet?'

'I'm a little busy now.'

'Won't take long.'

Harvey visiting the ITF didn't appeal to him, but he needed to speak to him.

'How soon can you get here?'

Harvey paused. 'Actually, I'm downstairs. Your security guy doesn't know what to make of me.'

Bill covered the extendible microphone. 'Shit.' Then he said, 'I'll be right down.'

'I'll be waiting.'

Bill disconnected the call and yanked his communication device from his ear. He stood up and cursed. He hated being played and Harvey turning up on his doorstep felt like the biggest play of all. He would hear him out. Nothing more.

Bill found Harvey in the room where he'd met with Simon only hours before. He shook off the strangeness of meeting all these people from his past—a past that wouldn't stop asking for favours.

Harvey sat at the table. His fingers grazed a mini disk the size of an old dollar coin. Bill closed the door, causing Harvey to look up.

His eyes raked over Bill's appearance and he smirked. 'This new planet suits you. You've got colour in your cheeks. Maybe even a tan. As soon as I get a minute, I'm going sunbathing.'

Bill stood by the door and folded his arms. 'Why are you here, Harvey?'

'That's no way to talk to an old pal, is it?'

'Oh, I'm sorry for not being clear. You've got ten minutes, so get to the point.'

Harvey clucked his tongue and Bill suddenly remembered Harvey's past as a geneticist and torturer. He shivered at the memory. Back on Earth, Harvey had used to experiment on people for a living and Bill had witnessed what that torture looked like on his employees. One in particular, a man called Vladimir, had a protruding eye and was missing half his face.

But things were different on Exilon 5. Bill was in charge.

'Always in a rush,' Harvey said. 'Got somewhere to be?'

Harvey said it casually enough, but someone had rattled him. Bill wondered whom his former adversary wanted to avoid in his circle.

'I'm a busy man, Harvey. I don't have time for bullshit.'

'Okay.' Harvey held his hands up. 'You win. If you've been monitoring chatter, which I know you have, you'll already know I met with one of the GS humans and got this.' He pinched the file between his fingers. 'I traded it for security detail.'

Bill pushed off from the doorframe and walked over to the table. 'So you're going in to the security trade now?'

Harvey shrugged. 'A few of my men show up and this particular GS human relaxes a little. Easy enough work.'

'What's so important on that file that you're prepared to trade with the GS humans for it?'

'I told you.' Harvey stared at Bill. 'Medical information outlining what testing was done to the Conditioned and the Elite.'

'I'm confused.' Bill leaned on the table. 'You want

medical data, but your colleague Patterson asked me for guns. Those two things don't sound related.'

'They're not. Patterson doesn't know I have the data. The guns are to show the Indigenes we are serious about attacking the GS humans.'

'And are you?'

Harvey laughed. 'No. We want your power, not theirs.'

That didn't surprise Bill. But Harvey's honesty did. 'So what's changed?'

'I found a better distraction.' He held up the micro disc. 'In here. What I have is just partial information. My contact won't give me more unless I get him access to his cable. So you can see, the force field puts me in a predicament.'

Bill frowned. 'Let me get this straight. You want *me* to remove the force field so you can get more useless medical data?'

Harvey laughed and sat back. 'Bill, you really have changed. I remember you hunting down every opportunity you could. First you sought revenge for your wife's death, then you took on a crusade mission to help the Indigenes. You're telling me you have no interest in never-before-accessed medical data on the Elite? If you don't, you're full of bullshit.'

Bill had an interest, but a trade like this would attract a heavy price. And according to Simon, giving the Elite enough power so they could transcend would be far worse.

'What if I negotiated a certain quantity of power? Would that facilitate a new trade with your GS human contact?'

Harvey shook his head. 'My contact wants as much power as possible. I don't think a new trade will happen without it. But I'm not stupid either. He gave me useless partial data on the Elite—early tests, not the later ones. My contact got lucky and stole this information. The chance of that luck happening twice is unlikely.'

Bill didn't understand. 'So if you got your information by chance and more power for your GS contact won't change that, why are you here?'

'I want to do a trade.'

Bill laughed; he couldn't help it. When Harvey stared at him, he pulled it back in and waited for him to explain.

'You know what I used to do for a living, Bill. I've been studying the data on the Conditioned, which is more readily available. From their data, I've extrapolated the likely tests to have been carried out on the Elite.'

'You *just* said the data was useless.'

'To ordinary doctors, maybe. Not to the geneticist involved in their creation.'

Bill pursed his lips. If Harvey could help stop Tanya's plans, he had to take the risk.

'We know they plan to go out with a bang.'

Harvey nodded. 'Transcendence.'

'Is it possible?'

'Unfortunately, yes. I don't know where they will settle once they do, but it won't be to a plane higher than one on Earth. What do you know about it?'

Bill knew better than to discuss the details with Harvey. 'So we come back to my original question. Why are you here?'

'I want status. I want to be reinstated as a legitimate geneticist with my own clinics. I want to reinvent myself on Exilon 5 because, right now, I'm a nobody. I travelled here under an alias and my job prospects are less than zero. But if you grant me permission to operate here again,

I could make a life for myself.'

Harvey seemed genuine in his request, but Bill knew where a legitimate practising license would lead. Harvey was addicted to power, prestige. He was another Charles Deighton, but worse, because he had knowledge that could destroy humans, and he could hide his darker side better.

But Bill couldn't ignore the opportunity to understand the GS humans better, in particular the Elite.

'Let me think about it.'

'Harvey slid the file across the table. 'Consider this a goodwill gesture. It contains good information about the Conditioned. It might not mean much without my analysis though.'

Bill picked up the coin and pocketed it. 'I said I'll think about it.'

Harvey stood; a trace of a smile was on his face. 'Don't wait too long, Bill. I have other ways of getting what I want.'

'I know, which is why I need time to think.'

Harvey flashed a smile. 'I look forward to hearing from you. You know where to find me, apparently.'

Bill watched him go, still not sure if taking Harvey's gift was a good idea. With a man like that, the smallest of acts meant a deal had been made. Bill had backed himself into a corner. To leave Harvey without an answer could mean serious consequences for him.

☼

Bill sat in his idling vehicle while he waited for Simon to show. It was close to 10pm and he played with the file in his pocket. He'd viewed its contents after Harvey left. It contained reams of data alright, but it could have been the alphabet in Hebrew for all he knew. Bill was no scientist. That's why he'd brought it. Maybe Stephen would have better luck.

Someone rapped on his side window, causing him to startle. Simon stood back from the vehicle as Bill climbed out.

'Fuck, you gave me a heart attack.'

'Sorry,' said Simon. 'I waited for you to notice me.'

Bill frowned. 'Why, how long were you there?'

'About ten minutes.'

Bill shook off his fright and slipped the file into the inside pocket of his coat.

Simon watched him. 'Where did you get that?'

Bill feigned innocence. 'Get what?'

'Don't play that game.' Simon pointed at his pocket. 'That.'

'An acquaintance.'

'You know I gave it to him, right?' Simon visibly tensed up. 'So why do you have it now?'

'I had no choice. Harvey gave it to me.'

'What do you plan to do with it?'

'Nothing right now. Harvey wants something that doesn't affect your situation.' Simon appeared to relax at that. 'He says he also has information on the Elite. Where did you get it?'

'One of the doctors left his bag unattended. But I don't think I'll be able to get more. That was a rare opportunity. Tanya is getting ready to implement the hosting idea.' Simon glanced around the deserted, flat landscape. 'When will Stephen get here?'

Bill checked his watch. 'Soon. He'll know where we are.'

Simon smiled. 'When I was changed, I wanted that ability. You know, to sense the location of other people.

My changes gave me telepathy and a higher brain function, but silent conversation is limited to the Elite.'

'How does that higher function work? How do you know so much about electricity? Were you trained as an electrician on Earth?'

Simon seemed hesitant to answer. 'I need to know that what I tell you will go no further.'

Bill nodded, intrigued.

'We have developed mind mapping, the ability to map the skills of another person on to our minds. The effect is only temporary since our brain can only retain a certain amount of information.'

Bill's mouth dropped open. 'Fuck, Simon. Since when?'

'Since four months ago, before we designed the machine to store the energy.'

'So you could become experts in, say, bomb building?'

Simon nodded. 'Theoretically, yes. But luckily Tanya has never asked for more than the machine. The Elite are a funny group who don't want for much.'

Bill snorted. 'Except everlasting life and unlimited power.'

'Well, when you put it like that... What I mean is their goals have been limited to preserving their lives, not taking others.'

'Except for their plans to sacrifice some of you.' Bill rubbed his unshaven face. 'Well, I suppose we can be grateful they haven't built bombs—'

The sound of approaching footsteps cut him off. He touched his holstered Buzz Gun. It could be Stephen but he saw only shapes in the dark.

When Stephen slowed to a walk, Bill steadied his racing heart and took his fingers off his gun.

Genesis Variant

Serena was with him. 'I'm sorry, Bill. We got caught up with something important.'

His heart raced again; he hoped Laura was okay. A cagey Stephen staring at Simon drew his attention away from his problems.

Serena had also locked her gaze on Simon. Bill didn't know what she was doing. Maybe she was trying to keep Simon's thoughts under her influential control.

'There's no need for that,' said Simon, rubbing the side of his head.

'We can't be too careful,' said Stephen.

'I can vouch for him, Stephen,' said Bill. 'Please, just hear what he has to say.'

He nodded at Simon, who launched into an abbreviated explanation of what he'd told Bill that afternoon.

'The Conditioned could really use your envisioning skill right now, Stephen,' said Simon.

Bill noticed Stephen flinch at that suggestion while Serena kept her probing gaze on Simon.

'I'll see what I can do,' said Stephen. 'But we have something else that might help. We've been testing a new device on Laura.'

Bill's heart barrelled down the side of a hill at the mention of her name. But he refused to ask about her. 'So what do you suggest?'

'We need to try something back in my lab.'

Simon shook his head. 'If Tanya accesses my thoughts, she'll have access to your tunnels.'

Stephen nodded at Serena, who stepped closer and produced a blindfold.

'Put this on, Simon,' she said. 'Tanya won't see what you do.'

Bill hesitated at the thought of going into the

293

district. 'Is this the only option?'

'I'm afraid so, Bill. We need to throw everything we have at this problem. This is bigger than our issue with the rogue Indigenes and humans teaming up.'

Simon grabbed the blindfold from Serena and put it on. 'Let's go. Tanya told me today their plan is to exist in technology on Exilon 5. If that happens, who knows what damage they can do?'

Or what Tanya would control. Bill nodded and strode towards the district. This problem trumped any promise he made to Laura to stay away.

36

Marcus couldn't believe it. The traitor.

Harvey had just come out of the ITF building. He shook hands with Bill Taggart like they'd just done a deal. What deal? Harvey was supposed to be taking down the ITF. He and Patterson wanted the ITF's power, and that plan required giving support to the rogue groups who had done nothing more than watch the GS lair for days now.

Two to each shift: one human one Indigene. Marcus and Clement had been paired together from the beginning. What did Marcus have to show for it? A killer headache from listening to Clement badger him about Harvey and Ollie, about how he needed to divide them with more lies.

And a deep-rooted desire to go solo.

He stormed away from his hiding place just as Harvey got in his vehicle parked outside the glass monstrosity on a street filled with old-world opulence. The car drove away. Marcus used to command similar vehicles on Earth. But here, he had to steal one.

Nothing more than a common thief.

He had no problem with the label, but he'd earned a better place in society through working for Gaetano. He refused to return to the bottom of the rung and wait another seven years to climb it.

Marcus returned to his stolen vehicle and ordered it to drive to nowhere in particular. He didn't care where he went. He should have floored it to race Harvey back to the construction site, but seeing Harvey all pally with Bill Taggart had turned his stomach. He was sick of everything. What he really wanted was to confront Buchanan about his meeting. The shocked betrayer would have no choice but to let him in on his plans.

Marcus changed his mind and returned to the construction site. The car parked in its owner's drive. From there, he walked the couple of miles back to the site and his giant hole, which could fit several chopped-up bodies. The thought made Marcus shudder. The hole beckoned him like a prison guard taunting him from outside a cell. He bypassed it and looked around, surprised not to see any sign of either Harvey or Ollie. He took advantage of the lack of supervision and went to the house to get his communication device from his room. The house was both quiet and empty when he arrived. Marcus planned to be in and out before either Harvey or Ollie caught wind of his diversion.

He slipped into his bedroom and made a call to Clement. The phone rang and rang. The dickhead Indigene kept him waiting until the tenth ring.

'Yes?' said a cautious-sounding Clement.

Marcus rolled his eyes. 'It's Martin Casey, your old buddy. Your pal. Listen.' He talked low and kept one eye on his closed bedroom door. 'We need to chat about some things. Tonight. Can you meet with me?'

A long pause followed. It irritated Marcus that the Indigenes had no clue about human technology. It had been the same deal in the attic of the Deighton Mansion.

'We're not on the schedule tonight,' said Clement.

'I know,' said Marcus. 'I need to talk to you about something. Not meant for discussion over the communication device, if you get my drift.'

Another long pause irritated Marcus to no end. Carl, his traitorous—and hopefully dead—best friend back on Earth, had been the exact same way.

'Okay,' said Clement finally. 'Usual spot at nine.'

'Okay.' Marcus rolled his eyes again. 'See you then.'

He slipped the device out of his ear and stole out of the house. Back on site, it appeared nobody had missed him. Normally that would have pissed him off, but today that's how he wanted it.

☼

Marcus arrived earlier than 9pm to make sure he didn't miss Clement. He stood by the boulders that marked the boundary for the GS land. It was the only place he and Clement had been. The Indigene hadn't turned up yet, but Marcus knew enough to know he probably watched from afar. The dark prevented him from seeing much. Even his magnification glasses didn't extend his vision beyond a few green feet. A sudden gust of wind alerted him to the presence of another. He twisted round but saw nothing. When he turned back, Clement stood a few feet from him, watching.

'Shit. Fuck!'

Marcus pressed his fist to his already racing heart. The Indigene did his best impression of a statue.

'How about a little warning next time?'

'I don't do warnings,' said Clement flatly.

'No, you don't do humour either,' muttered Marcus.

'What?'

'Nothing.' Marcus eyed the creature. 'Do you have any idea how creepy you are?'

Clement smiled. 'You brought me all the way out here to insult me?'

Marcus exaggerated his eye roll. 'Of course not, but an insult here and there doesn't hurt, especially for someone with thick skin like yours.'

'And I understand yours is thin.'

It was the way Clement said it, all creepy and low, that forced Marcus to drop the act. This Indigene knew more than he let on—and probably too much about Marcus. But at least the neural blocker kept the freak out of his head and put them on equal footing.

'Okay, yeah, I didn't bring you here to insult you. I came here to do business.'

Clement lifted his hairless brow. 'Business?'

'Things are changing on my side. I thought you'd like to know. I repeated the lies to both Harvey and Ollie, told them you were so desperate you would do anything for a truce with us,' Marcus bluffed. 'Not sure if they believed me, but they didn't look surprised, if you know what I mean.'

Clement's expression darkened in the black night. 'How have things changed, human?'

'Harvey told me he wants to protect the GS humans now. That's where their focus lies. He doesn't care what happens to the Indigenes.'

'Well, you need to find a way to get their focus back on us.'

'I will, I promised, but I need something from you.'

'What?'

'I'll pledge my loyalty to the Indigenes if you get me a meeting with your... what do you call them... elders?'

Clement smirked. 'What do you need to talk to them about?'

Marcus lifted his chin. 'I want to be changed into one of you.'

'Why?'

Was this Indigene playing games? 'Because you suggested it to me. You told me I had options.'

'I caught some of your thoughts before you turned on your neural blocker. I know you see the GS humans as a more attractive option.'

'I've changed my mind.'

Without Harvey's help, he didn't see how he'd get near them.

Clement paused for too long. Marcus didn't like the wait.

Then Clement said, 'How will your alteration benefit our truce with the humans? You have the ear of Harvey and Ollie. If you become Indigene, we lose that connection.'

Marcus had given that some thought. 'I was going to cement the idea in Harvey and Ollie's heads before I changed, you know, to make sure they wouldn't back out. But I'll only agree if your elders promise to change me.'

Clement glanced behind him suddenly, and that's when Marcus saw three other Indigenes step out of the shadows, all as menacingly tall as Clement. Marcus had not seen them before.

'We don't feel you would be a good addition to our race.'

'You can't back out, Clement. You promised.'

'I made no such promise, human. And you won't get near District Three.'

'Sure I will.'

'How?'

'The same way you get in.'

Clement laughed. 'There's more than one way in, human. Drop this idea.'

Marcus shook his head. 'So you're not going to help me, not even after I promised to help you?'

'If your human leaders wish to protect only the GS humans and leave us vulnerable, you've outlived your usefulness. We will find another human to manipulate.'

Marcus didn't care for the term "outlived", especially not in the Indigenes' presence. He'd used that term before when he frogmarched one of Gaetano Agostini's betrayers to their execution.

The group advanced on him and forced him to back up.

His heart thumped so loud he was sure the Indigenes could hear it. 'So that's a no to my offer?'

'That's a no,' said Clement.

'Okay.' He thumbed behind him. 'I'll be off then.'

'Are you sure you don't want to stick around, see how we hunt?' teased Clement.

Marcus was certain he did not. 'Maybe another time. See you on the next rotation?'

'Perhaps we'll see you sooner than that, human,' said one of Clement's associates.

He licked his incisor, causing Marcus to shudder.

Marcus retreated from the group, catching himself too late as he stumbled and fell over a low cluster of rocks. His bum hit the ground with a thud, prompting a round of laughter from the carnivorous group stood just three feet away from him. He turned and crawled away until he was clear, then got to his feet and ran.

A panting and swearing Marcus stopped to see Clement and the others run off in a northerly direction. Clement would be no ally to him after all. But Marcus wasn't giving up on the idea of alteration yet. With Harvey making his own plans, it was time for him to do the same.

He pulled his DPad out of his pocket and brought up a map of the area. Some of the Indigenes who'd lived in the Deighton mansion attic had discussed the location of District Three's entrance. It was nothing more than a metal hatch from what he recalled of their discussions. Marcus had a vague idea of its location, given the direction Clement and his associates just ran. He would go there, wait for someone friendlier to appear.

Then what, ask them if he could meet their elders? Ask to be changed into one of them?

Was that what he wanted?

Maybe, if it meant he could become powerful. The Indigenes on Exilon 5 were not the frightened rabbits he'd lorded over on Earth. Here, they had power. He saw the potential to be someone great among them.

The more he worked through his plan, the more ridiculous the idea became. But he had to try something. Of one thing he was certain: Marcus Murphy would not go down without a fight.

37

Stephen led a blindfolded Simon through the hatch entrance and down the stone steps while Serena and Bill brought up the rear. He sensed Serena's mistrust of the man the Elite GS humans referred to as "Conditioned". While Stephen had omitted to mention his envisioning skill had stopped working, his ability to see auras lit up the people around him.

The Conditioned produced auras in odd shades: rusty reds and green/blue combinations, different to the purer colours of the Indigenes. Simon's aura was a hesitant yellow mixed with a moodier grey—nothing that concerned Stephen.

They stood outside the outer door to District Three. A scanner swept over the entire group and the door opened. Stephen guided Simon through the environmental force field. In the thinner air, Stephen popped out his air filtration device, while Bill donned a gel mask. He noticed Simon had no trouble in either type of air. It was possible his lungs had been genetically altered to adapt to any environment, similar to the biodome animals and the Indigenes who underwent genetic reversal.

Similar to Laura.

The strong yellow depicting Bill's hesitation stood out. His friend didn't want to be here and Stephen knew the reason for his reluctance. But Laura was part of this next phase and he'd need her help to refine his experiment.

Stephen brought Simon to one of Anton's testing labs, cleared of work benches and equipment. They couldn't risk Simon seeing their equipment.

He stopped at the door when he saw who was in the room with Anton.

'Gabriel! Clement. What are you two doing here?'

'Clement and I heard you were battling against more than a few rogue Indigenes and humans. Thought you might need a hand. I was less than a courteous host when you and Serena last visited me.'

'You had a lot going on.' Stephen waved his hand. 'Where's Margaux? Did she come with you?'

'No. She's looking after things while I'm away. In fact, it was she who encouraged me to come.'

Stephen smiled. With Gabriel here, it felt like he had Pierre, his former elder, back.

He led Simon inside the room and said, 'You can remove your blindfold now.'

Simon pulled it off, blinking in the low light.

Anton moved closer, with the neurosensor in his hand.

When he reached for Simon, the Conditioned stepped back, his fear manifesting as a rusty red aura. 'What are you going to do?'

'Relax, Simon,' said Bill. His mask muffled his words. 'You won't be harmed here. You have my word.'

Anton opened his hand to show Simon a silicone casing. Inside was the flat, round disc made of amorphous metal. 'It's my neurosensor. We've tested it out on a volunteer and she was able to enhance her own ability while wearing it. If this works on you, we should be able to break the Elite's mind barrier and restore our abilities in their presence. If Stephen can improve his envisioning ability, we can deal with whatever comes next.'

Stephen felt Bill's edginess increase, saw him glance towards the door.

'We'd like to try it on you now, Simon,' said Anton.

Simon shook his head. 'If Tanya gets control of my mind, she'll know exactly how this thing works. She'll feel what I experience.'

'No, you won't be the one wearing it.' Anton nodded to Stephen. 'He will.'

Stephen kept his expression neutral when Simon glanced back at him. Both Gabriel and Clement watched him from one side of the room while Serena and Bill stood near the door. He couldn't let on that the neurosensor might be his only chance to get his broken envisioning skill to work.

'You're the closest thing to an Elite we have to test on,' said Anton. 'I'd like to see if I can push past your mind blockade. If we are to read Tanya's mind, we must practise first.'

Simon nodded, but his yellow aura said he wasn't convinced. 'Can't you just look into the future, tell us how this is all going to play out?'

Stephen prepared to rattle out an excuse when Serena reached out with her mind.

What's wrong? she said.

Nothing, I just...

He felt Anton muscle in on the telepathic conversation. *Why not try it? We'll probably still need others to use the neurosensor, but at least this way we'll*

304

Genesis Variant

predict what's coming.

Stephen huffed out a breath. *Because I can't. My ability hasn't been working for months.*

'What?' Gabriel said out loud

Bill had moved next to Anton. He poked him in the arm. 'What did he say?'

'He says his envisioning ability is gone,' said Anton.

'I didn't say that.' Stephen glanced at an alarmed looking Bill. 'It hasn't worked since they created that machine.'

Simon nodded as if he understood the problem. 'The machine produces radiation. And anyone who gets near it would carry some on their skin. A low enough level, but it might be enough to block your brain's abilities.'

'Radiation?' Stephen smiled. 'That's what I've been stressing over for months? I thought I'd lost my ability.'

Why didn't you tell me? Serena said.

I didn't want to bother you over nothing.

Your health isn't nothing, Stephen.

I'm sorry.

Bill and Simon both stared at him; he sensed their anxious energies.

'Could we get on with this, maybe talk about disappearing abilities another time?' said Bill. 'Simon doesn't have much time.'

Stephen nodded. 'I'm sorry. Of course.' He turned to Anton. 'Will the neurosensor work to bolster my envisioning ability?'

'It works to bolster any ability. We should try it,' said Anton.

The omicron rock could be a limiting factor.

'It should be able to penetrate it,' replied Anton to his silent thought.

'Okay,' he said, and Anton pressed the outer silicone casing to the side of his head.

Stephen felt an instant jolt of power that started out slow, but increased steadily. All of a sudden he became aware of Simon, sensing his ability to switch from independent to shared thought in a flash. But he put him out of his mind so he could concentrate on the future.

He closed his eyes. Serena stood next to him and used her influence ability to bolster his, like she used to do in the beginning. It felt like a pulsating wave across his mind. With the neurosensor attached, everything in his mind opened up; conduits in his mind widened to make the transfer of information easier.

Serena grabbed his hands and her touch delivered to him a much needed calm. He concentrated on the flashes of events not yet to occur that had been out of reach for a while now. Several images flashed through his mind. He latched on to one, but the scene blurred too much for him to make out detail. The neurosensor had widened the conduits all right, but the fast rate of information delivery made it impossible for Stephen to control.

'Take a deep breath and relax,' said Serena. 'Remember, you're not in control; the device is. Slow your thoughts down and the images will adjust.'

Stephen took a deep breath and followed her instructions. As soon as he slowed everything down, the images followed suit. He plucked one from the carousel which showed Simon leaving the district—an event yet to happen. Relief flooded through him and he smiled. He plucked another one of Laura loitering close to this room, watching while Bill walked through a tunnel. But a third selection produced his greatest fear.

It was of Simon inside their district. But it wasn't the Simon standing in this room. This one had a dark passenger.

Stephen released his frustration in one long breath and opened his eyes. 'I couldn't see far enough to see how this plays out, but I saw Simon inside this district. He wasn't himself.'

A worried-looking Simon nodded. 'Tanya plans to put a copy of her personality in my mind. And if you've seen it, that means I have no way to avoid that outcome.'

'Do you know what she's after?' Gabriel asked him.

'Probably the Nexus. She and the others want to transcend and they need power to do it.'

'But the Nexus won't help them,' said Serena. 'It resists foreign bodies—those not made from our DNA.'

'It has already helped them,' said Simon. 'We used the machine to siphon off some of the Nexus' power to heal Tanya.'

'But that was with the aid of a machine,' said Anton. 'If you or Tanya connected directly with the Nexus, you would experience it differently.'

'Were you able to access Simon's mind?' Bill asked Stephen.

Stephen nodded. 'Partially. I wasn't really trying, but it felt possible.'

'Good because I have an idea.'

'What?'

Everyone looked at Bill.

'Serena's an influencer. What if she accessed the Elite's thoughts, convinced them not to come here?'

Simon appeared to perk up at the idea. 'You would only need to access Tanya's mind. The others listen to her.'

307

Stephen looked at Serena. 'What do you think?'

She shrugged. 'It's possible. I'm willing to give it a go, but I would need to get closer to the caves.'

Simon nodded. 'I might be able to give you some cover if I turn off the cameras.'

'Okay, that's settled,' said Stephen. 'Let's agree a plan now because this can't wait.'

'What about Simon?' said Bill. 'Can we offer him immunity if this goes wrong?'

'If this works,' said Serena. 'the Elite will die of natural causes before they have a chance to imprint on him.'

38

Clement's withdrawal of his promise to change Marcus into an Indigene played on his mind. For an hour after his shift ended, Marcus had lain on his bed and thought too much about their meeting that day. It wasn't until he'd stared at the ceiling for too long that he remembered something else Clement had said: *There's more than one way in, human.*

More than one way inside District Three. Who would pay for that information? Harvey, Ollie? He didn't even know what their agenda was any more. But he'd worked for Gaetano Agostini long enough to learn a little information in your back pocket could prove useful.

There were no surveillance jobs on that evening, leaving Marcus with time to search for those alternative entrances. But when he drove out close to where he knew the main entrance to be, he looked around a stony landscape that was flatter than Carl's arse. Where to begin?

He got out and trekked around for a while, making sure to keep the car in sight. He'd brought a stronger pair of magnification glasses with him, a set he'd seen on the dresser in Ollie's room that worked better than the lame pair he'd been given. In the distance, two figures met. He zoomed in and saw one was Clement, the other an older Indigene. He looked away, then looked back to see they'd disappeared.

'What the hell?'

Marcus trekked out to the same spot and looked around. And there it was hidden in the dirt: one of the alternative entrances Clement had hinted at set into the soil at a forty-five-degree angle. Marcus would never have found the metal hatch camouflaged in rubble without Clement's tipoff. Using another filter on the glasses, he transposed a set of coordinates over the spot and jotted them down on his hand before returning to the car to watch the main entrance to District Three.

☼

Marcus rolled his neck. He'd camped out for hours watching the comings and goings at District Three. Two hours ago, he'd seen Bill Taggart and the GS human who'd met with Harvey and Ollie go inside with two Indigenes. Then the GS human emerged alone and disappeared into the black night.

Maybe Marcus had this all wrong. Maybe he didn't need to change into another species to get power. What if he could keep his human identity and still have a place in this new world?

Bill Taggart emerged next from the district. Marcus spotted a car parked close by. The ITF Director walked towards it. He had seen Harvey talk to this man who appeared to run things on Exilon 5. That meant Taggart had connections to the GS humans, probably dating back to when they were human and in charge on Earth.

Harvey had played both sides for long enough. Now it was Marcus' turn to get what he wanted.

He got out of his vehicle, which was almost invisible in the cloud-covered night. The distracted director didn't see him as he approached him from behind.

Marcus called out. 'Hey!'

Taggart stopped and spun round. His hard gaze and flashlight found Marcus. 'Who the fuck are you?'

'I need to talk to you.'

'I asked you a question.'

Taggart's flashlight pinned Marcus to the spot. He would need to earn this man's trust.

'My name isn't important—'

'I disagree...'

'—but who I know is.'

'Yeah?' Taggart eyed him. 'Who do you know?'

'Harvey Buchanan.'

Something registered on Taggart's face as he brought the light down to rest on Marcus' chest. 'You one of the boys over at the construction site in the west quarter?'

Marcus nodded, grateful the man who'd helped to bring down Gaetano Agostini didn't know his real name. He could still use his alias, but being this close to Taggart made him nervous, disguise or no disguise. If Taggart discovered his connections on Earth, he would probably stick him in some detention centre.

Taggart folded his arms. 'So, what about Harvey?'

'I have information on the GS humans that I think will be of value to you.'

'I'm listening.'

'First I want your promise of immunity.'

'Seems everyone wants that from me. And I'll tell you what I've told them. Depends on what information you've got.'

Marcus had to show trust. 'What if I told you that Buchanan and Patterson were helping the GS humans to access more power from your power station feed?'

A stony faced Taggart cocked his head. 'Is that so?'

'Yeah, they've been talking at the power station.'

The director laughed.

Marcus wasn't impressed. 'Something funny about that, friend?'

'You're a day too late, *friend*.'

Taggart walked away.

Marcus ran after him. 'Wait! What does that mean?'

The director didn't break his stride. 'It means we have it all under control.'

'So you're not going to help me?'

Taggart stopped and turned around. 'With what?'

'With immunity.'

'Tell me why you need it.'

'I just do.'

'You afraid of Buchanan, is that it?'

Marcus pretended to be scared. Nobody scared him. 'Something like that. You gonna help me?'

'Tell me your name.'

'Martin Casey.'

Taggart shook his head and smiled. 'Your real name. I'd recognise Buchanan's handiwork anywhere. The face manipulation is slightly off-centre. You must have been important to him. Did you come from Earth? What did you do there?'

Marcus knew a dead end when he saw one. 'Don't bother, friend. I'll sort myself out.'

Taggart turned back to his car. 'Whatever you say... friend.'

312

Genesis Variant

☼

Only one course of action remained open to Marcus, and it involved speaking with the one group he had yet to encounter. He knew exactly where their lair was; he and Clement had watched it for days. Why, he had no idea. But Marcus was starting to feel like the whole collaboration with the Indigenes was for show, to plant the seed of doubt among their race.

He drove to the GS boundary wall and ditched the car. He climbed over the boulders lining the perimeter and jumped down the other side. He began his walk to the back of the environ. The black night provided him with cover as he approached the rear. A hand on his shoulder stopped him cold and nearly gave him a heart attack. He spun round to see the GS human he'd seen with Bill earlier.

'What's your business out here?' the man snarled.

'None of yours. This is a free country.'

Up close, the GS humans looked more human than the Indigenes. It freaked Marcus out.

'You're trespassing on GS land so either you're on a suicide mission or you want something.'

Marcus pointed to the white, tarpaulin environ. 'What's in there? I see you lot coming and going all hours of the day and night.'

'What's it to you?'

'You want more power? I can offer my services.'

The GS human frowned. 'In exchange for what?'

Marcus shrugged. 'Everlasting life is a good place to start, I reckon.'

The GS human laughed. 'You don't want that, so I suggest you move along—'

'Halt! Who's out there?' said another voice. Two

313

Eliza Green

more GS humans rounded on their location. 'Simon? What's going on?' One of the GS pointed his weapon at Marcus. 'Who are you?'

Nervous sweat soaked Marcus' shirt. 'Someone who can help your leaders get what they want.'

'And what's that?'

'Let me meet them and we'll discuss it. Seems rude to have the chat out here.'

The one called Simon said, 'No, he needs to go.'

But then the freak grabbed his own head, like he was in pain. The other pair shook theirs as though something buzzed in their ear.

'She's detected him. She wants to see him,' said one of the other GS humans.

Marcus caught the look of surprise on Simon's face. He was sure he was helping the Indigenes and Bill Taggart with something and this "she" didn't know anything about it.

His reasons for being here had gone way beyond a simple request for immunity. Marcus wanted power and where else to get it but working alongside the most powerful beings on the planet?

One of the others grabbed his arm and pulled him along. He slipped his glasses on and saw the outline of their caves in the distance. What could he offer them? That depended on what they wanted.

He would throw everything at them, see what stuck. And if nothing worked, it didn't matter. Harvey had said the GS humans couldn't read others' thoughts, only their own.

He'd make up some shit when he got there.

39

From her hiding place, Laura watched as Bill entered the District and pressed his gel mask to his face. Her chest tightened at seeing her best friend, but she needed more time. She wouldn't string him along any more.

It was torture waiting for him to leave. Her heightened abilities sensed everything about him that was familiar and comfortable. She pushed back her longing to go to him. Arianna had even stuck by her side to, in her words, 'keep you from doing something stupid.'

The group with Simon were camped out in Anton's lab to test the neurosensor that Laura had tried out just recently. It was an amazing piece of tech that had completely opened up her ability. When the chatter died down, Laura emerged from her hiding place. All was quiet in the room. Eager for a progress report from Serena, she walked on, not hearing Arianna's silent warnings behind her.

When she was just a few feet from the room, *he* emerged. A stunned Laura locked eyes with her husband, who stared at her, then looked down at the floor. Her heart jolted from the surprise; the shock forced her to turn away.

315

A heavy-footed Bill strode past her, followed by Simon. And then she could no longer sense him.

Arianna appeared by her side. 'One day he'll understand why you had to do this.'

Tears pricked Laura's eyes. 'He encouraged me to come here. He kicked me out. And now he hates me.'

'No, he doesn't. He's just confused. He doesn't know how to act around you. You're going through a transition. That's all. When it's all over, you two can talk.'

Laura hoped that soon she'd decide on something worth discussing. She entered the testing room to find Stephen, Serena, Anton, Gabriel and a new Indigene she hadn't met before talking telepathically to each other. Her skill wasn't strong enough to join the silent conversation but her presence in the room caught their attention. They broke out of their huddle to look at her.

'What happened?' she said, feeling Stephen and Serena's concern weigh her down.

Bill was gone. Of course things were tense. She could do nothing about it right now.

'Stephen saw Simon attacking the district,' said Serena. 'We assume Tanya was using him as a vehicle.'

'We need to test this neurosensor out on the surface,' said Gabriel. 'We have to know when she plans to attack. Is it one day from now, one week?'

'What difference does it make?' said Laura. 'If they're coming, we can prepare.'

'If we can access Tanya's thoughts, Serena might be able to change her mind,' said Stephen.

Serena looked sceptical. 'I don't know if I can, but I'll try. To do that will require me to maintain a connection with Tanya.'

'All we need is time. Gabriel and Clement have sent word out to the other districts about the problems here. We must give the support time to get here,' said Stephen.

The blue-eyed Indigene called Clement stared at Laura. His intensity forced her to look elsewhere.

Gabriel paused. 'There's something else.'

'What?' said Stephen.

'I heard some chatter after you left, about the rogue humans and Indigene groups. That's why we came. Clement says the rogue Indigenes are using the humans, pretending to ally with them. As soon as their guard is down, the Indigenes will attack the weak points in the city and take control of the power station.'

Clement added. 'The Indigenes don't trust your alliance with the ITF to protect the treaty, Stephen, and they definitely don't trust the GS. They think you've become sympathetic to the humans and have lost sight of the dangers that can fill a complacent bond.'

Stephen sighed. 'They have a point. But they aren't our immediate concern.'

'No, the GS are,' said Gabriel. 'But when this is all over, you must get control of your district.'

'Can't you see when they'll get here?' said Laura, trying to push the focus back on the GS.

Stephen shook his head. 'I can't see very far into the future, but what I did see was her arriving before any support did. If we can stall her just for a while, we might be able to delay her plans to imprint on the minds of the Conditioned.'

Laura noticed Anton shudder. It had been eight years since he carried an imprint of Charles Deighton's personality but she imagined it had been traumatic enough that he'd never forget.

'Okay, so when should we try this?' said Serena.

'Now,' said Stephen. 'We're running out of time.'

Serena nodded, released a breath. 'Just me then.

317

Alone.'

'No, all of us.' Stephen grabbed her hands. 'We'll all help you. You'll wear the neurosensor but we'll provide you with our energy to see if we can bolster your connection with Tanya.'

Anton snatched up the neurosensor. 'Last one to the top is a rotten egg.'

☼

The others collected spare air-filtration devices, except for Laura who had no trouble with the oxygen-rich air. The group travelled by foot to the GS boundary wall. Even with her keen sight, Laura could not see the caves located about three miles away. She saw the environ well enough; it was closer.

'Okay,' said Stephen. 'Everyone needs to concentrate on Serena, give her whatever help they can. We just need to plant the seed of doubt in Tanya's mind.'

'Assuming I can access it,' said Serena with a huff.

Stephen squeezed her shoulder. 'I know you will.'

The display of affection between them tugged at Laura's heart. She missed her best friend.

Anton fixed the neurosensor to the side of Serena's head. 'We've already tested this on Laura and Stephen so we know your ability will be enhanced.'

'I know I need to find Tanya but what am I looking for?'

Laura remembered the Tanya from old, the one with impeccable manners, but also a suspicious mind. 'Look for a pessimistic mind. She trusts people close to her, but she also discards them if it suits her.'

'So I'm looking for a self-centred personality.'

Laura nodded. 'The former board members are all

selfish, but Tanya considers herself above them all. She placated them while on Earth, but she wants an outcome that will benefit her.'

Serena closed her eyes and the others followed her lead. Laura did the same, and focused on directing what little Indigene energy she owned to Serena. She located her signature, surrounded by a cluster of energies. Laura's energy felt the weakest, and she wasn't sure if she was doing it right, but she added it to the effort.

Serena cast her influence out like an invisible net. It raced over the terrain towards the caves, slowing when it got closer. Laura couldn't see the net, but she felt what Serena put out there, what Serena wanted her to see.

Her influence met resistance at the entrance point to the cave. 'That's as far as I can push. We need to get physically closer.'

They all disconnected from her, visibly exhausted. Laura not so much, but her efforts had not been as powerful as theirs.

'Let's hope Simon was able to disable the camera feed,' said Stephen, beginning the climb down to the GS side of the rock barrier.

The others followed, with Laura to the rear. She was slower than all of them. Clement waited for her and helped her down. She nodded her thanks. Was she really Indigene or just playing at it?

They reached the back of the environ and Serena tried again. Laura gave her energy to her, felt her attempts to push past the barrier to the cave. She felt a pop in her mind when Serena crossed over.

'I'm in. I can feel her. Her energy is more powerful than the others.'

'Can you read her mind?' said Gabriel.

'Yes, I can also sense the other Elite minds. They

just want to die. She wants to transcend and will do anything to reach that goal. The others follow her orders. She's weak, physically, but her mind is strong. I'll see what I can do.'

Serena spread her influence around the caves. It felt like water filling a container. By proxy, Laura also felt Tanya, too powerful for her untrained mind to handle. But Serena was better at this than her. She'd been human too once, except she'd taken to Indigene life like a duck to water. Laura couldn't hold on to one side or the other.

Serena's energy was fading. Laura felt her influence retreat out of the cave at an alarming speed. Her eyes jerked open just as Serena collapsed to the ground. The others, visibly exhausted, went to her.

Serena stared up at the sky. 'That's it. I've planted the seed of doubt. I can't maintain a connection. Her mind is too powerful. That's all we can do.'

'Which means in Simon's body, she'll be unstoppable,' said Stephen.

'Not necessarily,' said Serena. 'There are more of us than them. We'll be ready if they come.'

'And when the others get here,' said Gabriel, 'we'll be an army.'

'Come on,' said Anton, 'we should get back and prepare just in case Serena's efforts amount to nothing and Tanya changes her mind.'

The others ran ahead and Laura kept pace as best she could. Clement ran slower than the others, glancing behind him and checking on her progress. She blamed herself for this situation. The GS were her and Bill's responsibility, tied to the power structure that they both operated in the board members' absence.

How had they let things get this bad?

40

Simon followed the Conditioned pair as they dragged the trespasser into the observation room. Tanya was alert to their arrival. She was on the move.

He glanced at the cameras he'd promised he'd turn off for Stephen, to give them some privacy while they tested the neurosensor. But with an audience in the room, that option was no longer available to him.

The trespasser with the brown hair and dirt-streaked face stood in the room that rarely had visitors. Tanya must want to change things sooner if she was prepared to let a human stranger into their midst. The stranger smiled and looked around the room. Simon couldn't read his thoughts but that didn't matter. He didn't trust him.

Tanya appeared from the left side behind the platform, from the tunnel that led to the laboratories and the Conditioned's accommodation. She sat in her hover chair, back to her usual withered self, while her assistants surrounded her in a protective manner. But Tanya didn't need protecting; the Conditioned did. Except none of them realised that.

She leaned forward, and lifted her head with great

effort.

'Step forward please,' she said.

The stranger looked around at the others, then shrugged. Simon did not like this man.

The man placed his hands behind his back. 'Hello, er, lady.'

'My name is Elite One. You will address me as such,' Tanya croaked.

Her soft voice crackled but Simon still felt the power behind her words.

'My bad,' said the man. 'Elite One. My name's Mar —' He paused. 'Ah fuck it, Marcus. I'm here to help you get what you want.'

Tanya leaned on the armrests. 'And what is it you think I want?'

Marcus shrugged. 'You tell me.'

Tanya levelled a gaze at Marcus. Then she laughed. 'What I want is to get out of this skin. Can you help me with that?'

The stranger looked around again. 'Er, maybe. Tell me what you need and I'll be your servant.'

'And what do you want in exchange for this servitude?'

Marcus cleared his throat. 'To be changed, to become one of you.'

Tanya laughed again. 'Do you think I was born yesterday, son?'

The man looked her over. 'You look too old to use that line.'

Tanya smiled and shook her head. Simon couldn't tell if Tanya was merely stringing the stranger along or taking him seriously.

'Do you know who I used to be on Earth?' she said.

Marcus linked his fingers behind his back. 'No, I do

not.'

'I suppose there's a first for everything.' She glanced at Simon before her eyes cut back to Marcus. 'I used to be the chair of the World Government.'

Marcus' eyes widened for a second before he pulled his surprise back in. 'Nice to... meet you?'

'So you see, son, when I was human I ate assholes like you for breakfast. Tell me again what use you are to me?'

Marcus appeared to think about it. Tanya huffed and rotated her chair to go.

Marcus called out. 'Wait! Indigenes.'

Tanya stopped and turned back. 'What about them?'

'Would access to their lair be of any use to you?'

Tanya narrowed her gaze at him. 'What do you know about that?'

Simon wanted to know too. Who was this human?

'I... I've been watching this place, doing patrol for a man in charge. My buddy—' He airquoted the term. '—is an Indigene. He told me there were several ways to get inside the district. Not just the main one. Well, I found one. Would you like to know where it is?'

Tanya gave a slight nod. 'Possibly. Let me speak to my advisor first. Stay here and touch nothing. Simon?'

The stranger unclasped his hands and put them up. Simon climbed up on the stage and followed Tanya's hovering chair to the left and down the tunnel. Just clear of the tunnel, she opened the right-hand door that accessed the staging room and hovered inside. When Simon closed the door, she turned to face him.

'What the hell was he doing out there? How did he get this far? I don't have time to entertain this man. The doctors are ready to try hosting tomorrow morning. But,' she glanced at the door, 'if he could give us an advantage over the Indigenes, should I waste it?'

Simon saw his own chance to change her mind. 'I've never seen him before. He could be lying just to get you on side.'

'I had thought of that,' said Tanya. 'But we should give him a shot. You can keep an eye on him, make sure he doesn't step out of line.'

Simon felt something in his head, a tingling presence that Stephen had warned him to expect. They must be outside, possibly visible on the cameras he couldn't switch off. The influencer was close by. He studied Tanya, whose sharp focus turned blurry.

'I think we should get rid of him. He's obviously a con artist. We don't need anyone to help us get inside the district.'

Tanya looked up at him, her focus off. 'I guess you're right. We don't even know where he came from or how many he brought with him.'

Simon released a quiet breath. If Tanya was under Serena's influence, perhaps he could stop this whole thing.

'Are you sure it's the right time to begin the hosting?'

'Of course it is!' Her gaze softened again. 'Why? Do you think it's the wrong choice?'

'I do. The humans promised me access to the main feed tomorrow. We should try that and the machine first. There are no guarantees this Marcus knows of any secret entrance, or that we'd get anywhere near the Indigenes' district anyway.'

'You're resourceful, Simon. I trust you. That's why I want to use you as my host.'

He had expected that. 'But if I'm killed before I can get in there... The machine is safer.'

Tanya frowned. 'I hadn't thought of that before.' She looked up at him. 'What's your suggestion for that man out there?'

Memory loss must be a side effect of influence. They'd just discussed this. 'We should get rid of him.'

Tanya nodded, but said nothing more.

Simon kept pressing while she was in a state of indecision. 'Let's get in there and remove the stranger, then wait twenty-four hours before trying the hosting idea. I'm all for it, but I think it's too soon.'

Tanya nodded, pinning him with her watery gaze. 'If you think that's a good idea.'

'I do.'

He pushed her chair back to the room where her aides and two Conditioned waited with a now restless Marcus. Her chair hovered a few inches over the platform once more.

'Simon has convinced me of something, which, if I'm being honest goes against my thinking,' said Tanya.

Simon froze at her words and glanced at the unmanned monitors. He saw several figures dressed in dark clothing running away from the back of the environ. His heart squeezed in his chest until the figures disappeared. When it looked like Tanya hadn't seen them, he relaxed.

'So do we have a deal?' said Marcus.

His smirk made Simon's skin crawl.

'We do,' said Tanya. Marcus smiled. 'You will show us the secret entrance.'

She nodded to one of the Conditioned, who stepped forward and looped an arm around Marcus' neck.

'What the f—?'

'Take him to one of the spare rooms,' she commanded. Then she spoke to Marcus. 'My charges will watch you until we're ready to leave.'

'Get off me!'

Marcus struggled beneath the thick arm of his captor, who dragged him on to the stage and disappeared down the right-hand tunnel.

Simon contained his shock and looked at Tanya, whose eyes had narrowed.

'I couldn't figure out why it was so easy for you to convince me of a new course of action back there,' said Tanya. 'Then I came out here and saw on screen what you tried to hide from me. Indigenes, I presume? I felt something in my head.'

'I don't know what you mean.'

'Yes, you do, Simon. You tried to stall the hosting. And I don't blame you. I wouldn't want me in my head, either. But here's the thing; we've come to the end of the line, the Elite and I. If we don't do this, we die.'

'Tanya, please. The machine... it will do what you need.'

Tanya nodded to her aides, who jumped off stage and grabbed Simon's arms.

'It's nothing personal, you understand. It's just that you're more valuable alive than dead or missing. You're the strongest Conditioned here, which means my chances of survival are excellent.' She waved her hand at her aides and turned to go. 'Lock him in his room until the doctors are ready for him.'

Simon squirmed under his restraints. 'I don't want to be part of this, Tanya. I never agreed to this.'

Tanya turned back. 'I know, Simon. None of us wanted it to end up like this. My vision involved a much smoother transition into everlasting life. But this is how it has to be. It's just business.'

41

'I don't understand,' said Stephen. With the aid of the neurosensor, he read the future. 'Tanya changed her mind. I saw it, felt it. You influenced her.'

Their group had returned to the entrance of District Three. Gabriel Anton, Arianna, Clement and Laura watched Serena and Stephen where they stood with their hands joined.

Serena sighed. 'I felt it too. When Simon told her to hold off, she made up her mind to listen to him.'

'So why are they still coming?'

He pulled out of her grip and tore the neurosensor from his head. He'd just seen them arrive—a brown-haired human led the way—but he couldn't pin down when exactly that might happen. It could be a day, an hour from now.

Gabriel shook him, breaking Stephen out of his thoughts. 'Stephen, when are they coming?'

Stephen focused on the elder. 'I don't know.'

'Come on, we don't have time to mess around. Give us a ballpark figure. Day or night, at least.'

Stephen blinked at Gabriel. 'Day. Definitely day.'

Gabriel let go of his arms and paced. 'Let's assume the worst and that their arrival could happen at any moment. We can't rely on Stephen's accuracy. How are the others doing with the barricades?'

Anton replied. 'The north and east entrances are completely blocked.'

'That leaves just the south.'

Anton nodded. 'Under the Maglev train station in Victoria. But the entrance there is tight and the air too thin.'

'That won't matter if they have breathing apparatus,' said Laura. 'Bill, Jenny and I navigated the tunnels just fine. You mustn't assume they won't come at you from that spot.'

Stephen nodded. 'She's right. We should seal off that entrance too.'

'But it's more likely they'll gain access through one of the more obvious routes,' said Arianna.

'How strong did they appear to be?' said Gabriel.

Stephen shrugged. He'd seen Simon in his future reading. 'We don't know much about the Elite, but they want to use the strong Conditioned as vessels. We should get Bill down here. He spoke to Harvey Buchanan recently, who gave him information on them.'

Stephen turned when he felt Laura's hesitance.

She nodded and said, 'He needs to be here.'

'We'll have to use our combined abilities to fight them.' Stephen turned back round to the others. 'We know they want access to the Nexus. Under no circumstances should they be allowed to reach it.'

'So,' said Gabriel, 'we hold them off for as long as possible, then gather all remaining Indigenes to protect the tranquillity caves?'

'That's the plan,' said Stephen.

'But there are dozens of caves. How will we stop them from reaching them all?'

Stephen had never said it was a good plan.

He glanced at the neurosensor in his hand, then at Serena. 'Right now, our best defence is Serena. If she can convince them to stop, it might give us enough time to regroup, to keep them from the Nexus.'

'Then what?' said Gabriel. 'They won't stop until they succeed. And if the Elite are using Conditioned hosts, time will be on their side.'

'Then we must work out how to attack the Conditioned, discover their weaknesses.'

42

Simon woke on his bed to find a pair of Conditioned stood in one corner of his room, watching him.

He sat up and one of Tanya's guards sprung to attention.

'I'm not going anywhere.' He touched the side of his throbbing head. One of the guards must have knocked him out. 'No need to have a panic over it.'

The guard stepped closer and pushed down on his shoulder to keep him in place. 'Tanya says you're to preserve your energy for the transfer.'

Simon groaned and lay back down. Tanya may have control over his body but he still owned his mind. For now.

An hour later, two doctors, including Tanya's personal physician, Dr Jameson, entered the room.

Jameson slipped a blood pressure sleeve on to Simon's upper arm, then stuck a probe into the crook of his arm while he inflated the sleeve. The pressure built until Simon couldn't bear it any longer. Then the pressure subsided, but the voice inside his head nagging at him to do something stayed put.

'Your blood pressure is slightly elevated but other than that you're fine.' Jameson turned and walked to the door. 'Bring him.'

The guards pulled Simon to his feet and herded him along behind the doctor.

'You don't have to do this,' said Simon.

'It won't hurt,' said Jameson. 'It's a straightforward procedure. You've nothing to worry about.'

While the guards pushed him along the corridor, Simon wondered if the doctor knew of Tanya's plans to use his body as a vessel.

'She plans on killing me, you know,' he said.

Jameson turned briefly, then walked on. 'I know.'

They stopped outside the staging room. Jameson opened the door and waved Simon inside. He looked around and saw nine other Conditioned, all males. They sat on the Elite's beds while the Elite, in their almost dead-like state, occupied hover-chairs in front of them. The mind-mapping machine sat on a table in the centre of the room. Each of the Elite was connected to the machine via a wire and a small circle that blinked red, attached to one side of their dipped heads.

One bed remained and Tanya's chair was positioned in front of it. The guards forced Simon to sit on the tenth bed. He locked his gaze on Tanya, hoping to reason with her. She also had a blinking red circle on her lopsided head—a device to facilitate the imprint exchange, he assumed.

A second doctor in the room removed the blinking red circle from Elite Ten, then placed it in a round carrier on top of the machine. The carrier beeped once, and the doctor extended a small, thin wire from the machine. The wire squirmed when the doctor placed it on the neck of the Conditioned lined up with Elite Ten. The Conditioned winced when the wire pierced his neck. Simon watched it worm its way under the skin and up to the brain.

The doctor copied the procedure with the remaining eight until it was Simon's turn to be imprinted with Tanya's consciousness. He felt a sharp sting in his head as the device containing the imprint implanted somewhere in his brain. Instantly, he felt a second presence. Tanya. Her consciousness stirred, as though she'd been in a deep sleep.

Who's there? her imprint called out.

The real Tanya looked asleep in her chair.

He didn't answer her. The voice became more demanding. *Answer me, damn it.*

I'm here, he said, feeling like he had no choice.

This personality would not permit him silence.

Simon. It worked! But I can't see anything. Where am I? Can I control you? Simon's arm shot out to the front and he strained against an immovable force. With a lot of effort, he pushed it back to its original position. *Good... that felt very good.*

Tanya's consciousness continued to chatter. He had no idea how to shut her off.

I won't be quietened. I've been given a new lease of life.

Simon studied the barely conscious Tanya in corporeal form to his front. She hardly moved. It was her imprint who spoke to him inside his head.

'I need time to adjust to this. It feels... strange,' he said aloud.

We don't have time.

Tanya forced Simon to stand. The sudden movement made his head spin. He glanced at the other Conditioned who'd been forced into similar positions while their Elite counterparts sat immobile in their chairs.

332

In Simon's head, Tanya said, *Elite, how are you feeling?*

Good, they all replied.

Strong.

Never better.

Then Tanya's voice was no longer in his head; she took control of his voice box. It was his voice, but her words.

'We are strong, we are few, but with the right weapons, we will be victorious.'

The Elite controlled the Conditioned in the same way.

Weapons? said Simon, his voice reduced to thought.

'Oh, didn't I tell you, Simon? We've been working on ways to attack the district when our friend Marcus gets us there. We created temporary weapons experts, thanks to our mind-mapping technique.'

Simon hadn't thought it possible to use the mind-mapping machine for anything other than defensive purposes.

'Neither did we. That's why we tricked it into believing we needed those weapons for defence.'

When?

'After our Nexus treatments, when we felt strong enough to walk.'

Tanya spoke aloud, answering what were supposed to be his private thoughts. His heart sank at the realisation his thoughts would never be his own again.

'Oh, don't say that, Simon. You still have independent thought,' said Tanya. 'It's just that now I know everything you think about.'

☼

Simon spent the night in his room with just a bed and Tanya for company. He got little sleep thanks to the constant humming in his head. Tanya Li's imprint wouldn't shut off.

He found his voice and ground his fists into the sides of his head. 'Could you stop?'

The humming ceased. *Oh, you're awake then. Had I known, I would have ordered the others to gather sooner. We don't want you falling asleep on the job.*

Under his own steam, he got up and tried the door, which was locked. 'Why did you lock me in?'

I didn't want you running off with me in the middle of the night. I might be able to hear you, but you're still too strong for me.

Simon considered that. Maybe he had a chance to turn this around.

'Get the doctor; he's ready.'

It was Tanya's voice but Simon said the words. His own voice drifted into the background.

What has she planned?

'It's not a plan so much as a necessity. I need you more subdued than you are. I don't want to fight you *and* the Indigenes when we storm their district. You're stronger than me. I plan to use that.'

I thought you said you had weapons.

'We do,' said Tanya's imprint. 'But first you need a little something.'

The door opened and Dr Jameson burst in, brandishing a needle. He came close to Simon, who shrank back until he hit the wall. Jameson caught his arm and jabbed it with the needle.

Simon's mind turned fuzzy. Then he felt Tanya push to become the dominant mind. So far he'd restricted her power over him to voice only, but now, as his left arm jerked, Tanya fought to take control of his body. Possessing independent thought would mean nothing if he couldn't stop her.

Simon's dizzy spell forced him to sit. But the second he did, his body stood against his will.

'There's no time for rest, Simon. I need you familiar with our weapons.'

Tanya directed him forward. He fought against her, which only made her push harder. Half way down the corridor, he relented to her.

'That's easier, isn't it? After a while, it's useless to fight something that's meant to happen. I'm supposed to transcend and you're supposed to help me.'

You could have achieved that without using me as a sacrifice.

'That wasn't my intention. The Elite hadn't planned on including any of you in this. But our bodies are spent; nothing is left. We can't do this without you.'

Tanya pulled him along.

Simon pushed and found his voice. 'You're just an imprint of your real self. How's that going to work?'

Tanya replied out loud. 'Jameson says the imprint believes it to be the real thing. Think of me as a copy of myself, in every way. Soon my real body will die and along with it my mind. Jameson reckons that could happen a few hours from now.'

'That soon?'

'Our bodies weren't designed to withstand the extensive testing performed on us. That kind of change takes a millennium of evolution to achieve. Our current forms aren't hardy enough to withstand it. But preserving consciousness, even if it's a copy... well, that's better than death. If Charles Deighton hadn't succeeded in achieving mind occupation, then we wouldn't have known it was even possible.'

Simon's body halted at a closed door near the lab area. He waited to see what Tanya would instruct him to do next. His arm lifted and his hand turned the handle. Then she walked him inside. Still able to control the movement of his head, Simon looked around the room at the nine other Conditioned whom the remaining Elite occupied. They had created a half circle around a table with at least a dozen weapons on it. At the table stood another two Conditioned who checked the weapons and who were not part of the mind-hijacking experience. Dr Jameson stood off to the side, making notes on his DPad.

'These are our temporary weapons experts,' said Tanya out loud. The pair not part of the experiment both looked at Simon. 'Please demonstrate to everyone how to use the guns.'

The pair nodded and they each picked up a gun.

One of them said, 'The weapon contains a minuscule version of the machine in the environ.' He opened the side cover and showed the group. Simon saw a small ball of energy sitting in a containment field. 'The weapons fire bolts of electricity.'

How long does the energy last?

'About an hour per gun.'

Simon saw a huge problem with their weapon. He strained against the imprint to gain control over his voice box once more. He felt Tanya loosen her control over him.

'The Indigenes aren't harmed by electricity,' he said.

Tanya snatched back control. 'Actually, they are. It slows down their movements. They will most likely prepare for our arrival by carrying energy absorption devices on them. The devices can negate the effects of an energy blast if they've been modified enough.'

Simon was careful not to think about his recent meeting with Stephen and the others.

He felt Tanya tap into his thoughts. 'But it seems as though that meeting has already happened. They have an envisioner in their group.'

Shit.

'Don't worry, Simon. I would have discovered that in the end. You can still mask your thoughts from me, but soon it won't matter.'

The weapons experts fired a shot against the wall, close to one of the host Conditioned. The host flinched but didn't move. Simon worried about the impossibility of fighting against this internal occupation.

'It won't be easy to move us now,' Tanya said, 'but it will be over soon. And to answer your earlier question...'

Tanya gestured for one of the weapons experts to explain.

'We've adapted the gun to fire continually if it meets resistance from an energy absorption device. The onslaught will not only slow them down, but it will make them immobile.'

'For how long?' said Simon.

'Minutes at a time.'

What could they do in a few minutes?

'Plenty, Simon. We could reach their Nexus, for one.'

That's what worried him. Tanya didn't appear to catch that thought.

'We don't have much time,' she said. 'We've designed body armour to protect the Conditioned, so all the hosts need to suit up and get trained on these weapons. We leave as soon as we're ready.'

'What about using mind mapping to learn the layout

of their district?' suggested one of the Elite.

Dr Jameson looked up from his DPad and shook his head. 'Not possible. Your minds are already overloaded as it is.'

It was then that Simon realised he'd lost his working knowledge of electricity. That must have happened when Tanya merged with him.

'We had to sacrifice something,' she said. 'Now let's get trained on these, get our guest who's bellowing like a wild calf and find this secret entrance.'

43

Bill arrived twenty minutes after Stephen called him, armed with a backpack and a DPad. Stephen ordered the temporary removal of boulders to the main hatch entrance to allow Bill to pass and escorted him down into the district, where Bill put on his gel mask.

'We're all gathered in the core,' said Stephen. 'It's the only space big enough to run operations.'

Bill slowed. 'All of you?'

'Yes.' Stephen felt his hesitation, saw his yellow, indecisive aura. 'Laura's there. But I need both of you on side. Whatever your issues, they must wait.'

Bill sped up. 'Of course, I didn't mean...'

'I know,' said Stephen. 'Everything will work out the way it's supposed to in the end. Give it time.'

Bill flashed him a half smile. 'That's what I'm worried about.'

The core buzzed with active Indigenes who, on the back of Stephen's orders, were gathering large rocks in the middle of the room to use as barricade material.

'Where did all that come from?' said Bill.

'We began digging a new tunnel and we're using

debris from the dig to block access to the tranquillity caves.'

'Do you have enough material to block them all?'

'We will.'

Anton with Arianna, Gabriel with Clement and Laura with Serena directed different groups in the space. It might be a day or a week before the GS humans attacked. Stephen wished he had a better idea of the timing of the attack.

'What about spotters?' said Bill, as though he'd read Stephen's mind.

He smiled. 'You're getting good at that.'

'What?'

'Guessing what I'm thinking before I say it. Maybe we've been spending too much time together.'

Bill smirked. 'Maybe.'

'We have Indigenes up top who are keeping a lookout. They're limited on how far they can venture while the sun shines, but it's all we can do for now.'

'Well, I brought a few reinforcements with me. They'll help to keep an eye out for the same thing.'

'Thank you.'

A relieved Stephen led Bill over to where Gabriel and Clement directed a group of younger Indigenes to carry rocks to the five tranquillity caves in the south of the district.

The elder turned when they both approached. 'Ah, good, you're here too.' Gabriel nodded at Bill, who eyed the Indigene with eyes as blue as Serena's. 'This is Clement. He's from my district.'

'Nice to see you again, Gabriel. Clement.' Bill nodded. 'I wish it was under better circumstances.'

'Never mind that.' Gabriel directed the last of the young Indigenes. 'It warms my heart to see both sides working together.'

Stephen watched the young under Gabriel and Clement's direction, who, according to Anton, had shunned the rules of the district. Stephen wondered if the physical threat to their home was enough to change their minds.

He looked around at the combined efforts. Blocking the tranquillity caves would not be enough. They needed to find a way to stop the Conditioned.

'We should talk,' he said to Gabriel. 'Just the three of us and Serena. The rest can carry on here.'

Gabriel nodded while Stephen reached out telepathically to Serena and Anton.

Arianna, I need Serena for a moment.

Arianna nodded and took over from Serena. An anxious-looking Laura split her time between watching Bill and directing her group.

They relocated to the Council Chambers but Stephen didn't want to keep this discussion private. The entire district needed to understand the consequences they faced if they couldn't stop the attack.

Inside the room, Bill placed his bag down on the floor. He ripped open the zipper and pulled out a dozen electrified Buzz Guns with the capacity to kill. These same weapons had been used in the fight between the Indigenes and the board members from Earth. They had rendered the Indigenes useless in the fight against the genetically modified bodyguards.

'I don't know how useful these will be, but let's try them anyway.' Bill activated his DPad. 'I was preoccupied and forgot to discuss some information the last time I was here. Information from Harvey Buchanan on tests done to the Conditioned and Elite.'

Bill set the DPad down on the floor and pulled the

information until it was represented as a 3D image. Stephen watched while Bill sorted through the files and gathered three specific ones together. Stephen moved closer, as did Gabriel and Serena.

'I can't read medical data, so I'm hoping one of you knows what we're looking at,' said Bill.

Serena, who had once been a lab technician, pointed at the screen. 'These are results from the tests performed on the Conditioned. Blood test results. And here.' She pointed to a bunch of formulae that meant little to Stephen. 'These formulae show what was done to the Conditioned, from the beginning to—' She paused. '—up to three months ago. These tests go well beyond what my work as a lab technician did to our test subjects.'

Serena, as her former alias Susan Bouchard, had tested on patients with imperfect genetic code.

'So what do we know from this information?' said Gabriel.

Serena shook her head. 'This information says the Conditioned have the same mutations as the second-generation Indigenes, but without a complete picture of testing from start to finish, I can't say if they can do more.'

'One thing's for certain, they can block our telepathy and turn theirs on and off at will,' said Stephen.

'Or maybe they only have the ability to speak to each other,' said Serena. 'Their mutations appear to have been crafted more specifically than ours.' She studied the 3D files. 'It's possible their telepathy never switched on like ours did.'

'Didn't switch on?' said Bill. 'So the doctors selected what to activate and what to keep dormant?'

'That's my feeling,' said Serena. 'I don't know what they planned to achieve by making the Conditioned, but I assume the testing done on the Elite was far more extensive.'

'The Elite want to transcend, so that requires a strong mind, yes?' said Bill.

'Yes,' said Serena. 'It requires a mind capable of existing beyond a physical plane.'

Bill folded his arms. 'I don't see how that's possible.'

'The Nexus makes it possible for us to exist outside of our bodies. If the Elite, using the Conditioned as vessels, get inside the Nexus, I have no idea how their minds will affect it,' said Serena. 'You remember how it reacted to me? I ended up changing it. We don't know if their energies will make it better or kill it. Whatever, we can't take the risk.'

'I agree,' said Stephen. 'So what defence can we use against the Conditioned?'

Serena shook her head. 'We must treat them the same as one of us. Be prepared for strength, speed. We might have the edge over them on abilities. But that won't matter if they get inside.'

Bill uncrossed his arms and picked up one of the Buzz Guns. 'So let's hit them with everything we have.'

44

'We're almost there,' Marcus shouted back at Tanya.

Even though the sun shone, the man wore a pair of magnification glasses.

Tanya in Simon's body and the other Elite occupying the other Conditioned followed Marcus to a vast, flat area with nothing visible for miles. Fifty extra Conditioned bolstered their attack group numbers.

'Where is it?' said Tanya through Simon.

'Not far now.'

Simon observed Marcus. Tanya had placed her trust in this stranger without knowing if the secret entrance really existed. He'd tried to convince her to wait, to send an advance party to check, but Tanya's excitement about transcendence couldn't be tempered.

He considered fighting Tanya, to slow her down, but in the short time she had occupied his mind, she had gained more control over his body. Each time he fought her, the effort drained him a little more.

Up ahead, Marcus stopped and stared at a patch of land. Simon couldn't see what he looked at until he approached the area from a different side. Set lower than the eye could see was a hatch set at a forty-five-degree angle, covered in rubble and indistinguishable from the landscape, except for a rusted handle.

Marcus pointed down. 'There.'

Simon imagined the Indigenes had the main hatch entrance covered just east from here, which was twice as big and visible to the naked eye. This made it too easy. He had hoped for some resistance—a tank, perhaps. A tank would have slowed the Elite down, if only for a short while.

'The stranger did good,' said Tanya.

Marcus looked at her. 'What now?'

'Now you take us inside.'

Simon saw the shiver than ran through the brown-haired stranger.

'No fucking way. This was not part of the deal.'

Tanya smirked. 'If you want to live like another species, you'd better see how they live. Open it.'

Marcus opened the hatch and Simon saw stone steps descending into the darkness. Tanya pushed Marcus down the steps. He stumbled but managed them without falling.

The non-vessel Conditioned, wearing robes and no body armour, followed him.

Shouts surprised Simon as three soldiers who'd been camouflaged by the landscape suddenly sprang up from their flat positions. Shots followed. Buzz Guns. Tanya ducked as several Conditioned retreated from the hatch to protect her and the Elite. Some fell but others pushed forward to attack the humans. The sound brought new bodies to their location—this time Indigenes. They posed a greater challenge to the non-vessel Conditioned, but not by much. Their strength matched the Indigenes well. And since the Indigenes had never met them in combat before, that gave Conditioned the edge.

Simon tried to help the fallen, but Tanya held him back alongside the other Elite.

'I can hear everything you're thinking,' she said.

'I don't think that matters any more,' said Simon.

'Probably not. We'll reach that Nexus or die trying.'

Simon knew all about Tanya's plans. She didn't need to tell him.

Tanya chuckled. *I just wanted to remind you in case you forgot.*

Hard to. It's all you think about in my head.

Simon looked ahead to see the Indigenes had the upper hand in the fight against the remaining Conditioned.

'How about we even this fight?' said Tanya to the others.

The Elite nodded and their vessels joined the fight. Weapons at the ready, they fired at the Indigenes, who moved with speed around the Conditioned. Simon couldn't move as fast as the Indigenes, so when Tanya lifted his hand with the gun, his mind froze.

'Doesn't matter which one I hit,' she said. 'We need this to be over. They're not prepared for us. They didn't send enough.'

She fired at one male Indigene who had a Conditioned in a choke hold. His body resembled a blur of light as he clutched his victim. The fight slowed immediately and the Indigene looked up at her—or rather Simon—just as she fired again. The Indigene jerked and convulsed then fell to the ground while the Conditioned, with a sizeable burn mark on his torso, collapsed next to him. Simon ran over to the Conditioned and checked his pulse before Tanya could stop him. He couldn't feel one.

Collateral, said Tanya before she issued a vocal

command to the others. 'Let's get inside.'

Tanya ran down the stone steps. To get this far felt too easy. Stephen must have seen this and taken measures farther inside.

'We'll find out soon enough,' said Tanya.

Simon was sick of Elite One listening in on all his thoughts.

They gathered outside a door. Three Conditioned males milled around it, checking it over.

What are they doing? Simon asked Tanya.

'You and I were unable to use the mind mapping, but their empty brains could accept the information. These three are structural engineers—temporary ones anyway.'

It didn't take the trio long to get through the door. Tanya shoved Marcus through and Simon felt a new pressure on his chest when he passed through the environmental force field. Waiting on the other side were several Indigenes armed with Buzz Guns.

'Oh my God, do you feel that?' Tanya looked around, seemingly oblivious to the fact weapons were being pointed at them. 'The Nexus. It's so powerful. I can feel it calling me.'

Simon heard her laugh inside his head. Then he felt something, a tugging on his mind. An attempt to bend his will.

Serena.

'The Nexus is a hostile place, Tanya. It will kill foreign bodies.You must not go there.'

The tugging increased and with it he sensed Tanya's growing doubt. 'Yes, I believe it will kill me. But I don't understand. A moment ago, it called to me.'

'It's how it lures you to it, with the promise of power. But when you get there, it rips away the pleasure and leaves you borderline psychotic.'

347

The tugging, the bending increased the more Simon talked. Serena could be anywhere.

'Who's anywhere?' said Tanya.

His mind clouded over until he couldn't remember his last thought.

'I don't know. But it's a bad idea to go to the Nexus. We both risk losing our minds.'

'Maybe you're right...'

One of the Conditioned grabbed her weapon suddenly and fired into the group of armed Indigenes. That broke the spell and Tanya made Simon's body lunge for the weapon to reclaim it.

She shook Simon's head. 'What happened?'

Simon's thoughts remained fuzzy but Tanya's were sharpening with every second.

'Never mind,' she said.

She fired again at the group, who no longer moved. Simon heard voices descending on their location.

He felt Tanya's panic. 'Which way to the Nexus?'

Simon pushed against his arm but it lifted and pointed to a tunnel ahead.

'Your mind remembers the way. I can see the tranquillity cave now.'

She ordered half of the Elite to give their weapons over to the Conditioned. The non-vessels would protect them.

The group stepped over the unmoving bodies of the Indigenes. Simon pulled Tanya back to a human body— Marcus. He struggled to breathe in the thin air.

What about him? Simon said, losing power over his voice again.

'He's fulfilled his usefulness. There's nothing I can do for him now.'

There was one thing. Before Tanya could stop him,

Simon dragged him outside the containment field until Marcus gasped and drew in new air. Then Tanya reclaimed control of him and they walked on.

'You're too soft, Simon.'

Serena's influence got stronger the farther inside the district they got. The armed Conditioned made light work of any Indigenes who stood in their way. Their group entered the core, a central space inside the district. Simon was surprised to find it empty. He wondered if their efforts had been redirected to protecting the tranquillity caves.

How many caves are there, Simon? said Tanya in his mind.

I don't know. I was only in one of them.

She pressed against his thoughts as though she didn't believe him and was checking for herself. *You're telling the truth. You know the way to one, so that's the cave we hit.*

Simon resisted her advance, but the longer she occupied his mind the stronger she got.

There's no use in fighting me.

She marched him into the tunnel that Simon knew would lead them to the cave. They emerged at the other end to find a blocked, but unguarded, tranquillity cave entrance.

Tanya pulled him towards it. 'I can feel its raw power through the floor. I can't wait to get inside.'

Simon felt the vibrations too. It surprised him to find nobody there to stop them. Given how easily the Elite's guns had disabled the other Indigenes, maybe it was better they stayed away. In such a small, confined space outside the cave, the electricity from a shot would bounce around too much.

Those Conditioned who were not armed dismantled the rocks blocking the cave until they'd removed enough

Eliza Green

to squeeze through. Serena's influence felt stronger here. She pressed on his will again.

'Now I know what she feels like, I can fight her off,' said Tanya.

Three armed Conditioned shimmied inside the space. Simon went next and found Stephen, Arianna, Serena, Clement and Gabriel waiting for them on the other side.

'Stop her, Simon,' said Serena.

'I can't. She's too strong,' he replied.

Serena wore the neurosensor. She pushed harder, attempting to bend his will.

The Nexus is painful. The Nexus will destroy anything it does not recognise.

His desire to flee from the pain overwhelmed him, but Tanya pushed him farther inside the room. 'A little pain never hurt anyone.'

The other Elite stayed outside while three armed Conditioned fanned out to protect Tanya in Simon's body.

'Let me pass and you will live,' she said to the Indigenes.

'I can't do that,' said Stephen. 'My duty as elder is to protect the Indigenes in this district.'

Tanya laughed. 'From what, an old woman? All I want is a little of your power.'

'What you want is to transcend.'

Tanya shrugged Simon's shoulders. 'Yes, that too. But this could be over without more injuries or deaths.'

Serena continued to push her will on to Simon's mind. *His* mind bent while Tanya's resisted.

'You can stop that now, dear. I know what you feel like and I can resist.'

Serena huffed out a long breath as if the effort to influence had drained her.

350

'You will let me pass,' said Tanya.

Stephen stepped in front of her. 'No.'

While Tanya was distracted, Simon looked around at the dozens of floor units.

'You can't be everywhere in this room, Stephen,' said Tanya, snapping Simon's head back. 'You can't protect all of the units.'

Serena, Arianna, Clement and Gabriel fanned out around the room.

'But maybe we can,'said Serena.

Simon heard commotion outside and Bill's voice. 'Take their weapons!'

Tanya loosened her hold on Simon and in that short moment, someone charged him and knocked him to the ground. He hit it with a thud and a breath escaped his lungs.

An alert Tanya shoved Anton off her and scrambled back just as Gabriel, Arianna and Clement surrounded the armed Conditioned. A tousle with one caused a weapon to fire and sent all three flying.

'Arianna!' someone cried.

It was Anton. He scrambled to where she lay unconscious or dead—Simon couldn't tell.

Stephen and Serena were also distracted by Arianna's misfortune. While they weren't looking, Tanya crawled to the nearest hole. He wanted to shout out, to warn Stephen that Tanya was too close, but his voice box no longer listened to his command.

She slid into the hole and at the bottom, he landed on his neck. Through the pain, Tanya forced him to sit. A figure landed on all fours beside him in the hole. It was Stephen. He hauled Simon up the stone steps.

'You won't succeed, Tanya,' he grunted.

Simon's eyes closed as Tanya initiated the

procedure for connecting to the Nexus—a memory of seeing Stephen perform and explain the process. Stephen had a hand around his neck and was dragging him out of the unit.

Simon saw the Nexus reach out for him. Tendrils, fatter than the ones the machine in the environ attracted, slipped through a golden lattice. With Stephen's hand squeezing his airway, Simon couldn't breathe. He wanted to shout at Stephen, *Kill me*. If he were dead, Tanya would die too. *Snap my neck, break the connection.* The words remained in his head. He had lost control. He was just a passenger now.

Simon slipped out of Stephen's grip; he tumbled back down. Stephen scrambled after him and pinned Simon's body down on the cold, hard floor. With a grunt, he jammed his knee into Simon's neck and put all his weight behind it.

Simon, still with his eyes closed, saw Stephen's efforts as his body hovered over the scene, but also the Nexus tendril that hovered next to his arm.

The tendril waited, almost as if it hesitated to take him. Tanya gave one final push, then Simon heard a soft giggle as the tendril wrapped around his arm. One pull, then another. Her energy—his energy—merged with the fat strand of light.

Tanya had made it inside the Nexus.

45

Stephen lost his grip on Simon. He scrambled next to him on the unit floor and tried to break his connection with the Nexus. A dead body would give off no energy. He heard Simon's neck crack and opened Simon's eyes to see they were lifeless. He sat back with a huff, certain he'd made it in time.

Eager to put distance between Simon and the Nexus, Stephen hoisted his body over his shoulder and carried him to the top, where he lay him down on the floor above.

Bill squeezed through the barricade. 'I have the others rounded up. Did you stop—?'

Bill's words cut off as he took in the scene. He slid to the floor next to Simon's body.

He grabbed his old boss's face and shook it, then pressed two fingers to Simon's neck. 'I can't feel a pulse.'

Stephen glanced over at where the three armed Conditioned fought with Anton, Serena and a recovered Gabriel. A shot was discharged from one gun, followed by a 'No!' from Anton just as Gabriel fell to the floor next to Clement and Arianna, who still weren't moving.

Stephen stared at Bill. 'Help them.'

Bill scrambled over to the fight with a Buzz Gun in his hand. He gave a sharp whistle, and that's when Stephen saw an armed ITF member slip inside the room. His gun discharged and frightened one of the Conditioned enough to drop his gun. The others stopped fighting and Serena and Anton quickly disarmed them. Bill kept his weapon pointed at their group of three. One of the Conditioned who'd been restrained outside the door glanced at Simon on the floor. He looked weary, as though the fight had been drained from him, his mission somehow complete. Eight others with similar weary expressions smiled, and nodded.

Stephen's gaze shot to the presumed-dead Simon. He pressed his fingers to his neck and felt a pulse. It was weak.

'Serena!' Stephen called.

She ran over, slipping on the floor and landing on her backside. She slapped Simon's face.

'I think he's inside,' said Stephen. 'I don't know how... I killed him. The Nexus doesn't take dead bodies.'

Serena peeled open his eyes. 'He probably wasn't dead at the time.' She removed her fingers; his eyes sprang back closed. 'We need to go in after him. It's not too late.'

Stephen got to his feet and told Anton and Bill their plan. His eyes found an unconscious Arianna and Gabriel, who had both been hit with a close-range bolt of electricity. Clement stirred on the floor. Anton checked them over.

How are they? he asked Anton.

Not good. But we don't have time to discuss this. Hurry, and get them out of there.

Stephen nodded at Serena and they each took a unit. At the bottom, Stephen closed his eyes and concentrated

354

on the lattice. He waited impatiently for the Nexus to come get him. Amid his unsettled mind, the tendril danced before him but wouldn't latch on to his energy.

'I don't have time for this.'

He grabbed the tendril, which delivered a shock. But he fought the pain to hold on. The Nexus tried to release itself from his grip, but then yanked him inside as if it were irritated with him.

Stephen rode the rough treatment of the abusive tendril until he was safely inside. Not waiting for Serena, he searched the dull Nexus space, which had no users connected—he had ordered all other users out—and saw a single energy waiting in the space the curved Nexus wall surrounded.

'Simon!' he called out.

The energy turned to him. The Nexus had not yet found his energy. At least that was something.

Serena floated to his side. 'Is he responding?'

'Not yet. *Simon!* If you can hear me, follow my voice out.'

There was no answer. That didn't surprise him. He had no idea how much control Simon still had. But his energy was still intact, which meant Simon and Tanya were still one. When Anton had been possessed by an imprint of Charles Deighton, their energies had split when they got inside. But this time felt different to back then.

'We've been here once before, Stephen,' said Serena.

'This isn't quite the same. We had help the last time, more users to call upon. I couldn't risk it this time. I can't be sure what her altered presence will do to the Nexus.'

The Nexus became agitated, which manifested as a strong ripple that ran the length of its wall.

'We didn't have the new Nexus back then. I can use it to control them,' said Serena.

Stephen looked at her bright and beautiful energy. 'You're right. We still have time. Simon's joined energy hasn't figured out how to interact with the wall yet. Let's try it.'

46

Tanya became too strong for him, too giddy, from the moment she felt the power inside the Nexus. It was an addictive feeling, being that close to all this power. Simon had felt its strength without even trying the Nexus. Now Tanya was not only experiencing its power for herself but also accessing his memories of Stephen explaining how it worked.

'In order for this to work we must connect to the wall. That's where it holds its greatest power,' she said, drawing on information from Stephen's prior explanation.

She pushed Simon closer to the wall, but the nearer they got the more sluggish their movements became.

'Why are you fighting this?' said Tanya. 'This is how it has to be.'

Simon wasn't fighting anything. From the moment they had entered the Nexus, his mind had weakened to the point where he controlled nothing. Tanya was in the driver's seat now. She just didn't realise it.

'Well, answer me!'

She must have lost the ability to read his thoughts when they entered the Nexus. At least he would leave this world with just his thoughts in his head.

Another voice came through. It was Stephen. *We won't let that happen.*

How? he replied.

The Nexus amplifies connections in here. We can hear you, but not her.

Can she hear you? said Simon.

I don't think so. Serena is here too. She's commanding the Nexus to protect itself. That's why you feel a resistance. It has put up a barrier.

Tanya was getting impatient. 'Simon!'

He had no choice but to answer her. 'I'm not stopping you. This place is.'

She turned their joined energies towards the wall. 'Or your friends are. They know I'm too strong for this place. Help me to fight the Nexus' barrier.'

Tanya used his energy as a battering ram to fight against the force of the Nexus. The force slowed his body and mind down too much for him to do anything. If his body had connected instead of his mind, like up top in the environ, he was sure the raw Nexus power would have crushed him by now.

It's why we exist in energy form, said Stephen. *The Nexus is powerful. What you saw in the environ would only have been a fraction of this. Keep fighting the Nexus. Serena will command it to see you as an enemy.*

I have no control over my energy in here.

Try, Simon.

He did, but to little avail. He felt like a rag doll, being positioned and repositioned wherever the owner wanted. He couldn't drag Tanya away from the wall.

'Push harder,' Tanya commanded, and with that the impediment on his energy lessened. 'Feel that?' she said. 'It's weakening.'

358

It's weakening! Simon shouted to Stephen.

We know, Stephen replied. *Serena's trying to strengthen it. Just hold on.*

Tanya was back inside his head. 'I can feel it giving in. It's curious about me. It wants me to join. Whatever is stopping it won't hold out.'

That's what Simon feared.

We can't maintain the barrier. It's weakening, said Stephen.

Tanya thinks the Nexus is curious.

That's it, said Stephen. *If we can distract the Nexus, it might back off long enough for us to disconnect your body from the outside.*

Simon watched as a lone energy floated to the opposite side of the curved wall that Tanya was trying to access. The Nexus' defence firmed up as it tracked the lone energy. Serena, he presumed.

'We're losing it,' said Tanya. 'We need its attention back on us.'

She backed their joint energy up and charged at the wall. The Nexus' defences slipped enough for it to refocus on them.

'Again!'

Tanya backed up a second time and charged again.

The barrier was loosening. Simon could feel it.

'One more time.'

Serena! Simon heard Stephen shout. *We need to do more.*

Tanya charged at the barrier protecting the wall and, with a pop, it gave way. Their motion carried their energy straight to the wall. A hundred tiny tendrils appeared and wove around their joint energy to create a tight lattice.

Serena and Stephen's energy sped to their location

but an energy field kept them at bay. Behind the energy field, Simon could no longer hear Stephen.

He felt the beginnings of what Tanya had fought so hard to achieve: transcendence, the conversion of her mind and body into pure energy. The Nexus drew energy from them and added it to its own. He felt his hold on reality slip further away while Tanya's strengthened.

'This feels amazing,' said Tanya. 'I've never felt this strong before.'

The temporary feeling would remain as long as they stayed connected to the Nexus and its power. Simon felt something split their energy into two. His energy, smaller than Tanya's growing one, dislodged from the wall and landed with a thud on the ledge below it. While the tendrils appeared to feed Tanya's energy, they drew from his, tightening around his energy and squeezing until he could no longer fight the pressure.

47

No matter what they tried, Stephen and Serena could not get near the Nexus wall. It had created a cocoon of energy around the joined energies before weaning off Simon's weaker energy, until the pair had been separated. The Nexus continued to steal from Simon's energy while feeding new energy to Tanya.

'What's it doing, Serena?'

She was quiet beside him. Her attempts to distract the Nexus had failed. The Nexus always listened to her. If she couldn't stop it, then how could they stop Tanya?

'It's killing Simon. We have to stop it,' he said.

'We can't, Stephen. What the Nexus does with either of them is out of my control. It ignores my commands.'

'What now? She spends her days in here, trapped?'

'I don't know.' She sighed. 'This has never happened before.'

'We'll have to quarantine users—'

A sudden brightening of Tanya's already dazzling energy cut him off. Then the brightness faded to nothing.

'Where did she go?' Stephen drifted closer to the

wall; the barrier no longer impeded them. There was no sign of her. Simon's energy was barely a blip. Then it, too, disappeared. 'What happened?'

Serena moved closer to the Nexus and pressed her energy to its now calm wall. The organic being communicated only with her.

'I can't sense her. Maybe the Nexus killed her.'

'What's it saying?' said Stephen.

Serena disconnected from the wall. 'Nothing at all. It's calm. Everything feels... normal.'

'So that's it?'

'I don't know. But I'm not sensing anything new here. It's possible the Nexus became too much for her to handle. She was not one of us. She was a foreign entity inside here.'

Stephen floated to the exit and Serena followed him. 'We should check on Simon.'

He disconnected and climbed out of the unit to see Simon still lying on the upper floor. Laura sat on the floor beside him. She wore the neurosensor and had Simon's head in her lap. Her eyes were wet. Bill had hunkered down opposite her, but kept his distance.

Laura looked up when Stephen neared.

'How is he?' he said.

She shook her head. 'He died a few minutes ago. I tried to reach him with the neurosensor. I felt everything he did. He fought her for as long as he could. He felt no pain in the end.'

She placed Simon's head gently on the floor and tore the neurosensor from her head. She wiped her eyes and went over to where Anton tended to Arianna, Clement and Gabriel. Bill straightened up, looking like he wanted to go with her. He followed, but kept his distance.

Serena emerged from her unit. Stephen met her

362

Genesis Variant

halfway and pressed his forehead against hers. *You did everything you could.*

I have a connection to the Nexus. I should have been able to stop them.

A more alert Arianna drew his attention. But in all the commotion, he couldn't feel Gabriel.

He strode over to where they lay. Clement was sitting up while Laura tended to a blast wound on his shoulder. Arianna looked up at a relieved and smiling Anton. But Gabriel had a sheet over his head.

Stephen swallowed back a lump. 'Is he dead?'

He already knew.

'Gabriel took the brunt of the hit to save Arianna and Clement. The blast hit his heart. It was instant.'

'But we can heal...'

Anton shook his head. 'Not this time.'

Stephen peeled back the cover and touched Gabriel's peaceful-looking face.

'We need to tell Margaux.'

'Somehow I think she already knows,' said Serena.

Stephen pressed his forehead to the Indigene who had been like a father to him since Pierre's death. 'Goodbye, my old friend. This district will never forget what you've done for us.'

48

Chaos ensued in the core of District Three as the Indigenes rounded up the disarmed Conditioned. Bill ordered his men to watch the Elite, whose hosts wore energy absorption vests, similar to the ones Tanya and the board members had worn in the fight in New Melbourne eight years ago.

'Remove their vests,' said Bill.

He fumed at the turn of events, at the blatant disrespect shown for the Indigene's space and the Nexus. At least only Tanya out of the ten Elite had made it inside. According to Serena and Stephen, her energy had been destroyed along with Simon's.

Bill relieved the Elite of their vests while his men pointed the Elite's own weapons at them. In another corner of the room, the Indigenes pointed Buzz Guns at the Conditioned who didn't carry hosts. He would need some place more secure than an open core to house the GS humans who were now under his command. The invading numbers and the piled-up bodies told him approximately half of the GS 100 had accompanied the hosted Elite.

They'd found an extra person, unconscious and just

Genesis Variant

outside the environmental controls. A man with brown hair who had an alliance to Harvey Buchanan.

Bill left the Elite and walked over to Stephen where he oversaw the Indigenes controlling the Conditioned. Bill placed a hand on his shoulder when it seemed like the Indigene didn't notice him. Stephen jumped and glared at him. Then his expression softened.

'Bill,' he said softly. 'I'm tired of losing friends in this fight.'

'I know,' said Bill. 'Gabriel was a good man.'

'As was Simon.'

'He could have walked away from it all. But instead, he did everything he could to stop her.' Bill paused. 'I think we should talk.' He looked around. 'Privately?'

Stephen paused and looked around at the chaos. 'Okay, but let's keep it brief.'

They relocated to the Council Chambers. Stephen left the door open, which surprised Bill.

'A return to my policy. I don't like secrets. They're too hard to manage.'

'Listen.' Bill paced the room. 'We've won here today, even though it feels like we haven't. But I'll need to round up the remaining GS humans in the caves and contain them. Then I'll need to figure out what to do with them.'

'You mean kill them?' said Stephen.

Bill stopped pacing. 'It's not up to me to take anyone's life.'

'They are parasites, Bill. They don't deserve life.'

He stared at his friend. 'What happened to you? You are usually the moral compass around here. Now I'm the one protecting lives while you're gung ho about ending them.'

Eliza Green

'I've seen too much. I'm sick of it all.' Stephen slumped against the wall. 'Where does it all end?'

'You can't think like that. You give those thoughts power and you lose the democracy and trust you've worked hard to build here.'

Stephen waved his hand. In that second, Bill saw Pierre. Other than a brief encounter with him, he hadn't known much about the elder. According to Stephen he had been a stubborn man, and not easy to convince that change was a good thing.

'I've lost trust here already. But the Elite's attack on us was just one problem. Our focus must shift now to the rogue groups who wish to see the peace treaty torn apart.'

'I'm afraid the issue with the Elite isn't over.'

'What do you mean?'

Bill sighed. 'The doctors created the Elite and the Conditioned. If we don't destroy the medical data, what's to stop them from creating more? In a year, or five, we could be right back where we started.'

'But nothing happened when Tanya entered the Nexus.' Stephen frowned. 'It destroyed her energy. The Elite wanted transcendence. If the Nexus, the most powerful energy source on this planet, wouldn't give it to them, they will never achieve it. If we make that fact public knowledge, the doctors, the Elite, will stop chasing after it.'

'They may stop coming after you, but transcendence can be achieved through artificial means. There's nothing to stop them from creating an energy source more powerful than the Nexus. This fight isn't over.'

Stephen sighed. 'So what now?'

'Now, you must tend to things here. I need to visit

the caves, round up the others before they realise something's wrong.'

Bill heard a sound at the door. He turned to see Clement.

'I'm sorry,' Clement said. He raised both hands. 'I'll come back later.'

Bill waved him in. 'We're done talking.'

He prepared to leave but Clement stopped him with a hand on his shoulder.

'Don't go. I need to speak with both of you.'

'What's wrong, Clement?' said Stephen.

The Indigene with the blue eyes walked farther into the room.

In the middle of the room, he stopped and turned. 'That man we found, just outside the environmental barrier?'

Bill nodded. 'One of Harvey's associates.'

'He's part of the rogue group I infiltrated. He was my surveillance partner.'

Stephen shook his head. 'I don't understand.'

'Marcus Murphy is his real name, and I told him there were other ways inside the district. He must have followed me to one.' Clement looked contrite. 'I led them to the entrance we never thought they'd find. It was my fault Gabriel died.'

Stephen walked over to him and gripped the side of his neck. 'You are not to blame for their actions. It was nobody's fault.'

Clement nodded while Bill mulled over the name he'd heard from Jenny Waterson: Marcus Murphy. The associate who had run Waverley neighbourhood back on Earth.

☼

Bill left the district with a dozen armed men and women in tow, and drove to the caves using three cars. They parked at the boundary wall. Nobody stopped them when they climbed over and entered GS land. They arrived at the caves to find three Conditioned males waiting in the room with a dozen wall monitors on the left-hand wall and a raised platform at the back. His men raised their guns, but the trio lifted their hands in surrender.

'Are they dead?' asked one.

Bill assumed he meant the Elite. 'Just one. We have the others in custody.'

'Tanya?'

'Yes.'

The males looked relieved. 'We don't wish to fight you. Our only fight was with the Elite and what they had planned for us.'

'Are there more of you here?' The Conditioned nodded. 'And the original Elite?'

The Conditioned nodded at the raised platform. 'Back there. In the first room you come across.'

Bill jumped up on to the platform and took the right-hand tunnel, which led him to an area with one door on the left. He opened the door and saw a dozen beds inside, their headboards following the curved wall. In the centre of the room was a square, black machine on a table with wires protruding out of it. He assumed this was the mind-mapping machine that Simon had mentioned.

Ten old and frail Elite lay in repose, one to each bed. He checked two bodies and pressed his fingers to their necks.

A familiar voice caused him to turn. 'They're dead.'

'Harvey, what are you doing here?'

'Same as you. Checking on them.' He nodded at the

dead. 'They wanted transcendence, did you know that?'

'Not all of them as it turned out. Where can I find the doctors?'

He needed to confiscate all the medical data they held on the Elite and Conditioned.

Harvey shook his head. 'They're long gone, and so is your data. The labs here have been cleared out.'

Bill narrowed his eyes at the former geneticist. 'What do you know?'

'I monitored their movements from the second Simon and the others left here two hours ago. The doctors packed everything up and got the hell out of here.'

'I need that data, Harvey. Can you find them for me?'

'What's it worth to you?'

'What do you want?'

Although he already had an idea.

Harvey smiled as if he'd won. He may just have. 'Genetic manipulation clinics, three to start. A squeaky-clean record so I can run my business the way I've always wanted.'

'Harvey, in case you haven't noticed, getting one's face fixed isn't a high priority here.'

Harvey stuck his hands in his pockets. 'Take it or leave it. I want them operational in a week.'

Bill didn't see how to make that happen. 'I can do something in six months... but right now, there's too much going on.'

'Sorry, Bill, my terms are non-negotiable. The sooner you set it up, the sooner I help you find the doctors.'

'That's not going to work for me. You help me and I get you your deal.'

Harvey removed his hands and backed out of the

room. 'I won't compromise. My clinics come first. I'll be around, watching. When you change your mind, and you will, come find me on the Wave.'

Harvey vanished out the door just as one of Bill's team entered through another door on the opposite side of the room. He let out a low whistle.

An irritated Bill said, 'Get the Elite into cryogenic chambers. We may need access to their genetic information. And round up the remaining Conditioned. I haven't decided what to do with them yet.'

The officer nodded and Bill rubbed a hand over his tired face. He left his team to organise things in the caves and started the walk back to his vehicle. No matter what way he spun it, he couldn't do this without Harvey's help. If the doctors really were gone, Harvey might be the only one capable of reverse-engineering the tests done to the Elite and Conditioned, and deciphering the file Simon had copied.

But first, he had to talk to Laura.

49

Laura sensed Bill before she saw him. Not only did she recognise his familiar heavy stomp, but she heard his erratic thoughts, which sounded like a rumbling train in her mind. She used to say, 'Penny for your thoughts?' It still surprised Bill she could read him so well.

Truth was, she didn't need a rumbling sound to know when Bill carried too much load. It was his pacing, how he delivered a one-word reply when he was annoyed or distracted. Or how he changed the subject when she got too close to something that bothered him. And she knew his decision to let her go bothered him most.

She waited in her room—a temporary home away from home. Yet it felt less temporary and more like the place she needed to be. She wasn't done here; the last twenty-four hours had proven that. The fight against the Elite. Using the neurosensor on Simon. The Nexus. She'd barely scratched the surface of her abilities and this fight had woken up her desire to learn more. Clement had been helping her to understand some things.

She heard his voice, loud and clear, even though he was on the other side of the district. He was with Arianna, asking her how she felt. Laura sensed Arianna's physical weakness after being hit by a close-range blast of electricity, but at least she was improving. In a short time, Arianna had become a sister to her. Laura wasn't ready to lose anyone else.

She stiffened when Arianna told Bill where she was and offered to walk him there. Her heart fluttered in her chest at the thought of seeing him again. It had only been a few days and she'd seen him since, but things had been awkward between them. She didn't know how to talk to him any more.

'She's down there.'

Bill charged past the room, then backtracked and looked inside. His stride had purpose to it, but when he saw her, his energy dissipated, as though the fight had left him.

'Laura.'

His voice sounded cracked and broken. It nearly broke her heart.

'Bill.' She stood beside her bed and gestured to it. 'Please, sit.'

He did, but looked up at her when she remained standing. 'Aren't you going to sit with me?'

Laura needed a clear head and she couldn't have that with Bill so close. 'I'm fine here.'

She tucked her hands behind her back and leaned against the wall.

Bill scratched the back of his neck, indicating his discomfort. 'Eh, how are you?'

'I'm fine.'

'Were you injured?'

She shook her head. 'No. And Arianna and Clement will both be fine.' Her heart hurt to remember Gabriel. She had no idea how Margaux would take the news. 'I'm sorry about Simon.'

'Yeah.' Bill stared at the floor and blew out a breath. 'He made the ultimate sacrifice to protect the Indigenes. His sacrifice won't be forgotten.'

'I'll make sure everyone here will remember him too.'

Bill looked up at her. 'Julie can't wait for you to get back. You'll never guess who showed up at the ITF. Ben Watson, looking for a job. I put him to work with Julie. Turns out he's good—'

'I'm not coming back.'

She hadn't meant to just blurt it out.

Bill stood up fast. 'What? Never?'

'I don't know.' She turned away from him. 'All I know is these past few days have given me a chance to explore my Indigene side. I need more time to figure out who I am.'

'You're the one who didn't want to explore it.' She looked back to see Bill pointing a finger at her. 'I never stopped you.'

'No, you didn't, Bill. In fact, kicking me out was the most painful and liberating thing you could have done.' She saw him flinch at her use of the words "painful" and "liberating".

'So you *want* to be here?'

'For now. All I know is I'm not ready to return to my old life.'

'You mean your life with me?'

Bill sounded bitter.

Laura had feared this confrontation, the one where Bill would get so riled up he refused to listen to reason. He always pushed her away when things got too real.

'That's not what I'm saying at all.' At least she didn't think she was. 'Can you and Julie keep things running at the ITF in my absence?'

'Sounds like we don't have a choice. But don't expect your job to be there when you get back.'

His words cut her. 'You don't mean that.'

Bill's expression softened and he sighed. 'No, I don't.' He sat down on the bed and buried his head in his hands. 'I don't know. I want you to come home, but I also know you need this.'

Laura sat beside him and Bill looked at her. She climbed on to his lap and buried her face in his shoulder. His tension evaporated when he wrapped his arms around her.

'I miss you, Laura.'

She clung to him. 'I miss you too.'

They stayed that way for a moment.

'What will you do now?' she said softly into his neck.

'Concentrate on cleaning up the mess that happened here, I guess.' He paused, pushed her away. 'I'm sorry, Laura. This... you... it's all too much.'

He stood up and strode out of the room. As she watched him go from the bed, her heart wanted to run after him. But she didn't move.

Arianna appeared seconds later. 'You okay?'

Laura nodded and wiped away her tears. 'I will be. Am I doing the right thing?'

Arianna shrugged and entered the room. 'I can't answer that for you.' She tapped her heart once. 'But this never lies.'

Laura listened to what her heart was telling her. All she heard was silence.

50

Two weeks later

The funeral for Gabriel had been a sombre affair and not one Stephen could handle alone. Serena stayed by his side through the entire ceremony. Margaux had arrived from District Eight, already aware of her husband's demise. She'd been strangely pragmatic about the whole thing.

'I felt it before I got here,' she'd said when he spoke to her privately in his Council Chambers.

'I'm so sorry, Margaux. It's my fault. I wasn't paying attention.'

Margaux had grabbed his head and pressed her forehead to his. 'Nobody is to blame, Stephen. Gabriel would have died for what you and Serena fought to protect: our freedom. Before Gabriel left, he told me he might not return. We said our goodbyes.'

A normally erratic Margaux had occasional bouts of lucidity. This was one of them, and it had surprised Stephen to find her so calm in her lucid state.

'Don't feel sorry for me, Stephen. Gabriel and I had many years together. He will forever be in my heart.'

'I wish I knew what to do, Margaux. This is all too

much.'

Margaux had released him. 'You'll know when the time is right.'

She had followed with a series of nonsensical mumbles that told Stephen her lucid moment was over. She had crumpled to the floor and flipped between staring up at the ceiling and wailing. Her cries had brought a distressed Serena to the door.

'Is she okay?'

Stephen had looked down at the elder from District Eight. 'I don't think so. Help her.'

Serena had nodded and closed her eyes. Stephen had felt the room spin as her influence bore down on him, then passed through him. Margaux's wails had reduced to intermittent sobs. She had looked up at Serena, who had given Stephen a worried look.

'I think she should stay here.'

That had been two weeks ago and Margaux was still in District Three, sometimes lucid, but mostly out of it. Maybe it was better that way.

A week ago, Bill had returned to the district to report that Simon had been given a hero's burial on the surface. The Conditioned had been rounded up and placed in a secure location that only three others knew about. Stephen was one. Alongside the detainees, which included Marcus Murphy, the bodies of the Elite rested in cryogenic chambers.

'Best nobody knows where they are,' said Bill to Stephen as they discussed matters in the Council Chambers.

'Do you think you can separate the Elite consciousness from the Conditioned hosts?'

'Maybe. But I wouldn't know where to start.'

'Anton could help.'

Bill shook his head. 'Only you can know their location. It's safer. No, we need to find those doctors.'

'And Harvey Buchanan?'

'I'll use him as a last resort, but he won't budge until I give him his clinics.'

'Maybe you should do it. It's the lesser of the two evils.'

Bill folded his arms and stared at the ground. 'I'll think about it. I want to see if I can locate the doctors first.' He looked at Stephen. 'They're not even showing up on the Wave. Julie has Ben Watson all over it, but it's as if they've found another way to communicate.'

'That or they're all dead.'

Bill shook his head. 'Unlikely. We could be looking at a similar situation to what happened with the skilled workers on Earth. Robinson, Olsen and Hayes were forced to go underground, off the grid.'

'They might be worth talking to, Bill,' said Stephen.

'Maybe. But let's see if we can locate those damn doctors first.'

☼

That evening, as Stephen wandered the tunnels of District Three, he was reminded of the events that had taken place. Not just recent ones, but since the discovery of their human origins. He wondered if the Indigenes or the humans would ever find peace.

As he walked on, the noise of the other Indigenes dissipated to be replaced by a rare silence. He took advantage of the quiet lull and drew in a deep, calming breath.

The last couple of weeks had left him feeling

drained. He'd barely had time to stop, and he hadn't used the Nexus to heal. In that moment of peace, he felt the extent of his body's weakness and mind's fragmentation. The Nexus would piece him back together again so he could face the next chapter in this fight.

Stephen arrived at a different tranquillity cave to the one where they'd lost Simon and Gabriel. He still couldn't bring himself to visit it, even though a now-resident Margaux used it every day. According to Clement, the representatives there had put temporary leadership in place while Margaux was away. But Stephen sensed that Margaux as leader would be too erratic to command the same respect as Gabriel.

He jumped into a unit and connected to the Nexus. Inside, the power of the Nexus washed over him like warm water. Nothing gave him this level of comfort. Not even Serena. He couldn't imagine life without the Nexus.

Others who used the Nexus gathered as bright energies in a tight ball, at the centre of the curved wall. He avoided them and went straight to the wall, knowing a direct hit of the Nexus' power would be tough to absorb. But he needed a stronger hit than the gentle energy the gathered energies offered.

Stephen stuck his energy to the wall. The Nexus stung him at first, but the resistance let up enough for him to feel its healing power. It made him feel stronger, although he knew his mind would need more than one session to sort out. Also his envisioning skill, which had not returned, even after Anton had dismantled the machine inside the environ. With the radiation gone, his ability should have returned. Maybe the Nexus could help with that.

When the healing power of the Nexus weakened, he knew it was time to leave. He could only gain so much

Genesis Variant

from each session.

Except for a strange pulsating sensation, the Nexus had suffered no ill effects from Tanya's invasion. The sensation was probably due to the Nexus reclaiming its former balance; Tanya's energy would have introduced her mutated DNA into the realm. But the organic being seemed to handle it just fine.

Stephen disconnected and climbed out of the unit. He was surprised to find Margaux waiting for him.

'Is Serena with you?'

Margaux shook her head. She appeared to be lucid.

His loss of envisioning skill bothered him. 'There's something I wanted to talk to you about.'

Margaux smiled. 'Your reader ability.'

'I lost it when the GS humans built the machine inside the environ. Simon said it was because of the radiation. But the machine is no longer active and it still hasn't returned.'

Margaux pressed her hands to the sides of his head and closed her eyes. 'You still have it. Your mind fights against it because there's something it doesn't want you to see.'

Stephen frowned. 'What?'

'Like what will happen next.' She removed her hands and nodded towards a unit. 'Did you feel something in there?'

'Nothing unusual. Have you been in?'

Margaux nodded. 'Every day, but not for long. I don't like how it feels. It's different to ours in District Eight, you know.'

'That's because Serena commanded it to use the space more effectively. We got rid of the chasm and the wall now surrounds the energies.'

'No, not that. It gives off the oddest feeling.'

Margaux walked away. At the exit, she turned round. 'You need to see what your mind is blocking. Stop fighting it and it will come to you.'

She left a confused Stephen alone to ponder her advice. He wasn't fighting anything. He wanted his skill back.

He left the cave shortly after Margaux and walked around for a while. Stephen's restless mind refused to quiet down. He considered going hunting, if for no other reason than to use it as a distraction. Maybe Margaux was right and he was the problem, not his skill. Maybe he'd weighed his mind down with so much responsibility he'd forgotten how to access the ability that had manifested eight years ago after he returned from Earth.

Perhaps if he concentrated on the skill it would come to him. The neurosensor had helped before. It might help now.

He found it in Anton's empty lab and stuck it to the side of his head. With it on, he concentrated on the visions that the neurosensor had helped to unlock before.

Then he saw it, a glimpse into a near future without a timestamp. A new threat from the rogue groups. An attempt to break apart peace and return things to the way they were, pre-treaty.

But something else caught his attention, a new threat that he'd been too distracted to notice.

Chaos, unrest. Not just in his district, but in others. A deep sense of loss accompanied the threat that he could not yet see or quantify. But one thing was clear: It came from the place where he'd just been.

The Nexus was altering.

☼

The story continues in Genesis Cure.

Sign up for Eliza's newsletter at www.elizagreenbooks.com to receive updates on more in this series and *Genesis*, a teaser story set before *Genesis Code.*

WORD FROM THE AUTHOR

Wow, are we on book six already? When I started this series I never imagined the story would make it past three books. But I've had so much fun with this series I didn't want it to stop. The ideas kept coming and I wasn't ready to say goodbye to any of the characters. Thank you for joining me on this writing journey.

I wish I had a crystal ball to see beyond the next (and what feels like the final) book in this series. I don't want things to end, but I may take the series in a new direction, focus on new characters, maybe even do a few origin stories? That's the best thing about being an indie author. I can do what I want when I want.

Thanks to Sara Litchfield for editing my book and for your compliments on my much improved writing. In 2018, I undertook a massive re-evaluation of the series. Cue one labour intensive year where I reassessed and reworked all the books under the old Exilon 5 title (now Genesis). I learned a lot about the errors I was making in my writing and it pushed me to become a better writer. This business is nothing if not exciting!

Thanks to Kathryn for reading an early version of the book and for giving me notions (I mean ideas). I had killed off a character, but it was suggested said character needed a more creative (and satisfying) way to die. I thought about it and decided I wasn't done with him. Yes, we're talking about Marcus. Thanks to Tom, Iffet and John for jumping on board as early readers, and for hating Marcus as much as you did. I think one of you called him "such a shit." Haha! I loved writing that character so much. He has no filter!

Thanks to my launch team who devour any new book I write. I might only chat to you when I have a new book out, but you mean so much to me and make this process WAAY less stressful. (Believe me, it is incredibly stressful. I just LOOK like I have my shit together!) Reviews are the social proof I need to convince others to buy.

A quick word about piracy, because this topic is simply everywhere at the moment. You might know someone who never buys books and always downloads freebies from these pirate sites. But this practice kills author sales and potentially kills off series completion. If I can't support myself financially, I can't afford to write the next books. So if you ever hear anyone say, "What harm can it do?" tell them, lots. Tell them to source a copy from legitimate sources. Sign up to the author's newsletter, or wonderful sites like Bookbub where freebies and deals are announced. Or, request the book from their library.

So to end on a happier note, keep on reading those books. Together, we shall slay the dragon of banality!

PURCHASE OTHER BOOKS IN THE SERIES

Digital only

Genesis (Book 0)

(Get this teaser story for free when you sign up to my mailing list. Check out **www.elizagreenbooks.com** for more information)

Paperback and Digital

Genesis Code (Book 1)
Genesis Lie (Book 2)
Genesis War (Book 3)
Genesis Pact (Book 4)
Genesis Trade (Book 5)
Genesis Variant (Book 6)
Genesis Cure (Book 7)

Standalone series

Duality (a sci-fi mystery)

THE BREEDER FILES

THE FACILITY (Book 1)

An orphaned teenager. A brutal re-training facility. Will she choose freedom or rebellion? To find out more, visit **www.elizagreenbooks.com/the-facility**

BOOKS BY KATE GELLAR

Eliza also writes PARANORMAL ROMANCE under the pen name Kate Gellar. All books are available in ebook and print.

THE IRISH ROGUE SERIES

Dark witches and guardians are mortal enemies? Tell that to Abby and her four hot demon fighting men.

Check out **www.kategellarbooks.com** for more details.

REVIEWS

Word of mouth is crucial for authors. If you enjoyed this
book, please consider leaving a review where you
purchased it; make it as long or as short as you like. I
know review writing can be a hassle, but it's the most
effective way to let others know what you thought. Plus, it
helps me reach new readers instantly.

GET IN TOUCH

www.elizagreenbooks.com
www.twitter.com/elizagreenbooks
www.facebook.com/elizagreenbooks
www.instagram.com/elizagreenbooks
Goodreads – search for Eliza Green

Printed in Great Britain
by Amazon

66773566R00234